The baron waited while Lady Mary and Aubrey sat, his face a mask of concern. "As well you know," he began, "I have, for years, been tasked with running the Royal estates. As such, I have been working at the Palace diligently, but I fear that under our new king I can no longer carry out this duty."

"Why ever not, Robert?" asked his wife. "Surely the task is not so onerous?"

"I'm afraid events in the capital have spiralled out of control."

"How so, Father?"

"It seems King Henry has seen fit to arrest and execute Princess Anna and her people." He waited, watching their faces as the news sank in.

"Cousin Beverly!" cried out Aubrey.

"I'm afraid so," he replied. "Word is that all the Knights of the Hound have been executed for treason. I've no doubt that Baron Fitzwilliam will be arrested as well. I suspect that even as we speak, a delegation is being sent to Bodden."

"Uncle Richard would never conspire against the king," declared Aubrey. "Surely there's a mistake?"

"I'm afraid not, Aubrey. While King Andred might have been willing to accept the queen's bastard child, it appears his heir, King Henry, is not."

"Is Aubrey in danger?" asked Lady Mary.

"I hope not," said the baron. "Before I left my position I used my privilege to search through the Royal records. Any record of her working for the Royal Mage has been purged. There is nothing left to link her to the conspirators."

Also by Paul J Bennett

A Plague in Zeiderbruch

FATE OF THE CROWN

Heir to the Crown: Book Five

PAUL J BENNETT

Dedication

*To my brother, Ian Bennett, International Man of Leisure, whose insights helped
me get this series rolling.*

ONE

Hawksburg

AUTUMN 961 MC* (MERCERIAN CALENDAR)

~

Lady Aubrey Brandon, daughter of Lord Robert Brandon, Baron of Hawksburg, was bored. She sat on the front step of the manor house, staring down the pathway with all the concentration her seventeen-year-old head could muster. This was, of course, considerable, for beneath this young exterior hid an accomplished wielder of magic.

For more than a year she had travelled with the Royal Life Mage, Revi Bloom, as his apprentice. She had easily mastered her first spell, but now she sat, weary of her studies. It wasn't that she didn't find magic interesting, far from it, but the books Master Bloom had given her had long since ceased to be of interest, a victim of her growing awareness of the magic that resided within her.

She looked down at the book beside her, a treatise on the history of magic, and chuckled to herself. History was fascinating to some but to her, life was all about the here and now, the harnessing of arcane power. She thought back to Weldwyn; there, at least, she had managed to cast her first spell, that of healing the flesh. It had been put to good use, for during the siege of Riversend she had been called upon to use her spells to help the brave defenders of the city.

The sound of a carriage caught her attention, and she looked up to see a familiar sight coming down the lane. It seemed her father had returned early from Wincaster. She stood, her mind no longer occupied by stray thoughts and focused on his arrival. Tomlinson, the old coachman, was covered in dust and dirt, the carriage likewise filthy. Her father must have been in a hurry to return, and yet his duties in the capital typically kept him busy well into the winter months.

The carriage pulled up, and she moved forward to open the door, only to see her father preparing to exit.

"Father," she said, "what a pleasant surprise. We weren't expecting you back until the midwinter feast."

His face broke into a grin, "Good to see you too, Aubrey. Go and fetch your mother, will you? I need to speak to both of you right away. Bring her to the drawing room."

She wanted to ask him for more details but saw the look of determination on his face. Something important has happened, she thought, and was suddenly struck with a feeling of dread.

"I'll go and get mother immediately," she replied, hurrying away. Her mother, as usual, was easy to find. She would often sit in the library in the late afternoon and today was no exception. "Mother," she announced, "Father has arrived from Wincaster."

Lady Mary Brandon rose to her feet, setting down her book. "Something must be wrong," she said. "He usually sends word when he is returning."

"He wants to see us in the drawing room."

"Go and find your brothers," her mother said.

"I think he wants just the two of us," replied Aubrey.

"Very well, let us see what news he brings."

They made their way to the appointed room to find Lord Robert in his chair. He had discarded his cloak, dropping it to the floor and was just removing his boots as they entered.

"Robert," asked Lady Mary, "whatever is the matter?"

"Come, sit down, my love. I'm afraid there have been some...developments in Wincaster."

"You're worrying me, Robert. Tell me everything is fine."

The baron waited while Lady Mary and Aubrey sat, his face a mask of concern. "As well you know," he began, "I have, for years, been tasked with running the Royal Estates. As such, I have been working at the Palace diligently, but I fear that under our new king, I can no longer carry out this duty."

"Why ever not, Robert?" asked his wife. "Surely the task is not so onerous?"

"I'm afraid events in the capital have spiralled out of control."

"How so, Father?"

"It seems King Henry has seen fit to arrest and execute Princess Anna and her people." He waited, watching their faces as the news sank in.

"Cousin Beverly!" cried out Aubrey.

"I'm afraid so," he replied. "Word is that all the Knights of the Hound have been executed for treason. I've no doubt that Baron Fitzwilliam will be arrested as well. I suspect that even as we speak, a delegation is being sent to Bodden."

"Uncle Richard would never conspire against the king," declared Aubrey. "Surely there's a mistake?"

"I'm afraid not, Aubrey. While King Andred might have been willing to accept the queen's bastard child, it appears his heir, King Henry, is not."

"Is Aubrey in danger?" asked Lady Mary.

"I hope not," said the baron. "Before I left my position I used my privilege to search through the Royal records. Any record of her working for the Royal Mage has been purged. There is nothing left to link her to the conspirators."

"What if someone confessed?" asked Lady Mary, her voice rising in pitch. "She could be arrested."

"Fear not, my love. If they had made that connection, she would already be in the dungeons beneath the Palace. I have managed to see the so-called 'confessions' that were said to have been extracted from the prisoners; they are nothing but flights of fancy."

"None of the knights would confess," defended Aubrey. "I knew them all, and they were honourable to a fault."

"It matters not to the king," explained the baron. "He has fabricated these confessions to suit his own purpose. Our primary concern now is to keep you safe."

"Me?" said Aubrey in alarm. "Why?"

"You are a Life Mage," he continued, "perhaps the last in the kingdom, for it is said that Revi Bloom has been implicated in the plot. We must ensure your power remains hidden, for all our sakes."

"But I cannot give up magic," she protested.

"Nor would I want you to," he responded, "but we must find somewhere safe for you to practice, out of sight of prying eyes."

"What about the old manor?" interjected Lady Mary.

"I hadn't thought of that," replied the baron.

"You mean that old building behind the estate?" said Aubrey. "I thought it was unsafe."

"It is run down," agreed her father, "but I'm sure with a little work it would suit your purposes. It hasn't been used since the days of your great-grandparents. It was too small to house their growing family, that's why my grandfather built the manor in which we now live."

"So I'm to be hidden away?" asked Aubrey.

"No, dear," said her mother, "you would still live here, but use the old house to practice your magic. After all, you don't need much in the way of furnishings to cast spells. If anything, you want fewer things to break."

"I don't break things when I cast, Mother."

"I know, dear, I'm just teasing you."

"It would require some work to prepare it, I should think," her father interrupted. "I'd rather not involve the servants, so we'll have to keep this to ourselves."

"What about Tristan and Samuel?" asked Aubrey.

"I think it best that your brothers not know of this."

"But they know I can cast magic."

"That's all well and good, but let it appear that your interest has waned. You'll need to explain your absences while you study. I would suggest you go riding a lot as a cover."

"Fair enough," said Aubrey, then fell into silence.

Her father saw her struggling with something, "What is it, Aubrey?"

"Cousin Beverly," she confessed. "I can't bear the thought of them torturing her."

"I didn't say they tortured her," said the baron.

"I'm not a child, Father. I've heard what happens in the dungeons of Wincaster."

"I'm sorry, Aubrey, but there's little I can do about the past. I would send word to your Uncle Richard, but the King's Rangers might intercept it. I fear that I have become a target of interest to them and must tread carefully."

"Why would the rangers do that?" asked Lady Mary. "Surely their job is to keep the roads safe?"

Lord Robert looked at his wife with sorrowful eyes. "Much has changed in recent years, my love. The rangers now act as the king's eyes and ears. Of late, the roads have become much more dangerous for those who oppose the king."

"Are we in danger, Robert?"

The baron forced a smile, "Not for now, but we must be vigilant. We must be seen to support the king in all things, or we shall draw further attention to ourselves." He saw the look of despair on his family's faces. "Now, let us turn our attention to the old manor house. Shall we go and have a look?"

Aubrey stood in the large foyer that dominated the entrance to the old building. The room was dusty, with cobwebs covering the corners.

"Where do we start?" she wondered out loud.

"I would think the library might be the best place," her father answered. "It's likely to be a small room. At least that way we'll feel like we're making progress."

Aubrey glanced through an open door. "Judging by the bookshelves, I'd say that it's over there," she said, pointing.

"Let's go and have a look, shall we?" he said.

They wandered through the doorway, and she was instantly impressed by the decor of the room. "It's so cozy in here, though it's a little cold."

"I wouldn't go using the fireplace just yet," her father warned, "the chimney is likely clogged up. This place hasn't been used in decades."

"What were they like?" she asked. "My great-grandparents, I mean."

"I didn't know your great-grandfather, he died before I was born, but your great-grandmother was an interesting one."

"And by interesting, you mean?"

"I think the word I'm looking for is eccentric," he said. "She was a strong-willed woman, wouldn't take no for an answer. Even after they built the new manor house, she refused to move into it. She spent her last years here."

"What was her name?" Aubrey asked. "I've never heard you speak of her."

"Her name was Juliana," her father replied, "though I've forgotten her maiden name. She was always 'Nan' to me."

"And this was her only home?"

"Yes, she took great pride in it. All the furnishings and decorations were hers. My grandfather didn't care two twigs for such things."

Aubrey wandered over to the bookshelf that occupied the north wall. "I never realized there were so many books here."

"Yes, Nan was an avid reader, just like you."

She carefully withdrew a book, glancing at its spine. "This is a book of poetry by Califax," she remarked. "I thought he wrote plays."

"He did," responded her father, "but like all great artists he did so much more."

She flipped the pages, stopping as she saw the title page. "It's signed," she said in astonishment.

"She must have purchased it that way," he said. "Califax lived long before Nan."

"True enough," she said, returning the book to its position on the shelf. No sooner had she placed it, then the shelf collapsed, the wooden structure breaking beneath the weight of the books. Aubrey jumped back in alarm, casting an embarrassed look towards her father.

"The wood's likely dried out and rotten," he explained. "I'm surprised it's lasted this long. Let's move the books over here; we'll pile them against the wall for now. The bookshelf will need to be repaired eventually, perhaps even replaced."

Aubrey began removing tomes, carrying them across the room and laying them in careful stacks on the dusty floor. She returned to the shelf, grabbing another armful.

"What's this?" said her father.

"What's what?"

"I think I might have discovered something," he said.

She set her armload down, coming to see what her father had found.

He knocked on the back of the shelf. "What do you hear?" he asked.

"It sounds hollow. Do you think there's something behind it?"

"There's only one way to find out," he said, grinning.

They quickly removed the remaining books and began examining the shelf in more detail.

"There must be a lever or something to open it," she said.

The baron felt around the edge. He ran his fingers across the top of the shelf and paused, "I've found a latch of some sorts. I can just feel it with my fingers, hang on a moment." He moved across the room, singling out a chair to drag across to the bookshelf and stand on. "Ah, I see now, a rather simple latch."

She watched as he fiddled with something on the top and then they heard a clicking sound. "You seem to have done it," she said.

He hopped down from his perch, pulling the chair out of the way. "I should think we could swing this out now," he said, pulling on one of the shelves. It moved forward a fingers breadth, hinged on one side. "It appears to be stuck," he announced.

"Let me give you a hand," she offered, grabbing the end of the structure. As they both pulled, the shelf swung outward.

Aubrey turned her attention to what lay behind, "There's a narrow staircase that leads down." She poked her head through the opening to see where it led. "It looks like there's a room beneath the library."

"Let me fetch a lantern," he said, "and we'll take a look."

"Don't bother," she replied, "I've a better idea."

She started uttering an incantation and a moment later a small ball of light floated just above her palm.

"Remarkable," said her father, "I thought you were just a Life Mage."

"There's more to Life Magic than just the healing," said Aubrey defensively. "The orb of light is a universal spell."

The baron shook his head, "I have no idea what you're talking about."

"Universal spells can be cast by any mage, regardless of their school."

"What do you mean by school?" he asked. "I thought you were taught by the Royal Life Mage."

Aubrey let out a laugh, "I was, Father. A school is a particular way of looking at magic. Surely you've heard of the elements?"

"You mean earth, fire, water and so on? Of course."

"Those are the elemental schools. An Earth Mage could never call forth fire, nor could a Fire Mage control nature."

"And what about Life Magic?"

"Outside of the elements, there are four additional schools," she continued, "life, enchantments and of course the forbidden arts of death and hex magic."

"And so you're saying any school could use this orb of light?"

"If they learned how to cast it, yes," she said, eager to share her knowledge.

"Interesting, but perhaps we should save this discussion for later. We have more pressing business."

"What business is that?" she asked.

"Don't you want to see what's at the bottom of those stairs?"

"Oh, of course," she said. "Sorry, I was so engrossed in the discussion."

"Just like your mother," he beamed. "Now, lead on, Aubrey. You're the one with the glowing ball of light."

She returned her attention to the stairs and concentrated on the light. It drifted from her hands, floating down the stairs as she watched. She began to descend, the orb illuminating the way.

The stairs ended at a dirt floor. To the side, directly under the library, was a brick-lined room, matching the dimensions of the space above. There was little here in the way of furniture, however, save for a lectern in the centre which held a large tome, and a worktable and chair that lay against the north wall.

"What do you see?" called down her father.

"A rather bare room," she replied, "but with a book taking a place of honour in the middle."

The sound of her father coming down interrupted her perusal. She moved into the centre, allowing him access as she examined the lectern. The book was closed, so she floated the light over it to study it in more detail. It was leather bound, with metal clasps holding the pages together. She carefully reached out and turned to a random page, her eyes confirming what she already suspected. "It's a book of magic," she said, awe filling her voice.

"Magic? Are you sure?"

She waved him over, pointing to the page she had revealed. "This is just handwriting," she explained, "but this," she stabbed down with her finger, "is a magic rune, part of the magical alphabet."

"I've heard you mention that before," he said. "It's a universal language, isn't it?"

"Yes, that's right. It's the same in every tongue."

"Are you saying your great-grandmother was a mage?"

"I don't know yet, I'd have to read through this. It may just be random notes about magic."

Lord Robert smiled at his daughter's interest, "I'd say it's more likely she used magic. It seems she went to a lot of trouble to create this room. Why do so just for a book about magic? No, I think she must have been a mage, though why she didn't tell anyone is an absolute mystery to me."

"Perhaps the book can tell us more," she said.

"Well, I would suggest you get busy. It looks like it'll be a long read, even for you."

"What about the mess upstairs?" she asked.

"Don't worry about that," he answered in reply. "I'm sure this room is fine for your practice, now that I look at it. You study the book, I'll go and fetch us some food. I have a feeling we're not going to pry you from that," he pointed at the book, "until you've found your answers."

By the time the first flakes of winter arrived, Aubrey had studied the book in great detail. Now she stood before it, ready to resume practicing her spells. Setting the lantern on the table, she then moved to the dead centre of the room, by the lectern, to begin the incantation that would produce her customary orb of light.

The familiar words came quickly to her while she held out her hand for the glowing sphere to appear. As the last word tumbled out of her mouth, the customary ball of light burst forth, but far brighter than she had ever experienced before. She jumped back in surprise. With her mental concentration broken, the orb disappeared, returning her to the dim light of the lantern.

She cast her eyes about, but the room held no surprises, at least not that she could see. Perhaps, she thought, she had merely made a mistake in casting. She steadied her nerves and began the process anew, careful to use the correct pronunciation.

The orb reappeared, once more with a brilliant light. This time Aubrey didn't flinch, but instead, looked around the room yet again, trying to ascertain what was affecting her spell. Her eyes fell to the table. She had often sat there perusing the great tome and she wondered if perhaps it held something, for it was the only explanation she could think of. She had examined the lectern in great detail and the chair was nought but a simple wooden construction, incapable of hiding anything.

She kept the orb suspended and made her way to the table, intent on finding its secrets. She examined the top, the sides, even going so far as to crawl underneath it and inspect the underside, but to no avail. She sat down, once more looking about the room. It must have been some time, for she suddenly found herself in darkness, her spell expired. She recast the glowing orb, only to notice the light was dimmer, rather than the brightness she had come to expect. She glanced back to the lectern; had she missed something?

Returning to the centre of the room, she cast again, the orb once again blazing. She wished, not for the last time, that Master Bloom was here to explain things to her, but then grew stubborn. She knew she was well-educated; surely there must be some way to figure this out! She decided to move the lectern, to see if placing it near the table made any difference.

The wooden structure was too heavy to simply push upright, so she moved the book of magic to the table and then tipped the lectern, in order to drag it. What she discovered surprised her, for stone could be seen beneath its base. She stared down, not quite believing her eyes. Placing the stand back to its original position, she knelt, digging through the dirt floor with her hands. A moment later, a stone floor was revealed.

She sat up in surprise. Was the entire floor made of stone? Intending to find out, she rushed from the room to look for a shovel.

By the end of the day, she stood gazing down at the newly revealed floor. Made of carefully fitted grey stone, the real prize was the embellishments, for now, with the dirt removed, she saw the magic circle that had been hidden all this time.

She had read about magic circles, of course, but never had she seen one in person. It took up most of the floor, save for the north wall where the table sat, along with heaps of the newly displaced dirt. It was actually two circles, a smaller one within a larger, with runes of power that embellished the space between them. These circles, she knew, amplified the effects of spells cast within, enabling the caster to unleash greater power.

The sound of a distant voice interrupted her thoughts. In her desire to unearth this treasure she had lost track of time, and now her name was being called out, likely summoning her to dinner. She looked down at her hands, filthy from her work. The task of carting out the dirt would have to wait. For now, she must return to the manor and play the part of the disinterested daughter.

TWO

Bodden

WINTER 961/962 MC

~

A thin blanket of snow had settled over the land, giving it a peaceful look as Baron Richard Fitzwilliam stared out the window from his beloved map room. His thoughts were interrupted by Sir Gareth.

"How long till they come, Lord?"

Fitz turned from the windows, "Oh, I expect it will be some time, yet. It's unlikely they'd bring a siege to Bodden in the winter. How are the defences going?"

"They are going well, Lord. The new ditch is complete, and we've reinforced the main gate. When they finally do arrive, we'll give them a fight worthy of the trip to the Afterlife."

"Good," said Fitz, "and the training?"

"All able-bodied men are training hard. A lot of the women wanted to help too, Lord, so we've got them learning to use the bow."

"I shudder to think of the loss of life a siege will bring," said Fitz.

"They have given us little choice," Gareth reminded him.

Approaching footsteps drew their attention as a woman entered the room.

"Lady Albreda," said Fitz, "good to see you."

"Richard, Sir Gareth," she replied, nodding in greeting, "I come bearing news."

"Which is?" asked the baron.

"A group of riders approaches from the east. I've had them under observation for some time."

The baron looked to Sir Gareth in alarm, then returned his gaze to Albreda, "How many?"

"Fifty-three, to be precise," she answered.

"Rather an unusual number," he replied.

"They'll have a hard time sieging us with so few," offered Sir Gareth.

"Fifty or so men would hardly constitute a threat," the baron mused. "Can you tell us anything more about them?"

"Yes," she said, "three of them wear chain with metal plates, so I can only assume they are knights. The rest march on foot, and appear to be soldiers of some type."

"Perhaps they're bringing an ultimatum," offered Gareth.

"With fifty men and three knights?" said Fitz. "I hardly think that likely."

Albreda moved to the eastern facing window, "If you look to the great elm yonder, they should soon come into view."

Fitz turned his gaze to the window, conscious of the closeness with Albreda. "I see them," he said, "though I cannot make them out clearly. I wish I were younger; my eyes were so much sharper back then."

Albreda put a hand on his forearm, "Your eyes are fine, Richard, I can't make out details, either. They are, indeed, a long way off, but they do not appear to be brandishing weapons. In fact, now that they've cleared the elm, I see they have pack mules following."

"Pack mules?" said Sir Gareth in disbelief.

"Intriguing," said Fitz. "I wonder who they might be?"

"Shall I send out troops, my lord?" asked Gareth.

"No, let them ride closer. Send for Sir Heward, have him meet us at the gates to Bodden, perhaps he can shed some light on our visitors."

"Are we to fight, Lord?"

"We'll see what they want before I put any of my men in danger. We can talk to them from the gate-tower, but let's take no chances, have the archers man the walls."

"Aye, Lord," said Sir Gareth, turning to leave.

"Do you think them a danger?" asked Albreda.

"I have no idea," said Fitz, "but I intend to find out."

The gate that led into the village of Bodden was guarded by a ditch and drawbridge, a recent addition that Fitz took great pride in. In times past, he had considered such a defence, but the amount of work required was overwhelming. It was Albreda that had supplied the answer, for the Earth Mage had used her magic to move large amounts of dirt, thus creating the ditch.

They kept the drawbridge down, of course, for farmers frequently travelled back and forth, but when the strangers appeared, Fitz had ordered that the portcullis be lowered, blocking any entry. Now, they watched from the tower as the strangers approached. They were still out of bow range when Fitz turned to Sir Heward.

"Do you recognize any of them?" he asked.

"No, Lord. Nor their armour."

Fitz nodded his head in agreement. Armour was very personalized, and many a warrior could be recognized simply from what he wore. "I wonder who they are," he mused.

The visitors halted, and two of the knights rode forward while the third waited with the men. As they came within earshot of the gatehouse, they raised their visors, calling out as they did so.

"Who commands here?" came a suspiciously familiar voice.

"I do," answered Fitz. "Lord Richard Fitzwilliam, Baron of Bodden."

The two knights looked at each other and then one removed his helmet, riding a little closer. "It is I, Sir Rodney, Lord. We have come to serve you."

"Sir Rodney?" called out Fitz. "Surely not, he'd be an old man by now."

"I am indeed, Lord," the knight replied, "and yet, still able to swing a sword. I bring with me two gallant knights of your acquaintance, Sir James and Sir Randolph."

"Saxnor's beard," exclaimed the baron, turning to Heward. "Open the gate, I'll go and talk to them."

"Is that wise, Lord?" said Sir Heward.

"Fear not, they are old friends."

Fitz descended the steps while the portcullis was raised. As soon as it was high enough, he ducked under, making his way toward the two knights.

"Sir Rodney," he called out, "I see that old age has not dampened your spirits."

"My lord," Rodney replied, dismounting, "it is so good to see you again."

"Whatever has brought you to Bodden?" asked the baron.

"We heard of the rebellion, my lord, and have come to offer our service. We have even brought footmen with us to help in the cause, volunteers all."

"You are, of course, welcome here," said Fitz grasping Sir Rodney's hand, "though I fear it is likely to be a short rebellion. The king has, no doubt, heard of it by now, and soon an army will come to crush us."

"Then let them come," said Rodney, "and we'll make a stand that will live forever in the annals of history."

"You remember Lady Albreda?" asked Fitz, leading them through the gate towards the Keep.

"The Witch of the Whitewood?" asked Rodney.

"I prefer the term 'Druid,'" said Albreda, "though mage will do in a pinch."

"I meant no disrespect, my lady," said Sir Rodney. "You grace us with your presence."

"Tell us, Sir Knight," she continued, "how did you come to Bodden?"

"Well, not long ago, all the knights of the realm were summoned to Wincaster. Once we arrived, we were informed that the king was forming an army to march and suppress a rebellion in the north. Questions were asked, and when the king revealed that the baron, here, was guilty in a plot against the crown, the news did not sit well with some of us. The king immediately insisted that all his knights swear fealty to him, but we three left quietly and resolved to bring our men north, to aid Bodden."

"Did you see any sign of the royal army on your march north?" asked Fitz.

"No, Lord. We took the road westward and came up through Redridge to avoid the king's allies in Tewsbury. We heard that Marshal-General Valmar was to lead the army up through Uxley, then to Tewsbury and west along the northern road."

"And the rebellion? What do you know of it?"

"There are stirrings of rebellion in Wickfield and Mattingly. It is said even Hawksburg plotted against the king, though we only have his word for it."

"Valmar is a ruthless man," said Fitz. "I fear he will use his army to exact personal revenge for imagined slights."

"What shall we do, Lord?" asked Sir Gareth.

"Let us retire to the map room," said the baron, "and there, perhaps, we will find clarity."

He led them through the village, heading toward the inner Keep. They were about to enter when Sir Rodney halted suddenly. He stopped at the inner gates, a look of wonderment on his face as he stared at the broken portcullis.

"What happened here?" the aged knight remarked.

"Albreda," explained Fitz.

"The metal is twisted and broken," observed Rodney. He turned his gaze once again to the druid, "You are very powerful, my lady."

"I know," she replied, "and yet why, I wonder, do men always find it surprising? Can a woman not wield immense power?"

"I meant no offense," he reassured her.

"And I have taken none, Sir Knight. I am merely amused. Come along, we are almost at the Keep itself, and the baron will have fine wine waiting for us."

"I will?" said the baron, almost chuckling.

"Of course, Richard, what else would you have for such old friends?"

"Very well, I'll call the servants."

It turned out to be unnecessary to call anyone, for the faithful retainers of Bodden Keep had seen them coming. The entourage made their way to the map room, where wine waited for them

"Here we are," said Fitz.

"Just like old times," remarked Sir Rodney. "I see little has changed, Lord."

"I'm afraid much has changed," corrected Albreda. "Richard has lost his daughter, and the tyrant of a king wants him dead. Perhaps you enjoy this situation, Sir Rodney, but I get little entertainment from it."

"My apologies if I have offended you, Lady," said the knight once again. "I merely meant-"

"I know what you meant," said the mage, "and I know you mean well, but these are tumultuous times, and we have much to do."

"Yes, well," interrupted the baron, "shall we continue the discussion?"

Everyone gathered around the table where a map of Merceria had been laid out.

"We are facing an uncertain future," started the baron. "As Albreda has said, the king is coming for us, or at least his army is."

Someone chuckled.

"You find something funny, Sir James?" asked the baron.

"No, sorry, my lord, but I was just thinking of our new king. I doubt anything would convince him to command an army."

"I might remind you," continued the baron, "that he was with the army at Eastwood."

"Yes, my lord, though he had little to do with its command. I believe it was you, was it not, that controlled the army?"

"It was not," answered Fitz. "Admittedly, I dealt with the army of the Earl of Shrewesdale and Gerald Matheson lead the other half. The overall command of the army fell on the shoulders of Princess Anna."

The room fell silent for a moment.

"She shall be sorely missed," said Sir Gareth.

"Indeed she shall," added the baron, "but now we must consider our future and make plans."

"What think you, Sir Rodney?" said Fitz.

"I think we should go on the offensive, Lord," replied the aged knight. "If rebellion truly is building in the north, perhaps we can fan it into an open flame."

"An interesting idea," replied the baron. "I shall have to think it over. In the meantime, gentlemen, I would suggest you see to your men and then get some rest. You've had a long ride, and no doubt you are weary. We'll reconvene in the morning and see what we can come up with."

They all filed out of the room save for Albreda, who remained by the window, gazing east. Fitz saw the other knights out then turned, surprised to see her still present. "Something troubling you, Albreda?"

She kept staring out the window as she replied, "Something's wrong."

"You suspect a trap from these knights?"

"No, it's not that, I'm sure they're quite devoted to you. No, it's something else. I am troubled by my visions."

"How so?" he asked.

"I was sure that Beverly would survive all this," she turned, casting her arms about the room. "She should be here, right now, helping us plan this. I saw it."

The baron moved over to her, placing his hands on her shoulders, looking directly into her eyes. "Beverly's death has greatly pained me, but we cannot undo the past. Perhaps your visions are untrue, or you have somehow misread them. Could it have been a vision of the past?"

"No," implored Albreda, "she was here, talking with you, holding Nature's Fury."

"The hammer? How could that be possible? Aldwin only completed it after Beverly's death."

"How indeed?" Albreda mused aloud.

THREE

Queenston

WINTER 961/962 MC

D ame Beverly Fitzwilliam, Knight of the Hound, opened her eyes to
see the small hut she had slept in, and briefly wondered where her
hut-mate, Hayley Chambers, was. The furs on the other sleeping mat lay
undisturbed, and it was then she remembered that the ranger had been sent
south, on a scouting mission to Kingsford.

The knight let out a deep breath, watching it frost in the cold morning
air. All she wanted was to sink farther into the furs that made up her bed,
but duty called. She reached out to the pile of clothes beside her and pulled
her gambeson under the furs, the better to warm it up before putting it on.
The sounds of the camp crept through the thin walls; the snorting of horses
and the hammering of iron echoing as the smiths went about their work.

She finally braved the frigid morning and stood, climbing into her
clothes as quickly as she could. Looking around, she chose to leave her
armour in her hut, but strapped on her sword as she stepped out into
daylight.

Queenston had been a camp when they left, yet now it boasted more
than two thousand individuals. The bulk of those were from Weldwyn, for
King Leofric had sent an army of 'volunteers' to help in the struggle to rid
Merceria of the shadow behind the throne. In addition, Princess Anna had
promised free land to any farmer willing to make the journey. Now, the
large numbers of commoners who had arrived were preparing for the
spring thaw as they readied their farms.

It was, for all intents and purposes, a town, though the buildings were cruder than most within the kingdom. She took it all in, relishing in the vitality that the village now held, reminding her of the people back in Bodden.

She made her way eastward, toward Royal Hill, the mound of earth beneath which sat the ancient flame portal. At the exit to the cave, the Dwarves had built the first stone structure, and this had become known as the Manor House, though it was little more than a single room.

Wanting to check in on her horse, she made her way to the pasture. Lightning saw her as soon as she cleared the stable master's hut and trotted over to her, nuzzling affectionately. She was rubbing the great horse's head as she heard a voice call out.

"Bev, good to see you."

She turned to spot Hayley, her horse covered in snow and mud, trotting towards the pasture. "When did you get back?" she asked.

"Early this morning," the ranger replied, "I've been up with the princess."

"I'm on my way up there shortly," said Beverly. "Anything exciting to report?"

"Give me a hand with my horse, will you, and I'll tell you all about it," she said, dismounting.

"You look tired, Hayley."

"Exhausted. It was a long ride, but well worth it. Kingsford is in revolt."

"What makes you say that?"

"I was down there and saw them flying a red flag. I didn't go in, of course. I might have been arrested as a King's Ranger."

"The red flag of rebellion? That hasn't been used in...well, I don't even know the last time it was used."

"The princess is calling everyone together to talk things over. With any luck we'll be able to convince them to join our cause, then we can winter in an actual city."

"Don't be ridiculous, Hayley, we can't all leave Queenston. Besides, the gate is here."

"True enough, I suppose, but I'd certainly like to sample a real ale again. The stuff they brew here is horrid."

"You obviously don't share Gerald's sense of taste."

"How is the general?" asked the ranger. "He had his hands full when I left."

"He still does, I'm afraid. Getting everyone to work together has proven to be challenging. No doubt we'll hear more about it when we get to this meeting."

They hurried about their task and then made their way to the manor, entering to find the room crowded. Many visitors stood around the crude table in the middle of the room. Beverly passed by Arnim, Nikki and Revi to take up her customary place to Anna's left, making sure not to disturb Tempus who lay snoring. The old dog never left the princess's side but could wake in an instant when needed.

Gerald Matheson stood to Anna's right, wearing a serious expression. Hayley took up a position to Revi Bloom's side, their hands touching briefly. It made Beverly long for home and the smith that waited for her, but she chided herself for the weakness and pulled her mind back to the task at hand.

The meeting was rounded out by Herdwin, the Dwarven smith, Kraloch, the Orc shaman, Telethial, leader of the Elves, and Commander Runsan, the leader of the Weldwyn volunteers. Noticeably absent were the Kurathians, but that matter was settled as voices were heard outside. They stepped into the room, led by Commander Lanaka, leader of the mercenary horsemen.

"My apologies, Your Highness," he said as they entered, "but by the beard of Saint Matthew it's cold out there."

Beverly chuckled, as did most of the others. The Kurathians were from a distant shore, and their customs strange, but intriguing.

"Tell me, Lanaka," said Gerald, "is it a long beard?"

The Kurathian broke into a large grin, "Not so much. He kept it trimmed close to his face."

"So he was a civilized saint," he jested.

"Indeed. It is said that of the five saints, he was the holiest."

"So it was not as long as Saxnor's," returned the general.

It was an old game and one they both shared, each trying to outdo the other with tales of their Gods, though Beverly had to remind herself that the Saints were mortals.

"If you two are done bantering," interrupted Anna, "we have business to attend to."

"Of course," said Gerald, "sorry, Highness."

"Now," she continued, "Hayley returned early this morning. Would you like to give an account?"

"Certainly," replied the ranger. "As many of you know, I set out two weeks ago to ride to Kingsford and ascertain the situation there. There was some hope that perhaps the duke might be persuaded to support our cause. What I found, when I arrived, was quite surprising, for they were flying red flags from the battlements."

"Red flags?" said Lanaka. "I'm afraid I don't understand."

"In Mercerian culture," explained Anna, "it is the symbol of rebellion. It appears our friend, Lord Somerset, is upset with King Henry."

"Did you get inside?" asked Beverly.

"No, the gates were closed with lookouts on the walls. If they identified me as a King's Ranger, I could have been locked up."

"What do you propose we do?" asked Lanaka.

"We must send a delegation," replied Anna. "If the city can be persuaded to support us, it will be a great benefit. Not only will it give us a solid, defensible base of operations, it will also open up our supply lines from Weldwyn. At the moment, they are sending things to Falford and then they are lugged overland to Queenston. The docks at Kingsford would be much more convenient."

"So we march the army south, in winter?" asked the Kurathian.

"No," said Gerald, "not yet. We'll send a small group to talk to the duke. If he supports us, as I'm hoping he will, we'll make arrangements to march south."

"So we'll winter in a city?" asked a hopeful Revi.

"Don't get too comfortable, Master Mage," continued Gerald, "I haven't finished. I have plans to take Colbridge before spring arrives."

Voices erupted around the room. "You can't be serious," declared Arnim. "You can't siege a city in the middle of winter, the men would freeze."

The general held up his hand to forestall any further objections. "This is all conjecture at the moment, and we have to gather more information, but I've given this a great deal of thought."

"What do you think of this, Highness?" asked Telethial.

"Gerald has told me his intentions, but we shall speak no more of it for the moment. I gave Gerald and Beverly the task of coming up with a plan to retake Merceria and their strategy is sound. A lot of it depends on the movements of our enemies, of course, but we know the king's army will not march in the snow. If we act quickly, we can gain an advantage before he has time to redeploy his troops."

She gazed around the room to see all faces focused on her. "The first step is to visit Kingsford. I will go there myself, along with a suitable escort, though not at the head of an army. To that end, I'll be taking Gerald, Beverly, Hayley and Revi. Arnim will be in charge here while we're gone. If things go well, we'll return to arrange for the army to be shipped to Kingsford."

"Shipped?" asked Revi.

"Yes, King Leofric has volunteered ships to help us transport troops, when needed."

"Won't the river freeze up?" asked Lanaka.

"No, not till much later in the season. We still have a month or more before that happens."

"So we'd only be looking at a short march to the river," said Herdwin. "I like that."

"Is that how you plan to take Colbridge?" asked Arnim.

"Possibly," Gerald confessed, "but more information would be needed concerning their defences. The walls of Colbridge are said to be in a bad state of disrepair, and we'd need an assessment of their troop complement before we strike. Of course, there's always the hope the city might also be in rebellion, though I suspect that's unlikely."

"Why so?" asked Revi.

"The Duke of Colbridge is a strong supporter of the king," said Anna.

"So much so," added Gerald, "that the duke once sought to marry his son to the princess."

"So an assault it is," said Hayley.

"Let's not get carried away," warned Gerald. "The first step is to visit Kingsford. Once that's done, we can make further arrangements."

"And if Colbridge is too heavily defended?" asked Arnim.

"Don't worry," replied Gerald, "we have a number of plans. We'll adapt as we go."

"That sounds suspiciously like improvising," said Revi.

Gerald smiled, "That will be all for now, please see to your training. We need the troops ready for the coming offensive."

They filed out, save for Anna, Beverly and Gerald. Sophie entered the room bringing food, which she passed around. Tempus opened his eyes at the young maid's approach but promptly went back to sleep.

"How's the training going, Gerald?" asked Anna.

"It's a lot of work," he admitted. "I've got to balance Humans, Orcs, Elves, Dwarves, not to mention foreign mercenaries."

"And Trolls," added Anna.

"Yes, those too, though Tog handles them well enough. At least Beverly, here, has a handle on the horsemen."

"Yes," said Beverly. "They're quite good. Not as heavily armoured as knights, but still experienced men and excellent horsemen. They're eager to learn, and I've managed to tame their wilder nature."

"Wilder nature?" asked Anna.

"Yes, they have a tendency to get carried away in battle and ride head-long into danger."

"Not unlike Mercerian knights," added the princess.

"Some knights, yes, but I can break them of that habit. It takes discipline to make them truly effective, and that's made easier by not having to deal with nobles and their sense of entitlement."

"What about the Orcs?" Anna asked her general.

"They've proven to be remarkably easy to train. I have two companies of Orc Spears now, but I never thought they'd take to it. Kraloch seemed to think their individual personalities wouldn't allow it, but that hasn't been my experience."

"In terms of their effectiveness," said Anna, "how would you rate our troops?"

"If we use the volunteers as a baseline," said Gerald, "then I'd say the Orcs are very useful. They have a longer gait than Humans and can move about quite quickly, even in formation. Of course, they're not all armed with spears, I also have some Orcish bow. Their natural strength allows them to use larger bows than the volunteers, though not as effective as the Elves or Dwarves."

"So they can stand in the line of battle?" asked Anna.

"Yes, though they might be better employed on the flanks where their movement advantage can be used if necessary."

"And the Elves?"

"Well, we've seen the effect the Elven bows have in battle, I only wish we had more. Same goes for the Dwarves with their arbalests, though their shorter legs slow them down considerably. We have some Dwarven axemen, or axe-dwarves if you prefer. They're the heaviest armoured troops, bar none. Herdwin tells me Dwarves never retreat."

"It's true," says Anna, "but with good reason. Their slower speed means they could never escape their traditional enemies. Their only option would be to fight to the death or surrender."

"They don't surrender either," said Gerald. "In short, they're solid. They're best suited to any critical defensive position."

"How about the Kurathians?" asked Anna. "They seem quite capable."

"They are," admitted the general. "They're as good as the Weldwyn volunteers and experienced as well, we're lucky to have them. It's the Trolls that still confound me. I haven't managed to figure out how to employ them, yet. Their leader, Tog, seems to know his business, but they're not a warrior race, despite their fearsome reputation. At least the Mastiffs are useful, and their handlers are experienced."

"Yes," said Anna, "I've spent some time with them. Tempus seems to like them."

At the mention of his name, the great dog's head rose, and he let out a bark.

"We were lucky they joined us," said Beverly. "We'll need them when we have to face the king's knights."

"Yes," agreed Gerald, "but I'd like to keep them in reserve. The king's army has never faced them before, so we should use them sparingly. We don't want a repeat of Beverly's tactics."

"Agreed," said Beverly, "but I believe that since then the Kurathian's have been making some changes."

"How would you prevent that from happening again?" asked Anna.

"They've placed some archers among the hounds to keep the enemy at range, at least until they're released. Of course, we can only use them once in a battle. We'll have to be sure to deploy them when they can do the most damage."

"You two seem to have considered every option," said Anna. "You've become quite the tactician, General."

Gerald blushed at the compliment. "Let's not get carried away, they haven't fought together in battle yet."

"I've seen you working with them all in their separate units. How do you think they'll do when you put them all together?"

"We shall have to see. I've organized the army into smaller companies, each led by a commander. It'll lessen the burden of command and allow delegation to senior leaders. Each race will have its own leader, capable of interpreting orders. Of course, the real test will come with battle, but I'm confident in the progress we've made so far."

"You're changing the shape of warfare, Gerald," mused Anna.

"How so?"

"Never before have so many races been united into a single army. Not only that, but delegating control is something that's almost never done. The troops must have confidence in you."

"Why wouldn't they?" queried Beverly. "After all, he's the saviour of Weldwyn."

Gerald blushed again, "I might remind you there were a great many people involved in saving that kingdom, not just me."

"But you led them, General," said Beverly. "That's what made the difference."

FOUR

Kingsford

WINTER 961/962 MC

❧

G erald looked to the woman beside him. "Nervous?" he asked.
"Very," she replied. "I've never been married before."

"Relax," he soothed, "it's not as bad as it sounds, though if it were my choice, the ceremony wouldn't be performed in the middle of nowhere."

"Better to be wed before we set out," the nervous woman replied. "Where's my future husband?"

"He'll be along shortly," said Gerald. "He is a rather busy man, after all."

They were in a glade, near the outskirts of Queenston. Anna had selected the site for its natural beauty, a choice that Gerald whole-heartedly agreed with. A small stream nearby, trickled as they waited, lending a relaxing air to the ceremony.

He heard a noise, then looked to see Arnim Caster approaching the party, another man following. "It appears he found someone to perform the oath, a Weldwyn volunteer by the looks of him," said Gerald, "though he's likely a follower of Malin."

They came closer, and the man held out his hand. "Greetings," he said, "My name is Carver, Desmond Carver. I see to the volunteer's spiritual needs."

"Strange to see a Holy Father in the army," said Gerald.

"I was a Holy Brother before volunteering," the man replied. "Is this the bride?"

"It is," said Gerald.

"I hope you're not nervous, my dear."

"No," the woman replied. "I've waited a long time for this."

"Then let us begin," said the officiant.

"Do you, Arnim Caster, take Lady Nicole Arendale..."

His Grace, Lord Avery Somerset, Duke of Kingsford sipped his wine absently. He was staring down at a list of figures, his mind elsewhere, when someone entered the room. He looked up at the intrusion, only to recognize one of his captains standing before him.

"Captain Harcourt, is something wrong?"

"No, Your Grace," the man hesitated. "Well, actually, I suppose something is wrong, my lord."

"Well, spit it out man, what is it?"

"There's a knight demanding entrance to the city."

"Just one?" the duke mused. "I would have expected more. I suppose it was inevitable that the king should hear of our rebellion. Did he give you a name?"

"No, my lord, but she did say she represented someone important."

"She? You're saying this knight is a woman?"

"Precisely, Lord."

"With red hair?" he asked.

The captain shifted nervously, "Aye, my lord."

"I can't believe it!" yelled the duke. "For Saxnor's sake man, don't just stand there, go and open the gate. Give them leave to enter the city and bring them straight here."

"Yes, Lord." The captain turned to leave, but the duke's next words caused him to pause.

"And while you're at it, call out my guard. We must have a guard of honour to welcome Her Highness."

"Highness, Lord? I thought we were rebelling against the king."

"We are, Captain, we are. If that red-headed knight is truly Dame Beverly, then there can be no doubt that Princess Anna must be alive and well. Be off with you, quickly man."

The captain scurried out the door to attend to his duties. The duke tried to return to his lists, but the imminent arrival of the princess took hold of his interest, and he swept them into a pile, to be dealt with later.

"Marsdon," he called out, only to find the old steward already present, startling him by his answer.

"Yes, Your Grace?"

"Saxnor's beard, Marsdon, you old fool, you were nearly the death of me, sneaking up on me like that!"

Marsdon smiled. It was an old game, one that he knew the duke appreciated.

"We're expecting a royal guest," continued the duke. "It appears word of Princess Anna's death may have been a tad premature. We'll need rooms for her party, and tell the kitchen to prepare a meal fit for a royal."

"Have we any idea of the number in the party, Your Grace?" asked the faithful servant.

"No, but I'll send word as soon as we know. I expect it's only a few, after all, there isn't an army at our gates. I'm sure the good captain would have told me if there had been."

"Will you want it in the great hall, my lord?"

"No, I think something more intimate. If I remember correctly, the princess isn't one for ceremony. I shall want my officers in attendance, can you arrange that?"

"Of course, Your Grace, though it will take some time. Who would you prefer for the guard of honour?"

"Whoever is closest, we haven't much time. Have the rest join us here as soon as they can. I expect there will be much to discuss."

"Anything else, Your Grace?"

"No, that's it for now, Marsdon. I shall leave the details up to you."

"Certainly," the old man replied, "then with your leave, Lord, I shall retire."

"Yes, yes of course, off you go."

The faithful servant shuffled out leaving the duke in a somewhat flustered state. A royal visitor meant protocols to follow, clothing that must be changed into, and he hadn't much time. He rushed from the room, calling for his manservant to come and dress him.

Dame Beverly led the small procession to the duke's estate. She halted and then turned to look at the column following her. Gerald and Anna rode behind, with the rest of the travellers arrayed in two's just beyond.

The duke had lined up a row of soldiers; each standing with spear and shield, while a captain bowed deeply.

"On behalf of the Duke of Kingsford," the man said, "welcome to our city, Your Highness."

"Thank you, Captain," said Anna, dismounting.

Beverly watched as the duke exited the building, a rather opulent house with ornate marble pillars out front. He was an elderly man, with long hair and a neatly trimmed beard. They had met before, but she couldn't help but notice how much he had aged since their last meeting, just under two years ago.

"Your Highness," he said, through laboured breath.

"Lord Somerset," replied Anna, "you honour us by your presence."

"It is I that is honoured," replied the duke. "Had we known of your coming, we would have organized something more fitting to your station."

"We don't need any special treatment, Your Grace. I believe you know General Matheson, my army commander?"

"Army?" the duke's face went pale. "Surely you're not here to arrest me?"

"No," replied Anna, "far from it. We have seen the flag of rebellion flying from your ramparts and have come seeking your help."

"Your army," he asked, "is it nearby?"

"It is some distance from here," she replied, "but perhaps we should discuss this in more comfortable surroundings, rather than outside?"

"Of course," said the duke. "I'm sorry to have interrupted you. You were introducing your party?"

"Yes," she continued, "as I said, this is Gerald Matheson, general of my army. You've met Dames Beverly and Hayley before, along with Master Revi Bloom and Tempus, but I don't think you've met Sophie, my Lady-in-Waiting."

"Pleased to meet you all," said the duke graciously. "Now, if you'll come this way, you can make yourselves comfortable inside, where it's warm. I'll have someone take the horses, shall I?"

They followed him inside where he led them into a comfortable looking sitting room. Servants were standing by to take their cloaks while another stood ready with wine, serving them as they sat.

"I must thank you for your hospitality, Your Grace," said Anna. "We didn't know what to expect when we received word of your rebellion. Can you tell us what led to it? I fear we've been out of touch for the last few months."

"Well," started the duke, "where should I begin? Of course, we all rejoiced when you returned to Merceria after a year abroad, but then, shortly after your arrival, we started hearing rumours that you had been arrested and tried for treason. Then, almost a month later, came word from King Henry that you and all your followers had been executed for said treason. I must say it was just too much to take. You have been popular here ever since you saved our city early last year. The final straw came when the king summoned all his knights to Wincaster."

"All of them?" asked Gerald.

"Yes, every single one of them. King Henry wanted them to repeat their oath of allegiance to him. It left us completely devoid of protection. How can a king deprive his own people in such a way? Why, if Westland decided to attack, we should have little to defend ourselves with."

"I can assure you, Lord," said Gerald, "that Weldwyn has no such thoughts. Don't you have a large garrison?"

"We do now," said the duke, "but it wasn't always so. Ever since the attack in the spring of '60 we've been more vigilant. I've doubled the garrison, and the town guard has been resurrected."

"And what do you place your numbers at, if I may ask?"

"We stand ready to defend our walls with more than a thousand men. Of that, the bulk are footmen, but we have three hundred archers, some of those using crossbows. It is cavalry we are weak in. The king took our knights, leaving us with no horsemen, though I daresay they're not too useful when defending a walled city."

"And your defences?" Gerald asked.

"In fine shape," he replied. "We wouldn't be going against the king if they weren't, and it's not just us."

Anna leaned forward at the news, "Whatever do you mean?"

"Have you been out of the country? I thought everyone knew," said the confused duke. "You were the people's princess. When word of your demise at the hands of the king spread, so too, did the talk of rebellion."

"Where did it start?" asked Gerald.

"It is rumoured to have started in Bodden," the duke explained, "and it's said it spread through the north like wildfire."

"Bodden?" said Beverly.

"Oh yes, I can only imagine the effect that the report of your death must have had on your father."

Beverly looked to the princess, "We must send word at once," she said, "before the king can send troops."

It was Gerald that answered, "We will, in time, but the king won't march in winter, and you're needed here. Have no fear, we'll get word to the baron eventually, long before the king can make his move."

"You spoke of an army," interrupted the duke. "Where have you raised it? I haven't heard of any recruitment."

"We have stitched together a patchwork army of allies," explained Anna, declining to give more details. "You have ample supplies here for the city?"

"Oh, yes," said the duke, "we're well prepared to hold out."

"Good, for we have allies in Weldwyn," she said.

"Westland? Why in the Three Kingdoms would they help? They've wanted to destroy us for years."

"We saved their kingdom last year," said Beverly, "and now, in return, they've pledged to help us take back the crown."

"Well, I'm glad to hear it, though the thought of Westlanders on Mercerian soil worries me."

"They owe us," said Gerald, "and the truth is they feared us as much as we did them, but they are a decent people, not terribly different from us. I'm sure once you meet them, you'll see for yourself."

"So what is the next step?" asked the duke. "I shall issue a proclamation to the city, of course, but what then? Have you a Royal Standard?"

"We have a flag," said Anna, "but it's not a Royal Standard. Sophie, if you would?"

Her servant dug into the satchel she carried, pulling forth the flag that had served them so well in Weldwyn. Hayley took one end, while Sophie stood, holding the other to display it for the duke.

He looked rather pleased by it. "The red flag of rebellion over a green bar. Saxnor himself couldn't have picked a finer flag, but surely your coat of arms should be present?"

"No," said Anna. "This is a flag for the people of Merceria, not my personal emblem. We fight for everyone, not just the Royal Family."

The duke appeared overcome with emotion. He dabbed at his eyes with a kerchief. "You make me proud to serve you, Highness."

"Thank you, Your Grace," said Anna. "Now, there are many things that need to be done. We have an army to move and preparations to make for the spring. I would like to send word to Weldwyn that they can start shipping supplies to Kingsford if that's all right with you?"

"Of course, Highness," he replied, "I am at your disposal."

"Excellent. We'll rest the night here. In the morning, Gerald and Hayley will return to Queenston while Beverly remains here with me to make arrangements."

"Queenston?" said the duke. "I don't understand. Where is that, in Weldwyn somewhere?"

Anna blushed slightly before answering, "It's best you don't worry about it for now. Suffice it to say our army is nearby, but we will need to bring it to Kingsford to continue with our plan."

"You will winter here?" asked the duke.

"Some, yes," said Anna, "but the bulk will continue downriver. We mean to take Colbridge before the spring."

"I shouldn't advise that, Highness," said the duke. "Lord Anglesley is a strong supporter of the king. He's likely got a large garrison of loyal troops."

"We shall see," said Gerald. "We've sent in some scouts to assess their defences. I expect we'll hear back within a fortnight or so. In the meantime, you'll be dealing with shipments coming from Falford."

"Surely you mean Aldgrave," said the duke. "It's just a few hours ride across the river."

"No," said Gerald, "Falford is better able to handle the boats we'll need for transport. Ferrying goods across the river here would take too long, and we're told Aldgrave has its own problems."

"I see," said the duke. "I'll do all I can to facilitate things."

"Thank you, Your Grace," said Anna. "And now, if it isn't too much to ask, we'd like to retire, for it's been a long ride."

"Of course, Your Highness."

Gerald stood, extending his hand, "Thank you, Your Grace. We'll keep you informed of our plans as they develop. We won't know more until our scouts return from Colbridge."

Lord Somerset shook his hand firmly. "Of course," he said.

FIVE

Infiltration

WINTER 961/962 MC

The gates of Colbridge were immense, for long ago it was a major trade centre. As the great swamp to the south expanded, however, it choked off access to the sea, and the city began its slow decline. With its usefulness to the kingdom vastly reduced, it had become a place forgotten and neglected, its population dwindling.

Arnim looked about as he and Nikki entered the once great city, now with its ancient stone walls crumbling and its streets unkempt. The town guard mirrored the neglected city; instead of watching as people came and went, they spent their time in the pursuit of gaming or even sleep, one snoring loudly in the gatehouse.

The road here was uneven, the cobblestones ill-fitted, broken, or simply missing. Arnim chose to walk in the mud beside the street, dirty boots being less treacherous than turning an ankle. Alongside him, Nikki took it all in. She had been born and raised in Wincaster, and until last year, had never left the Mercerian Capital. But now, with her new husband, she found herself, once again, in a strange city.

They made their way through the streets, pausing only to ask directions to a suitable inn. Finally, they settled on The Mermaid, a run-down place that had seen better days, like most of the establishments around here.

Arnim paid for a week in advance, and then they made their way up to the sparsely furnished room.

"Not the best of places, I'm afraid," Arnim said, sitting glumly on the edge of the bed.

"Oh, I don't know," said Nikki, "I've slept in worse." She looked over, noticing a look of concern on his face. "What is it, Arnim?"

He turned his gaze to her, "I would have liked to have taken you somewhere nice, now that we're married."

"There'll be time enough for that when the war is over," she stated. "I'm happy being here with you."

He smiled, an action that was rare these days for the knight. "So," he mused, "where do we start?"

Nikki opened the shutters to look outside. "The docks are over there. I think we should start by investigating them. When we take Colbridge, we'll need to bring in supplies somehow."

"Why?" asked Arnim. "Colbridge lies too far south to be of any real strategic value. Of course, it was different when the river was open to the sea, but now it's just an inconvenient garrison we must deal with."

"You're letting the gloom of this place get you down," she said.

"Can you blame me?" he retorted. "The whole city is like some abandoned, neglected, forgotten place."

"The king seems to think otherwise. Did you notice all the soldiers?"

"Yes," he said, warming to the challenge, "there are far more troops here than I would have thought."

"Why do you think that is?" she asked.

"They're up to something. King Henry could have just ordered them to seal up the walls and wait it out. Instead, he's sent troops from Wincaster."

"How do you know that?" she asked. "We only just arrived."

"I saw men in the king's livery, his household troops. They were drinking at a tavern called The Rose."

"That would be worth checking out," she said, "perhaps you can make contact with some of them, feel them out."

"Good idea," he said. "We need to gather as much information about these troops as we can. Where will you start?"

"I'm going to arrange our exit plan in case we need it. There should be smugglers hereabouts, especially with Weldwyn right across the river. I'll try to track one down. We may need to leave in a hurry if the duke gets wind of what we're up to."

"You might need to grease some palms, have you enough coins?"

"More than enough for what I need to do. How about yourself?"

Arnim hefted his purse, "I've plenty, but we should stash some here as it is not a good idea to walk about with so much." He gazed around the room, looking for somewhere to hide the coins.

"Do you remember Riversend?" she asked, looking at the floor.

"Ah, yes. The hidden floorboard, but isn't that a little obvious?"

"I have a variation on that," she said. "We'll put it right under the bed so that the frame sits atop it."

Arnim looked at the bed and grumbled, "I suppose that means I'll have to move it. It looks quite heavy."

Nikki walked over to the bed, bending slightly to push on the frame. "You know, it would help if you weren't sitting on it."

Arnim rose, coming around to her side. She began pushing on the bed, but he grabbed her around the waist.

"What are you doing, Arnim?" she giggled. "That's not how you do it."

"Oh, I don't know," he replied. "I can think of more than one way to move a bed."

The next day found Arnim wandering the streets, observing those that passed by, determined to identify any military troops he might see. He paused at a weaponsmith, intrigued by the conversation he overheard.

"That's far too much, my friend. What else have you got?"

"Well," replied the smith, brandishing a new blade, "I have a shorter sword here. It's seen some use, but it still has an edge to it. How much did you want to spend?"

Arnim moved closer to observe the transaction.

The purchaser dug into a small purse but found it difficult to extract the coins. He settled for dumping them out on the counter.

The smith looked disappointed. "That won't get you much," he said, "at least not a sword, at any rate."

"How about an axe?" suggested Arnim.

"What was that?" asked the customer, turning at the intrusion.

"An axe is usually much cheaper," the knight continued, "as it doesn't require as much work to forge."

"A good point," added the smith. "I have several here you could choose from, all the way from a small hatchet up to a great two-hander."

"I haven't really used an axe," complained the customer. "I'm afraid I wouldn't be able to wield it."

"It's easy," offered Arnim. "I could show you if you like?"

"That's very kind of you, sir, but I don't even know you. How do I know you aren't working for the smith, here?"

"I've never met him before," complained the merchant.

"That's easy enough to settle," said Arnim. "My name is Richard Arendale."

"Glad to meet you, Richard, my name is Rowan Spencer. Are you new to Colbridge?"

"I am," replied the knight. "I heard the duke was looking for soldiers and thought I'd make my way down here. It's always nice to have a little coin in the purse."

"Have you found employment yet?" asked Rowan.

"No, I only arrived last night. How about you, what's your story?"

"I'm part of the levy. We've been enlisted to beef up the defences, though for the most part, we've been doing manual labour."

"You don't say?"

"Oh yes. Now that rebellion is in the air, the duke is all concerned about reinforcing the city walls, and we're desperately short of people. Why don't you come and join us? We could always use another pair of hands."

"A fine idea, Rowan. Are you billeted nearby?"

"We're the levy, not a regular company, so we all live in our own homes, but the headquarters isn't too far from here."

"Then lead on," said Arnim.

"Hey," called out the smith, "what about your weapon?"

"My mistake," said Rowan, scooping his coins up and dropping them back into his purse. "I'll come back later for a weapon. It's unlikely I'll need it for some time anyway. It's not as if anyone is going to attack in the middle of winter. Come along, Richard, I'll introduce you to our captain."

Arnim was led up the street by his host who proved to be most talkative.

"Colbridge is an old town," Rowan was saying. "Have you been here before?"

"I'm afraid not," Arnim replied. "I was raised in Wincaster, though this city is very similar."

"I imagine it is, but Colbridge is much older. It is the second city of the kingdom."

"Second city?"

"Yes, Kingsford is the first city founded by our ancestors, while Colbridge followed soon after."

"Interesting," mused Arnim.

"Of course," his host continued, "back then it was a bustling port city, and one of the most populous of the entire realm."

"Was? What happened?" Arnim said, feigning ignorance.

"The Great Swamp, that's what happened," explained Rowan. "It's been spreading for generations, even closed off the mouth of the river a while back."

"Couldn't they just clear it out? Surely it wouldn't be that much work."

"It's not just the plants, it's the creatures that lurk there that are too terrible to mention."

"How long ago did this happen?" asked Arnim.

"About two hundred years ago, give or take a few decades. They tried clearing it out many times, but they lost too many ships. There hasn't been a seagoing vessel at our docks for many generations."

"But surely the river is still navigable?"

"Oh, aye, the river provides trade opportunities, but they pale in comparison to what we did in our heyday. Of course, when the foreign trade dried up, so did our population. People sought out opportunities elsewhere. Well, those that could afford to, at least."

"And so now you have a large city with a much smaller population."

"Exactly," agreed Rowan. "For years the city has been neglected. The walls were built long ago when money poured in from overseas trade, but now there are no coins in the coffer, and the walls are tumbling."

"Surely it can't be as bad as that? What about all the troops you have here?"

"That's from the Royal Purse, or so I'm led to believe. It appears the duke is in the king's favour, a benefit for staying loyal, I suppose."

Rowan paused, looking left and right, "Ah, we're almost there. Just up ahead you'll see some men standing around."

Arnim glanced up the street to see what his host had predicted. The men looked more like common labourers waiting for their assignments, for none of them were carrying weapons.

"How many are there in the levy?" he asked.

"I'm told there's only about two hundred of us. This is the northern company, but there's another in the south end of the city."

"So what do we do now?"

"Just wait. The captain will appear soon enough, and then we'll have plenty to do."

As if on cue, the captain arrived; a dour-looking man with a humourless face. Pushing his way past the crowd, he opened the door and entered the building, leaving the men to follow him in. Arnim and Rowan waited until the crowd thinned and then joined the end of the line.

The captain sat at a table, a ledger placed before him. As each man came up to him, he asked their name, scribbling it into the ledger with his quill, and then dropping a meagre few coins into the waiting hand. At Arnim's approach, the officer looked up.

"I haven't seen you here before," he commented.

"I just arrived in Colbridge," Arnim offered.

The captain looked him up and down, nodding to himself, "You look able enough. Name?"

"Richard Arendale," he replied.

The captain wrote the name down in rough lettering, then dropped three coins into Arnim's palm. "You'll be working on the north wall today. Report to Sergeant Hawkins. Rowan, here, will show you the way."

Arnim moved aside and waited, while his new friend collected his pay.

"Come along, Richard," said Rowan, "we must hurry. Sergeant Hawkins is not one to welcome tardiness."

They hurried off to their day of labour.

Nikki sat, nursing a cider. The common room of The Mermaid was busy, and she cast her eyes about, examining each of the patrons. In order to carry out her assignment, she needed information, and the tavern on the first floor of this inn was likely to be the best place to find it.

Most of the people here were simple workers, though the occasional merchant showed his face. People came and went, the entire room constantly humming with conversation. It was nigh on noon when she finally overheard something of consequence. Two men were talking in hushed tones, something about an incoming shipment and their eagerness to avoid the town guards. It immediately piqued her interest, and she shuffled closer, the better to listen.

"Who's bringing it in?" asked a swarthy fellow.

"Garan," replied the elder of the two, a white-haired man.

"When can I get it?"

"Tomorrow morning."

"Can I pick it up here?"

"No, of course not. Come down to the Pearl and speak to Harriet."

The swarthy fellow shook the older man's hand then left, leaving his companion to finish his ale in peace.

Nikki considered approaching the man but then thought better of it. She waited till he finally left, then rose from her table, determined to locate the Pearl by following him. Of course, she had no idea if he was making his way there directly, but decided it was worth the gamble.

The white-haired fellow wandered down the street, taking his time. He stopped to chat with a local merchant who was unlocking his door, forcing Nikki to duck into a doorway to avoid discovery. She looked around, aware that anyone who had seen her would think her actions suspicious, but no one seemed to take any notice. Breathing a sigh of relief, she returned her attention to the white-haired man. He had continued down the street, and she stepped out of the doorway to follow. This individual appeared to know everyone, for he stopped on multiple occasions to talk to vendors. On at least one of these occasions, she spotted coins changing hands, and then she understood; her target was collecting money, likely payment for protection. It was an old racket and one she was all too familiar with. This was getting more interesting by the moment.

She managed to get a little closer the next time he halted, enough to hear part of the conversation. What she heard confirmed her theory, for the merchant was obviously not happy with having to pay. It seemed this fellow was well known throughout town, for his appearance brought instant obedience. Nikki became more convinced that he represented the local power hereabouts and resolved to continue following, hopefully to the Pearl.

Her efforts were finally rewarded as her target's meanderings brought them to the docks, which lay on the west side of town. There, he entered a tavern, its placard proclaiming the name for all to see, The Pearl. She halted, watching from a distance; it wouldn't do to enter the place without an appreciation for the type of clientele. She spent the rest of the day observing, taking note of the people coming and going.

That evening Arnim and Nikki met back at The Mermaid. They were both tired but knew there was still work to be done.

Nikki sat on the bed, removing her shoes, "Did you make any progress today?"

"I did," said Arnim. "I joined the local militia."

"And?" she prompted.

"And not much else," he confessed. "I spent the day doing heavy labour. The troops are mainly being used to haul away broken bits of stone, but I did make some valuable observations."

"Where were you working?" she asked.

"The north wall. It seems there are a few sections that have crumbled over the years. I'm no engineer, but I think the stone they used is the wrong type. There are large cracks everywhere. I don't imagine it would stand up to a siege for very long."

"So why are they clearing out the rubble?" she asked. "I would think it would help hinder an attack."

"I'm sure it would," he admitted, "but they've brought in some large timbers. I think they're going to try bracing what's left of the wall."

"Valuable information," she said. "I would think, considering what you've observed, that it would be the perfect place to assault."

"Yes, though perhaps a little too easy to defend, if they put their minds to it."

"Care to explain?" she asked.

"If I were in their shoes, I'd let the wall fall, then lead the attackers into a trap. With the right preparations, it could be deadly."

"How would they do that?"

"By funnelling their enemies through the hole, and then boxing them in. I saw them building some barricades nearby."

"How do their numbers look?"

"They have a lot, but their quality is doubtful. I suspect most of them have been called to arms with little or no training; half the militia doesn't even have real weapons, just pitchforks and knives."

"Knives can still kill," warned Nikki.

"Yes, but almost useless in a battle. How about you? What did you find?"

She smiled, "I think I've located the lair of the local crime lord. I'm going to try contacting him tomorrow. If anyone can arrange things, it would be him."

"Be careful, Nikki, they're likely to be dangerous folk."

"Hey, it's me, remember? I'm used to people like that."

Arnim broke into a grin, "Maybe they should be worried?"

"That's more like it," she replied. "Now get over here. My back is sore from standing all day, and I need you to rub it."

The next day found Arnim once again hauling stones, in a chain gang of sorts, with the larger rocks passed along the line to be stacked out of the way. Other men shovelled smaller stones and dust into wicker baskets and buckets to be taken away, out of his sight. It was back-breaking work, but at the noon break, as he quenched his thirst at the water barrel, he overheard the captain say something interesting.

"Sir Nigel," the man said, "I didn't expect to see you here today. Is there a problem?"

"Nothing urgent," replied the knight, "but I need some advice. We have a new contingent of knights due here by the end of the week, and I'll need more stabling."

"Surely not," said the captain. "Wilkerson has stables enough for at least two dozen."

Sir Nigel frowned, "Would that it was enough, but the king has seen fit to double our numbers."

"How many are we talking about?"

"By the time they arrive, we'll need stabling for fifty."

"Fifty! Saxnor's beard, that's a lot. Surely the king doesn't expect an attack?"

"I doubt it," said the knight, "but I'm sure we'll start becoming more aggressive come spring. His Majesty may wish to use Colbridge as a starting point for his coming campaign."

The captain looked at the wall, "I thought all this was just to keep the troops busy. Surely we're not going to war?"

Sir Nigel cast his eyes about, but Arnim, ever on the alert, bent to the task of watering himself to avoid suspicion. "The rebellion is spreading, and the king wants it crushed as quickly as possible. Come spring, troops will be on the move, for he wants it all handled by summer. Now, you do me this favour, and I'll see to it your name is mentioned. Come summer, there'll be rewards for those that came to the king's attention."

The captain's back noticeably straightened. "Carsons, down by Silverstones Ave."

"Thank you," replied the knight, extending his hand. "And remember, no one else is to know of this."

"My lips are sealed," promised the good captain.

Arnim turned, ready to resume his work but a voice called out, halting him in his tracks.

"You there!" yelled the knight.

Arnim froze, then turned slowly. "Who me?" he asked.

Sir Nigel walked toward him, "Don't I know you?"

"I don't believe so," he replied.

The knight was not having any of it. He strode over, halting just in front of Arnim, staring into his face as his mind struggled to think. "I've seen you somewhere," he said. "Where are you from?"

"Wincaster, Lord," he replied, trying to sound courteous.

The knight's face suddenly dawned in recognition, "You're one of those bastard Knights of the Hound. Guards! Seize him!"

Arnim reacted quickly, drawing his knife and stabbing forward. Sir Nigel was armoured in chainmail but had forsaken his helm and coif this day, thinking himself safe within the walls of the city. Arnim's knife plunged forward, striking the knight in the throat. It wasn't a deep cut, but enough to stagger the man backward, clutching at his wound.

Arnim turned and ran as fast as his feet could carry him, while a hue and cry arose behind. He went for the nearest cover, a small alleyway, and ducked down the narrow confines. Voices echoed off the buildings as he sprinted and then a man appeared at the end of the narrow passageway, his sword raised. Arnim slowed his pace, his knife ready for a fight.

His enemy's blade slid forward, but Arnim ducked to the side, the edge tearing across his tunic but doing little damage to his skin. His knife struck out, and his target dropped his blade, clutching his injured arm. Arnim sprinted away, past the injured soldier, turning right, running farther into town. He cast his eyes about, desperate to find some place of safety, but he was unsure of the layout of this great city.

Ahead of him, others had taken up the cry, and a group of men with spears jogged toward him. Seeing a door to his immediate right, he pushed it open and ran in, only to crash into someone. He lashed out wildly, knocking them to the ground, and then looked around. He was in a tavern, and as his luck would have it, it was full of soldiers. They'd heard the cry of alarm and were standing, but his sudden appearance had taken them all by surprise. He spotted a set of stairs and rushed toward them, but there were men everywhere, and then he suddenly felt the impact of something hitting the back of his head. His vision blurred and he staggered forward, intent on reaching his destination, but hands dragged him down, and then he fell, his desperate struggle ended by the blackness that overtook him.

Nikki entered the Pearl. The place was ordinary enough, with the smell of cheap alcohol permeating the air. She sat on one of the bench seats that lined the walls, a small table before her. Soon, a woman walked over.

"What'll it be?" she asked.

"I'm looking for a man called Garan," she said. "I understand he frequents this place?"

She noticed a slight look of fear on the woman's face. "Why in the Three Realms would you want to see him?" she asked.

"I have a business proposition, one that could be quite profitable to him."

"I'll see that he gets the message," the barmaid replied. "Come back tomorrow."

"I'll stay," Nikki said. "I've a feeling I won't have to wait long. Take him this," she said, passing over a coin.

The woman looked at the gold. "This is Westland money," she said in appreciation.

"Yes," said Nikki, "and there's lots more where that came from. What's your name?"

"Harriet," the woman replied.

"Well, Harriet, there's a gold crown in it for you when you come back."

Nikki kept her eyes on the woman as she left, tracking her movements. Harriet ducked behind the bar and whispered something to the barkeep, who looked in Nikki's direction and then nodded. A moment later, Harriet left the room, using a door behind the bar as her egress.

It didn't take long for the door to reopen. A dark-haired man, complete with ponytail entered the room, heading straight for her table. He sat down without introduction. "You wanted to see Garan?" he asked.

"Yes," she admitted.

"What's this about?"

"I have need of his services. I need to get some people out of the city."

"How many," he asked.

"Only two, but I'd prefer it to be kept quiet."

He looked to his hand, which held the gold coin she had passed on earlier. "This is Westland gold," he said. "Do you work for them?"

"No," she responded, "though I've done work for them recently. I have plenty more where that came from, Garan."

He looked up in surprise. "What makes you think I'm Garan?" he asked.

"I've been watching this place for a while. You always travel with an escort. Either you're Garan or the Duke of Colbridge."

"You're a smart woman," he said, "perhaps too smart for your own good. What makes you think I wouldn't just kill you and take the money?"

"I've done this type of negotiation before. I know not to have it all on me. What's your price?"

"When would you need transport?" he countered.

"Sometime in the next few days. Perhaps as early as tonight, but more likely a day or two from now."

"And you wish to avoid any unnecessary entanglements, I suppose?"

"Yes," she admitted, "and I'm willing to pay extra for your discretion."

Garan looked around the room in thought. "I can do it, but it'll cost you."

Nikki smiled, pulling forth a purse and dropping it on the table. "How about this for the first half, the rest on delivery?"

He lifted the purse, testing its weight, then peered inside, smiling. "This will do nicely," he said. "You said there's just two of you?"

"That's correct, myself and one other."

"Very well," he replied, pocketing the purse. "When you're ready, come here and look for Harriet. She'll bring you down to the docks where we'll have a boat ready."

"Isn't the river frozen?" Nikki asked.

"Only partially. Don't worry, we know where the ice is thickest. We'll take a boat if it's thin. Otherwise, we'll guide you across the river, will that do?"

She stared at the man's face, trying to gauge his trustworthiness. "Very well," she replied, "I'll next see you when it's time to leave."

SIX

The Duke's Guest

WINTER 961/962 MC

Mather Reed put his feet on the table, leaning back in his chair and rocking it on two feet. He placed his hands behind his head, intertwining his fingers and closed his eyes, imagining a different life, with beautiful women at his beck and call.

He was startled out of his reverie by the sound of a door opening, and his eyes flew open to see a woman standing in the archway, her face masked by the shadows of her winter cloak.

Suddenly conscious of his pose, he lowered his chair and removed his feet from the table.

"Can I help you, Miss?" he asked a moment later.

"Are you the jail keeper?" she countered, her voice melodic and sultry.

"That's me," he said, rising to his feet and puffing out his chest. "Mather Reed, at your service."

The woman entered, her eyes barely visible until she removed the hood to reveal a woman of substance; hair carefully set, clean face, and a smile that would charm a Holy Father. Mather immediately knew this was a woman of means.

"I understand you have prisoners here," she continued.

"All sorts, Miss," he replied. "Is there one, in particular, you were interested in?"

"As a matter of fact, there is," she replied, coming closer. She paused before him, the table holding her at arm's length, "I understand you apprehended a spy?"

Mather's face scrunched up in thought. "A spy? I don't think so," he replied, and then a look of understanding took hold. "Ah, you mean the traitor?"

She smiled, and his heart melted. "Yes, that's the one. I heard one of the knights captured him?"

"Yes," said Mather, "Sir Nigel brought him in."

"A Knight of the Sword," she said, "how interesting."

Mather warmed to the task now, the smile on her face drawing him in.

"Well," she continued, "I should go, I don't want to keep you from your duties."

"No, wait," he blurted out, desperate to keep her in the room. "Perhaps you'd like to see him? It's not every day we have a traitor in our midst."

She halted, giving him hope, a sly smile curling the ends of her mouth. "How intriguing. Perhaps I will let you indulge me; I've never seen a traitor before."

"Let me fetch my keys," he said, "and then I'll take you down there."

"Isn't it dangerous?" she asked. "What if the prisoners overpower you?"

He laughed, "They're secure enough. Beyond this door here, is a hallway which leads to the cells. The cells themselves are locked, and only my companion, down in the guard room has the keys."

"I thought this was the guard room?" she asked, her voice dripping like honey.

"No, I'm just the jail keeper. I look after all the important stuff. There's another man down the hallway that holds the keys and feeds the prisoners; it makes it harder for them to escape." He halted at the door, pulling forth a key from his pocket and inserted it into the lock. It clicked as he turned it and then he pulled on the handle, swinging the door outward. "After you," he offered.

He stood close to the door, forcing her to brush past him as she entered, the smell of her perfume captivating. As soon as she was through, he followed, turning to face the door. "Just have to lock the door," he said, "can't be too careful with these rogues."

Hands reached around him from behind, the heady scent of perfume once more drifting to his nose. "I like a man that knows his job," she whispered in his ear.

He never spoke again. The slim dagger drove up, expertly placed beneath his ribs, and Nikki guided his limp body to the ground, carefully extracting the weapon as she did so. She turned her attention to the hallway, lit by a single oil lamp that hung from the rafters. The jail keeper had told her all she needed to know. She could see the end of the hallway, blocked by a stout wooden door, while on either side there were wooden doors with barred windows. She moved to the door on her right and peered through, only to be met with an empty chamber.

She pursed her lips in disappointment and then moved to the door opposite. She heard a faint noise coming from beyond it and peered through the window. Like its companion behind her, the room was a modest size, perhaps no more than twelve feet or so in depth. It ran the length of the corridor, a good twenty feet, with a window opposite that opened into the courtyard, letting in enough moonlight to illuminate the occupants.

Nikki counted six men, though in the shadows she couldn't identify which one was Arnim. She let out a bird whistle, trying not to be too loud. There were stirrings on the floor, where the men lay, but none rose. Fearful that the noise might alert the guard, she lifted her dress, pulling forth the lock picks she kept tucked in her garter, and then bent to the task at hand.

Working in the shadows was not ideal, but years of practice had honed her skills. Soon, after a satisfying sound, she felt the door unlock. She pushed gently, swinging it open quietly to peer in while waiting for her eyes to adjust to the darkness before stepping inside. Moving the lock picks to her left hand, she drew her dagger in her right; these were criminals, after all. Creeping forward slowly, she looked at each man in turn, finally settling on the familiar shape of Arnim Caster.

She almost let out a gasp when she saw him, for he had not been treated kindly by the guards; he had a swollen face with clothes bloodied and tattered. She reached out, gently shaking him. "Arnim," she whispered.

He murmured something, and then his eyes opened as she leaned over him in the dark. Suddenly, his hands shot out, grabbing her by the throat.

"It's Nikki," she called out softly, not resisting.

The hands dropped. "Nikki?" he murmured.

"Come on, let's get you out of here," she said, offering her hand.

He took it, hauling himself to his feet. Despite his injuries, he smiled. "I knew you'd come," he whispered, "but how did you find me?"

She led him out to the hallway, her hand grasped firmly around his. "When you didn't turn up at the inn, I came looking," she said. "It didn't take long to hear about the arrest, it's all over town."

She paused, letting go of his hand.

"What are you doing?" he said, as she turned back to the door.

"Locking the door," she said, pulling it closed. "It'll add to the mystery."

Arnim was confused but said nothing as Nikki started in with her lock picks.

A moment later and all was done. "There," she said, "everything back where it should be."

Arnim saw the dead guard blocking the exit and hauled him out of the way.

"You should take his sword," said Nikki. "I'm sorry, I don't know where yours went."

"That old thing? I won't miss it; I have King Dathen's sword back in Queenston. I'm glad I didn't bring it with me."

Nikki opened the door to the main office, the key still sitting in its lock. She stood aside, waiting for Arnim to exit. A moment later she stepped through, locking the door behind her.

"Come on," she said, "we have to get out of here. With any luck, they won't find anything amiss for some time."

She was about to leave when Arnim grabbed her hand.

"Wait," he said, scanning about the room, "I'll freeze out there."

"Don't worry," she replied, "I've stashed some clothes nearby. This isn't my first jailbreak."

He looked at her in surprise, but she just smiled. "Now come along, my love, we've got to get to the docks before someone raises the alarm."

She led them across the road and down a side street where they halted. Nikki reached behind a water barrel and pulled forth a sack, extracting a bundle of clothes which she then tossed to Arnim. He dressed quickly, pulling the woollen tunic over his head only to see her holding out a pair of boots.

"You thought of everything," he said.

"Like I said," she replied, "not my first jailbreak. I know how petty guards can be."

He pulled on the boots while she stripped out of her dress. "Time for Lady Nicole to disappear," she said, "and get back to good old Nikki."

Arnim watched as she laced up her new outfit. "Aren't you forgetting something?"

She looked at the smile on his face, "There'll be plenty of time for that later, my love. We have to get out of here."

"No, I meant your hair. You can't wander about town dressed like a commoner with hair like that, it's a dead give-away."

"Oh yes, I forgot," she said, mussing her hair. "Better?"

"Much," he replied, "now lead on, we haven't much time before dawn."

She led them through the city, cutting down alleys and keeping close to the shadows. Soon, they approached the docks, the telltale smell of the river revealing its proximity.

"We're almost there," she said, "The Pearl is close by. We have to contact someone called Harriet and then they'll take us across the river."

A few more side streets and they came out at the edge of the water. The

Pearl was close by, its sign swinging in the cool breeze that blew across the river.

"It's colder than I would have thought," remarked Arnim. "I'm glad you brought me these clothes."

"Are they warm enough?" she asked. "We have a lot of ground to cover once we're on the other bank."

"They're fine," he said. "Now let's get a move on, I want to be across the river before the sun comes up."

They made their way along the street, walking in the open as if they belonged. The sounds of the tavern drew nearer as they made their way to the entrance.

Arnim led, opening the door to feel the warmth of the room envelope him. He stepped inside, holding the door for Nikki who moved past him, heading to a nearby table. A moment later, they were seated.

It didn't take long for their arrival to be noticed. Harriet came over, stopping in front of them. "I see you made it," she said.

"Yes," said Nikki, "I hope everything's arranged?"

"It is," she confirmed, "I'll just get you a drink to warm you up while they prepare the boat." She disappeared into the back room after a quick word with the barkeep. Another server dropped two tankards on the table, the ale sloshing over the rims.

Nikki was about to take a sip when Arnim's hand stopped her. "Hold a moment," he warned, "something doesn't feel right."

She placed the drink back on the table, her eyes scanning the room. "People are leaving," she said quietly. "They know something's about to go down."

Arnim looked to the doorway. Two large men stood there, their hands resting on the hilts of their knives.

"What do we do?" asked Nikki.

"Is there another way out?" he asked.

"Yes, around back, behind the bar, but they'll have that covered."

"Saxnor's balls," said Arnim, "we'll have to fight our way out."

"Then what?" said Nikki. "We still need to cross the river. It'll take forever to launch a boat."

"The river's frozen," said Arnim. "We can make it across on the ice."

She looked at him in horror, "The ice can't possibly be thick enough to hold us."

Arnim stood, ignoring her protest. He had his tankard in his right hand, his left resting on his hip, near to the sword he had stolen.

"A toast!" he yelled out loud, drawing the attention of all in the room. He moved toward the door slowly, his face to the crowd, "To our good King

Henry, may his reign be short." He turned suddenly, using the tankard to throw ale into the face of one of the door guards.

Taken by surprise, the man gasped, raising his hands in reaction. Nikki, having discerned her husband's plan, struck out, the dagger slipping silently into the second man's gut.

They didn't wait for a reaction, rather they pushed forward, forcing the men to the ground. Arnim's left hand punched the man's face, breaking his opponent's fingers as they were clutching at his ale-soaked eyes. The guard fell heavily while his companion joined him on the floor, clutching his stomach. Nikki leaped over him, rushing through the doorway, Arnim close behind. They paused only a moment to take their bearings.

"This way," yelled Nikki, "there's stairs down to the water."

Yelling erupted behind them, and they heard the call to action as they rushed toward the river, descending the stone steps quickly onto a short wooden pier. Standing at the end, the darkness hid the distant shore, but the ice below was easy to see. Arnim lowered Nikki, joining her a moment later. He took a step, and hearing a crack, froze in place.

"What was that?" Nikki cried out in alarm.

"The ice," he replied. "Move slowly, make for the far bank."

They headed off across the ice, moving as slowly as they dared. Shouts came from the steps, and then the voices drew closer. Arnim risked a look over his shoulder only to see half a dozen men crowding the wooden pier.

"Faster, Nikki," he called out, "they're catching up to us." As he took another step, his foot slipped out from under him, sending him to his knees with a loud noise as cracks radiated out from where he had hit. He rose slowly, his eyes riveted on the ever-spreading cracks. Men were lowering themselves onto the ice behind him, and he risked another glance, then turned his eyes toward Nikki. She was a good twenty paces or so in front of him, making steady progress.

Shifting his attention back to his pursuers, he withdrew his knife. Three of them were coming close now, spread out so as not to break through.

Arnim drove the knife into the ice, creating more cracks. One of the pursuers must have realized what he was doing for he suddenly turned, scrambling back toward the dock. The other two, however, moved closer, prompting Arnim to repeat the action.

"You won't do it," yelled one of them, "you'd go down with us."

Nikki had turned upon hearing the voice. "Arnim, no!" she screamed, but it was too late. He drove the blade down a third time, and suddenly the ice broke.

Arnim pitched forward as the ice disintegrated beneath his feet, plunging into the frigid water. He stabbed down again and again with his knife, trying to find a chunk thick enough to hold him up. Finally, his knife stuck in, and he hung on for dear life.

His pursuers, however, were splashing about, now intent on their own fate, forgetting their quarry. The cold quickly sapped his remaining strength, and he lost any feeling in his legs. Struggling to hold onto the knife handle, his hands lost feeling by the moment. He managed to keep his head above the water, but try as he might, he couldn't haul himself up onto the ice; his strength was spent. He watched as Nikki drew closer, but more cracks appeared.

"No," he cried out, "the ice is too thin, save yourself!"

"I waited years for you," she yelled, "I am not giving up on you now."

He stopped struggling, resigned to his fate, for surely it was the only way she would be convinced to leave him. Closing his eyes, he was about to release his grip when a thought struck him.

"Crawl," he cried out. "You need to spread out your weight, or the ice will crack."

He watched her lower herself to a prone position, then she began to inch forward. It seemed to take an agonizingly long time until her hand was there, right in front of him. He reached out, unable to feel anything, hoping she could pull him out. She grasped his forearm and hauled back with all her might, rising to a sitting position to do so.

Slowly he emerged from the water, his body resisting his best efforts to help. Finally, he lay on the ice, unable to move, but Nikki worked feverishly. He felt her cloak cover him and then she removed his scabbard and belt. This, she looped around his ankles and then she headed for the far bank on all fours using the belt to drag him.

He fought to stay conscious, his mind fogged by the cold. Ice and snow passed by him as he looked left and right, struggling to make sense of everything. He felt a bump and then, to his amazement, he saw grass poking through the snow; they had made it to the far bank.

SEVEN

War Council

WINTER 961/962 MC

~

With the return of Nikki and Arnim to Kingsford, the princess called a council of war. Now, they all sat around the table, eager to learn details.

"Can it even be done?" asked Revi. "Moving an army in the winter time is problematic, to say the least."

"Yes," replied Gerald, "though there are numerous difficulties."

"All right, supposing we get them to the city," continued the mage, "then what? We have no siege engines. It would be impossible to breach the walls."

"Arnim and Nikki's report tells us otherwise," Anna reminded him. "There are numerous weaknesses we can exploit."

"Well, I guess there is the advantage of surprise," said the mage.

"I've marked the weak spot in the walls," said Arnim, "and from what Hayley tells me, the Trolls could easily batter it down with stones."

"The Trolls will be a surprise," cautioned Hayley, "but the defenders will still be expecting an attack on the walls, they've been reinforcing them for weeks now."

"I have other ideas," said Gerald, "but of greater concern to me is getting the army to Colbridge in the first place. We have a winter march ahead of us and a lot of terrain to cover."

"You had this idea back in Weldwyn," said Anna, "what makes you so nervous now?"

"I'm not nervous, but there are a thousand details to arrange. Getting all our allies to work together has been...trying."

"As in," questioned Nikki, "they're trying to kill each other?"

"Not directly," replied Gerald, "but the Orcs and Elves still won't work together; it's hampering the tactics I'd like to use."

"How so?" asked Arnim.

"I have to deploy the Orcs and Elves with a separation between them. In addition, I've got to deal with Weldwyn Volunteers who don't want to be anywhere near the Kurathians."

"Can you blame them?" asked Revi. "The Kurathians did invade their kingdom, after all."

"Yes, that's true," said Gerald, "but I never thought through all the problems that have been cropping up."

"It doesn't sound too bad," soothed Anna. "You can change the marching order so they're not together and then line them up for battle with Humans between the other races. That should separate them nicely."

"It's much more complicated than that," defended Gerald. "To begin with, their marching speeds vary. The Elves are fleet of foot while the Dwarves lag far behind. The Kurathian foot marches slower than the volunteers, not to mention that the Orcs outpace everyone except the horses. Add into the mix the setup of camp each night, and the problems multiply."

"Are you saying that we risked our lives for nothing?" growled Arnim.

"No, the information is very useful," said Gerald, "and I'm confident I can take advantage of it, providing I can successfully move the army."

"So then tell us," prompted Anna, "providing you can get the troops to work together, what is the plan you've been brooding over?"

Beverly looked up in surprise, "I thought you'd already know, Highness."

"No," said Anna, "Gerald hasn't told me anything."

"Sorry," said Gerald, "I've been overwhelmed with things."

"You need a staff," suggested Beverly.

"A what?" asked Nikki.

"A staff," she repeated. "A group of people that can assist in planning and executing his orders. He needs people to run messages, carry orders, and act with his authority."

"Yes," agreed Anna, "that's a marvellous idea. I should have thought of it."

"Why would you say that?" asked Gerald. "I've never heard of Mercerian armies using a staff before."

"No," agreed Anna, "but I've read of foreign lands. Our ancestors came here from across the Sea of Storms, the library at Uxley has books that tell of times before that. The army that expelled our ancestors was organized along similar lines."

"You had a staff, of sorts, when we marched to Eastwood, Highness," Beverly reminded her.

"That wasn't really a staff," interjected Gerald, "that was a group of advisors. What she's suggesting now is people to do the heavy lifting."

"Yes," agreed Anna, "though they have to have enough leadership skills to carry through with things, so you don't have to organize every little detail."

"They'll have to know how to talk to all the races," warned Arnim.

"No," said Hayley, "there's a better solution."

"Which is?" asked Arnim.

"Pick your aides from each company," explained Hayley. "Surely there's enough of them that speak our language?"

Revi smiled, "I knew she was more than just an archer."

"Who said I'm just an archer?" she asked, turning her attention to the mage.

Revi blushed, "Why, no one, it's just an expression."

"Can we get back to the subject at hand?" asked Gerald.

"What do you need from us, Gerald?" asked Anna.

"I've already arranged some things with Weldwyn. I need someone to go to Falford and meet with Osbourne."

"Who's Osbourne?" asked Beverly.

"Osbourne Megantis," offered Revi, "he's a Weldwyn Fire Mage."

"Yes," agreed Gerald, "and the man who's going to make sure the ships can move down the river in case it's frozen."

"Will that work?" asked Hayley.

"He assures me it will."

"And the ships?" asked Arnim. "What are they for?"

"They'll carry our supplies," replied Gerald. "Even as we've been planning, they've been stocking up on things for this eventuality. The plan is to have them rendezvous with us here, at Kingsford, and then parallel our march downriver. They'll be within sight the whole time and able to come to our aid if needed."

"Will they be carrying troops, too?" asked Hayley.

"Yes," he confirmed, "they'll pick up some hand-picked troops when we meet them."

"Hand-picked?" asked Arnim.

"Yes, I've discussed an idea with Beverly, but I think we'll keep it a secret for now, the fewer that know about it, the better. I'll brief the princess once the meeting is over."

Anna smiled, "You're being rather crafty, Gerald. I like that."

"I'll go to Falford," offered Hayley. "When should I leave?"

"We'll all go back to Queenston first," said Gerald. "You'll leave for

Falford when the army starts moving south. The boats move quicker, but will likely take a day or two to load up. Whoever gets back here first will simply wait for the others."

"The distance shouldn't be too great," said Revi. "Shellbreaker can keep an eye out for both sides."

"Excellent," said Anna, "then I suggest we get some sleep, we've a long journey back to Queenston, and then we're on the march. The war to retake Merceria is about to begin."

Anna exited the building, Gerald following her out. She was just descending the steps to the street when a commotion drew their attention.

"Yer Highness!" a voice called out.

The guards were swift to respond. The Duke of Kingsford had insisted on posting sentries wherever the princess travelled, and now they apprehended a man who was clearly overexcited. Anna turned toward her carriage, ignoring the calls, but something in the voice made Gerald pause. He looked toward the commotion. The guards had swarmed the man, and he now lay pinned to the ground by a knee on his back.

"Halt there," called Gerald as he moved toward them.

The guards backed away, save for the soldier who held the man beneath him.

"Get off of him," the general commanded.

The soldier looked surprised by the order but did as he was commanded.

Gerald knelt, extending his hand, "Let's have you on your feet, Edgar."

Edgar Greenfield took his hand, hauling himself up. "As I live and breathe, I thought the princess dead, so I did."

"She's alive as you and me, Edgar. Come along, we've much to discuss. Tell me, how did you come to Kingsford? The last I heard of you was months ago."

Edgar blushed, "I was livin' down in Stilldale, so I was. Found me a nice widow to settle down with, but she took all me money and kicked me out. Now I'm back to being a messenger." He looked Gerald in the eye, "Sorry 'bout creating the noise back there, but I was sure you was both dead. It were like seein' a ghost, so it were."

Gerald guided him toward Anna, who had turned at the disturbance. "Much has happened, Edgar. It's good to see you."

Edgar bowed as they drew closer. "Yer Majesty," he said.

"Highness," corrected Gerald.

"Edgar," said Anna, ignoring the comment, "your reports over the last year have been particularly illuminating."

"Pardon?" said the old warrior.

"They've been very useful," Anna reiterated. "Come, ride with us in the carriage. You must tell us what you know of the kingdom."

Tempus was asleep inside the carriage and opened his eyes as they entered, much to Edgar's surprise.

"You remember Tempus?" asked Gerald. "Don't worry, he remembers you."

Edgar took a seat, looking uncomfortable as he did so. "I thought you was all dead," he said. "I travelled up to Bodden and told the baron so. Even had his daughter's hammer as proof."

"The baron is well, I trust?" asked Anna.

"Oh aye, he was, though not so much after I told 'im 'is daughter was dead."

"She's quite alive," said Gerald, "and with us here in Kingsford."

"Well I never," said Edgar.

"So what news have you?" asked Anna. "We know so little of what is happening in the capital."

"Things in Wincaster is gettin' bad, I'm afraid," said Edgar. "The king, he called all 'is knights to swear loyalty. Said he was going to raze the north. There's been rebellion there, you see. I 'eard Baron Fitzwilliam started it all."

"Do you know how he plans to do that?" asked Anna, her face a mask of concern.

"'Fraid not. I were eager to get out quick as I could. I was planning on heading to Westland for safety. I don't reckon I like the sound of what's 'appenin'. What is it you're doin' 'ere in Kingsford?"

"We're taking back Merceria," said Gerald. "Kingsford is our next step."

"Next step?" said Edgar. "What was yer first?"

"Raising an army," said Anna.

"You 'ave an army?"

"Of sorts," said Gerald.

"Do you 'ave one or not?" asked Edgar.

"It's a difficult one to answer," said Anna. "It's more of a collection of allies."

"An alliance?" asked Edgar, then his expression broke into a grin. "You've made an alliance with the Westlanders, haven't you?"

"Partially," said Gerald, then he saw the look of confusion on Edgar's face. "We also have Elves, Orcs, Trolls and foreign mercenaries."

"Wait, did you say Trolls? You 'AVE been busy," said Edgar.

"On that, I think we are in agreement," said Anna.

Edgar's return to the princess's service had put her in a good mood. She had him write out everything he could think of and now sat pouring over his scribbled notes.

Gerald found her this way, sitting in front of the fireplace, stray pieces of paper spread across the floor. "Anything of interest?" he asked.

"Yes, lots," she answered, without lifting her head.

Gerald picked up a note, scrutinizing it. "I don't know how you can find something useful from all these random observations. Look at this, for example. This note says two dozen knights left Wincaster heading west, how does that help us?"

"If you remember Arnim's report, he said that Colbridge was expecting another two dozen knights. Edgar keeps very accurate dates on his notes. These knights that left Wincaster must be the ones expected in Colbridge."

"How does that help us?" asked Gerald.

"It at least confirms Arnim's report," explained Anna. "Anyway, it's just an example, but I can use a similar process to estimate what's happening in the kingdom."

"And what do you think is happening?"

"Nothing good, I'm afraid," answered Anna. "If Henry is sending an army north, no good will come of it. We may have to change our plans."

"I was hoping we could trap him on the Kingsford-Wincaster road. If he heads north, it will complicate things immensely."

"Indeed," she said, "but there is some good news."

"Which is?"

"He's put Valmar in charge of the army. It's marching to Tewsbury. I rather suspect they plan on wintering there; that should give us time to secure Colbridge."

"Yes, his incompetence is to our advantage, but we need eyes in the north," said Gerald. "I wish Revi had more of those gates for us to use."

"He does," said Anna, startling her old friend. "He has two more gate locations worked out; we just haven't had time to explore them. I had hoped that once we secured Colbridge, we'd have time to investigate them."

"Did he say where they were?"

"Yes," admitted the princess, "one by Wickfield and the other near Redridge."

Gerald's face broke out into a grin, "That's marvellous news. I couldn't ask for two better locations."

"Don't get too carried away," warned Anna, "we don't even know if the locations are still viable, they could be dead ends."

"Then how did he find them?"

"He was looking through more of those ancient Saurian records back in Erssa Saka'am."

"Erssa what?"

"Saka'am. It's the name the Saurians use for their home city. You know, the one with the huge ancient temple?"

"I never heard it called that before," admitted Gerald.

"It is a mouthful, I grant you. It's in their native tongue. It means 'place of magic.'"

EIGHT

The March South

WINTER 961/962 MC

They returned to Queenston to marshal the troops for the winter march. The Duke of Kingsford had promised to arrange supplies and billeting for them once they arrived, but the army first had to cross the miles to the great city.

Gerald sat on his horse, watching as the troops formed up, Beverly beside him. He was in a foul mood, the steadily falling snow having crushed his optimism.

"The Elves are already on their way," reported Beverly. "They're fast, the snow doesn't seem to slow them."

"They have the advantage of being the first through the snow. The going will get more difficult as additional troops trudge through it. I assume Telethial is leading them?"

"Yes, General," said the red-headed knight.

"We're not on parade, Beverly, you can call me Gerald. Are the Kurathians lined up?"

"Lined up and ready to go on your command."

"Give the order then and let's get this army moving."

Beverly rose in her stirrups and waved. The Kurathian leader, Lanaka, saw the motion and barked out commands. Moments later, the mercenaries moved forward, their light cavalry spreading out in front.

"They are very experienced," said Beverly, "but I wish they had heavier armour."

"It would only slow them down," said Gerald. "They're excellent light cavalry and perform their jobs well. We can't make them into something they're not."

"I understand," said Beverly, "but with no real heavy cavalry, how are we to counter knights?"

"I have an idea or two," said Gerald. "Don't worry, we've lots of Mercerians joining us in Kingsford. You'll get your heavy cavalry, but you must be patient. You don't want knights anyway, do you?"

"I'd be lying if I said they wouldn't be useful."

"After we take Colbridge you'll get time to train your horsemen. I'm hoping we'll have lots of heavier armour by then."

"How do you reckon on that?" she asked.

"We'll just take it from the king's knights."

"You make it sound so easy."

"Easy? No, I suspect it will be rather difficult, but we have a surprise for them, several in fact."

Beverly grinned, "You can be quite devious at times, Gerald."

"I learned from your father." He looked to Beverly, who was staring down at the ground. "Don't worry, I'm sure he's fine."

"I'm not worried about my father," she said, "he knows how to defend Bodden."

"I was talking about Aldwin," said Gerald.

Beverly blushed, for in truth her smith was all she could think about for the last few days. "I miss him terribly," she confessed, "and I've been gone for ages. What if he's moved on? He could be married by now, he certainly wasn't lacking for attention."

Gerald reached out to her, touching her on the forearm. "If that's what you think, then you're vastly underestimating the man. Aldwin loves you, he's willing to wait decades."

"But he likely thinks me dead," she objected.

"It doesn't matter," said Gerald. "I didn't stop loving my wife because she died. She'll always be a part of me. This isn't like you, Beverly, you're usually so confident. What's the matter?"

"I'm worried," she confided. "It feels like events are moving out of our control. What if this attack fails?"

"It won't fail," promised Gerald, "I won't let it. You have to have faith."

"How can you be so sure?"

"What makes you think I'm sure? I have doubts, just like everyone else, but I know it's a solid plan. You have an important part to play, do I need to replace you? I can have Hayley take your place if you like?"

"No," she replied, "I know the plan better than most, it just seems so...unorthodox."

"That's the beauty of it," he said, "and I don't think they'll expect it."

As the Kurathian mercenaries finished filing past, Gerald looked north to where the rest of the army gathered. "Who's next?" he asked.

Beverly withdrew a paper from her saddle, unfolding it carefully. "Looks like the Orcs."

Gerald frowned.

"Something wrong?"

"No, they're wonderful troops, and I wish we had more of them, but they move quickly. They'll catch up to the Kurathians in no time and then they'll have to slow down."

"I had to use them to separate the Kurathians from the Weldwyners," explained Beverly.

"I know. I just wish it were easier. Here comes Kraloch now."

The Orc shaman walked in front of his troops while Orc hunters ran to either side of the column. Behind him were the disciplined Orc spearmen, though Gerald had to remind himself they weren't 'men'.

"They're impressive," said Beverly. "I daresay I wouldn't want to face them in battle."

"You already have," said Gerald in surprise, "or did you forget the Battle of Eastwood?"

"Believe me, I'll never forget, but those Orcs weren't disciplined like these. I can see why the ancient Elves were afraid of them, they're a forbidding sight."

"I wouldn't mention that around the Elves," Gerald reminded her. "I don't think they'd ever admit to being afraid of anything."

"The Orcs will be followed by the Weldwyn Volunteers, led by their cavalry. I wish we had more of them."

"I wish we had more of everything," added Gerald, "but we must make do with what we have."

They waited as the Westlanders marched past, grins lighting their faces.

"They're eager," commented Beverly. "They think it's a grand adventure."

"Let them," said Gerald. "Few men would serve knowing the true horror of war. I only hope that most of them will live to remember this day."

Beverly looked at him in surprise, "Having regrets?"

"No," he replied, keeping his eyes on the troops, "but it's not easy sending someone out to battle."

"There are those that would disagree," said Beverly. "Valmar, for instance."

Gerald snorted, "Valmar doesn't care about his men. I won't lead someone into battle without a hope of living through it. Men aren't cattle to be led to the slaughter."

"That's what makes you a great general," said Beverly.

Gerald blushed, "Yes, well, who's left?"

"The Dwarves," she replied, "followed by the Trolls and then the supply wagons. I thought it best to bring the mastiffs up at the tail end of the column."

"A good idea," he agreed. "Where's Anna? I would have thought she'd be here with us."

"She's at the back, with the dogs. It seems she's grown rather fond of them."

"I'm surprised, they're quite aggressive."

"They seem to have adopted Tempus as their pack leader," she explained, "when you're not around, that is."

"I still find that rather disturbing," said Gerald.

"What? That they bow down to you?"

"Yes, it makes me uncomfortable, as though I've got something locked up inside of me, waiting to get out."

"Think of it this way," offered Beverly, "you've just got a way with dogs. Did you have one as a child?"

"I did," said Gerald, "his name was Calum. He was a scruffy looking beggar but a great companion."

"What happened to him?"

"He was killed by the raiders that murdered my parents."

"I'm sorry," said Beverly, "I never knew."

"No reason why you would," offered Gerald. "That was years before you were born. Your father had dogs on occasion, but after you came along, he sent them away. I think it took all his attention to look after you."

"Are you saying I was a handful?" she asked with a smirk.

Gerald laughed, "You still are, Beverly, you still are."

The column halted for the day. Arnim was looking north, along the track they had taken when Beverly came up behind him.

"Problem?" the redhead called out.

The knight turned to see her approach. "It's the Dwarves, they should have been here by now."

"But the rest of the army is already here, weren't they ahead of the wagons?"

"They were, but their pace slowed down the column, so they sat beside the road and allowed everyone else past."

"So then, where are they?" mused Beverly.

"I was just wondering the same thing. Shall I go and investigate?"

"No, I'll go. Your horse looks winded, and Lightning here, has lots of energy left. Go and find Gerald and let him know, he'll be anxious for news."

"I will," promised Arnim, turning his horse and heading south.

Beverly rode back up the track. They referred to it as a road, but it was little more than a trail, and even then it was only the passage of their own troops that had created it. It was getting dark by the time she found the Dwarves. They were marching south, but much slower than expected. Being short of stature, the snow, which had been a minor inconvenience to the other troops, was a major obstacle to them. She halted and waited while the Dwarf captain trudged up to her.

"I'm sorry, Commander, but we can make little more progress this day. How much farther is the camp?"

"It's some distance, I'm afraid," she replied. "Are your troops tired?"

"Exhausted," he admitted, "they're not used to this kind of weather."

"You should camp here. I'll ride back to the column and let them know. Will you need food?"

"No, each Dwarf carries three days rations, and we can see to our own camp. We'll try to catch up to you in the morning."

"Very well," said Beverly, "I'll let the general know." She turned Lightning and galloped off, the great beast navigating the snow drifts with ease.

Beverly found Gerald sitting by a large roaring fire along with Princess Anna and her usual assortment of advisors, including the company commanders.

"Beverly," called out Gerald, "what news?"

"I'm afraid it's not good. The Dwarves are having a rough time with the snow. It's going to slow us down."

"We should carry on without them," said Telethial, "let them catch up as best they can."

"No," objected Kraloch, "that would diminish our forces. We must wait for them."

"We can't," objected Arnim. "The longer we wait, the worse the weather will get. We have a limited window to take Colbridge; if we wait too long, their reinforcements will arrive."

"A valid point," said Anna, "but it's the general's decision to make. What do you suggest, Gerald?"

The old warrior looked around the fire before speaking, "I'll not split up the army. They've been training to work together, and leaving the Dwarves behind will play havoc with my plans. We need some way of speeding them up. Revi, is there a spell you can use?"

"I'm a Life Mage, not an Enchanter," replied the mage.

"Not entirely true, my friend," said a voice. They all turned to see the approach of the Kurathian mage, Kiren-Jool.

"What do you mean?" asked Revi.

"From what you've told me," the mercenary continued, "you've already started using enchantments. Your spell of tongues belongs to my school of magic."

Anna looked at Revi in surprise. "Are you saying that Master Bloom has mastered two schools of magic?"

"Yes," continued the Kurathian, "that's exactly what I'm saying. As an Enchanter myself, I know what I'm talking about."

"Remarkable," offered Revi, "who would ever have guessed."

"It doesn't surprise me," said Hayley. "I know how special Revi is."

The Life Mage blushed, "I'm flattered, of course, but I know of no such spell that would work in this circumstance."

"Wait a moment," said Beverly, "can't an Enchanter enhance someone's endurance? Surely that would let them march longer without tiring."

Kiren-Jool stared into the fire as he answered, "I'm afraid it doesn't work that way. Oh, I could use the spell, but I wouldn't have enough power to affect all the Dwarves, perhaps only a dozen or so, assuming I was fully rested, of course."

"So what do we do?" asked Anna.

"We drag them," a voice boomed out.

They all turned in surprise to the Troll leader, Tog, who seldom spoke.

"How do you propose we do that," asked Arnim, "by their ankles?"

"No," replied the huge troll, "we drag them on wooden platforms."

"Like a sled?" asked Gerald. "We'd need horses for that, surely."

"No," persisted Tog, "we Trolls will pull them."

"Do we have enough rope?" asked Gerald, looking to Beverly.

"Rope we have in plenty, King Leofric was generous in that regard. He thought we'd eventually need it to make siege engines."

"Will the Dwarves agree to that?" asked Arnim.

"What makes you ask that?" responded Herdwin.

"They are a proud people, stubborn in the extreme," offered Arnim.

"Where did you get that idea?" asked the Dwarf.

"I've heard they never surrender," suggested the knight in defence.

"It's true that we never surrender, but we're very pragmatic. I suppose you've heard that Dwarves never retreat as well."

"Of course."

"Do you know why?"

"I confess I don't," replied Arnim.

"Dwarves are short of stature, with shorter legs than most races."

"I remember," said Arnim, "they marched slower than us when we put down the rebellion back in '60."

"Yes," added Anna, "but they marched longer hours to make up for it."

"Agreed," said Herdwin. "Us Dwarves know that others can easily outpace us. If we were to retreat from a battle, we'd be cut to pieces on the march."

"So you're saying they won't mind being dragged?" asked Arnim.

"Not at all," said Herdwin. "In fact, if I may be so bold as to say so, they'd be happy to do it if it meant participating in the upcoming campaign."

"Then sleds it is," said Gerald. "Now, we'll need to cut down some trees..."

The conversation soon devolved into planning mode and carried on into the wee hours of the night.

The sun rose to a beehive of activity. While the Elves stood guard, the rest of the army concentrated on the task at hand; cutting down trees, then hewing them into square-cut timbers. The first platforms were tied together and tested, but friction with the ground proved too much, even for the Trolls.

It was Anna that found the solution, remembering something she had once read. She oversaw the creation of runners, planes of wood that ran on either side changing the wooden platform into a true sled, rather than a simple raft design. By the time the Dwarves came into view, they had two workable models, with more in the works.

There were roughly a hundred Dwarves and one hundred and fifty Trolls. If it hadn't been for their armour, each Dwarf could have simply been carried by a troll, but the heavy Dwarven chainmail almost doubled their weight.

In the end, the sleds proved quite useful, for they not only provided transportation for the Dwarves but some of the army's supplies too, as traditional wagons often bogged down in the snow. The sleds, on the other hand, had runners that would ice up, making them even easier to move in the frozen landscape. If there had been enough time, Gerald would have insisted on more, but the weather was closing in, and he was eager to continue the march.

· · ·

They arrived in Kingsford with little fanfare. It had taken them a little over a week, a fast march considering they were crossing wild country. The majority were happy to see the warmth of a billet, but the Elves, Orcs and Trolls refused to enter its walls, preferring to remain in the countryside. The Human and Dwarven troops soon flooded the city; a strange collection of Mercerians and foreigners, swelling the taverns with their business and overwhelming shop keepers. While this was happening, those in charge met with the duke, eager for news of the ships.

Gerald hoped to find their allies in residence, but the ships had failed to arrive. Revi sent his familiar, Shellbreaker, upriver only to discover the ice had slowed their progress. It looked as though it would be several more days before they would make it to Kingsford and so the troops had time to rest.

There was still lots of planning to be done. For now, the duke added Mercerian troops into the mix, including some much needed armoured cavalry. All of this had to be taken into Gerald's plans for Colbridge, and while the extra troops were a blessing, they complicated things considerably.

Now he had to adjust the order of march in addition to reorganizing his supply train. He finally decided to create his staff by recruiting from each company. He placed Beverly in charge, though during battle she would assume command of the cavalry. He started with appointing six people, but this proved inadequate to the task, and it rapidly expanded to twelve. He had a representative from the Orcs, a hunter by the name of Marguk, who proved able to learn the common tongue of man with considerable ease. Telethial appointed her own representative, an Elf named Elunien, while Herdwin represented the Dwarves at their request. The Weldwyn Volunteers, the Kurathians, and the Mercerians each supplied three staff members.

Gerald relied on Anna's knowledge of history as they struggled to organize things, but it still took many hours until he was satisfied. He began issuing orders, only to reveal yet another problem; the staff members were indistinguishable from regular troops. They settled on having them wear sashes, identifying them as a member of the general's staff. A quick visit to each company to explain the situation was all it took, and things began to fall into place.

Late at night on the third day after bringing the army to Kingsford Gerald was restless. Most of his staff had turned in for the night, but the general couldn't sleep, and so he decided to go for a walk to clear his mind. He dropped in to see the princess, but Anna lay fast asleep. Sophie suggested he take Tempus with him and so he found himself wandering through the city of Kingsford, the giant mastiff in tow.

The streets were empty, save for the rare appearance of a town guardsman. These men wandered the street at night, carrying lanterns on the lookout for troublemakers. They didn't bother Gerald, for most of them knew the general by sight, and those that didn't couldn't help but notice Tempus.

They wandered around aimlessly while Gerald thought things through. The duke had added close to five hundred additional troops, bringing his total to almost sixteen hundred soldiers. He knew Beverly would be glad of the extra cavalry, but he had to carefully consider where to place his foot and archers in the line of battle.

It was while pondering this exact thing that he turned onto a side street. His thoughts were interrupted by the sound of people. He looked up to see a tavern, its windows letting the light escape into the night.

Gerald halted his battle planning, at least for the moment, diverted to other pursuits. "What do you think, Tempus? A nice tankard of cider?"

Tempus looked up at him, drool dripping as his massive tongue hung out the side of his mouth.

"Very well," said Gerald, "a tankard it shall be, but just one, mind you, we don't want to overdo it." He resumed his walk, the great dog trotting along at his side.

He was just about to reach for the door when it flew open. Two soldiers stumbled out, bumping into Gerald and sending him tumbling to the ground.

He looked up in disgust only to see the men punching and hitting one another. Tempus growled, but Gerald ordered him to stay. The smaller of the two men kicked the other, a rather rotund individual, in the groin, sending him to the ground. Now, the attacker straddled his target, sending a rain of blows down on him, which his opponent feebly tried to block with his hands.

Gerald regained his feet, moving to prevent the onslaught. He grabbed the smaller man by the shoulder, but his target lashed out wildly, striking Gerald in the face, knocking him back.

Tempus didn't hesitate, launching himself across the short distance. A moment later, the great dog stood over the man, pinning him to the ground beside the second individual.

"Get him off me!" demanded the shorter man, his voice slurred by drink.

The portly one tried to rise, but Gerald planted his foot on the man's stomach, keeping him down. "Stay where you are," he commanded. "What do you two think you're doing?"

A reply came from beneath Tempus, "He's a filthy Westlander."

"What of it?" demanded Gerald. "That Westlander came here to free our kingdom from oppression. You should be thanking him, not attacking him." He turned to the other combatant, "And you, you should know better than to pick a fight with an ally. What's wrong with you people?"

"Get this beast off of me," demanded the Mercerian, "I'll show him who's oppressed."

Gerald moved up beside Tempus. "Do you know who I am?" he asked.

"No," replied the subjugated man, "why? Does it matter?"

"You struck me."

"What of it?"

"I'm General Gerald Matheson, perhaps you've heard of me?"

Beneath the great dog, the struggling stopped.

"Do you know the punishment for striking a superior?" Gerald pressed.

"A fine?" squeaked out the voice.

"It's death," said Gerald, fed up with the man's nonsense.

The Mercerian turned deathly pale. "I'm sorry, my lord, it's just the drink talking, I didn't mean anything by it."

"There's no excuse for this type of behaviour." He put his hand on Tempus, touching him lightly on the head, "It's all right boy, let him up." Turning his attention back to the other man and asked, "How did this start?"

"In there," the Westlander said, pointing to the tavern.

For the first time since his encounter, Gerald became aware of the noise in the background. He looked to the doorway while the sounds of a fight wafted out.

Ignoring the two men on the ground, he stepped toward the doorway. "Come along, old boy, I might need you."

He caught sight of something out of the corner of his eye as he entered and instinctively ducked as a tankard sailed past his head, smashing against the wall beside him. The entire tavern was one massive brawl. A man had ducked down behind the bar, likely the owner, while two women cowered behind an overturned table in the corner. Someone dragged another patron over a table while a third threw punches.

Gerald called out, ordering them to stop, but his voice was carried away in the yelling and screaming. Two men rolled past, clutching at each other's throats and then Tempus let out a tremendous bark. The ear-splitting sound easily cut through the noise, reverberating throughout the room, seeming to shake the very walls.

The fighting paused, as if by magic. Everyone turned to stare at the door and the great dog that stood guarding it, his teeth bared.

"This will cease now!" Gerald commanded, his voice finally heard. "You will return to your billets at once or by Saxnor's balls I'll have the town guard in here and hand over every last one of you. I will not see my soldiers act in this manner."

He hadn't meant to lose his temper, but it had all been too much. The last few weeks had been a nightmare to organize, and he would not see it devolve into a petty fight.

The tavern began to clear, and he watched them leave. So intense was his fury that none of them would meet his gaze and it wasn't until they had all left that he realized what a significant risk he had taken, for if they had refused his command, he would have been powerless to stop them. He looked down at Tempus, rubbing the great dog's head in affection, "It's good you were here, old boy. I couldn't have done it without you." Tempus wagged his tail.

The very next day, Gerald put the Humans to work making more sleds, keeping them busy, and more importantly, too exhausted to fight.

When the boats from Weldwyn finally arrived, two days later, they met Hayley at the dock, along with a man dressed in robes.

"Osbourne Megantis, I presume?" asked Revi.

"Indeed," the man replied, "and you must be the esteemed Master Revi Bloom. Dame Hayley has told me all about you."

"Indeed," said Revi, bowing deeply. "May I introduce Her Highness, Princess Anna of Merceria and General Gerald Matheson."

"Pleased to meet you," said the Weldwyn mage, "though I must apologize for our tardiness. We would have been here a few days ago, but the river ice has thickened considerably."

"You managed to make it," said Gerald, "so the plan must have worked."

"It did," said the Enchanter, "though it took some time to get it perfected."

"I wonder," said Anna, "if the ice will slow our advance. Perhaps we should wait until spring?"

"No, Highness," replied Osbourne, "I can get the ships through. As I said, it was more about learning the actual technique. Melting the ice with magical flame is very easy in theory, but if it's not done properly, it simply re-freezes. I think I've solved that problem. Give the crews the night to rest, and we shall be ready to get back at it at first light."

"Excellent," said Anna, "then the advance to Colbridge can begin."

NINE

Colbridge

WINTER 961/962 MC

G erald let out a breath, the chilly winter air misting it before his eyes. "It's cold," he observed.

"Not as bad as I expected," said Anna. "How are the troops doing?"

He looked to the marching army. They were heading south, following the riverbank while keeping their supply ships in sight at all times. "Their morale is good," he said, "far better than I would have thought after a long march."

"They're competing," said Anna.

"What do you mean?"

"They're trying to outdo each other. The Mercerians from Kingsford want to out-march the Weldwyners, and the Weldwyners can't stand to see the Kurathians out-pace them."

"Ah well," said Gerald, "at least it keeps them moving. How are the others doing?"

"The whole army is in good spirits. I think they're all expecting victory. You know, you're developing quite the reputation."

"I'm just doing my job," he grumbled, glancing out to the river.

He watched as the Fire Mage, Osbourne, stood at the prow of the lead ship, waving his hands. A moment later, an area of flame appeared on the ice a few yards ahead of them, its colour the distinctive blue of magic. Nothing happened for a moment, and then with a cracking noise, the top of the ice turned back to water. The ship kept sailing, easily smashing through the now thin ice.

"Quite effective," said Anna. "It is a clever idea."

"It would have worked better had we more mages," mused Gerald. "Our Weldwyn Fire Mage can only cast so many spells in a day; it's actually slowing us down."

"Not really," said Anna. "We still have to take time to set up camp each day. The progress so far has been excellent, much better than I would have expected, especially considering it's winter time."

He watched the ship inch forward. "I remember when we sailed upriver to Falford the first time."

"Yes," said Anna, "and you didn't like the water. You got over it by the time we left, though."

"I suppose I did," he replied.

Anna returned her attention to the army marching by, "Where's Beverly? I haven't seen her all morning."

"I sent her and Hayley ahead of us with some hand-picked troops."

"Oh? What do you have in mind for them?"

"I'd rather not say at this time," he replied, "it's a bit of a long shot, but Arnim's report gave me an idea."

"Don't you trust me?" she asked, her face a look of disappointment.

"I trust you completely," he replied quickly, "it's the ears of others I don't. If word got out about what I have planned, the tactic wouldn't work. I'll tell you about it later when I can be sure no one else is listening."

"Fair enough," she said, lapsing into silence.

A loud popping noise grabbed their attention, and they looked once more to the boats.

"What was that?" asked Anna.

"The ice," explained Gerald. "Sometimes when Osbourne casts his spell, the ice cracks into great chunks. I noticed it earlier."

"It's a good thing we're not trying to be stealthy," said Anna.

"Yes," he agreed, "if whoever commands the troops at Colbridge has any ability, he'd know we're coming by now."

"Why do you say that?"

"We're getting very close. I'm sure he would have heard of Kingsford's flipping to our side. Unless he's a fool, he'll have put out scouts to detect an enemy's approach."

"From what Arnim and Nikki told us, there are Knights of the Sword present."

"Yes," he agreed, "and likely this Sir Nigel is in charge of the defence. Beverly recognized the name; he's one of the senior knights of the order."

"Surely the duke would be in charge," countered Anna.

"The duke has no experience in these matters, and the poor condition of the walls tells us he has no interest. I rather suspect he was happy to have someone else take over his troops. This way, if he loses, he can claim to have taken no part in the fighting."

"I remember the duke," said Anna. "He wanted me to marry his son, do you remember?"

"I do. I remember threatening the son."

Anna turned in disbelief, "You threatened the son of a duke? You never told me that."

"He was being obnoxious and said some unkind things about you."

"I'm flattered," she said, "but you could have gotten yourself into some terrible trouble; you were only a guard at the time."

"It worked out in the end, and that's all that matters."

"You can still surprise me from time to time, Gerald."

"That's what I'm here for, Anna, to surprise you, and keep you safe."

The troops were moving quickly and soon came the Trolls with the sleds that carried the Dwarves. A cheer erupted from the passengers as they were pulled past.

"They seem happy," remarked Anna.

"And well they should be, they get to ride in those things, it's much better than trudging through the snow."

"We should get moving," she said. "The only unit left is the mastiffs, and they're some distance back to keep them from scaring the troops."

They fell in behind the Dwarves, well out of earshot.

"Tell me, Gerald, what is the biggest threat?"

"The knights," he replied, without any hesitation. "It all hinges on the knights."

"Why do you say that?"

"They can do the most damage to us. I suspect they'll be held back and used at a crucial moment. When that happens, we shall have to be ready for it."

"How will we know the right time?"

"We will have to tempt them. Knights are very effective but notoriously unreliable in battle. They'll attack whatever they think will give them the most glory."

"And you think that is..."

"You," he smiled.

"So I'm to be bait?"

"That's one way of looking at it, but don't worry, I'll keep you safe."

"I'm not worried," she replied. "I trust you, but what makes you think I'm their prime target?"

"That's easy," he said. "Once they know you're with us, they'll realize that killing or capturing you would end the entire rebellion."

"But the rebellion was spurred on by rumours of my death, wouldn't the same thing happen if they actually caught me?"

"I don't know, but at least the rebel army would be destroyed."

"I won't be captured again," declared Anna, "I'd rather die."

"Don't worry, you'll be perfectly safe, I guarantee it."

"How can you be so sure, Gerald? You can't always control a battle, the unexpected sometimes raises its head."

"I'll take precautions to protect you, Anna. If things go badly, we'll get you aboard the boats. They'll look after you in Weldwyn, if necessary."

"If it comes to that, I'm not going without you."

"If it turns out like that," he said grimly, "I'll probably already be dead."

"Then let's make sure the plan works."

"I'm with you on that," he said. "Now, where's that hound of yours?"

"He's back with the pack," said Anna.

Gerald glanced over his shoulder, "I still can't see them."

"Don't worry, they're not too far behind us."

"Don't they normally bark or something?"

"They do," she replied, "but they can smell you, Gerald, and so they're calm."

"I still find that disturbing."

"Of course you do."

By nightfall, the advance scouts reported that the walls of Colbridge were in sight. Early morning would see them forming up for battle, but for now, it was sufficient to put out pickets to watch for enemy raids.

Gerald wandered the camp, visiting his warriors. It was strange to think that not so long ago he was just a simple sergeant in Bodden. If it hadn't been for a strange twist of fate he might have remained there till his dying days, and he wondered, not for the first time if the Gods meddled in the affairs of men.

As he wound his way through the camp, he listened to conversations drifting by. There was the usual jesting of comrades; bragging of past conquests both on and off the battlefield, and their prowess in combat. Many of these men had never seen battle before, and he wondered how many would have to die before there was an end to this war. His fit of melancholy was interrupted by familiar voices, and he found himself approaching a campfire, around which sat Arnim and Nikki. Revi was there too, though he sat quietly, petting his familiar, the black bird known as Shellbreaker.

Gerald moved toward them, "I hope I'm not interrupting anything?"

"Of course not, General," said Nikki. "Come, join us, we've some cider here if you'd like?"

"No, thank you," Gerald replied. "I must keep my head clear, there is too much to look after."

"Don't worry," said Arnim, "I know exactly what I'm to do tomorrow."

"I never doubted it," said Gerald, "but it will be exceedingly dangerous; we've never tried something like this before."

"We were all at the siege of Riversend," Revi reminded him.

"Yes," agreed Gerald, "but we were the defenders. Now, the shoe is on the other foot, and we have to attack. Have you scouted the city?"

"Yes," replied the mage, "thanks to Shellbreaker, here, we have a very good idea of their numbers. It's much as Arnim reported, they haven't changed anything."

"Good, then we can proceed with my plan. Now remember, Arnim, the timing is extremely important. If you linger in the breach for too long, you'll take massive casualties. After the siege, we still have to conduct a campaign, so we can't afford significant losses."

"I won't let you down," promised Arnim, then chuckled.

"Something you want to share?" asked Nikki.

Arnim's laughter died down, "I was just trying to imagine the look on Sir Nigel's face when I ride up to the gate to demand their surrender."

She nudged him with her elbow, "You have the sickest sense of humour. With all this death looming, how can you find something so entertaining?"

"I'm happy, and why wouldn't I be. I have you by my side. If I die tomorrow, it will be with a smile on my face."

"Well," she retorted, "if you die tomorrow I won't be happy at all. You will look after yourself, Arnim Caster, do you hear me?"

"Of course," he said, with an exaggerated nod of his head.

"Revi," prompted Gerald, "why the long face?"

"It's Hayley," added Nikki. "He misses her, but he won't admit it."

"She's my lucky charm," mumbled the mage.

"Let's hope her luck rubs off on us all tomorrow," said Gerald. "I'm sorry I had to take her from you, but she and Beverly have a very important role to play."

"I understand," said Revi.

"You should get some sleep," prompted Gerald. "You all should, it'll be a busy day tomorrow."

"You should follow your own advice," suggested Arnim.

"Hah! That's a good one," said Gerald. "Me, sleep before a battle, if only I were so lucky."

Gerald turned and left them, wandering off to the next fire.

"Where's he going?" asked Revi. "Shouldn't he sleep?"

"He won't sleep," said Arnim, "he'll probably find Tempus and wander the lines all night long. He'll be tired in the morning, but the rush of battle will keep him going."

"And how about you?" asked the mage. "How will you sleep tonight?"

"Quite well," replied the knight, standing. He held out his hand to Nikki, "Come along, my love, it's time we were abed."

"Good night, Revi," said Nikki, "we'll see you in the morning."

Lord Reginald Anglesley, Duke of Colbridge, gazed out from the battlements of the city. The rising sun had burned off the early morning mist to reveal enemy troops arrayed to the north. He had hurriedly dressed in his best armour and now stood, watching the enemy's movements.

Sir Nigel, the commander of the Knights of the Sword, walked up beside to join him in his observations.

"Well?" asked the duke. "What do you make of them?"

"Rabble," replied the knight, "no doubt about it. I rather suspect they were hurriedly armed and are likely poorly led."

The duke moved closer to the parapet to get a better view. "What is that flag?" he asked. "I don't recognize it."

Sir Nigel swept a discerning eye over the enemy lines. "A red bar over green. I've never seen its like. I see the banner of the Duke of Kingsford, his men are deployed over there," he pointed. "The others I don't recognize. There's also a strange banner over yonder that looks quite foreign."

"That's the banner of the Kurathian Princes," said the duke. "I've read about them."

"Kurathians!" the knight spat in disgust. "They're nothing but mercenaries. They can't be counted on."

"I might remind you that Merceria was founded by mercenaries."

"Yes," objected the knight, "but we've come a long way since then. You must feel a great sense of relief."

"Why is that?"

"Because you have the Knights of the Sword to serve you, Lord. We have never been defeated in battle."

"I wish I had your confidence," muttered the duke.

"Let me ride forth now, Your Grace. I can polish off these usurpers in no time."

The duke was about to reply when movement caught his eyes. "Something's happening."

Sir Nigel focused his attention back to the enemy line. More troops joined them, emerging from the distant tree line and began forming up. A small group moved quickly forward, bows clearly visible in their hands. "Elves," he swore. "I remember seeing them at Eastwood. Luckily, there aren't too many. Shall I ride forth?"

"No, I think we should wait, there may be more troops arriving. One must have a good idea of the enemy's strength before attacking, don't you agree?"

"There is wisdom in your words, Your Grace."

They watched as another group emerged, this time on the eastern flank of the rebel line. These moved much slower and the early morning sun glinted off of armour.

"Dwarves," said the duke. "How in the Three Kingdoms did they get Dwarven troops? They don't live anywhere near here."

"It seems they're full of surprises," commented Sir Nigel. "See how they're anchoring the end of their line? An important placement, they must think highly of them."

"So we have a large group of Human troops flanked by Dwarves and Elves. I wonder what else they might have up their sleeves. Where's their cavalry?"

"I expect they're keeping them in reserve," said Sir Nigel. "Though I doubt they'd compare favourably with our knights. Look, I see a rider leaving their lines."

He pointed, and the duke watched as a lone rider headed for the main gatehouse. "Let's get down there and see what the villain wants."

It was a short walk from the wall to the gatehouse, which stood in the northeast corner of the city. Soon, they were staring down from the crenellations while the sole rider halted just before the massive doors.

"Who are you," called the duke, "that dares bring an army to my doorstep?"

"My name is Sir Arnim Caster," called out the rider, "Knight of the Hound and servant to Princess Anna of Merceria."

"Lies!" called out Sir Nigel. "You are nothing but a traitor and a scoundrel."

Ignoring the jibes, the messenger continued, "I am here on behalf of the princess to request you to lay down your arms and surrender the city. Do so now, and you will avoid unnecessary bloodshed."

"Hah," called out the duke, "it is you that shall shed blood today. You and your rebellious army."

"Is that the answer you wish me to take to the princess?"

"I tell you what," offered the duke, "take your army and depart and I shall have no quarrel with you. What do you say to that?"

"Alas, I cannot agree to such terms. A siege will result in a great many deaths, on both sides. I offer to meet you on the field of battle. Let us settle this with honour."

"Honour? You have the gall to talk to us of honour? You're the ones fighting against the rightful king. You are nothing but traitors."

"I take it then," said Sir Arnim, "that you refuse the offer of battle?"

"We do," called out Sir Nigel. "Let your army come and grind themselves to death on our walls."

"Very well," Arnim said, then turned his horse to leave but halted for a moment. "I have one more message for you, Your Grace."

"Which is?" called out the duke.

"Before the week is out, this city shall be ours. When the walls come down, and they will come down, all those that oppose us will be put to the sword. I implore you to tell your troops not to resist the inevitable assault."

"Begone, vagrant!" yelled the duke. "I've had enough of your insolence."

The messenger rode off toward the troops formed up to the north.

The duke turned to his military commander, "What now? Do they expect to starve us out? Surely they realize we have lots of food."

"They haven't the men for an assault," said Sir Nigel, "and where are their siege engines?"

"Perhaps they thought we'd offer battle."

"I rather suspect their commander is inept. Maybe he thought we'd just cave in?"

There was some activity in the enemy ranks. The rider had returned, and now a small group of horsemen could be seen heading to the rear of their lines.

"What in the name of the Afterlife are they doing now?" demanded Sir Nigel.

The answer came shortly as new troops began to appear. The rebel line split in half, moving left and right to open up a gap in their centre. The reinforcements filled in the gap, their green skin clearly visible.

"By the Gods," swore the duke, "what are those?"

"Orcs," said Sir Nigel, visibly paling.

"Where in Saxnor's name did they come from? There aren't any Orcs in this part of the realm, are there?"

"It appears there are now, Lord."

"How many of the beggars are there?"

Sir Nigel calculated quickly, "I'd say there are two hundred, or so. I've seen them before, at Eastwood, but never formed up with spears. It's most unusual."

"This whole attacking army is unusual. I daresay they've scraped together a rather hodge-podge collection of forces. How can they possibly control them all?"

The duke watched for some time while the enemy carried out their manoeuvres.

"I see the princess has moved her standard," said Sir Nigel.

"Yes," the duke agreed, "she's hiding behind the green-skins. I heard they were tough at Eastwood."

"At Eastwood, they greatly outnumbered us, my lord. Here, the numbers are much more in our favour."

"Are you sure of that, Sir Nigel."

"It is apparent that the rebels have more troops than we thought possible, but they still lack sufficient numbers to take the city, Your Grace."

"I wish I had your confidence."

"What would you like to do? Shall I sally out with the knights?"

"No, let them wear themselves down on our walls first. I'd like to see what they have planned. How will they attack, do you think?"

"I suspect they'll try a ladder assault; they don't have any siege engines to pound the walls with."

"We must be wary of this enemy leader, whoever he is. He might have a trick or two up his sleeve."

"I doubt it, Your Grace. He shows little aptitude for properly deploying his troops."

"Let us hope you are right, Sir Nigel. I wouldn't like to be surprised."

～

Gerald sat astride his horse, just behind the Orcs, with Anna beside him as their archers moved forward.

"They'll form a skirmish line ahead of us," he advised her.

"Don't you normally put them on the flanks?"

"Yes, but I have Elves and Dwarves to anchor the lines. This cloud of bowmen before us will draw out their archers."

They watched in fascination. There were close to three hundred archers, all of them Human, though they were a mixed bag of nationalities.

They advanced steadily, spread out to avoid concentrated enemy fire. Soon, they were within range, and arrows began flying toward the north wall of Colbridge.

"It's not very effective," said Anna.

"It doesn't have to be, watch."

It didn't take long for the royalists to counter with crossbows, their bolts striking out with accuracy.

"We're taking casualties," said Anna.

Instead of looking south, toward the city, he looked west, to the end of his line. The Elves, on cue, began moving forward. They only advanced a short distance and then started loosing off their arrows with deadly accuracy. "Our archers have drawn out their crossbowmen. The Elves are famously good shots; now they can pick off their opponents."

Crossbowmen fell, but only a few. Those that remained took cover behind the parapet.

Gerald turned to a mounted soldier waiting behind him. "Signal one," he called out.

The man reached into his satchel to pull forth a green flag that he affixed to a staff. He hoisted it into the air, waving it about.

Moments later the Trolls appeared from the edge of the woods behind them, each pulling a sled piled with rocks. They passed through a gap in the line of footmen and continued their progress south where they faced the flat walls of Colbridge.

Someone on the walls must have noticed for the crossbowmen reappeared, sending a rain of bolts toward the new threat. Most of the shots did little, but at least one Troll fell, a quarrel lodged firmly in his leg.

Slowly they drew closer and then halted, dropping the reins. Trolls are immensely strong, and now they ran to the back of their sleds to heft up rocks. These they threw across the distance to crash against the crumbling walls of Colbridge.

The Elves moved closer to more accurately control their shots. The first rocks smashed against the wall, making loud cracking noises as bits of stone broke away from the structure. It didn't take long for cracks to appear. They were small at first, but the repeated strikes were proving effective. One rock struck a parapet, clipping a crossbowman and carrying his upper torso into the town beyond while his lower fell out of sight.

Another Troll went down, and Anna gasped, "They're taking casualties. How much longer?"

"The next group is moving up, and the first group will withdraw as soon as they do. Where's Revi?"

"Right here, General."

"Don't go anywhere, I'm going to need you very soon."

Gerald turned to Arnim, "Send word for the men to prepare. As soon as the wall comes down, I want you taking them in. You know what to do?"

"Yes," said the knight, turning his horse and galloping off.

"Will there be enough of them to take the breach?" asked Revi.

"No," said Gerald.

"Then for Saxnor's sake," added the mage, "why are you sending them?"

"We must draw them out," said Gerald.

"But the casualties..."

"The Men of Kingsford volunteered, they know what they were getting into."

A large rumble echoed across the battlefield as a portion of the wall collapsed. The men of Merceria moved forward, yelling in triumph, Arnim at their head.

It was agonizing to watch. Gerald wanted to be there, to lead them himself but knew he was needed here, to watch over the battle. Even so, his nerves were taut, his body working through his tiredness on pure adrenalin.

He could only observe as Arnim led them on. They were soon at the base of the wall. The collapsed structure had formed a ramp of rubble, and now the men struggled to climb it, to gain entry into the city beyond.

Gerald could imagine the experience, for years before he had climbed through a breach after the siege of Bodden. The sight then had sickened him, and now he wondered if, perhaps, he had made a mistake.

"They're faltering," cried out Revi.

"Send in the men of Weldwyn," ordered Gerald. "Have them support the attack."

"But they're stuck in the breach!" came a voice.

Gerald swung around in anger, directing it at an aide. "You," he jabbed a finger, "send word immediately. The Weldwyn Volunteers are to support the attack."

The rider wheeled his horse about, riding off to do the general's bidding.

Sir Nigel ran up to the duke, his bloodied blade still held in his hand. "We're holding them at the breach, Your Grace. Our defences are working perfectly. They're throwing their men away, exhausting their manpower."

"Prepare your knights, Sir Nigel. When the enemy breaks, I want you riding them down. We'll massacre them as they run and then follow the rabble into their own lines."

"With pleasure, my lord. This will be the shortest siege in history. I shall bring you the head of the princess."

Sir Nigel made his way to the great gatehouse. The Knights of the Sword were already formed up, waiting for the word to ride forth. Their commander took up his position at their head and raised himself in the stirrups, turning his mount to face his men.

"The enemy is retreating," he announced. "They have ground themselves to dust on our walls. Now, it is time for us to ride forth and bring death to them all. Onward to glory!"

With a cheer from his men, the portcullis was raised as the soldiers in the gatehouse worked the massive winch. A moment later, men ran forward, pushing open the great doors and then standing aside to let the riders through.

He led them out of the city, the morning sun reflecting off their armour. Out rode fifty of the finest soldiers in the realm; the unstoppable force that is the Royal Order of the Knights of the Sword.

"What a glorious day," Sir Nigel shouted, but the jangle of his armour and the noise of hooves drowned out his voice.

They cleared the gate and then turned north, forming into a wedge with Sir Nigel in the lead. He spotted the enemy footmen running for cover, some dropping their weapons as they streamed back toward their own lines. The green-skinned Orcs moved left and right to let their compatriots through the line, breaking up the formation.

"Now is our chance!" yelled Sir Nigel. "We shall bring death to this usurper!" The knights broke into a full gallop, heading directly for the standard of the traitorous princess, and the weakened rebel line.

TEN

Assault

WINNER 961/962 MC

❦

G erald watched as the line wavered. "Let them through," he cried out, "they've done their part."

"Enemy cavalry approaching," warned Anna.

"Yes, I see them," said Gerald. "Master Bloom, are you ready?"

"Yes, General."

"Hold a moment longer, we must wait till they've committed to their charge."

The tension built as Gerald forced himself to count to ten, rolling his shoulders as he did so.

"Wait...Wait...Now!"

Revi began the incantation. The air buzzed with magical force as he traced the runes in the air. A small light appeared in his hands, growing brighter as he continued his chant. The mage focused his attention on it, levitating it as it glowed even more. Soon, it was above them all, a huge beacon in the chilly winter sky.

"Are you sure this is going to work?" asked Anna.

"We've lured out their knights," offered Gerald, "and now it's time for Hayley and Beverly to do their part."

"A nasty surprise for them," said Anna. "Will they be able to see the signal, Revi?"

"Trust me, Highness," responded the mage, "Hayley has the eyes of a hawk."

～

Beverly's leg began to cramp, and she uttered an oath.

"What was that?" asked Hayley.

"I said my leg aches. I need to stretch them soon. How much longer, do you think?"

"There's the signal," answered the ranger.

"Let's go," said Beverly, rising to her feet. Behind her the men stood, appearing from the undergrowth as if summoned by some spell. They were on the west side of the river, looking across the frozen water to Colbridge.

They began making their way down to the ice while Hayley led her own group, a band of Orc archers.

Halting at the river's edge, Beverly cast her eyes about until she spied the markers. She and the ranger had spent the better part of the night crawling across the river, marking the thicker parts of the ice flow with stones and now they began the crossing in two single-file lines.

It all hinged on surprise. Arnim had told them the gate to the docks was left open and lightly guarded, but if the defenders saw the attack coming, it would be a simple enough task to close it.

No one was in sight on the far side as they began their trek across the ice. To Beverly's mind, the bank seemed such a long distance away. She kept expecting someone to call out, but no one raised the alarm. The ice was slippery, and so they took their time, careful not to make any sound.

They were halfway across when Beverly spotted an observer. A man stood by the docks, his eyes shielded from the sun as he stared over the frozen water.

Beverly tried to pick up the pace, but the unforgiving ice forced her to slow down when her foot slid forward, almost tumbling her. The observer turned suddenly, perhaps finally recognizing the coming threat. He ran toward the gate, but an arrow hit him in the leg, causing him to fall. A moment later a second shot struck him in the back. She glanced to the side to see Hayley, her bow in hand. The ranger nocked a third, but it was unnecessary; her target lay, unmoving.

The docks drew closer until Beverly finally reached up to the wooden planking and hauled herself onto the pier. She paused for only a moment to help the man behind her and then sprinted towards the gatehouse where the doors were wide open. A bored guard leaned against the frame, smoking a pipe, his eyes closed. Beverly's blade struck the man down before he could react. She paused, letting her men catch up to her. Hayley was off the docks now, her Orcs outpacing her to the gatehouse.

The ranger halted to catch her breath, "Well, that was exciting."

"Everything's gone well, so far," said Beverly. "You know what to do?"

"Of course," she replied, looking over her Orcs. "I've got all my hunters."

"And I have mine," the red-head returned. "I'll see you when this is over."

"Yes," said Hayley, "and no arrows in the back this time."

"Agreed."

They headed into the town. The city itself appeared deserted. The inhabitants, perhaps fearful of siege engines, had taken to hiding indoors, leaving the streets bare of traffic. Beverly spied only one person, an elderly woman walking with a cane, trying to hustle along when the invaders came into sight. Beverly dispatched a warrior to see her safely home and continued on her way.

Hayley headed directly north, turning east as the duke's residence came into sight. The great walls of the city had been designed to hold enemies at bay while allowing those within the city to reinforce the walls quickly. The crenellations faced outward, but the interior lacked these defences. This now worked to Hayley's advantage as her Orcs formed a line and let loose with their arrows.

The onslaught was completely unexpected and the crossbowmen, their attention focused solely towards the enemies outside the wall, fell quickly, their armour insufficient to protect them from the Orcish volleys. Most of the remaining royalists abandoned the wall, running to whatever safety they could find. A few of them tried rushing their adversaries, only to be cut down by Orcish blades.

Beverly headed northeast, trying to get her bearings. The city was a maze of streets, and she temporarily lost her way, darting down a side street to a dead end. They emerged from the alley to a startled group of militia who took one look at the armoured warriors and fled. She cast about trying to orient herself as one of the men pointed out the church tower.

"This way," she called, leading the charge once more.

It seemed to take forever to get to the gate tower. The gates had been closed after the knights left, but there were still guards here. They were mainly atop the wall, looking out at the battle unfolding before their eyes.

Beverly waited until her men caught up and gave them a moment to catch their breath. They had been recruited from the heavier cavalry and were well armed and armoured. Their thick chainmail hauberks were heavy and slowed them down, but the protection the armour afforded was well worth it.

She peered around the corner of the building to watch the gate tower. Only one guard stood at the ground level, while the others remained within the structure, presumably intent on the battle outside their walls.

Waving her hand, Beverly advanced at a jog, sword at the ready and shield unslung. The guard heard her before she attacked and was fumbling for his weapon even as her sword struck him down. Leaving her victim convulsing on the ground, she rushed past, pausing at the door. There, just inside, was a set of stairs that presumably led up to the winch room, her target. Detailing two warriors to guard the door, she led the rest upward, their heavy footsteps echoing in the stone tower.

The winch room was large, holding a massive drum around which were attached the chains that lifted the portcullis. The two soldiers here were staring out the arrow slits to the north. One heard their approach and turned to face Beverly. She stabbed out, her sword penetrating the links of his mail, and he fell loudly to the ground. The remaining fellow, fortunately for him, was on the other side of the mechanism. Hearing his partner go down gave him time to draw his own weapon.

"Draw the portcullis up," yelled Beverly as she struck out.

Her opponent was slippery, dodging her first attack. He struck, the blow easily absorbed by her shield. She pushed back, the force of it sending him to the ground where she smote him in the leg with her sword. He screamed in agony, dropping his blade, and she kicked it away, then turned her attention back to her men.

They had grabbed the levers that worked the portcullis chain and were now heaving them back, the mechanism clanking loudly as it did its work.

She yelled down the stairwell as she ran. Her men outside rushed under the portcullis as it rose and now removed the bars that held the outer doors in place. The doors squealed as they protested the effort, but they swung open, revealing the cold, clear air of the wintery countryside.

Sir Nigel looked left and right. His knights were no longer in a tight formation as some horses, perhaps more excited, ran ahead. The green-skinned Orcs were shortening their line, moving their spears closer together, but the Knights of the Sword were committed. The horses' hooves were thundering, sending snow and dirt flying into the air.

Hearing a yell to his right, Sir Nigel quickly cast his gaze in that direction but all he saw was a horse rearing up in panic, and then the knight beside him went down, disappearing from view as the charge advanced.

He heard a rending sound behind him and a blur appeared out of the corner of his eye. He risked a glance to see an unbelievable sight; massive dogs were running amongst the knights, tearing into their formation. He tried to spur on his horse, but the hounds were closing in and running faster than his heavily encumbered mount. His horse lurched forward when a hound bit into its leg, and then the mighty Mercerian Charger went down. The knight commander catapulted himself from the saddle, hitting the ground and rolling to avoid injury.

Rising to his feet, he saw the line of Orcs ahead of him, watching with great interest. He yelled at them, taunted them, but they remained in place, much to his frustration. From behind him came a low growl, and he turned to see his worst nightmare; a massive hound with blood-soaked teeth, advancing towards him.

Gerald looked on as the mighty Kurathian Mastiffs tore into the Knights of the Sword. It was almost too much, and he had to briefly avert his eyes as horses had their legs pulled from under them. The screaming was the worst part, for the animals weren't dead, merely critically injured. The dogs also tore into the riders as they fell, but he had little sympathy for them; they had sworn to serve the tyrant, Henry.

"The yellow flag," yelled Gerald.

His aide pulled forth the signal, waving it in the air as high as he could. The mastiff handlers moved, ready to tame the wild dogs, but the animals had their blood up and were lost in their frenzy. Gerald rode forward, using his horse to push through the line of Orcs. He halted as he reached the front line, dropping from his mount. Tempus appeared beside him, his faithful guard, and the general moved into the field toward the scene of carnage and destruction.

He had only taken a few steps when the mastiffs first noticed him. The nearest let out a loud howl, and they all stopped what they were doing to look in his direction. Gerald continued moving forward, and as he did so, the great beasts began to bow their heads before him. The handlers rushed in, reattaching the leashes and muzzles. Gerald called the Orcs forward, and they began to pick their way through the field, finishing off any knight that refused to surrender.

The stench of death washed over Gerald, but he couldn't let it distract him. He turned back to the north. "Double Flags," he called out. The aide dutifully waved two of the pennants, the signal for the general advance. The entire line started lumbering forward.

The Kurathian horsemen were heading for the main gate, which they could clearly see was now open. Gerald halted, letting the troops surge past him. He was immensely tired, and the loss of life, on both sides, weighed on him heavily.

It was Anna that snapped him out of it. "We've won," she announced. "You've done it."

He looked up at her on her horse. He tried to form words, but fatigue overwhelmed him. What tumbled out of his mouth made no sense, and then he fell heavily to his knees, bereft of energy.

Anna called out for Revi, but Gerald couldn't focus, the whole world began twirling about. He felt himself fall to the ground, only able to watch as Anna bent over him. Revi came into view over her shoulder, looking down into his face.

"What's happening, what's wrong with him?" asked Anna.

"Exhaustion, I think," said Revi. "He needs to sleep."

"Beverly," stuttered Gerald, "command..."

"Relax, Gerald," soothed Anna. "Beverly will take over, you need to rest, you've overworked yourself."

"Hardly surprising, really," uttered Revi Bloom. "I don't think he's slept properly in days. When was the last time he ate?"

"I'm not sure," said Anna. "I haven't seen him at mealtimes for three days. He's been so busy."

Sounds echoed in Gerald's mind as his vision left him.

Gerald awoke to a soft bed and a warm fire in a well-appointed room. The first thing he saw was Sophie, sitting beside him.

"He's awake, Your Highness," she said.

Anna came into view, "You gave us quite a scare there, Gerald."

"What happened?" he asked. "I remember feeling...strange."

"You passed out," she replied. "Revi says you've been missing too much sleep. You haven't been taking care of yourself."

"The battle..." he started.

"Is done. We were victorious. You're in the duke's quarters in Colbridge."

"What's the tally?" he asked. "How many did we lose?"

"Not as many as we feared. Beverly can give you a number later, but you need to rest. Here, have some broth."

He smelled the hot liquid and then she lifted a spoon to his mouth. Sipping it gingerly, he felt its effects as he swallowed it.

There was a knock at the door.

"Enter," said Anna.

"Your Highness," said Beverly, entering the room. "I have a full report for you." The red-headed knight paused as she took in the scene. "Gerald, you're awake!"

"Try to hide your disappointment, Beverly," he said. "You're not the general, yet."

The knight smiled, "I have no desires on that front, General, trust me. It's been a headache keeping things under control.

"Why? What happened?" asked Gerald, pulling himself into a seated position and ignoring the broth held before him.

"Nothing good, I'm afraid," replied the knight. "The men got a little out of control after we entered the city. I'm afraid there's been all kinds of trouble."

Gerald felt sick, his stomach turning at the mere thought. "Out of control, how?"

"Looting mostly, but also assaults. I'm afraid several women have been attacked."

"We must round up those guilty," commanded Gerald. "Get my armour; this has to be dealt with at once. I will not tolerate this kind of behaviour in my army."

"It's already been taken care of," said Beverly. "I had my cavalrymen round them up, and the Orcs were a great help. We've got several men in detention, awaiting judgement. There's really nothing for you to do that can't wait."

"Get me Kiren Jool," demanded Gerald.

"The Kurathian Enchanter?" asked Sophie.

"Yes, he can get me back on my feet, can't he?"

"I believe so," said Anna, "but surely it can wait."

"No, it can't," said Gerald. "Discipline must be enforced as soon as possible, while the memory of the crime is still fresh. If the men think we'll look the other way to this kind of behaviour, we're just as bad as the people we're fighting."

Anna turned her attention to her maid, "Go and get his armour, Sophie, I can see he won't listen to reason. Send one of the pages to collect Master Jool, and Master Bloom if he's available."

Sophie scurried off on her tasks while Anna tried again to spoon feed Gerald. "You're not making this any easier, my friend."

"I'm fine," complained the general.

"Then show me by eating this broth, and I'll let you get dressed."

Gerald knew he was outranked, "Very well."

She handed him the bowl and spoon, watching as he devoured it.

"There, that's better," she soothed.

Sophie returned, a tunic in her hands. "I have his clothes here, Your Highness.

"Thank you," she replied. "Beverly, go and collect all the leaders, they'll need to make their reports. We'll see them in the duke's dining hall, that way our general can sit and conserve his strength. Any word on the mages, Sophie?"

"I sent word, Highness. The Kurathian should be here shortly. He is within the keep, but Master Bloom is in the stables down in the city."

"What's he doing down there?" asked Gerald.

"Healing the horses," said Beverly. "We're going to use them for our heavy cavalry."

He was about to get out of bed when he paused, looking around the room expectantly.

"What's the matter?" asked Beverly.

"I hoped for a little privacy while I get dressed," said Gerald.

Beverly blushed, "Of course, General, I'll wait for you outside."

"Let's clear the room," said Anna. "Gerald will join us downstairs once he's dressed."

It didn't take long for everyone to assemble in the dining room. Gerald, the final one to enter the packed room, was about to sit down when Anna indicated for him to take the seat at the head of the table.

"That's yours," he insisted.

"Nonsense, you're the general. It only makes sense that you should be at the head of the table."

He sat, looking around at the assembled guests. "Please, be seated," he said.

They all took their seats while servants scurried about serving drinks.

"Before we begin," announced Gerald, "I'd like to start by recognizing the actions of some of you. The battle could not have been successful without your participation this day."

Those assembled watched in expectation.

"Sir Arnim," continued Gerald, "you withdrew the assault at just the right time."

"It was your idea," said the knight, "I would never have thought of a feigned withdrawal."

"Nevertheless, your timing was perfect. It drew the knights out, allowing us to eliminate the threat."

Arnim bowed his head in acknowledgement as the others clapped.

"And of course I would be remiss if I didn't mention Dames Beverly and Hayley. You and your troops are the reason we are sitting in this very room today. Without your help, we never would have been able to gain entry to this city."

"Yes," agreed Anna. "You have both displayed courage and initiative. When this war is over, I shall have many rewards to hand out."

"I'm sure I speak for Hayley when I say we were only doing our duty," said Beverly. "It was the general's plan."

"Nonetheless," said Gerald, "I am grateful that you were able to pull it off, it was a difficult task."

"You surprised me today," said Anna, "though I daresay I shouldn't have been."

"How so?" Gerald asked.

"I knew about the river assault, but what inspired you to fake a retreat?"

"I had to lure their knights out. I knew they wouldn't just blindly charge our lines without being tempted in some way. It had to look like our line was faltering. Kraloch and his Orcs did an amazing job of closing the ranks as they approached."

"It is your training," offered the shaman. "We have adapted well to strict discipline."

"You have all done a remarkable job," said the princess, "and I'm very proud of each and every one of you. Now, much has happened since the battle and we must get to the crux of the matter."

"Beverly," began Gerald, "let's start with you."

Beverly produced a note, passing it to him. "Here's a list of the casualties," she said. "Remarkably light, considering the circumstances."

He looked at the numbers and then laid them down on the table. "I trust Revi is still healing them?"

"Yes," she said, "though he's had a chance to rest and recover his energy, I suspect he'll be kept quite busy for another day or so."

"You mentioned the horses earlier. How many of them did you manage to save?"

"Enough for a company of heavy horse," she replied. "I've already picked the men, and we're making use of a lot of the knight's armour."

"How many knights did we capture?"

"Only seven, General, the rest were killed. I'm afraid the Mastiffs are deadly fighters."

"Did we lose any of our dogs?"

"Three were killed, though a number suffered injuries. They're on the list to be healed once our soldiers are tended to. We could really use another Life Mage. I wish Aubrey were here."

"What of the duke?"

"He died fighting on the wall," offered Hayley. "He was taken down by arrows when he wouldn't surrender."

"A fitting fate for the man," declared Gerald.

"His son, Lord Markham, is in custody and under guard," added Beverly.

"I met him long ago," said Gerald, "and I must admit I don't have a very high opinion of the young man. Leave him there for the time being. Now, tell me about what happened when the troops entered the city."

They all looked around the room, avoiding his gaze.

"Someone must know what happened? Give us your opinion, Beverly."

"Well," she began, "the assault across the river was a great success. My group captured the gatehouse while Hayley's Orcs cleared the northern wall. The gates were opened, and the Kurathian horsemen rode in."

"Are you saying it was the Kurathians that caused all the problems?"

"No," she retorted, "we didn't get any reports of trouble until after our footmen entered. The gates were getting crowded with our troops, and so a number of them decided to climb through the breach in the wall. I'm afraid we hadn't planned for that, and they got out of hand."

"I confess," said Arnim, "that I must bear some of the blame. It was my idea to have them use the breach. I hadn't reckoned on their behaviour deteriorating so quickly."

"What, precisely, happened?" asked the general.

"They rushed the wall and were inside before I could get there," said Arnim. "A tavern nearby was their first destination. Once the ale flowed freely, there was no stopping them."

"What is the extent of the damages?"

"Three buildings burned, seven townsfolk killed and a number assaulted."

"Assaulted how?" asked Anna.

"Mostly beaten up or stabbed but at least three women were molested."

"You mean raped?" clarified the princess.

"Yes, I'm afraid so."

"Are these men under arrest?"

"They are, Highness, I saw to it myself."

The room fell into an awkward silence. It was Gerald that broke it, "We are fighting a war to liberate this realm from a dark presence. These people are Mercerian and deserve to be treated as such. The vast majority of inhabitants of this city don't support the king, nor do they care, one way or the other, who rules. They have the right to live in peace and safety. If our troops commit acts like this, we don't deserve to rule them."

"What are you saying?" asked Commander Runsan, the Weldwyn leader.

"I'm saying," said Gerald, "that justice must be seen to be swift and effective.

"Our ancestors used to hold military tribunals when men were to be punished," offered Anna.

"In Merceria it is usually the king that makes these decisions," countered Gerald.

"Yes," said Anna, "but it might be seen as more merciful if the men themselves had a say. For too long our nobles have meted out justice on a whim. The people must see true justice, not just a commander's decision."

"She has a point," offered Arnim. "We have a chance to change the way things work."

"Yes," agreed Anna. "I want the men to understand that justice will be fair for all, not just the nobles. We must have the rule of law."

"Very well," said Gerald. "We'll convene a court made up of captains and commanders. Have you a suggestion, Highness, on how such a thing might be done?"

"As a matter of fact, I do. Give me a day or two, and I'll have it all organized."

"Very well, in the meantime, keep your men on alert and away from the drink. Any man found drunk will stand duty outside the city walls, in the snow."

It took only two days to organize the trials. A tribunal was constituted for every major offense where the accused did not plead guilty. Each soldier would be judged by his own captain, as well as two captains from other companies. A senior officer, commander or higher, would act as the facilitator, making sure each trial was conducted fairly and in an unbiased manner.

Minor offenses were to be handled by company commanders directly. In the end, trials were required for a total of six men. Two of these were found guilty of theft and damage to property and sentenced to hard labour. They were transferred to the city jail for their sentence to be carried out.

Four men, however, had been found guilty of either murder or rape and were sentenced to death. Scaffolding was erected in front of the duke's residence, and a large crowd gathered to witness the event.

Gerald watched in disgust. He was not a man to hand out punishment lightly, but these men deserved what they had been given.

They were shaking and pale as they were led up to the scaffold. Each stood on a box and then a loop of rope was dropped over their necks. Anna stood beside Gerald, watching them intensely.

"You don't have to be here, Highness," offered Beverly.

"This is not the first time I've witnessed a hanging," she replied. "If I am to rule this kingdom, then I must be willing to witness the punishment dealt out. It is my responsibility."

"This will send a clear message," offered Arnim. "No one will dare break the rules when they've seen the consequences."

"I wish that were true," said Anna, "but my heart tells me otherwise. People have short memories; a year from now no one will remember this."

The prisoners stood in a line with ropes draped over their heads. The hangman looked to the princess.

"Carry out the sentence," she said, "and let all those present bear witness."

The nooses were tightened, and then, one by one, the boxes beneath them were kicked out from under their feet. Two of them died instantly, their necks snapped by their body weight, but the other two twisted painfully as the life was choked out of them.

Finally, they stopped twitching, and Gerald turned to Anna, "It is done, Your Highness."

"Yes," she replied, "but next time, let's make sure the hangman knows his job better. It doesn't look good when a man suffers in death."

"Agreed," said the general.

"Good," she replied, her sombre mood disappearing almost instantly. "Now that the unpleasant business is done, we have much to discuss."

"We do?"

"Of course, we still have a war to win."

ELEVEN

Albreda's Plan

SPRING 962 MC

B aron Fitzwilliam called a council of war in the map room, insisting that not only his knights be present, but his captains and sergeants as well. Now, they stood, crowded around a map of Merceria, eager to see what the coming campaign season might bring.

"I say we attack Redridge," offered Sir James. "The defences are likely weak, and it would cut off their only source of iron."

"Impractical," refuted Sir Rodney. "While it's true we would interrupt their access to iron, it would have little effect on them for some time as their troops are already equipped."

"We must attack somewhere," complained Sir James. "What would you suggest?"

"I think we should wait on the king to make the first move," he replied, "then we can react without over-stretching our rather limited resources. What say you, Baron?"

Everyone turned their attention to Baron Fitzwilliam, who sat, staring out the window. Upon hearing his name, he turned, stroking his beard absently. "I think there is merit in both ideas," he began, "but we must gather more information first."

"Surely we must act!" burst out Sir Randolph.

"And we will," appeased Fitz, "I assure you, but there is no point in striking until we know the location of the royal army."

"Perhaps Albreda could help?" suggested Sir Gareth. "Surely her animals could tell us more?"

"While I admire your faith in me," began the mage, "it is not as practical as it sounds. Finding an army in the countryside is simple, but locating soldiers in a city is not the best deployment of my resources. Birds do not know the difference between knights and soldiers. No, I think this kind of thing is best done by people. I believe someone will have to infiltrate Tewsbury before we march."

"Tewsbury?" asked Sir James.

"Yes," said Fitz, "Albreda and I have been talking, and we feel it most likely that the king's army will spend the winter months there."

"I agree," said Sir Heward, "Tewsbury is the biggest city in the area and controls the road to Wincaster."

"Very well," said Sir James, "Tewsbury it is, then. How many men should we send?"

"I have it in mind to send three," offered the baron.

"Three? Is that all?" Sir James responded.

"Which three?" asked Sir Rodney.

"I've given this careful thought," said Fitz, "and decided that whoever goes must be able to blend in easily with the local population. I've consulted with Albreda, and she feels that she is best suited to the job."

"How so?" asked Sir James. "No offense to Lady Albreda, but she's only a woman. How is she to recognize the types of troops, their weapons and armour and so on?"

"Do you think," asked the mage, "that I am incapable of knowing these things?" Her gaze bore down on Sir James, causing his mouth to shut and his face to grow crimson. "I am more than capable of this task, but I will be accompanied by Sir Heward and Aldwin."

"The smith?" gasped Sir Randolph. "I understand your affection for the boy, my lord, but surely he is no warrior."

"Precisely why he would be ideal," countered the baron. "Aldwin is not so young as you might imagine and he is familiar with all matters of arms and armour. Who better to evaluate their strength than a smith? I will remind you it was he and Albreda that freed us from the king's imprisonment, allowing us to retake Bodden."

"Indeed," said Sir Rodney, "and for that, we are truly thankful. I can see the wisdom in it, but I am curious why Sir Heward? Surely he would be recognized?"

"I will escort them to the edge of the city," replied the huge knight, "though I will not enter unless absolutely necessary."

"Sir Heward," said Albreda, "will be there to protect us on our journey. Should we encounter difficulties, he will explain that he has managed to escape from Bodden. Do any of you doubt his prowess?"

"No," offered Sir James, "he has proven himself."

"When do you leave?" asked Sergeant Blackwood.

"Not for some time," offered the baron. "The roads are still covered in snow. I suspect it will be some weeks before it melts and then another few days for the ground to harden. I shouldn't like to have them bogged down in the mud."

"And in the meantime, what do we do?" asked Sir Rodney.

"We train," replied the baron, "and continue upgrading our defences."

"While I shall go eastward," said Albreda, "and see what my animal friends in the Wickfield Hills have noticed."

The room fell silent at the statement.

"Surely not," Sir Rodney said, interrupting the silence. "The trip would take far too long, and you'd never be back in time."

"Nonsense," countered the mage, "I can be into the hills in less than a day."

"Impossible," scoffed Sir James.

"Have you not heard of magic?" she queried.

"What are you going to do, turn into a giant bird and fly there?" he continued.

"Even a bird couldn't fly that distance in such a short time," added Sir Gareth.

Albreda gave them both a steely look, "I don't need to explain myself to either of YOU."

She returned her gaze to the baron, "Richard, I promise you I will be back in plenty of time for this plan of yours to commence. I merely want to keep an eye on things. I wouldn't like us to ride straight into an advancing army."

"A valid point," said Fitz. "I cannot stop you, but I do hope you will be careful."

"Of course," she returned. "Now, I think we've all had enough of this discussion. Shall we perhaps retire to the dinner table? All this planning has worked up a healthy appetite."

"Very well," agreed the baron. "Let us get to it."

Albreda halted her horse just shy of the forest. "This will do nicely," she said.

"Are you sure you don't want me to go with you?" offered Aldwin.

"I'm quite capable of looking after myself," she said, "and you need to return these horses to Bodden."

At the smith's look of concern, her face softened. "I promise you I will look after myself, Aldwin. Now, get back to the Keep before they lock you out for the night," she said as she dismounted, handing the reins to him.

"I still don't understand how you intend to travel so far in so short a period of time."

"Do you remember the circle of stones?" she asked.

"Where you made Nature's Fury? Of course, why?"

"I shall use it to traverse a great distance. It is something I learned some time ago."

"You can travel through the air?"

"Not quite, Aldwin, but I can travel to another stone circle which lies to the east."

"You are truly a powerful mage," he said.

"Yes," she admitted, "but let's not tell the others for now."

"Then why are you telling me?"

"I trust you," she added. "There's something about you that I can't quite put my finger on. You've a part to play in this unfolding drama, I'd bet my life on it."

"Didn't you think the same of Beverly?"

"I did, and still do. There's more to this than either of us understand."

"That's fair. I don't understand any of it."

She smiled at him before continuing, "Don't worry your head over it. You know I have visions, correct?"

"Yes, but what has that to do with things?"

"I saw Beverly again."

"But she's dead," said Aldwin.

"I know, and yet somehow she still appears to me, and I am at a complete loss to explain it. Perhaps her death holds some secret that we have yet to unravel. I must now admit to you that I lied at the Keep. It's not for scouting that I'm going to the hills. Something is calling to me from a vision."

"Then I should come and protect you," he offered again.

"Trust me, I'll be fine," she said. "There is little in these parts that would harm me. No, you should be off."

She watched as he turned his horse about, trotting to the south and the safety of the village. Albreda turned her attention back to the woods and resumed her progress, soon entering the dense underbrush. She had walked less than half a mile when a familiar growling noise came to her ears.

"Ah, Snarl, so good of you to greet me."

The large wolf stepped from the greenery, coming close enough to let her hands caress his face.

"We have work to do, my friend, for events are unfolding, and I must try to decipher their meaning. We go now to the stone circle."

By nightfall, they had arrived. The stones stood in mute testimony to their ancient power. Albreda stepped to the centre of the circle, looking down at her faithful companion, who sat at her side. They had travelled thus on many occasions, and the wolf appeared almost bored with the entire process. She smiled, then looked up to the stones, raising her hands into the air.

She began the incantation; a high pitched keening that cut through the darkness. Soon, she felt the energy as the stones came to life, the runes on their surfaces glowing and then a crack of thunder and a flash of light erupted into the night air.

Instantly, her surroundings shifted as she lowered her hands while waiting for the stones to dim. The air smelled sweeter here, and she could smell the river nearby; they had arrived. Snarl stood, stretching his limbs.

"Come along, my friend. The work begins now."

TWELVE

The Hills

SPRING 962 MC

Beverly walked across the large open area, still wondering at its name. It was really just a field, but the Dwarves laying out the city plans for Queenston had insisted on calling it the Royal Commons.

The army had, for the most part, remained in Kingsford. A garrison occupied Colbridge, of course, but the bulk of the troops had marched to the ancient riverside city to wait out the rest of the winter. Only a few select units returned to Queenston; the Orcs, Dwarves, Mastiffs, and a few Humans.

The newest unit to be formed was the heavy cavalry, whom Beverly handpicked from the existing horsemen. They were armed and armoured as knights, though none but herself claimed that title. Unlike knights, they were taught discipline and tactics. She wanted them to be reliable troops, not wild warriors who attacked with reckless abandon.

Of course, the real reason for the return to Queenston wasn't the troops, but rather the gate that sat beneath Royal Hill. Its magical flame allowed almost instantaneous travel to and from the temple of Erssa Saka'am, the Saurian pyramid that controlled access to ancient portals.

Beverly mulled all this over in her mind as she approached the stone manor house, finally arriving to see the others waiting for her.

Anna and Gerald sat at one end, while Revi, Hayley and Lily sat to one side. Arnim and Nikki had remained in Kingsford to look after the troops along with most of the commanders. Beverly took her place, carefully stepping around Tempus, who dozed on the floor.

"It looks like we're all here," said Anna. "Would you care to begin, Master Bloom?"

"Certainly, Your Highness," began the mage as he stood, tugging slightly on his robes to straighten them. "As you know, some time ago I identified an additional set of coordinates."

"I thought you said two?" interrupted Gerald.

"I did, though I thought it better to start with the one that lies somewhere in the Wickfield Hills."

"I was under the impression you knew exactly where it was," said Gerald. "What do you mean 'somewhere'?"

"Oh, I know its exact location," defended the mage, "I'm just not familiar with the area enough to say how close it is to the towns and such."

"Regardless of its exact location," interrupted Hayley, "it will allow us to gather news from the north. It's likely only a day or two from Wickfield itself."

"I take it," said Anna, "that you are familiar with the area?"

"Quite so, Your Highness. I've spent many weeks there due to my ranger responsibilities, though I daresay that was some time ago."

"Good," said Anna, "then I think it's best you accompany Revi when he goes through."

"I should like to accompany them as well," requested Beverly.

"You surprise me," said Gerald. "I would've thought your new company of horse would keep you busy."

"It would only be for a few days," she defended, "and I'd like to make sure the two of them are kept safe."

"We're more than capable of looking after ourselves, Bev."

"Agreed," said Anna. "What's the real reason, Beverly? Is there something you're not telling me?"

Beverly blushed, "I..."

"Go on," urged Gerald, "we shall think no less of you."

"I want to try and make contact with Albreda."

"Albreda?" said Revi. "How do you intend to do that?"

"It's said that nothing happens in the Whitewood without her knowing of it," offered the red-headed knight. "If I were to enter the eastern edge of the wood, I might be able to contact her."

"How long would this take?" asked Gerald.

"The woods likely lie a few days to the west of the gate."

"It's rough country," interjected Hayley. "Are you taking your horse?"

"No, I'd traverse on foot," she replied. "The woods are too dense for horses to make any decent progress."

"So that's a few days travel," offered the ranger, "with a layover of a few more to try to make contact."

"That sounds like a long trip," stated Gerald.

"Not really," said Revi. "It's likely we would need at least that long to make contact with Wickfield, and if it did work, we'd have an archmage to help us."

"Archmage?" said Gerald. "I don't think I've heard you use that term before."

"It refers to a mage of considerable power," explained Revi. "From all I've heard and seen, she is a formidable caster. If we convince her to join us, it will give us a tremendous advantage."

"Very well," said Anna, "it's worth the risk. What about your cavalry?"

"I'll see to them," said Gerald. "There's little else to do here other than make plans."

"Excellent," said the princess, "then it's all settled. When do you want to head out?"

"I thought," said Revi, "that we might leave first thing in the morning. We have to traverse to the epicentre of the grid and then open the gates."

"He means," clarified Hayley, "that we have to return to the pyramid first." She turned her attention to the mage, "Honestly, Revi, sometimes you can be so..."

"Scholarly?" suggested the mage. "I'm afraid it's in my nature."

Morning found them atop the pyramid in the Great Swamp. The old Saurian priest, Hassus, watched with interest as Revi began the casting sequence that would expand the green, magical flame to allow them to step through.

Hayley turned to Beverly, "Are you all set?"

"Of course," replied the knight. "I'm getting very used to this sort of travel."

"So am I," said Hayley, "though it would be nice if we could use it to get to a tavern. I haven't had a good ale since we left Kingsford."

Beverly chuckled, then turned her attention back to the mage. Revi had almost finished the ritual, and she was just in time to see his final actions as the surface of the flame rippled, revealing a darkened chamber.

"It worked," she said.

"Of course," stated the mage. "Would you care to go through first?"

Beverly drew her sword. "By all means," she said, stepping forward to come close to the flame before bracing herself as she touched its surface. She felt the familiar tug and then was in a dimly lit cavern, the flame having diminished as she travelled through, and now she waited for her eyes to adjust.

It appeared to be a room of stone, much like that of Uxley. Revi had suggested they all followed the same layout and looking around, she was apt to agree. The familiar three corridors were leaving the chamber, so she turned her back to the solid wall and headed down the centre one.

She had only gone a few steps when a noise from somewhere ahead halted her progress. She peered into the darkness trying to discern whatever was there as the flame behind her jumped to life again, throwing distant shadows.

"Hayley, is that you?" she called out.

"Of course, were you expecting someone else?"

"No, but there's something up here."

"Hang on, I've got a lantern. Give me a moment, and we'll cast some light on the subject."

Beverly heard the ranger fumbling about, and then the familiar sound of steel striking flint. A brief spark of light flashed followed by a soft yellow glow as the lantern came to life.

The knight let her eyes adjust once more, then glanced down the hallway. "I don't see any footprints."

"No," agreed Hayley, coming up behind her. "In fact, the whole floor is clean. Look, it's been swept recently."

"You mean..."

"Yes, something is living here, or should I say someone. It's very unlikely an animal would sweep the place."

"Hello," called out Beverly, "we mean you no harm. Come out and show yourself."

"I don't think that will work," said the ranger.

"Why?"

"We're in a Saurian temple, remember? If there's someone here looking after the place, it's likely one of them."

"You're right," agreed Beverly. "We should back up to the flame and wait for Revi."

"Agreed. Then he can use his spell of tongues."

Hayley turned around, retracing her steps to the altar, taking the light source with her. Beverly stood rearguard, then started backing up. She noticed a brief flicker of movement just before a spear came sailing through the air towards her.

"Look out!" she cried, swinging with her sword. It clipped the end of the spear, causing it to deflect to the side of the corridor. "Someone's not happy we're here."

The corridor filled with a soft green light as the altar came to life once more. Seeing no one in front of her, Beverly turned and sprinted back to the flame, quickly turning as she arrived.

"Revi, there's someone here," Hayley rushed out. "You need to cast your spell of tongues quickly."

"One moment," replied the mage, "I need to get my bearings."

It felt like an eternity until the air began to tingle as the mage cast his spell. Beverly felt her skin itch slightly. "What did you do?" she called out.

"I cast the spell on all of us," he said. "You should now be able to speak to whoever it is."

"Don't I have to see him first?" she asked.

"Yes, of course. Why, haven't you seen them yet?"

"No, but I've heard someone moving and whoever it is, threw a spear at me."

"Where are they?" asked Hayley.

"Off to the left, I think."

"That corridor branches back around to here," said Revi. "I remember the floor plan from Uxley. Go ahead and block the way, Beverly. We'll move around to take them in the rear."

Beverly stepped forward cautiously, her sword out in front. Taking up a position by the side passage, she peered around the corner, but only blackness met her gaze. She heard Hayley and Revi heading down the other side, then some muttering just before Revi's light spell burst into existence, flooding the area.

Beverly peered around the corner again to see a small figure emerge from the far corner, its face turned toward the light. It grasped a crude looking spear and raised its arm, making ready to hurl the weapon.

"*We come in peace*," she called out and was startled by the sound escaping her lips, for she spoke in Saurian.

The creature turned its head to look at her, and she saw it blink. "*Who are you?*" it called out.

Beverly stepped around the corner, scabbarding her blade. "*I am Dame Beverly Fitzwilliam*," she said, holding her hands to her side. "*We have come from the great temple at Erssa Saka'am.*"

The words appeared to have a soothing effect on the creature, for it lowered his spear. "*Greetings honoured guests*," it said. "*I am Gort, guardian of the temple. Long have I waited for word from my brethren.*"

Revi and Hayley came up behind him, the orb of light now clearly displaying his features. He was a little taller than Lily with speckles of blue here and there on his otherwise green skin. His head bore a crest which continued down his back, giving him more of a reptilian look.

He somehow identified Revi as a mage quite readily and bowed his head. *"I am sorry if I caused offense,"* he said.

"It is we who are sorry," replied the mage. *"We have come a long way and didn't expect to find anyone here. How long have you been the guardian of this gate?"*

"A very long time," replied Gort, *"as long as I can remember. There used to be three of us, but the others passed into the darkness."*

"I am sorry to hear of their passing," said the mage.

The diminutive lizard dipped his head in acknowledgement. *"Tell me, why have you come here? Are all of my people now dead?"*

"No," said Revi, *"quite the reverse actually, they thrive, though they live very far from here."*

"Why did they not return?" he asked.

"They had forgotten how to use the flame," explained the mage. *"It was only when we rediscovered the secret that this type of travel could resume. Tell me, what do you know of the area? Have you gone outside?"*

"Of course," Gort replied, *"I regularly hunt in these hills, else how would I survive?"*

"He has a good point," said Beverly.

"We are Humans," continued the mage. *"Have you seen others like us, in the outside world?"*

"Yes, they live in a village outside of these hills."

"He must mean Wickfield," whispered Hayley.

"I daresay he does," replied Revi, switching back to the common tongue, "but we need to go and visit it. *Tell me, Gort,"* he continued, effortlessly resuming the Saurian tongue, *"could you take us there?"*

"I shall lead you to the edge of the hills, but I will go no farther for I fear these people are warlike and may seek to do me harm. They remind me of Elves."

"That will do nicely, thank you," added Hayley.

"I will be going west," announced Beverly. *"Know you of the Whitewood?"*

"It is some distance from here," replied the Saurian. *"I suggest you go north and then follow the river west, it will guide you as easily as may be."*

"Thank you," said Beverly, looking to her companions. "I shall see you in a week?"

"Probably more like ten or so days," replied Hayley. "Whoever returns here first will wait on the others, agreed?"

"Agreed," said Beverly, "though you can't wait forever. I would suggest if I'm not back in two weeks, you return to Queenston without me."

"And if we don't return?" asked the mage.

"Then I shall have to come looking for you. I can't operate the gate, remember?"

"We'd best get moving," suggested Hayley. "It's still early, and we want to get out of the hills by nightfall if we can. These are dangerous lands."

"*Gort,*" said Revi, "*will you take us to the other Humans now? We have to visit them. When we return, we'd be happy to take you back with us to the Great Temple.*"

"*Certainly,*" replied the Saurian, "*you should be on your way at once, and I will remain here to guard the temple. Follow me, and I will lead you to the exit.*"

Revi tugged at his tunic, "Are you sure I have to wear this?"

"Of course," said Hayley, "you can't just wander into the village in your wizard's robes."

"Why not?"

"It may be under the king's control, and you'd be placed under arrest. I won't have you rotting in jail again."

"It's just so...constricting."

"I think it suits you," she said. "Now remember, you're a farmer up from Hawksburg."

"What about you?" he asked.

"Me? I'm a ranger, remember? No one's going to ask questions of me."

The edge of the village could clearly be seen, with the spire of the church visible above all else.

"We're being watched," noted the ranger.

Revi looked about, "I don't see anyone."

"Up in the bell tower," she said, "though I suspect we'll see others shortly."

The road through the village was straight, heading directly to the river beyond with a makeshift wall at the southern end. Two men, presumably warned of their approach, made their way out of a nearby building and took up a position behind the row of barrels.

"Halt," cried out the taller of the two as they drew nearer.

Hayley reached into her tunic and pulled forth her ranger's token, brandishing it before her. "I'm a King's Ranger," she called out, "make way."

The men lowered spears, pointing them directly at her. "A friend of the king will find no safety here," one threatened.

Hayley halted, grabbing Revi's arm to prevent him from advancing. "What's going on here?" she asked.

"Do you not recognize the flag?" the guard asked, pointing to the top of the church.

She glanced up; a makeshift flag pole was attached to the bell tower, but with the windless day, the flag had not been visible. Now, her eyes focused on it, taking in its meaning. "The red flag of rebellion," she said at last. "It seems to be spreading."

"What would you know of rebellion?" asked the guard.

Revi stepped forward, despite Hayley's protestations. "I am Revi Bloom," he said, "have you heard of me?"

"Aye," replied the guard, "though we'd heard you were dead. Killed along with the people's princess."

"The people's princess?" mused Revi. "You mean Princess Anna?"

"That's the one," he replied. "There's no other."

He smiled, "Then, my friend, I bring you joyous news, for Princess Anna is alive and well. Not only that, but Kingsford and Colbridge have fallen to her armies."

"How do I know this isn't some sort of trick?"

At this, Hayley spoke up, "Is Elwind Marhaven still the reeve here?"

"Aye, he is, what of it?"

"Then go and fetch him. Tell him Hayley Chambers wants to speak to him."

They watched as the guard spoke to his companion, who then ran off.

"You know the reeve?" asked Revi.

"Of course, I regularly patrolled the area around here. The reeve was appointed by the Baronet of Wickfield. He never spends any time at his estate, he's too comfortable in Wincaster, so he pays the reeve to look after things."

"And you suspect this Marhaven fellow will be friendly?"

"I think so," said Hayley.

Revi detected some hesitation in her voice, "Is there something you want to tell me?"

She blushed, "Well, he might have been a little enamoured of me at one time."

"Enamoured?"

"Yes," she replied.

"And just how enamoured was he?"

"Well, he might have proposed at one point."

"Is he likely to bear a grudge? I mean, Hayley, you did rebuff him, didn't you?"

"I wouldn't be standing here now if I hadn't. Don't worry, he's a decent enough fellow. I think everything will be fine."

The man that came to meet them was younger than Revi had imagined, with chiselled good looks and a crop of black hair tied back with a strip of leather.

"Hayley Chambers, what a pleasant surprise," the reeve called out.

"You're looking well, Elwind," the ranger called back. "I trust all is peaceful?"

He halted before them to look them over. His attention to Revi was brief, but he let his eyes linger on the ranger for a while before answering. "There is a gathering storm, I'm afraid. We have word that the king has sent troops to quell the rebellion."

"And yet you still offer resistance," said Revi. "Are you that sure of victory?"

"Our understanding," continued the reeve, "is that the army will move west, to attack Bodden first. The villages here are small and unimportant in the politics of the realm. The king has troops here and so believes us to be loyal."

"And yet you still fly the red flag," offered Hayley, "why is that? Surely you would be better off to fly the flag of the realm?"

"No, the people here have suffered too much and refuse to pay the king's taxes. This new offensive was the last straw. When word came down calling on us to increase taxes and send half our food to the army, they'd had enough."

"What of the Royal Garrison?" asked the mage.

"The Wincaster bowmen? They're supporting us. Despite their name, they were recruited from the area. Most of them have families here, and they'll not see them suffer. That's why we've begun fortifying the place."

"If the army comes, this barricade will do little to dissuade them," said Hayley.

"True, but if they come in force, we'll cross the river into Norland. Better to face the raiders than the wrath of the king, but enough of this banter. Come, let's get you inside where we can catch up on old times."

He led them past the makeshift barricade and down the single street that ran northward. "The captain has posted lookouts in the bell tower," he explained, "and we've set up a command centre in the church itself." He turned left, leading them to the indicated building. "Captain Wainwright commands the archers."

"I'm afraid I don't know him," offered Hayley. "Is he to be trusted?"

The reeve halted, looking directly into her eyes, "You've changed, Hayley. You never used to distrust anyone till they gave you a reason."

"I've been through a lot in the last two years," she replied.

A group of soldiers stood around a table. At their entrance, the man at its head came toward them. "You're Revi Bloom?" he asked, without preamble.

"I am," exclaimed the surprised mage.

"Then I have need of your services," the man replied.

"And you would be?" asked Revi.

"Sorry, I should have introduced myself. I'm Captain Harold Wainwright, Captain of the Greens."

"The Greens?"

"Yes, the Wincaster bowmen."

"Ah," replied the mage, "I see now, the green tunics, it all makes sense."

"Are you here to help?" pressed the captain.

"We will help if we can," replied Hayley, "but there's just the two of us. I'm not sure what we can do."

"I have a number of wounded men," explained the captain. "We fought off Norland raiders last week when they tried crossing the river."

"I can take a look at them," offered the mage. "Where are they?"

"They're in the back. We've turned the Holy Father's office into a sick room. Halion," he called out, "take the Life Mage to the wounded."

"Aye, sir," came the reply.

Hayley watched as Revi was led away, then turned her attention back to the captain. "What kind of strength do you have?"

"A company of archers, and thankfully we're at full strength, or at least we will be when the mage heals my men."

"So you have bows, but what about spearmen?"

"The local militia has been called up," offered the reeve.

"And how would you rate their training?" asked Hayley.

"Little to none, I'm afraid," he answered.

"You need more men to man the walls," she observed.

"Agreed," said the captain, "but there are no more to call."

"What about Mattingly," she asked.

"It's a good distance from here," replied Captain Wainwright, "and they'd have to march through Hawksburg to get here."

"Not if they paralleled the river," said Hayley. "I've made the trip on several occasions. It's an easy enough path."

"We know little of the garrison there," offered the reeve, "but we'd welcome any help they might be able to send. Are you offering to go and talk to them?"

"I'm not sure we can spare the time," she said. "We have to rendezvous with another member of our party."

"It would mean a lot to us," offered the reeve, "to me, especially."

"That horse left the barn a long time ago, Elwind. I'm with Revi now."

A look of surprise crossed the reeve's face. "The mage? You can't be with a mage."

"Says who?" she demanded.

"Mages don't have relationships. They're married to their craft."

"Are you an expert on mages, now?" she retorted. "Trust me, I've known Revi for some time, he's dedicated, but I wouldn't say he's married to his craft."

As if by magic, Revi Bloom returned. "All done, Captain," he said, wiping his hands with a cloth.

"That fast?" asked the reeve in disbelief.

"What can I say," said Revi, "I'm very efficient at my job. They'll be weak for a day or two due to blood loss, but I expect them to recover fully."

"I must thank you," said Captain Wainwright. "We need every man."

"The good captain would like us to go to Mattingly and see if we can bring the levy here."

"The militia?" asked Revi. "Won't they need it themselves?"

"If the king strikes, he'll likely attack Wickfield first," offered Hayley, "it's closer."

"What about Beverly?" Revi asked.

"Precisely what I was thinking."

"I suppose we could leave a note with Gort," offered the mage.

"Who's Gort?" asked the reeve.

"A mutual friend," responded Hayley. "Revi, can I talk to you in private for a moment?"

"Certainly," he responded.

They hustled outside then she looked around, careful that no one was about to overhear their conversation.

"They need reinforcements," said Hayley. "What if we sent them some troops from Queenston?"

"That won't work," said Revi, "they're needed in the coming offensive. We have no idea when or even if the king will attack here. No, it has to be the levy at Mattingly, unless you think Hawksburg could help."

"No, they're too close to Tewsbury. I rather suspect they'll have their own troubles soon enough."

"The trip to Mattingly will take too long, Hayley. We still have to get back and make our report."

"We could return to Queenston and get a couple of horses. That would speed up the trip considerably."

"Yes," he agreed, "but we'd still have to wait for Beverly. There's no telling how much longer she'll be."

"Then we'll have to leave her a note if she's not there already."

"How long would it take, do you think?"

"To get back through the gate and return with horses? No more than a day I would say, and we'd more than make up that time on the way to Mattingly."

"It sounds like a good idea," said Revi. "I suggest we get moving on it right away. How soon can we leave?"

"First thing tomorrow," she offered. "If we leave before sunup, we can be back to the gate long before dark."

"You'd best say your goodbyes tonight then," he said. "Though I suspect the reeve will be sorry to see you go."

Hayley saw the look on Revi's face. "Hey, I'm your lucky charm, no one else's, remember?"

Revi coughed to hide his discomfort, "Of course, I know that. What do you take me for, some love-struck youth?"

The ranger kissed him tenderly.

"What was that for?" he asked.

"Just for being you," she replied.

Beverly Fitzwilliam started out heading north to the great river and then turned westward, following its southern bank while it meandered across the land. The distant trees of the Whitewood drew closer until finally, she entered their shadows. The woods here were thick with undergrowth that hampered travel.

Hours after entering the forest, she stumbled across an unexpected sight. It first came to her attention when her boot made a cracking sound. She looked down to see a bone, crushed beneath the weight of her foot. Pausing in her steps, she cast her eyes about. As they adjusted to the vibrant colours of the wood, she detected hints of a bone here and there, along with the glint of metal. She investigated further only to find a sword, still gripped in a skeletal hand.

A battle had taken place here some time ago; the bones picked clean, the woods engulfing the bodies. She remembered Albreda's reputation and decided this was as good a place as any to call forth the druid.

"Albreda," she called out, "it's Beverly, I'm here. Come and find me!"

Her voice echoed in the great wood, but only silence greeted her. She continued her journey, heading deeper into the Whitewood, calling out occasionally as she went.

The afternoon wore on. As she knelt by a stream, she heard the snapping of a branch. Standing, she drew her sword, her thirst now forgotten. Her eyes scanned the trees, but it was her hearing that told her the truth; there was movement all around her.

At first, she wanted to lash out with her sword, but her mind soon got a grip on her emotions. This was the lair of Albreda, she reminded herself, and no harm would befall her here. She scabbarded her sword and waited.

Moments later, a wolf came out of the undergrowth. It approached slowly, eyeing her the whole time as she stood, silent and unmoving. Soon, others joined it, surrounding her. Beverly remained still, scanning the trees, ignoring the wolves.

"I am here to see the Lady of the Whitewood," she announced.

"And so you have found me," came a voice in reply.

Albreda stepped from the shadows, her face wearing a look of surprise. "Beverly," she called out, "is that really you?"

"Yes," the knight replied.

Albreda crossed the intervening space quickly to embrace the red-headed knight. "By the Gods," she said, "this is too good to be true. I knew you must be alive, I just knew it."

Beverly, surprised by the act, returned the hug.

Albreda withdrew, holding Beverly at arm's length, "Look at you, healthy as a horse and alive. I knew the reports of your death had to be wrong, my visions would have seen it."

"My father, is he well?" Beverly asked.

"He is," replied the mage, "as is Aldwin."

Tears of relief came to Beverly's eyes at the mention of her smith.

"Yes," said Albreda, "he's been mourning your loss, though. We'd been told you were dead. Tell me, how did you come here?"

"Revi has unlocked the secret of the gates," she replied.

"Gates? What gates are those?" Albreda asked.

"It's a long story," the knight said. "What's been happening in Bodden?"

"They sent knights to arrest your father and put him in the dungeons, but we rescued him."

"We?"

"Yes, Aldwin and I. We had some help from the local garrison, of course. That's quite the smith you've got there, I must tell you."

"Aldwin helped rescue my father?"

"Yes, isn't that what I just said. You'd be proud of him, Beverly."

Beverly felt an immense sense of relief. Albreda must have seen it, for she used a hand to wipe a tear from the knight's face.

"How did you know I'd come here?" asked Beverly. "I expected to be here for weeks before you showed up."

"I was drawn here," replied the mage. "I had a vision, though I didn't expect it would be you."

"Weren't you at Bodden?"

"I was, but I left there just yesterday."

"Yesterday? But Bodden is such a long way away."

"Yes," agreed Albreda, "but I can travel from one end of this wood to the other in the blink of an eye."

"How?"

"There are circles of stone that hold great power," the witch replied. "Come, I will take you to Bodden."

"I don't have a lot of time," warned Beverly. "My friends will be expecting me back at the gate soon."

"I can have you back in two days, will that suffice?"

Beverly's face lit up, "Yes," she replied. "Please, lead on."

"Excellent, we can be back in Bodden in time for dinner, well a late dinner, anyway. Come along."

She led the knight deeper into the woods, talking all the while. "Your father has some help. A few of his old knight friends from long ago came, and they brought men with them."

"Wait, you say he was placed under arrest?"

"Yes, by a noble from Wincaster and a group of knights. Aldwin and I rescued him and his loyal men from the dungeon, then we took back the Keep. One of the king's knights joined us, a man named Heward. Do you remember him?"

"Yes, I do. I served with him at Shrewesdale."

"Excellent," said Albreda, hurrying through the woods, "he's sworn to your father's service now. He did mention that he knew you, but I wasn't sure if he was telling the truth. Did I mention Aldwin?"

"Yes, he helped you," said Beverly as she strained to keep up, both in walking and listening.

"Your father was most distressed to hear of your untimely demise," continued Albreda. She halted suddenly, causing Beverly to almost bump into her. The mage turned to her, a smile on her face, "I just remembered, your father said that if you were alive, he would allow you to marry whomever you pleased."

"My father said that?" asked Beverly. "Are you sure?"

"Quite sure, my dear," replied the mage. "Now, where were we?"

"You're taking us to one of these circles of stone," offered the knight.

"Ah yes, it's around here somewhere." She gazed about and then called to one of the wolves. The creature came to her, and she bent over, touching her forehead to that of the wolf. A moment later she straightened back up and then turned suddenly. "It's over here," she said, "I'm afraid in my excitement I'd lost sight of where we were."

They entered a clearing and Beverly was immediately struck by a familiar feeling. "I've seen this before," she said, "or rather, something just like it."

"Really?" asked Albreda. "Where?"

"In the Forest of Mist, far to the south. It bore the marks of the Meghara."

"Meghara," said the witch, "I've heard that name before. She was a mage of great power."

"Actually," corrected the knight, "it was several. The Orcs told us Meghara is a title."

"Interesting," mused the mage, "but we have other things to concern ourselves with for the time being. Step into the circle, Beverly, and I'll cast the spell. You might find yourself a bit disoriented when we appear at the other end of the forest," she said as she began the incantation.

THIRTEEN

Events in the North

SPRING 962 MC

The walls of Bodden drew closer as Beverly and Albreda made their way south. So much had happened since she last saw the village she called home, and yet its familiarity still drew her in as if welcoming her home.

As she expected, guards were on the gate, and a shout of recognition caught her attention. She looked to the gatehouse to see a young woman, bow in hand, waving. The doors to the village opened, and Beverly noticed a small crowd gathering. They had been under observation for some time, for the area around the Keep was kept clear of obstructions, and now the knight saw familiar faces gathering around her as she entered.

"Welcome home, Lady Beverly," said Sergeant Blackwood. "It's good to see you safe."

"Where's the baron?" asked Albreda.

"We've sent word of your arrival. I rather suspect he'll be along momentarily," the sergeant replied.

Beverly shook the hands of many. These were men she had led on countless patrols, and she knew them all.

"My dear!" called out a familiar voice.

She turned to see her father, hurrying toward her, his face a mask of tears.

"I'd been told you were dead," he exclaimed, embracing her. "I'm so happy you're well. I thought I'd never see you again."

She hugged him tightly, relishing the affection. "I was so worried about you, Father," she burst out. "We heard there was rebellion in the north."

"We?" asked the baron.

"Oh yes," interrupted Albreda. "Richard, there is much to catch up on. Perhaps we should adjourn to the map room."

"Of course," responded Fitz, "though perhaps there is time for one more welcome."

He stood aside, and Beverly saw Aldwin, just behind her father, standing nervously, his face framing an anxious-looking smile. Beverly didn't hesitate. She stepped past the baron and immediately embraced the smith. A flood of emotions swept over her as she leaned back to stare into his steel grey eyes. They drew her in, and she pressed her lips to his, embracing the feeling and ignoring those around her. It seemed to last forever and yet when they finally stopped, she wanted nothing more than for it to go on. Aldwin was grinning while tears streamed down his face. The red-headed knight wiped her own tears of joy and then kissed him again.

"Come along now," said her father, "there'll be plenty of time for that later. It's time we get to the Keep."

The group started moving and Beverly, heedless of protocol, grabbed Aldwin's hand. "You must come with us," she said, "I don't want you out of my sight. Saxnor's sake it's good to see you, Aldwin."

He squeezed her hand in response, too emotional to speak. They made their way through the village and to the gate that led into the Keep. Here, she paused, taking a closer look, for some sort of construction was going on.

"That was my fault, I'm afraid," offered Albreda.

"Why? What happened?" asked Beverly.

"She tore down the portcullis when we rescued the baron," said Aldwin.

"Come along," prodded Albreda, "we've much to discuss and so little time. We must make haste if I'm to get you back to your friends in time."

They proceeded across the courtyard, the central Keep looming before them. Aldwin halted, just short of the door, causing Beverly to turn in surprise.

"I'll meet you in the map room," he said. "I have to get something."

"I'll wait," said Beverly, unwilling to part with him.

"No, you go ahead," he insisted, "I'll only be a moment. It will be worth it, trust me."

She hesitated, watching him leave, and then resumed her march.

.   .   .

The map room remained exactly as she remembered it. She could almost see herself as a little girl, playing with the small carved wooden blocks that represented the troops of Bodden Keep.

Baron Fitzwilliam had always used the map room as his central meeting place, but now Beverly wondered if, perhaps, they had outgrown it. It felt crowded as she entered. In days past her father would meet with his top knights, and Gerald, of course, but few others. Now the place was packed with knights and the leaders of the footmen.

"Come along, my dear," called her father, "I have a spot for you over here."

She pushed her way through the crowd, finding herself at the head of the table, beside the baron.

"We've been discussing plans," he started, "but perhaps, before we continue, you should fill us in on your adventures. I rather gather, from Albreda's account, that you've been quite busy."

"I have, Father," she replied, perhaps a little more formally than she had intended.

The tone was noted by her father, who turned to look directly at her. "My dear, what's the matter?"

"I will marry Aldwin, Father," she said, ready for a fight.

His answer completely disarmed her, "Of course you will."

"That's it?" she replied. "No argument? No discussion of my duty?"

"Beverly," began the baron, "when you were born, I promised your mother that I would do everything in my power to make you happy. I'm afraid as the years went by, I lost sight of that. In days of old, it would require the king's blessing for a noble to marry, but now, in these trouble-some times, the realm is changing. The old ways no longer hold us back. You have my blessing to follow your heart."

Beverly, momentarily at a loss for words, simply hugged her father. "Thank you," she finally managed to squeak out.

The baron coughed as she released her grip. "Now," he said, "where is that young smith of yours?"

"Right here, my lord," came a voice.

As if on cue, the crowd parted. Aldwin stood there, his hands gripping a warhammer, its surface catching the light, reflecting it about the room. Beverly looked on in amazement while the smith approached. The room fell into a hush as Aldwin held out the hammer in the palm of his hands.

"I made this for you," he simply said.

The weapon was exquisite; its head a finely crafted piece of art. She took it reverently, feeling its weight in her hands. "Aldwin, it's beautiful, it must have taken weeks."

"Indeed," added her father. "He had to make a special forge."

"Yes," added Aldwin, finding his voice. "It's made of sky metal."

"I know," replied Beverly, "you had to write to a Dwarf to get advice."

"How..." he stumbled.

"I've met Herdwin," she said, a smile creeping across her face. "He told me about your letter."

"When did this happen?" asked the baron.

"We had escaped the dungeons of Wincaster," she answered, "and took refuge in Herdwin's smithy. He's an old friend of the general's."

"General?" asked Fitz.

"Yes, sorry," she replied, "I meant Gerald."

"Sergeant Matheson is a general?" blurted out Blackwood.

"Indeed he is," said Beverly.

"Saxnor's balls," said Blackwood, "if you're making general's out of sergeants, sign me up!"

"Perhaps I'd best start at the beginning," offered Beverly, ignoring the sergeant's outburst.

"That would be helpful," suggested Albreda.

"As I told you we were captured at Wincaster," the knight continued, "but managed to escape. The princess, Gerald, and I, that is. We hid out at Herdwin's place, and he helped smuggle us out of the city. There, we met up with the rest of our group and headed south."

"And who, exactly, is the 'rest'?" asked Fitz.

"Dame Hayley, Sir Arnim Caster, Revi Bloom and a woman named Nikki who helped us."

"Why south?" asked her father. "Surely Bodden would have been safer for you."

"We discussed it, but the king would have been looking for us. Heading south kept us from their net."

"Clever," mused Albreda, "though I suspect there's more to it."

"Yes," agreed Beverly, "but that's something best left for another day. During our adventures, we managed to make some friends and then travelled to Weldwyn to seek help."

"Westland? I'm surprised," blurted out Sir Rodney. "They've been our enemy for generations."

"We travelled there last year," Beverly reminded him, "and they're a lot like us. Once there, we discovered they'd been invaded, so we helped them defeat their enemy. There was talk of marrying the princess to one of their princes, but I'm getting off topic. They've sent troops to help us take back Merceria. Kingsford has pledged to our cause, and we've taken Colbridge."

"You've been quite busy, from the sounds of it," observed the baron.

"It was all Gerald's doing," she continued, "he managed to keep the alliance going against all the odds. We've got Humans, Elves, Dwarves, Orcs, and even Trolls all working together."

"You HAVE been busy," added Albreda.

"Wait," said the baron, "you say you control Kingsford and Colbridge?"

"Yes, that's correct."

"What's your next move?" he asked.

"The general wanted to march to Wincaster down the great road, but we heard of trouble in the north. Rumour has it there's an army at Tewsbury, led by Marshal-General Valmar. The princess won't march on the capital with the north in danger."

"Perhaps we might be of assistance there," offered the baron.

"How so, Father?"

"I've been contemplating a move against Tewsbury, but I'm stretched to the limit. Tell me, how did you come to find Albreda? We've been so happy to have you here that we've given it little thought."

"Revi Bloom managed to unlock the secrets of gate travel."

"Gate travel?" said Fitz. "I've never heard of it."

"There are ancient portals that allow instantaneous travel, much like Albreda does in the Whitewood."

The baron looked to the witch, who simply shrugged, "I would have told you about it eventually, Richard. A girl must have her secrets, you know."

He barked a laugh, "Well, it seems there are all sorts of surprises this day. Tell me, could you bring an army through these gates of yours?"

"It takes time," Beverly continued. "A small raiding group would be easy enough, though."

"Your main army is at Kingsford, I assume?"

"Yes, they're preparing for the spring offensive."

"If we could lure Valmar out of Tewsbury, could you conduct raids against his supply lines?"

"Yes, I have just the troops for that," she replied. "The Orcs are masters of that type of warfare."

The baron smacked the table with the palm of his hand, "By Saxnor's beard, we have him."

"I'm afraid I don't understand, Richard," Albreda confessed.

"We shall lure him out of his hiding place," announced the baron, "and draw him down the road to Bodden. Beverly, do you think your army can come up the Redridge road? We could smash Valmar's army at the crossroads."

"I'm sure Gerald would see the wisdom in it," she cautioned, "but we'd have to take the town of Redridge, and that might slow us down."

"Wait," piped in Sir Rodney, "when we came to Bodden we took the Redridge road. They had a small army there, along with a fortified keep. I can draw you a map if that would help."

"I'd appreciate that," said Beverly. "Any information you can provide would help us, we have little enough. Do you know who commands there?"

"I believe it's the Earl of Shrewesdale, or at least it was when we passed through," supplied Sir Rodney. "I remember seeing his standard there, hanging from the keep."

"Not to be negative," interrupted Sir Gareth, "but I see insurmountable problems here. How are we to coordinate our armies at such great distances?"

"I can help with that," offered Albreda. "I'll travel with Beverly to their base of operations. Once things are arranged, I can return here with news."

"But surely the distances involved..." began the knight.

"I can return to the Whitewood in an instant," she replied.

"I thought you needed the stone circle," said Beverly.

"My child," she replied, "I can return to the stone circle from anywhere, it is merely less taxing to do it from another circle."

Fitz shook his head in disbelief, "The more I learn about you, Albreda, the more I am impressed. Tell me, all those years ago, could you have escaped so easily?"

"Of course, Richard, but it didn't suit my purposes."

"Well I, for one, am glad you're on our side," he replied.

She placed her hand on the baron's arm, "As am I, Richard, as am I."

"Now," continued the baron, "let us clear the room. I have much planning to do. I'll need Albreda and Beverly here with me, the rest of you I'll recall later, once our plans are made."

The assembled group began to disperse.

"Stay, Aldwin," called the baron, "you're almost family now, and I'd value your input."

The smith remained, a confused look on his face. Beverly moved to stand before him, "I'm sorry, Aldwin, I should have spoken to you first."

"I don't understand," he said.

"I told my father I wanted to marry you, but I never asked if that was what you wanted."

He looked to the baron, "And what, exactly, did your father say to that?"

"He told me I could marry whomever I please," she replied.

"And?"

"And it would only please me to marry you if you would have me."

In answer, he leaned forward, kissing her softly on the lips. "It would please me greatly," he said, "for it is something I have often wished for, but never, in my wildest dreams, did I think that such a thing could come to pass."

Albreda grabbed the baron's hand, "Come along, Richard, I think the young people would like some privacy."

"But it's my map room," exclaimed the baron.

"Indeed it is," replied the mage, "though for once I think you should make an exception."

The baron looked at Beverly and, seeing the look of love that passed between her and the smith, capitulated, "Very well, we shall give them their privacy."

FOURTEEN

Mattingly

SPRING 962 MC

~

"I'm glad we went back for the horses," said Hayley.

"Yes," agreed Revi, "and it let us pass on what we've already learned. I've never been to Mattingly before, have you?"

"Of course, many times," she replied, "though not since the rebellion broke out."

The terrain along the south bank of the river was mostly flat, with small groups of trees here and there. As they cleared one such cluster, the village came into view.

Hayley halted, the better to examine the distant group of buildings. "I see a flag," she said, "but it's not red."

"Oh?" queried Revi.

"It looks like a Royal Standard."

"Surely the king's not there himself."

"No, of course not, but one of his royal companies is."

"Can you tell which one?"

"No, there isn't enough wind, it's hanging limp. We shall just have to visit them."

"With a Royal Garrison?" said Revi. "Have you lost your mind?"

"Hey now, I'm a King's Ranger, remember? We'll make some discreet enquiries and try to learn the full story. Besides, I'm your lucky charm?"

"I'm beginning to wonder if there's a limit to how much luck we can have. Very well, lead on, and I shall follow."

They continued riding, the details of the village becoming clearer as they drew closer.

"They don't appear to have much in the way of defences," commented Hayley.

"No," agreed the mage. "A simple barricade and even that has an opening. I imagine the rebellion has not spread here."

As they rode up, a soldier moved to intercept them.

"Who goes there?" he called out.

Hayley withdrew the token from about her neck. "A King's Ranger," she called out.

At the sight of the talisman, the guard visibly relaxed. "Welcome to Mattingly," he said, "you'll find the captain in the tavern. That's our head-quarters."

"Thank you," she said. "Come along, Moxbury, we shouldn't keep the captain waiting."

Revi looked confused for a moment, then quickly recovered. "Of course, Miss," he replied.

They rode past the barricade and headed directly for the tavern. It was easy to spot, for few buildings in this small village were as large as The Green Unicorn. They tied their horses to the tree outside and then made their way in.

The last time Hayley had been here was four years ago. At that time, the place was the centre of the village, packed with people exchanging their opinions. Now, with the prospect of war in the air, the tavern was almost deserted. A group of soldiers sat at a table, nursing their ale, while the barkeep, an elderly looking man with a wispy grey beard and sideburns arranged bottles behind the bar.

Their entrance caught the attention of the soldiers. One of them stood, making his way toward them. "At last," the tall blond man said, "fresh meat."

Hayley pulled forth her ranger's token, halting the man in his tracks. "Sit down," she commanded, "I have business here. It is no concern of yours."

Revi marvelled at the look of fear on the soldier's face as he returned to his seat. "Is everyone afraid of the rangers?" he whispered.

"Only the guilty," she replied, heading for the barkeep. "It seems quiet in here today."

The proprietor looked up from his work, recognition dawning on his face. "You," he said. "What do you want?"

"Just information," she replied. "What's the situation here?"

"I only talk to customers," he obstinately replied.

Hayley tossed some coins on the counter, "Does that loosen your tongue?"

He scooped up the coins. "Business is bad since that lot arrived," he nodded his head in the direction of the soldiers.

"How long have they been here?" asked the mage.

"They came in the middle of winter. Their captain is a man named Griffon."

"How appropriate," mused Revi, "it seems that word follows you around, Hayley."

In answer, the ranger punched him lightly on the arm.

"We had our arguments in the past," continued the barkeep, "but you were always truthful to us. Compared to this lot, you were sent from the Gods."

"Is that an apology?" asked Hayley.

"For what?" asked Revi.

"The last time I was here, we almost came to blows."

Revi looked at the barkeep in surprise.

"It's true," the grey-haired man continued, "something killed our livestock, and your ranger friend here was supposed to hunt it down and kill it."

"Let me guess," mused Revi, "it was a gryphon."

"Actually," said Hayley, "it was a whole family of them, but I wouldn't let these people kill them."

"So what happened?"

"They flew off to the south, abandoning the area as far as I know. Did they ever return?" This last question she directed at the owner.

"No, thank the Gods."

The soldiers made a show of getting up. They were quite noisy and dropped a few meagre coins on the table, laughing as they did so. Wandering over to the door, Revi overheard their crude comments directed Hayley's way. He waited till their backs were turned before he acted, waving his hands in the air and incanting. He held back part of his power, not releasing his full potential, but the effect was exactly as he desired. The soldier in the lead let out a large yawn, overcome with fatigue. He stumbled at the doorstep, his companions colliding with him as he tried to reach out for support. They all tumbled to the ground in confusion. Revi stifled his laugh and turned his attention back to the conversation, ignoring the events at the door.

"This Captain Griffon has been lording his control over everyone."

"Meaning?" asked Hayley, a look of concern on her face.

"He wants women, particularly young ones for his own pleasure, but we got the last laugh."

"How so?"

"We sent all the children into the woods. The hermit will safeguard them."

"Hermit?" remarked Revi.

"He means Aldus Hearn," said Hayley.

"Aye, that's the one," added the barkeep.

"Aldus Hearn?" mused Revi. "Where have I heard that name before?"

"He's an Earth Mage," said Hayley, "and a rather powerful one, if truth be told. I met him some years ago."

"When you found the gryphons?" asked Revi.

"As a matter of fact, yes. I believe the princess has also corresponded with him over the years."

"So what do we do now?" asked the mage.

"How many soldiers are here?" Hayley enquired of the tavern keeper.

"Two dozen or so. They're an awful lot; ill-disciplined and greedy, but they're very faithful to their captain."

"Hmmm," mused Revi, "perhaps we can do something about that."

"There's only two of us, Revi. What can we do?"

"I would hazard a guess that if the captain were removed, the townsfolk would likely support us, is that correct?"

"Without a doubt," offered the barkeep, "but we're not trained warriors."

"Then I suggest we look for this Aldus Hearn," said Revi. "I rather think he might be useful in all of this."

"Very well," agreed Hayley, "I'll take you to him."

"Just like that?" asked Revi.

"I know where he lives," replied the ranger, "and it's only a short distance away."

"Excellent," said Revi. "Now barkeep, I want you to spread the word quietly. When we strike, we'll need everyone turned out with pitchforks and knives; anything that might be used as a weapon, actually. Don't worry, you won't have to fight, just put on a show. Do you think you can do that?"

"Of course," the man replied, "but how will we know when the time is right?"

"Oh, don't worry, it will be quite obvious," the mage replied cryptically.

They found Aldus Hearn's home in a small clearing in the woods after a pleasant ride from the village. The hut stood just as Hayley remembered it; a decrepit looking wooden structure, smeared with mud that was falling off in many places.

"It looks abandoned," observed Revi. "Are you sure he still lives here?"

"It's as I remember it," she replied, "but don't be fooled by the outside appearance, it's supposed to look that way."

"What have we here?" called out a voice.

They turned to see a man, dressed in a long brown robe, coming toward them. His bushy grey beard poked out from beneath a somewhat tattered hood.

"I'm Revi Bloom," said the mage, "and this is..."

"The ranger, Hayley Chambers," the man finished. "We've met before. I am Aldus Hearn, the protector of these woods."

"How do you do?" said Revi.

"Did you say Revi Bloom?"

"I did, why? Have we met before?"

"No," replied the druid, "but I've heard of you. I believe we have a mutual acquaintance."

"You mean besides Hayley, here?" said Revi.

"Yes. Over the years I've been in correspondence with Princess Anna. I believe you know her."

"We both do," added Hayley, "in fact, we're in her service. What has she told you?"

"Well," answered Hearn, "I must admit I haven't heard from her for a while, but last she mentioned, you were the new Royal Life Mage. An important position to be sure."

"It keeps me busy," replied Revi, "though truth be told I don't serve the king anymore. I suppose technically that doesn't make me a Royal Life Mage."

"You still serve the princess," said Aldus, "that's royal enough for me. I rather gather this isn't a social call."

"While it's good to see you again," remarked Hayley, "I fear things in the north are, how shall I put it, unsettling? How have YOU been? It's been some time since we last spoke."

"Well enough," replied the elderly druid, "though I fear the village has not fared so well."

"Yes," agreed Revi, "it's about that very topic that we came to see you. I wonder if we might have a word or two?"

"But of course," said Aldus, "come inside, I'll make you some tea."

He pulled open the door to reveal a pleasant looking room. "Never mind the exterior," he explained, "I generally don't like visitors, and it serves to keep them at bay. Now, shall I put on a pot of water? Have a seat, over by the shutters. Open them up, will you, Hayley? Let's have some light in here."

They both sat down while the old mage fussed with a kettle.

Revi looked about the room, his eyes coming to rest on a shelf cluttered with books. "I see you're an avid reader."

"Indeed I am," replied Hearn, "though I seldom see new books to keep my interest."

"I should very much like to exchange books with you when this war is over," said Revi.

"I would be delighted, but we have much to do before then," said Hearn, as he dropped some herbs into the kettle. "Tell me, what brings you hither?"

"The village has been occupied by soldiers of the king," said Hayley.

"Indeed it has," agreed the elderly mage. "What of it?"

"We heard you have helped keep the children safe," said Revi.

"I have," Hearn agreed. "There are tunnels within the woods that they are hidden away in. They are quite safe, I can assure you."

"What about wild animals?" asked Revi.

"I've told them to keep their distance," explained Hearn, digging through his shelves for cups.

"Would you help us take back the village?" asked Hayley.

Hearn stopped his rummaging and looked at them, perhaps to gauge the depth of their commitment. "I normally don't involve myself in such matters, but I think I will make an exception. What did you have in mind?"

"Well," said Revi, "I was thinking..."

Bronson Thallinger peered out into the darkness. "Did you hear that?" he asked.

His companion, Garman Evans, looked doubtful, "You're imagining things, Bron. Would you just relax? We're in the middle of nowhere. Who in their right mind would threaten a Royal Garrison?"

"But what about the rebellion?" asked Bronson.

"Easily squashed," replied Garman. "These farmers won't stand up to soldiers. You mark my words, by summer this whole mess will be done with, and we'll be back in Wincaster enjoying the pleasures of the city."

Another noise came from the dark, and this time both men took notice.

"Did you hear it that time?" asked Bronson.

Garman stared into the darkness. "I did. Go and fetch the captain, something's up."

Bronson ran off, leaving his comrade alone at the thin barricade. Through the village of Mattingly he ran, and then hurried into the tavern.

Captain Griffon sat at a table, nursing his ale when the messenger arrived.

"Sir," Bronson called out, "there's something going on at the barricade."

"Which location?" asked the captain.

"South," the soldier replied.

The captain stood, downing the remainder of his drink in one gulp. "Very well, let's take a look. Lead on."

They exited the tavern, making their way to the makeshift barricade that gave some semblance of protection against attackers.

Garman, who had been staring into the darkness, turned at their approach. "They're out there, sir. I can hear them."

Bronson took up his position at the improvised wall. "Weren't those trees farther back?" he asked.

"Don't be absurd, man," replied the captain, "trees don't move."

Another rustle drew their attention. Garman climbed up onto the barricade, steadying himself on the top of the barrels as he gazed south, trying to identify the distant noise. Suddenly, an arrow struck the soldier full in the chest, knocking him back off of his perch. He fell to the ground, clutching at the wound.

Captain Griffon ducked behind cover, Bronson doing likewise. "It appears you two have made a discovery," he said. "Poke your head up and see if you can make out the bowman."

Bronson was about to protest but realized the futility of it, for in the king's army the captain's word was law. He furtively poked his head above the cover, but all he could see was the tree line.

"Do you see him?" asked the captain.

"No, but I swear the trees are getting closer."

"It's just a trick of the shadows. Keep your eyes peeled."

A light suddenly appeared, hovering in the air, then slowly advanced past the barricade until it was directly over their heads, just out of reach.

Bronson turned towards another rustling sound to see a tree directly in front of him, its branches reaching across the barrels. He felt a slap as the leaves smacked him in the face and then the great bulk moved forward, upsetting the heavy barrels that formed the makeshift defences. He heard a yell and looked to his left.

The captain struggled as the branches tried to entangle him. "What sorcery is this? We must have fire."

Bronson backed up, his mind racing as he tried to make sense of all he witnessed.

The captain somehow managed to draw his sword and slash out at the branches, finally freeing himself. He backed up as the last of the barrels was pushed aside. Bronson saw his commander getting ready to give an order, but all that came out of his mouth was a gigantic yawn, and then Captain Griffon collapsed to the ground.

Bronson tossed away his sword, turned, and ran with all the energy he could muster.

The small garrison, alerted by the calls, poured out of their billets. Pulling on their scabbards and belts, they hurried to form a short line. Bronson, screaming as he ran past, ignored them and headed directly north.

The ball of light grew in intensity as it floated into the village. Doors opened, and the townsfolk emerged, axes and pitchforks at hand. The line of soldiers closed their ranks and began to form a loose circle. A sergeant yelled out orders, his raspy voice carrying across the cold night air until an arrow took him in the throat and he collapsed, forever silenced.

The soldiers were nervous and leaderless as a voice called out for their surrender. At first, only one soldier tossed his weapon to the ground, but soon, others followed, until their resistance collapsed.

Aldus Hearn stepped forward, flanked by Revi and Hayley. "Lock them up in the church," he said. "We'll deal with them in the morning."

The villagers poked and prodded their new prisoners, herding them toward the place of worship.

The voices of children began calling out, and soon the village was alive with excitement as parents were reunited with their offspring.

"A good night's work, I should say," offered Hearn.

"It was Revi's plan," said Hayley, "and I must say it worked brilliantly."

"What now?" asked the elderly mage.

"We must send help to Wickfield if we can," said Revi, "though I daresay there's few enough spare people here to be of assistance. Mattingly needs its own men here to protect it."

"I will bring help to Wickfield," offered Hearn, "and if I can, perhaps convince a few to come with me. Will that suffice?"

"It will have to," said Revi.

"Thank you for all you've done," said Hayley, "we couldn't have done it without you."

"You're quite welcome, young lady," he replied, "but what of you and Master Bloom? What will you do now?"

"We must return to make our report," she replied. "The princess is awaiting us. We've already taken far longer than we had anticipated and we still have to locate our comrade."

"I'm sure Beverly is back at the gate by now," offered Revi.

"The gate?" said Hearn. "Would that be a magical portal of some type?"

"It is," confirmed Revi. "I figured out how to use it."

"Fascinating," mused the elder mage. "I shall have to take a look at it sometime in the future."

They watched as the last of the prisoners was marched off under heavy guard. "I'll finish off here," promised Hearn, "and if I find anything of interest among the captain's letters, I'll bring it to Wickfield. You'd best be off before you miss your rendezvous."

"Very well," said Hayley, "we'll just go and get our horses."

Aldus Hearn smiled, "No need, here they come now. I took the liberty of calling them."

"Calling them?" said Revi.

"Well, I am an Earth Mage, after all."

The weather turned warmer as they made their way back to Wickfield, promising a hot summer. They were following the river again, for the road would have taken them out of the way to Hawksburg. They were pondering this very topic as they rode.

"What do you think Aubrey has been up to?" asked Hayley.

"Knowing her, she's likely been studying. I left her with some books about magic."

"Should we visit her? It's not too far from here, you know."

"Much as I would like to, I fear we've already taken far too long on this trip. We were only supposed to be gone a few days, and already we've been over a week. The army is ready to march, and Gerald is waiting on our report to make some decisions."

"I suppose you're right," she replied, then changed the topic. "Tell me, what did you make of Aldus Hearn?"

"An interesting fellow," said the mage. "I should love to have the chance to sit down and talk with him at length, once this war is over. Do you think he'd be interested in marching with the army?"

"Hard to say, I don't know him well."

"But you introduced us," said the mage.

"Yes, but I only met him once before, back when Mattingly had a problem with their livestock."

"He seems very competent," mused Revi. "I have a feeling we've only seen a small sampling of what he is capable of. Let's hope he decides to join us."

"I'm sure he will, eventually, but he's needed here to help hold the north."

They mulled the situation over quietly as they rode. Hayley, deep in thought, unexpectedly broke the silence, "Revi? Can I ask you a question?"

"Of course," he replied, "anything you like."

"Do I distract you from your studies?"

"What do you mean, 'distract'?"

"It's just that I've been told a number of times that mages don't marry.

Most people believe that mages can't reach their full potential with the distraction of a relationship."

"That's all a load of nonsense, Hayley."

"How can you be so sure?" she asked.

"Think of it logically. We know that magic is passed down from generation to generation, correct?"

"Yes, I've heard that too."

"Well then, if mages didn't marry, who would carry that magic? We'd have no mages after only a generation."

"I suppose I never thought of it that way," she mused.

"I think most mages marry, it's just that the history books only ever talk about their magic. It's the same with heroes of the past. Think of a great warrior or great leader. Do you hear about their families? Of course not, and yet they must have had them, or they wouldn't have had descendants."

"You're right," agreed the ranger. "When you put it that way it seems quite obvious."

"Of course, if we should have children they would likely eclipse us in the history books."

"Why would you say that?" she asked.

"Well, with my magical potential and your ranger skills they would be unstoppable." He grinned, his boyish nature showing through.

"Does this mean you want to have children?"

Revi blushed, "Eventually, of course, but let's get this war over with first. Besides, we're not even married yet."

"We don't have to be married to have children, Revi."

"I know that, but I'm old fashioned."

"Is that a proposal?" Her eyes lit up.

Revi, who by now was beet red, coughed. "Well...that is to say...I should very much like to propose...eventually."

Hayley reached out to place her hand on his arm. "That's all right, Revi, there's no hurry. We'll finish this war off first, then we can look to our own future."

Three days later they arrived at Wickfield. The first sign of civilization was a small group of men in a boat catching fish on the river. They waved as Hayley and Revi rode by, seemingly oblivious to the brewing war.

"They look so calm," mused Revi. "I wonder if they know the danger they're in."

"The king is likely more concerned with Bodden," said Hayley. "Baron Fitzwilliam is more of a threat to the king than these villagers."

"True," he replied, "but it wouldn't take many men to subjugate the area."

"Yes, but any he left here would be less he'd have to attack Bodden."

"How can you be so sure?"

"I've spent a lot of time with Beverly," she replied, "and, after all, I am a Knight of the Hound."

"True," agreed the mage, "in fact, there are only three of you now, so it's a very select group."

"I'm sure the princess will reconstitute the order once the war is over."

"I don't think she will," speculated Revi.

"Why would you say that?"

"The days of knights are over, I think. There is a new world coming, one in which the common man has as much of a say as the noble."

"Wherever did you get that impression, Revi?"

"The princess wants justice for all and a legal system where all folk are equal under the eyes of the law."

"That doesn't mean there won't be knights, though," she warned. "Beverly has already begun training a professional company of heavy horse. I think it's only a matter of time until people realize how truly effective they can be."

"Knights, heavy cavalry," said Revi, feigning ignorance, "what's the difference?"

"Oh there's quite a difference," the ranger began with enthusiasm, "knights are very unreliable in battle. It's true that they're very effective when they get in among the enemy, but they seldom follow orders and often go charging off on their own. Imagine harnessing all that military might into a highly disciplined army. They would be unstoppable."

"Unless the enemy has mastiffs," Revi added.

"Well, I grant you, there is that," she said, "but they're very rare on the battlefield. We likely have the only mastiffs in this entire land. If it hadn't been for Beverly, they would have ripped us to shreds." She looked at Revi, who was grinning, "but you knew that, didn't you?"

"I did," he confessed, "though I must admit to some amusement at watching your passion shine through. Your whole face lights up, it's wonderful to see."

"Speaking of wonder," continued Hayley, "I wonder where Beverly is now? We've been away for so long, she's likely looking for us."

"I know exactly where she is," said Revi.

"Oh? How is that?"

He pointed toward the village, "I can see her right there."

Hayley looked to see the distinctive red hair and smiled. "She must have grown tired of waiting for us. Who's with her?"

"I don't know," replied the mage, "likely someone from the village."

As they drew closer, recognition dawned on the ranger's face, "It's Albreda."

Finally, they were close enough to talk and they both dismounted. Hayley looked at Beverly with a keen eye.

"Something's different," she mused. "Is that a new weapon?"

"It is," replied Beverly. "It's 'Nature's Fury'. Aldwin made it for me."

"Nature's Fury?"

"Yes, Albreda enchanted it."

Hayley turned to Revi, "Why is it you've never enchanted anything for me, Master Bloom?"

"I'm a healer," he replied, "what would I enchant?"

"A valid point, I suppose."

"Here, take a closer look," offered Beverly, handing over the weapon.

The ranger examined it in detail. "Very impressive work. What kind of metal is this? I've never seen its like before."

"It's called sky metal," offered Albreda. "Aldwin took great pains to find it."

"Albreda, it's good to see you again," said Revi, "though I'm surprised to see you here. Surely we're a long way from your home."

"I was drawn to the eastern edge of the Whitewood by a vision," she replied. "It was there that I found Beverly."

"And you just happened to be carrying this hammer?" asked the mage.

"No, of course not. We went to Bodden."

Revi wore a look of surprise, "That would take weeks, wouldn't it?"

"I think you forget your geography, young mage. The distance to Bodden is scarcely more than the distance to Mattingly."

"Through thick forest and overgrown hills," defended the mage, "and if you took the road, it would be almost twice as far."

"True enough," said Albreda, "but as it turns out, we used another mode of transportation."

Beverly, about to speak when she noticed a brief shake of Albreda's head, quickly changed the subject, "Albreda gave this weapon the power of the earth."

"What exactly does that mean?" asked Hayley, returning the warhammer.

"There are a number of spells on it, but I've yet to use it in battle. I'm told it will speed up my attacks, as it unleashes a fury of blows. I've seen the effect it had on a chest plate. It punched clean through."

"I thought you hadn't used it in battle?" asked Hayley.

"I didn't, Aldwin did."

"You've seen Aldwin? You must tell me all about it."

"Later, this is neither the time nor place."

"Well," interrupted Revi, "we should be on our way. We have to return to Queenston. It was very nice of you to escort Beverly, Albreda."

"Oh, didn't I mention it?" said Beverly. "Albreda's coming with us. I've been in discussion with my father, and we have a proposal for the general."

"Then we'd best get a move on," said Hayley, "or we won't get to the gate before nightfall."

FIFTEEN

The War Comes North

SPRING 962 MC

The chill morning air had laid a layer of frost across the grounds but Lady Aubrey Brandon's excitement at the day's activities had thoroughly warmed her on her walk to the old manor house. She removed her coat as she entered the casting room, eager to continue her studies.

The tome left by her great-grandmother had proven to be of immense benefit. Already, she had learned a few new spells, though most, in truth, were variations on her healing. Today, she had decided to expand her knowledge and try a spell of a different nature. It was referred to as 'spirit walk', and she wondered what that might portend.

Tossing her coat onto the table, she made her way to the centre of the casting circle, wherein lay the lectern with the book open to the new incantation. She had read it over many times, and yet still the words were difficult to articulate, the mindset requiring the utmost concentration.

She closed her eyes and took a steadying breath. The first part of the spell was easy, the incantation flowing from her mouth effortlessly. The magic circle, now cleared of all dirt, began to glow and she felt the power pour into her. The words continued, and she began to trace the intricate patterns that would release the magic within. Small lights appeared in the air before her, forming ancient runes of magic and then she heard a sharp snap.

After a momentary sense of falling, as if the floor had given way beneath her, she staggered back. Someone stood in front of her, and it took her a moment to realize it was her! She looked down to her hands to see them glowing slightly, the residual magic still evident. Something felt wrong, and she struggled to focus her mind. Everything was somehow muted as if most of the colour had been drained from the view before her.

She watched as her body slumped to the floor and her mind struggled to come to terms with her situation. She looked down at her body, which now looked devoid of life and then panic set in. Had she managed to kill herself?

She could sense the floor, where her feet supported her, but couldn't feel it. It reminded her of a cold winter day, years ago, when she had stayed out too long, and her feet had turned numb. Was this what death was like?

She stepped over her own body with a sense of dread to stare at the book of magic. She tried to flip the page, but her hands passed through the book as if it didn't exist.

"Calm yourself," she said aloud, her voice echoing slightly. "This is a spell of spirit walking. I must be in the spirit realm."

She turned, walking to the stairs, but when she tried to ascend them, her feet passed through, leaving her with no way to escape her prison. Reaching out with her hands, she learned that they, too, passed through the bricks. The room had been quite chilly when she had entered, but now she felt...nothing; neither hot nor cold.

Walking around the room, she examined things in detail, growing ever more used to her surroundings and their representation in the spirit realm.

Finally, she perceived a tug. It was almost a compulsion and then she felt herself being pulled back into her physical body, the spell having expired.

It all ended with another audible snap, and then she opened her eyes to see the room, once again returned to its natural state. The cold stone floor pressed against her cheek and she laughed aloud for this was proof enough that she was still alive. She rose, returning to the book, now even more determined to understand all its contents.

Resolved to master this new incantation, she delved into the book with great intensity. The pages were littered with notes, often scribbled in the margins, and these she paid particular attention to. According to her great-grandmother, concentration was required in the spirit realm to navigate successfully, a mentally draining exercise. After three weeks of careful study, she decided to re-attempt the casting.

She prepared herself carefully, getting a full night's rest and eating sparingly that morning. She took the precaution of laying furs down on the casting circle, the better to keep her body warm while she was out of it. It was quite easy to see the problems with the spell, for her physical form would be left unattended and alone. To her delight, she found the spell could be cancelled at any time, though there was a warning not to be too far from her body when doing so or she might risk remaining a spirit for all time. It was then that the full danger of what she was about to attempt hit home.

Standing before the tome, she began the incantation. This time the words came more easily to her mind, and the spell spilled from her lips almost without thinking. There was the anticipated snap, and then she stepped back as her body fell to the floor. Perhaps, she mused, in future, she might lay down to cast the spell to avoid bruising.

She waited for her mind to adjust to the change in colours. It was almost like dunking one's head in a bucket of ice, while the brain tried to keep up. She closed her eyes, concentrating on the spell, feeling a sense of calm washing over her.

She opened her eyes to the new world unfolding before her. The room still looked the same, but the hues were somehow off as if an artist had mixed together the wrong colours for his canvas. She made her way to the stairs, pausing at the lower landing. Concentrating on the stone step, she lifted her foot. It was a strange sensation, for she could see the step beneath her, but couldn't feel it. Up she went with a sense of euphoria at her success.

The library above was as she had left it. She was about to head to the front door and then remembered she didn't need to. Taking a deep breath, she stepped through the wall to the outside world.

The grass was beneath her feet now, the early morning dew still evident. She knew it was a chilly day, with a stiff breeze coming from the east, and yet she couldn't feel it here, in this strange otherworld. The rustle of leaves was muted as if cotton was in her ears. It all took so much effort that she had to close her eyes a moment to concentrate.

Her study of the book indicated the spell would have a lengthy duration, perhaps as much as an hour or two, and so she set off toward the town, determined to take in the sights.

She had only taken a few steps when the wind carried a scream that pierced right through her. Looking eastward, a plume of smoke greeted her eyes. She instinctively rushed toward it, concerned by the thick black cloud that bloomed in the air. Clearing the estate grounds, she found herself on Teland Street, a crowd rushing towards her in a panic. She tried to get out of the way, but they ran through her, a most distressing feeling. Looking up the street, she saw soldiers; they were torching the town, setting fire to the thatched roofs. A sense of dread overwhelmed Aubrey as she realized they were wearing the king's livery.

She sprinted to her family's manor house in a panic, fearful of what might have befallen them. The sight that greeted her sent a shudder through her body. Soldiers swarmed the front lawn, picking over the furniture and clothing that had been dumped there. Others were ransacking the house, but the true horror was the tree, for the great oak which decorated the estate had been used to hang her entire family.

She fell to her knees in anguish, her eyes riveted to the scene before her. No one had been spared. Whoever was in charge here had killed them all; Mother, Father, her brothers Tristan and Samuel, even the servants. She wanted to retch, but her spiritual form had no such stomach for it.

A shout dragged her attention from the scene before her to spot a well-dressed man, a noble by the look of him, though she knew not his identity. He gave an order, and she watched as two men carried her father's desk from the house. The noble pointed at a wagon, and the two soldiers loaded it up.

Aubrey screamed in rage, to no avail. No one could hear her, and they continued their orgy of plunder uninterrupted. Her fingers began the movements, her voice uttering the words that would put them to sleep, but nothing happened. It appeared that normal spells would not work here, in the spirit realm.

"We found a few more servants, my lord," a soldier announced.

"Ask them where the coins are and if they give you any guff, tell them Duke Valmar is here. That ought to sweat it out of them."

"And if they cooperate?"

"Grab it and then kill them. Remember, no prisoners. We will crush this rebellion once and for all."

Another man ran up to them, his helmet removed. He bowed respectfully and waited.

"Well man? What is it?" demanded the duke.

"There's another building back behind the estate, Lord."

"Well don't just stand there, go and search it!"

Aubrey's mind panicked. They had found the old manor house! If they were to discover her body, she would be trapped here forever. She fled the scene, rushing back to the casting circle and her physical form.

She dispelled the incantation, hearing the now familiar snap as her spirit once again joined her body. She rose, conscious of the necessity for speed. Grabbing her cloak, she was about to leave when her eyes were drawn back to the book. Closing the massive tome, she tucked it under her arm and rushed up the stairs, not a moment too soon for as she exited the library, the front door opened, revealing a startled soldier.

His unpreparedness saved her, for as he struggled to draw his sword, she cast the sleep spell and he let out a deep yawn before falling silently to the ground. She ran forward, spotting his companion. She swung at him with the book, its metal-bound spine smashing into the man's face, felling him instantly. Not bothering to look back, she ran for the trees.

Now in comparative safety, she halted, fighting the panic. Her mind was in a whirl, her family dead, her village put to the torch; it was all too much for her to handle. Tears streamed down her face as it shook her to her core. She took a deep breath, letting it out slowly. It would do no good, dwelling on the horror. Instead, she must take action, the time to grieve would be later when she was safe.

Her father raised horses; the mighty Mercerian Chargers that were so prized by knights. She turned and ran for the stables, determined to escape. The attached pasture ran parallel to the main road into town, and she noticed a group of soldiers running in her direction. As they drew closer, she recognized one of the local militia, likely retreating from the attackers. She waved at them, only to see them alter course, making for her location.

"My lady," called out their leader, "you have to get to safety."

"No time, Hugh," she said. "We must get to the stables. I won't give them the satisfaction of getting the horses."

"I don't know how to ride, my lady," returned the sergeant.

"It doesn't matter, we'll just chase them out of the stables. I'll open the gates, and with any luck, they'll run off. What's happening in the town?"

"It's terrible," the man said through tears, "they're raping and pillaging. Anyone who stands up to them is taken down by a swarm of soldiers. It's like a scene from the Underworld. We're all fleeing for our lives."

"Hugh, you go and find whomever you can. Tell them to head north, to Wickfield. I'll try to join you after we've taken care of the horses. The rest of you head to the stables; you know what to do."

"Aye, Miss," said the sergeant, turning around and running off.

Only two enemy horsemen were at the stables, light cavalry by the looks of them. They were dismounted and had apparently just arrived, for one held the reins while his companion headed toward the stable doors. Aubrey's spell of sleep took care of the horse minder, while her soldiers took out the other, cutting him down after a brief fight.

Her men rushed inside while she mounted one of the cavalry horses. "Can any of you ride?" she called out.

One of them called back, "I can, Miss."

"Come and take this other horse. Ride as fast as you can to the western edge of town. Find anyone fleeing and tell them to head north, the hills are too dangerous. Lead them onto Wickfield if you can."

"Surely the army will come after us?" he protested.

"Perhaps, but we can flee into Norland if we have to. Keep them as safe as you can. We'll follow you shortly."

She returned her attention to the stables. The remaining town militia had opened the large barn door and chased the horses out to the courtyard. The massive beasts were mulling about mindlessly, nibbling on the sparse grass that was in evidence this early in the spring.

Aubrey rode among them, trying to shoo them away, but still, they milled about, much to her frustration.

"They don't want to leave," called out a soldier.

"I can see that," she replied. "Never mind, we'll have to leave them, we don't have time. At least the king's men will have to chase them down, perhaps it will buy us some time."

"Where to, Miss?"

"This way," she called, trotting northward. "We'll cut across the Dunwin farm and then turn east to find the road to Wickfield. Hopefully, we'll see others we can help." She trotted off, careful to ease her pace so that the soldiers could keep up.

They arrived at the Dunwin farm to find it deserted. Though the king's soldiers had not yet reached this far, the smoke in the distance had likely warned the inhabitants of the approaching destruction. The small group rode across the fields, past grazing cows that looked up in mild interest at the travellers.

It didn't take long before they spotted the first of the refugees. A large line of survivors headed towards them from the town as smoke drifted from torched buildings. The small contingent of militia halted, trying to make out details and then Aubrey heard a noise. It began as a distant thunder, growing louder as they listened. She turned to see the cause; a group of Mercerian Chargers cutting across the field, led by her faithful pony Lucius. She had not ridden him since she was a little girl, yet the beast still remembered her, trailing her from the stables with the other great warhorses on its heels.

"It seems we were successful after all," mused one of the soldiers.

"So we were," she agreed, "but we have more pressing business." She turned to look down the road, south, to where the tail end of the refugees were still fleeing the town. A half a dozen horses were lined up behind them, their shiny armour leaving no doubt to their identity.

"Knights!" she swore.

"What do we do now?" asked the soldier.

She glanced around, taking in all she could. "You men get behind that bush over there, the one that lines the road. When I stop them, I want you to hit them, and hit them hard."

"But they're knights," he protested.

"You will have surprise," she said, "and their focus will be on me, I will see to it. Make sure you strike swiftly, for you'll only get one chance."

They grumbled, but they did as they were commanded. Aubrey trotted her mount to the roadway, waiting as the townsfolk fled northward.

The knights sat waiting, likely to initiate a charge to inspire more fear. Aubrey remained still until the last villager passed, and then turned her horse sideways so that her flank faced south, toward the enemy riders.

The sight must have intrigued them for they cautiously advanced northward, drawing closer by the moment. Soon, they were within hailing distance, and one of them lifted a visor to reveal his face.

"Stand aside," he called out, "and make way for the Knights of the Sword."

"These people are not soldiers," she replied. "Be gone and see to your master."

The knight looked to his companion, who simply shrugged.

"I'm afraid we can't do that," he replied. "Surrender yourself in the name of the king."

"He is no king of mine," she angrily retorted.

"Traitorous cur," called the knight, flipping down his visor as he spurred his horse into a gallop.

Aubrey focused her attention and started casting. The world around her became a blur as she saw the runes of power in her mind. She let loose with her magic, a simple spell of slumber, but with all the power she could muster. The visor hid the knight's face, yet the effect was clear, for his horse veered to the side of the road, its rider falling from the saddle with a crash.

His companions, who had watched in amusement, now reacted with panic, unsure of what had transpired. As a group, they rode forward, intent on blood.

Another spell flew from her hands, but this time it was a mount that was her target. The mighty steed stumbled in its new state of drowsiness, sending the rider tumbling. The others knights pulled back on their reins, halting their advance, their attention firmly on the young woman before them.

"Now!" she called out.

The soldiers, her soldiers, ran from cover, their swords flashing in the sun. They mobbed the knight closest to them, pulling him from the saddle and finishing him off with their blades.

The three remaining knights wheeled their horses about to meet this new threat, the mysterious mage all but forgotten.

Aubrey saw a sword rise and fall, the knight driving it into the arm of one of the militia. His victim fell to the ground, rolling to avoid the horse's hooves.

One of her men grabbed the knight's leg as he rode by. It was a desperate move, but the added weight pulled the rider off balance. His horse reared up, and the king's man fell from the saddle with a sickening thud as his helmet struck the ground.

The two remaining horsemen cut right and left, keeping the others at bay. Aubrey concentrated, her hands tracing patterns as she did so. A horse slowed, the spell of slumber not quite powerful enough to fell the beast, but it hampered the knight's efforts. One of the militiamen struck out, taking the knight in the small of the back. The knight slumped forward, dropping the reins, and then fell from the saddle to land, unmoving.

The last of the king's men stood in his saddle, swinging his sword down with all the might he could muster. A footman tried to dodge, falling back, but the blade cut into his face, leaving a ragged gash that bled profusely. As the defenders retreated, the knight surged forward, intending to run them down from behind.

As one of the fleeing men struck out wildly with his sword, the blade slid across the chainmail that protected the rider's leg, and the man lost his balance, stumbling. The knight turned in anticipation, raising his visor to see his enemy.

A dagger flew through the air, hitting him squarely in the face. It was not a killing blow, but the rider yelled out in pain, dropping his sword to remove the blade from his face; it was the last thing he managed to do. The footmen advanced, taking advantage of the situation. Swords stabbed forward, and the enemy dropped to the ground, his horse bolting off as he did so.

Aubrey dismounted, coming to the aid of her men. Two had suffered wounds, one a nasty gash across his face.

"Hold still," she called, placing her hands upon him. She uttered the magical words, and then the wound healed, closing the cut and leaving only a red line where the gash had been.

"Strip them," she ordered, "and bring their horses."

"It will take too long," the man replied.

"Then throw the bodies on the back of their horses and lead them. We'll strip them later."

"This one is alive," called out a soldier.

"Finish him off," she said, "we have no time for prisoners."

A knife flashed through the knight's visor, ending his protests. The soldier stood, looking about at the carnage. "We did it," he said.

"Yes," she admitted, "but we must hurry. It won't take long for others to follow and we need to be away from here as quickly as possible."

Two days later found them on the road to Wickfield which ran some forty miles or so, most of it through fairly flat terrain. The refugees were strung out in a long line, many abandoning their goods along the route in an effort to lighten their load and reach the safety of the northern village.

When word came of riders to the north, Aubrey grabbed two men and rode to intercept them, prepared for a fight, but what she saw took her by complete surprise.

Revi Bloom rode toward them, flanked by Dames Beverly and Hayley, while a third woman accompanied them.

"Cousin," she called out.

"Aubrey?" replied the red-headed knight. "Saxnor's balls, what happened?"

"They burnt Hawksburg," she called back, her voice full of emotion. "They killed everyone, burned the city to the ground. Valmar and his men are looting. It's a nightmare."

"You're safe now," soothed her cousin. "We'll get you to safety, all of you."

"How do you intend to do that?" asked Revi. "Have you seen how many people there are?"

"We'll use the gate," said Beverly, turning to the mage.

Her look gave him no choice but to acquiesce. "Very well," he said, "though it will take a long time." He gazed once more at the refugees, "A very long time."

"Are you being followed?" asked Beverly.

"Not that I know of. How did you end up here, of all places? I thought you were dead."

"I've heard that a lot lately," Beverly replied, "but I can assure you I'm quite alive, and so is the princess. Now, let's see to these people of yours. Hayley, ride south and keep your eyes peeled. Just to the back of the line, mind you, don't go wandering off. Give a shout if you spot any sign of pursuit."

"You think they'll follow?" asked the ranger.

"I doubt it," she replied. "If what Aubrey says is true, they're likely half drunk on stolen ale. I don't think they'll pursue when there's still plunder to be had."

Hayley rode off, leaving Aubrey at a loss for words.

"Perhaps," offered Albreda, "an introduction might be in order?"

"Of course," said Revi, "may I introduce Lady Aubrey Brandon of

Hawksburg," he turned to Albreda, "and this is Albreda, Mistress of the Whitewood."

"I've heard of you," said Aubrey. "You helped with the recent rebellion, didn't you?"

"I did," the witch replied, "and I'm helping with this war of yours, too. Now, let's get you looked after, shall we." She turned to Revi. "Master Bloom, where is this gate of yours?"

"It is west and slightly north of here," the mage replied.

"You cracked the secret of the gates?" asked Aubrey in surprise.

"Yes, some time ago, but I'll bring you up to speed later. I trust you've kept up with your magic?"

"Of course," she smiled, "and, you might say, I've made a monumental discovery."

"Which is?" asked Revi, his interest obvious to all.

"I'll tell you about it later," was all she said.

SIXTEEN

Return to Queenston

SPRING 962 MC

∽

Albreda stepped out from the cave to see the settlement of Queenston spread before her.

"You've been busy," she commented.

"Yes," confirmed Beverly. "Her Highness thought it best we secure a safe place to build up our army."

"How many people are here?" she asked.

"With the refugees coming from Hawksburg? I'm not sure, but I should think we will have over a thousand soon, maybe even double that when the army is in town."

"I don't see many troops," the witch said, looking around.

"They're mostly in Kingsford, waiting to march."

Small groups of villagers from Hawksburg filed past them as they stood, observing the town. Revi had been operating the gate for hours, teaching Aubrey as he did so. Almost a quarter of the refugees had arrived, but many more were yet to come.

"I'm surprised we couldn't just gate directly here," mused Albreda. "My spell of recall would work that way if you had a magic circle here."

"Revi says everything is tied to the temple in Erssa Saka'am, though he doesn't know why."

"What do you think?"

Beverly thought it over a moment, "I suppose it's more secure that way. You would have to control the main temple to allow access."

"Seems reasonable to me," replied the mage.

A voice called out from below, "Beverly!"

They looked down to see two people walking toward them with a large dog following along.

"Your Highness," replied the knight, "what are you doing here? Shouldn't you be in Kingsford?"

"We were," replied the young princess, "but we were eager for news."

"Yes," agreed Gerald. "What took you so long? We expected to come here and find you already back." He stopped talking, his thoughts interrupted as he recognized Beverly's companion. "Lady Albreda? I must say this is a pleasant surprise."

"I bring greetings from Baron Fitzwilliam," the witch replied.

"But how..."

"That's a long story, I'm afraid, one that will have to be told at a later date. For now, let us gather together, as I have much news to impart. Beverly has filled me in on your activities, but I must tell you what the baron has been up to. Do you have somewhere we can talk in private?"

"Of course, come this way. We have a hall we can use."

"Are you coming, Beverly?" asked Anna.

"I'll wait for Aubrey, Your Highness, if that's permitted."

"Your cousin? You found her?"

"Yes," she replied, "but I'm afraid it's not good news. They've sacked Hawksburg."

Anna cast a glance at Gerald, who wore a shocked look. "Very well, catch up with us when you can, we'll be in the meeting hall."

Beverly returned to helping the refugees after they came through the gate. It was late evening by the time they all arrived. Finally, Aubrey stepped through the flame, followed shortly by Revi Bloom.

"You look tired, cousin," said Beverly.

"I'm exhausted," she replied, clutching a book. "So much has happened. Did the horses make it through safely?"

"They did, though I'm surprised you brought them. You didn't know about the gates, so what were you intending to do?"

"I simply didn't want them falling into Valmar's hands," explained Aubrey. "I didn't expect them to follow me. It was actually Lucius."

"Your old pony?"

"Yes, the old fellow came after me and the rest just trailed along behind."

"Well, we can certainly use the mounts. What have you got there?" Beverly asked, pointing at the book.

"It's a spell book. It belonged to my great-grandmother."

"She was a spellcaster?"

"Yes, a Life Mage, in fact. I've been studying it. I can't wait to tell everyone what I found. Revi has filled me in on your adventures. It seems I missed quite a lot."

They stood looking at each other for a moment, and then Beverly noticed a look of sorrow pass over her cousin's face. "I'm sorry to hear about your family, Aubrey. I know it must pain you."

Tears sprang from the young woman's eyes, running down her cheeks. "They hung them up like slabs of meat, Beverly. It was horrific!" Her anguish turned into great wracking sobs, overwhelming her. Beverly quickly stepped forward, embracing her suffering cousin, holding her tight.

"There's nothing you could have done to save them," the knight said. "They would have killed you too if you'd been there."

She held onto her a little longer until she felt the tenseness release. Aubrey stepped back, wiping her eyes with the back of her hand. "It was Valmar," she said through clenched teeth. "I recognized him."

"You saw Valmar? You were lucky they didn't catch you."

"I was in spirit form," she replied. "They couldn't see me."

"Spirit form? There's obviously more to this story," said Beverly, "but we should find the princess first, as you'd only have to repeat it. Come on, I'll take you to my hut, and we'll clean you up a little. You can leave your book there, it'll be safe."

They arrived at the stone structure, now known by all as the Manor House. Inside, the others were already present and deep in discussion. As they entered, Gerald was speaking, "The strategy is sound, but the matter of timing worries me."

He noticed the new arrivals, greeting them as they entered, "Beverly, Aubrey, good to see you. Come and have a seat. Albreda, here, was just filling us in on the baron's plan to lure Valmar out of hiding."

"Valmar burnt Hawksburg," said Beverly. "How do we know he hasn't moved on Wickfield or Mattingly?"

"We thought of that," said the princess, "but it is more likely that Valmar will return to the comfort of Tewsbury. His main objective is still Bodden, and if he were to take those villages, he'd have to leave a garrison, depleting his forces. I rather suspect Hawksburg was more about enriching his own pockets."

"Are you telling me," burst out Aubrey, "that he killed my family just for their wealth?"

"I'm afraid so," offered Gerald. "Valmar is a greedy man. He covets wealth and power above all else."

"But now," offered Beverly, "we have a chance to make him pay."

"Yes," agreed Gerald, "providing we can draw him out."

"So what is the plan?" asked Aubrey.

"Baron Fitzwilliam has an idea," began Gerald. "He plans to send a force of cavalry to Tewsbury to offer battle."

"What if Valmar refuses?" asked Aubrey. "After all, he's behind city walls, all nice and safe."

"The duke outnumbers us by a significant degree," he explained. "I doubt he'll hesitate at a chance to take out the baron once and for all."

"Once he emerges from his hiding place," continued Albreda, "we'll make a small stand and then withdraw, luring him westward."

"Isn't that dangerous?" Aubrey asked. "I'm no tactician, but surely with the numbers you're talking about, it would be suicidal?"

"I'll be there to help," offered Albreda, "and we'll be taking some precautions. The horsemen will retreat westward, keeping the enemy just close enough but out of reach. Valmar will be eager for a victory. It would cement his position as Henry's right-hand man."

"While they're advancing," interrupted Gerald, "we'll have raiders hitting them from the Wickfield Hills. Their lightning strikes will be aimed at their supplies and camps. We'll harry them all the way."

"And when they get to Bodden?" asked Aubrey.

"They won't, that's where we come in," said Beverly. "The Bodden foot troops will be waiting at the junction of the Tewsbury and Redridge roads. They'll make a stand, and we'll reinforce up from Redridge. The difficulty here is that we'll first need to take Redridge itself, and quickly at that."

"How much time will we have?" asked Arnim.

It was Anna that answered, "Assuming the baron marches quickly, we'll have to return to Kingsford then march to Redridge. Based on our past accomplishments, I should say we'd have, maybe, three days to take Redridge once we get there."

"Is that enough time?" asked Arnim.

"It will have to be," answered Gerald. "Any more, and we won't arrive in time to help the baron."

"What do we know of Redridge?" asked Aubrey.

"More than you might think," offered Beverly. "I ran into Sir Rodney in Bodden. He travelled through Redridge on the way north. I have some notes he sent along."

"Sir Rodney?" asked Gerald. "I thought he was dead. I haven't seen him for ages."

"He's quite alive, I can assure you," answered Beverly, "and he sends his regards."

Anna took the notes, scanning them over quickly. "It looks like the only real trouble will be the tower keep; there are no other defences."

"We need a better idea of their numbers," stated Gerald.

"I still have another waypoint to investigate," offered Revi, "and it's in the Margel Hills, near Redridge.

"We still have to worry about the north," insisted Arnim. "If Valmar doesn't follow the plan, a lot of people could suffer."

"Here's what I suggest," started Gerald, "we'll send Orc scouts through the gate to Wickfield. Their job will be to harass Valmar's advance. We'll also reinforce Wickfield and Mattingly with a company of foot, enough to give him second thoughts about attacking. Hayley, you and Revi will travel through the gate to this new location. Take some men with you. Your job will be to observe the enemy troops and count their numbers, if possible. The rest of us will return to Kingsford and commence the march. When you come back to Queenston, you'll have to find us on route. Can you do that?"

"Unquestionably," offered Revi, "though it might be easier to simply make our way out of the hills and meet you on the road."

"You'll have to make that decision once you're there. I have no idea how rough those hills are. In any case, you will rendezvous with us. We'll halt short of the town, I don't want to blunder into an unknown situation."

"Do we know much about the tower?" asked Arnim.

"Sir Rodney described it as a round keep," said Beverly.

"Could the Trolls reduce it?" asked Hayley.

"I doubt it," replied Gerald, "not in three days, at least. Given enough time we could build siege engines, but that would take too long, and with our timeline, we can't wait. We'll have to deal with the army and then take the tower by storming it."

"Maybe they'll surrender?" suggested Nikki.

"Perhaps," said Gerald, "but I doubt it. Redridge is ruled over by Lady Penelope's brother. He'll likely be as fanatical as her."

"Does that make him an Elf too?" asked Arnim.

"That's a good question," commented Anna. "We know Lady Penelope is an Elf, but we don't know if she assumed someone else's identity. Perhaps she looks and acts like a Human with the same name, someone whose identity was stolen. The Baron of Redridge could be a fellow conspirator, or someone who is under her power, perhaps controlled by some sort of magic."

"So then, how do we deal with him?" asked Arnim.

"Simple," said Gerald, "if he fights back, we kill him. This is war, and he's on the other side. Only if he surrenders do we have to deal with the larger issue of his role in all of this."

The room fell silent for a moment as everybody contemplated the plan. Finally, Albreda spoke, "With your permission, Highness, I will return to Bodden. The baron will be eager to begin his expedition, and we should get started right away."

"Very well," Anna agreed. "How long will it take you to get to Bodden?"

"I will be there before the end of the day," she said, much to everyone's surprise.

"How is that possible?" asked Revi.

"Are you not familiar with the spell of recall, Master Bloom?"

Revi blushed, "I'm afraid you have me at a disadvantage."

"I can return to one of my stone circles at any time, but the spell takes some time to cast."

"Ah," said Revi, "now I understand; it's a ritual."

"Yes," admitted Albreda, "though I was under the impression it was known by many."

"No," said Revi, "as a matter of fact, I don't think I know of any mage, save for yourself, that can perform that spell. Certainly, none of the mages of Weldwyn know of it. May I ask who taught it to you?"

Albreda gave him a stern look, "No one taught me. I learned it all by myself."

The implications hit Revi like a brick. "You're a wild mage," he declared.

"What's that?" asked Hayley.

Princess Anna supplied the answer. "A wild mage is one who comes by their talents naturally, without any structured training. They are said to be exceedingly rare."

"Yes," admitted Revi, "and they are said to be quite dangerous."

"Well," said Albreda, "I certainly am that. Thankfully, I'm on your side. Now, I have work to be done. Much as I have enjoyed this meeting, I must leave. Beverly, see me out, will you?"

"Certainly," replied the knight, "with Her Highness's permission, of course."

"By all means," said Anna, "and thank you again, Albreda, for your assistance."

"It has been my pleasure, Highness."

Albreda left the room, Beverly walking quickly to catch up. "Do you need somewhere to cast?" she asked.

The white witch halted a bow's length from the building. "No, this place will do as well as any other. Do you have a message for me to take back to your father," she waited a moment, "or Aldwin, perhaps?"

Beverly blushed.

"I think I have the idea," said Albreda. "Now, make sure I'm not interrupted while I'm casting, this can take a bit."

By the time Beverly finally decided on a message, the mage had already begun her spell. The knight watched in amazement as Albreda started calling on arcane forces. The air buzzed as if a swarm of bees had arrived, causing stray strands of her red hair to stand up as Albreda continued her incantation.

A swirl of air enveloped the mage, like a small tornado that ran about her, pulling small particles of dirt from the ground. The miniature sandstorm held Beverly's fascination as slowly, her view of the caster was obscured.

Some time passed before the knight realized she could no longer hear the voice that commanded it. The swirl of air slowed, the dirt dropping once more to the ground, revealing the centre as an empty space, devoid of its conjurer.

"That was very different," the knight mused out loud.

"What was?" came a voice.

She whirled about to see Hayley.

"I just watched Albreda use her spell of recall."

"I bet Revi would have liked to see that too," offered the ranger.

"I'm sure he would," said Beverly, "and I can imagine his reaction; 'not bad for a wild mage'."

"I think you're reading too much into his comment," said Hayley. "He respects Albreda."

"I'm glad to hear it, for I think that she's going to be in our lives quite a lot in the future."

"What's that supposed to mean?" asked Hayley. "Not that I have any objection, of course."

"It seems my father has grown quite fond of her."

"Did she tell you that?"

"No," admitted Beverly, "but I've seen how they look at each other."

"And you disapprove?"

"No, quite the contrary, I'm happy to see my father enjoying life again. It's been a long time, and I like Albreda."

"You hardly know her,"

"I'll admit I haven't spent a lot of time with her, and yet I somehow feel a kinship. Her fate and my father's are intertwined, I can feel it."

"Interesting," reflected the ranger, "I would have said it was you whose fate was intertwined with hers."

"Don't you have a mission to start?" asked Beverly.

"Yes," replied Hayley with a smirk, "I suppose I have."

SEVENTEEN

Redridge

SPRING 962 MC

Hayley knelt, taking great care as she looked over the cliff.

"What do you make of it?" asked Revi.

They were in the Margel Hills, looking down on the village of Redridge, which lay some distance off.

"I can see the keep quite clearly from here. It certainly dominates the area."

"I could have told you that. I see things much clearer through Shellbreaker's eyes than you can."

"There are some things I have to see for myself, Revi."

"I suppose," he brooded. "I wish I could put my familiar's visions into your head, I think you'd find it so much easier."

"No thanks," she responded, "I have enough trouble dealing with my own thoughts, I don't need a bird in there as well."

"That's not quite how it works," he argued.

"I can clearly see soldiers walking about," she continued. "Knights, by the look of them."

"There's only one stable," added Revi. "I had Shellbreaker fly closer, but I couldn't see too many horses. I'd say there's fewer than a dozen of them."

"I'd agree, but there's lots of footmen."

"Yes," added Revi, "and they have decent armour as well. If they dig in, this will be a tough fight."

"Are they?" she asked. "Digging in, that is."

"I spotted some new earthworks at the north end of the village."

"That would make sense. If they anchored the south end with the keep, they'll need something for the north end. With their backs to the hills, they're in a perfect defensive position."

"I'm a little surprised," commented Revi. "This is not at all what I was expecting."

"Why would you say that?" asked Hayley. "You've been here before; we marched past back in '60 on our way to Bodden.

"That was different," said Revi, "we were in a hurry, and it was dark. I don't remember much about that march except being tired all the time."

"It was a rather harrowing experience, I grant you," she replied, "but I would have thought you'd remember it."

"I was busy healing people, if you remember."

"True," she admitted. "Anyway, all the maps show Redridge as being on the road, but what they don't show is the way it turns into the hills. In reality, you have to approach the village from the west. That shouldn't be a surprise, after all, Redridge is a mining town. The mines are in the hills. It only makes sense for the village to butt up against them."

"I'm afraid it will make an attack a little harder," contemplated the mage. "I rather suspect they know that Colbridge has fallen. They look like they're expecting us."

"On that, we're agreed. The keep is likely thick with archers."

"Crossbowmen," corrected Revi. "I saw some on the roof."

"Even worse," she replied. "It's one of the few weapons that can hurt the Trolls."

"So where does that leave us?"

"They have fortifications on both flanks. We'd have little option but to attack the centre and try to break through."

"I imagine they'd be expecting that."

"Yes," she agreed, "that's where I expect they'll put their knights."

"So what do we do now?"

"I have an idea," she offered. "Let's move farther along to the north. Somewhere near here will be the trails heading into the mines."

"How is that going to help us?" asked Revi. "We don't need to attack the mines. Besides, the terrain is rough, certainly not easy for an army to navigate."

"I don't think we'll need an army," she replied. "Come along."

They made their way north, following the cliffs as best they could. The terrain was, indeed, tough to navigate, and Hayley thanked her bootmaker, on more than one occasion, for making such sturdy footwear. The rocks here were often sharp and projected out from the ground seemingly at random. She wondered how Revi was making out, encumbered as was usual, by his voluminous robes. He didn't complain, but his progress was slow, and she could see the concentration on his face as he methodically picked his way among the rocks.

Soon, they were looking down on a small trail.

"This line," she said, "heads east, into the hills. If we follow it, we should find the mine."

"What are we expecting?"

"I believe it's an open-air mine," she explained. "A rather deep bowl will have been dug so that they can extract the iron ore."

"Surely an underground mine would be more suitable," the mage countered.

"No, it's more dangerous and makes it harder to keep an eye on people. I've heard stories over the years. Many of the people I arrested would have been sent here."

"As slaves?" asked Revi. "I didn't think Merceria used slaves."

"We don't," she replied. "At least we haven't for centuries. No, they would have been sent here as prisoners, to serve out their sentence in hard labour."

"So, essentially the same thing," suggested the mage.

"Not at all. Prisoners serve a limited sentence and then they're released. Slaves live out their lives in servitude."

"If you say so," he replied. "What's a typical sentence?"

"Three to five years is common enough," she replied. "Anything more serious is usually a death sentence."

"I thought King's Rangers acted as judge, jury and executioner."

"Some do, but we're not supposed to. The original charter called on us to bring criminals to the cities for sentencing. Carrying out a death sentence on the spot is a more recent thing."

"When did that start?"

"With King Andred," she replied, "or his father. I can't remember which one, exactly, but it's a rather recent change."

"How much daylight do we have left?" he asked.

She gazed skyward, "Not long, I'm afraid."

"Then perhaps we'd best return to camp and follow up in the morning. I can send Shellbreaker out to see where this trail leads, and then we can head directly there when we return."

"Very well," she agreed. "Mind your step, though, it's very uneven here. I wouldn't want you to twist an ankle or something."

Revi chuckled.

"What's so funny?" she asked.

"You needn't worry about me," he replied. "If I did get hurt, I'd simply cure myself."

"Good point," she replied. "Sometimes, I forget you're a healer."

Darkness had fallen by the time they returned. They had travelled for almost two days to reach Redridge, for the gate location had proven to be in a most inhospitable place, smack dab in the middle of the hills. The Orcs that accompanied them set up a camp each day, while the mage and ranger had moved about on their excursions.

The smell of freshly roasting meat drew Revi's attention immediately.

"Finally," he said, "something decent to eat."

At their approach, the Orc shaman, Kraloch stood, "It is good to see you returned safely. Did you find anything of interest?"

"Yes," the mage replied, "though I wish the news were better. It seems our foes have a very defensible position."

"Come, have something to eat. Perhaps inspiration will come to you."

"It already has, apparently. Or at least it came to Hayley."

The shaman looked to the ranger, "You have an idea? Tell me."

"It may come to nothing," she replied, "but I want to see the mine. I have a suspicion it may be lightly guarded."

"And if it is? Then what?" asked the Orc.

"Perhaps we can convince the workers to rebel."

"An interesting idea," offered Revi. "I'm sure a group of prisoners flooding down the road would cause chaos to their lines."

"True," agreed Kraloch, "but what if they simply run into the hills?"

"I don't think they will," replied Hayley. "The terrain is very rough around here and food scarce."

"We didn't have any problem finding food," countered the shaman.

"Yes, but you're skilled hunters and have weapons. The prisoners will have no such advantage."

"I concede the point," said Kraloch. "Now have some meat, it will give you strength."

Revi finished a mouthful before speaking, "Aren't you afraid they'll detect the fire?"

"No, we are a long way from the village, and the fire is small."

"You're very skilled at this sort of thing," observed the mage.

"It is our way of life," Kraloch responded. "When on the hunt, we do not wish to alert our prey."

Hayley smiled, knowingly.

"What are you smiling at?" asked Revi.

"Kraloch didn't mention it," she said, "but we're also downwind from the village. Any smell will carry away from them."

"You're enjoying this far too much," said the mage.

"Aren't you?" she replied.

"No," he stated. "Much as I enjoy your company, I'd rather be in a nice warm building somewhere."

"No doubt deep in study," offered Kraloch.

"Yes," agreed Hayley, "and on the verge of a monumental discovery."

They both chuckled as Revi blushed.

"All right you two, that's more than enough fun at my expense," said the mage.

They rose early, the crisp morning air showing their breath as they moved.

"Are you sure it's spring?" asked the mage.

"This is nothing," responded Hayley. "I remember having an especially cold day up near Mattingly. I woke up to find myself covered in a thin layer of snow."

"What did you do?"

"I moved around a lot to warm up. Don't worry, by the time we make the mine, you'll be sweating heavily."

"All ready?" called out Kraloch.

"Yes," said Revi, "let us continue this journey of exploration."

They made their way north, retracing their steps to the pathway that led to the mines. Soon, they were heading eastward, the road clearly visible beneath the cliffs they now traversed.

"I hear noises," cautioned the ranger.

"Halt a moment," said Revi, "and I'll send Shellbreaker ahead to get the lay of the land."

He sat down, tracing runes in front of him with his eyes closed.

"Why does he sit?" asked the Orc.

"So he doesn't fall," explained Hayley. "He often moves about as he's looking through his familiar's eyes."

"A wise precaution. Do you see anything, Master Bloom?"

"Yes," he responded, "a large cut into the hills, more like a pit. And there are lots of people there."

"Do you see any guards?" pressed the ranger.

"Not as many as I expected. They seem to be mainly confined to the outer perimeter."

"Likely to prevent escape," said Hayley.

"I agree," continued the mage. "I would estimate there to be somewhere in the range of two hundred or so people working the mines. They look like slave labour."

"Prisoners, more likely," countered the ranger.

"I think you're right. I'm having Shellbreaker circle around to the roadway again. I want a better look at the entrance to the mine."

Hayley and Kraloch watched Revi as he bobbed his head, simulating the bird's movement. The mage suddenly sat up straight, letting out a cry, and then fell backward, to lie on the ground.

"What happened?" yelled Hayley in alarm.

Revi mumbled something and then sat up, shaking his head and cradling his left arm. "Someone shot at Shellbreaker, clipping his wing."

"Is he safe?" asked the Orc.

"He is now, but that was a close call. I think we'd best keep our distance."

"Agreed," said Hayley. "You had me scared there, for a moment."

"I'll be fine," the mage responded, "but my arm is sore from sympathetic pain."

"What's that?" asked Hayley.

Kraloch answered, "When bonded to an animal, any pain felt by the familiar will be shared with the mage."

The ranger's face wore a look of concern, "Does it still hurt?"

Revi stood, rubbing his arm. "I'll be fine. Once Shellbreaker returns I can heal him."

"Can't you heal your own arm?" she asked.

"It doesn't work that way. It's my familiar that's wounded, I'm just feeling his pain."

"We should get out of here," responded the Orc. "You have a good idea of the layout of the mine. I suggest we return to camp and prepare to leave."

"Agreed," said the mage. "Shellbreaker will rendezvous with us there."

Sometime later they huddled around what was left of their camp. Shellbreaker sat on Revi's shoulder, his wound healed, but still weak from his encounter. All their belongings had been packed up, ready to go, and now only the glowing embers of the fire remained.

"What's the plan?" asked Kraloch.

"We move south, out of the hills, and meet up with the army," suggested Revi.

"I have a better idea," interrupted the ranger.

"Let's hear it," said the Orc.

"I propose that I remain here with half the Orcs," she replied. "Revi, you and a suitable escort will make your way south to locate the army. Once they come within range of Redridge and are preparing to attack, you send Shellbreaker to me, here."

"To what end?" asked the mage.

"I intend to disrupt the enemy from the rear. A few arrow shots here and there will keep them hopping. They'll either have to abandon the pit, or reinforce it to keep order."

"A good idea, though I'm loathe to part with you. Couldn't I stay?" he asked.

"No," she admitted, "much as I would like that, you have to get word to the general. The timing here will be important. If I create a disturbance too soon, they'll simply suppress it and if I'm too late...well, then it will all be for nothing."

"I'll likely be gone for a week, maybe more," he said.

"I'll be fine. I'm a ranger, remember?"

"Yes," agreed Kraloch, "and she has a fine group of hunters with her."

"Very well," the mage acquiesced, "we'll carry on as you've suggested." He rose, stretching his arms as he did so. "I'll see you in a week, hopefully no more."

Hayley stood, "Hey now, you're not going just yet. I want a kiss before you go, as a good luck charm."

Revi stepped around the fire, kissing her gently.

"What about me," asked Kraloch, "don't I get a kiss for luck?"

Revi looked at him in disbelief, "Why would I do that?"

"I thought it was a custom," the Orc responded. "Your race has such strange behaviours."

Hayley laughed.

"What's so funny?" asked Kraloch.

"I was just enjoying the look on Revi's face," she replied.

EIGHTEEN

The Outing

SPRING 962 MC

⁓

Aldwin gazed at the distant walls of Tewsbury. "It looks quite formidable," he said.

"And so it is," added Sir Heward, "but we're not assaulting the city. You'll notice the gates are still open."

"I'm surprised," admitted the young smith. "I would have thought they'd be locked up inside."

"Why would you think that?" asked Albreda.

"Aren't they at war?" he asked.

"In their minds, the war is a long way from here," she explained.

"Yes," agreed Heward, "and they won't expect an attack from Bodden, we haven't the troops."

"And yet," queried Aldwin, "isn't that exactly what we're going to do, offer battle?"

"Not yet," replied the knight, "you two still have to get inside and poke about. We need to know what kind of troops they have and how many."

"I wish you were going with us," remarked Aldwin. "I'd feel a lot safer with your axe nearby."

Heward barked out a laugh, but a stern look from the mage stopped his merriment.

"Sir Heward cannot accompany us," she said. "The danger of him being recognized is too high. Now come, it's time we dismounted."

"We're not taking our horses?" Aldwin asked.

"No," she replied, "they would complicate things. If we need to get out of the city, we may have to drop from the wall, and we can't do that with horses."

Aldwin's gaze swept the distant defences, "Surely the wall is too high. If we jumped from there, we'd probably kill ourselves."

"You forget my magic," she said calmly. "I can conjure vines to help us climb down. Now, if you're ready, we'll make our approach."

"Very well," he said, dropping to the ground and handing off his reins to Sir Heward.

"I'll be right here when you return," promised the knight. "Be careful in there."

"Of course," said Albreda, "your concern is comforting but unnecessary. We shall be fine. Come along, Aldwin, it's time for us to enter Tewsbury."

They walked out from their concealment in the woods to take up the road. In the distance, they observed carts and wagons hauling things into the city.

"It looks quite busy for early spring," he remarked.

"Yes," agreed Albreda, "likely Valmar has called on all the farmers to bring their remaining food stocks to the city to feed his troops. He must be getting ready to march."

"To Bodden?"

"Likely, but he might have decided to pacify the north first. That would mean taking Wickfield and Mattingly. We shall have to be on the lookout for information. You remember the plan?"

"Of course," he responded, "I'm not a complete idiot. All I have to do is enter a tavern or two and listen to what people are saying."

"Yes, but try to avoid getting into any conversations. We don't want the soldiers knowing that we're strangers."

"It's not as if I'd tell them anything," he replied.

"True, Aldwin, but neither of us knows the town very well. People that live here will know the locals and such. A simple slip up could ruin our chances of discovering what we need."

"I'll keep that in mind," he promised.

The gate to the city proved remarkably easy to penetrate. The bored guards looked on with disinterest as they walked in, caring little to interrogate newcomers. Past the gatehouse they went, until the cobblestone streets of Tewsbury lay beneath their feet. Here Albreda halted, grabbing Aldwin's arm as she did so.

"This is where we'll split up," she announced. "You go and find a tavern where soldiers hang out, and I'll see what I can discover at the stables."

"Which tavern?" he asked. "This city must have many."

In response, Albreda simply pointed upward. Aldwin looked to see a falcon flying overhead, and then it dawned on him. "You have a familiar," he said.

"Kerwin is not a familiar," she said, "just a friend of mine. I'll call him down to me and get the lay of the land, but let us move into an alley first, I don't want to draw attention."

She guided him between the buildings, then gazed skyward. The bird of prey sailed down, landing lightly on her outstretched arm. Pressing her forehead to the bird's, she went motionless while Aldwin looked about nervously. A moment later, the bird flew off and Albreda opened her eyes.

"There's a tavern just up the street called 'The Eagle and Dove'. You'll find soldiers there, though at this time of the day there shouldn't be too many. You have the coins the baron gave you?"

Aldwin tapped the pouch that hung from his belt, "Yes, right here."

"Good," said Albreda, "go and buy some drinks and keep your ears open. I'll be just down the street where the knights keep their horses. I'll meet you back at the tavern shortly."

"Very well," he said, heading toward the sound of laughter.

"Oh, and Aldwin?" she called out.

He halted, turning to look at her, "Yes?"

"For goodness sakes, be careful, I'd hate to have to explain your death to Beverly."

"Don't worry," he called back, "I'll behave myself."

She watched him enter the tavern, a small knot forming in her stomach. Perhaps she would have been better off to come here alone, she thought, but then quickly dismissed the idea. Aldwin was a grown man and could look after himself.

She continued down the street until she found what she was looking for; a small pasture, attached to the stables. Leaning on the fence, she looked about as a group of knights trotted their mounts back and forth on the grassy turf.

There were three of them, all told, but they soon grew bored with the exercise and brought their horses to a halt.

"Manson," called out one of them, "come and take the horses, man, we need a drink."

The aforementioned squire ran forward, taking the reins as the men dismounted. The knights took almost no notice of the youth, simply tossing the reins and then walking off with not so much as a simple thank you.

Manson struggled to hold onto them all, calling for a stable boy to help.

"Can I be of assistance?" Albreda called out.

"Pardon?" replied the man.

"I have some experience with horses," she replied, coming closer. "It looks like you're a little short-handed."

He glanced back at the stable, but no one was forthcoming. "Very well," he said, surrendering a pair of reins.

She took the leather straps, placing her hand on one of the horse's foreheads to give it a pat. "Magnificent beasts," she praised.

"Yes," Manson replied with pride, "they're Mercerian Chargers, the finest breed in the Three Kingdoms."

"Indeed," said Albreda, "and I'd wager quite intelligent, for horses."

The handler looked at her with a confused look. "Intelligent? Why would you say that?"

Albreda was quick to respond, "Well, they learn things quickly, do they not?"

"You obviously know nothing of horseflesh," he said. "These are just dumb beasts. It's the riders that train them that make the difference."

Albreda was about to object but thought better of it. "I take it the knights are expert horsemen, then?"

"There are none finer," said Manson with pride. "The Knights of the Sword are undefeated in battle, the finest warriors in the land."

"Undefeated?" she asked in surprise.

"Of course," he replied.

She was about to correct him but decided to let him have his moment, for he was likely ignorant of the events that had taken place at Colbridge. He led her into the stables, a large structure with many stalls.

"You have a lot of mounts here," she said, "doubtless a king's ransom in horseflesh."

"Yes," he beamed. "We have two companies of knights, more than a hundred to be exact."

"More than enough to deal with the rebels," she added.

"Of course," he agreed, "not to mention all the foot troops. When the marshal-general finally marches on Bodden, he'll put an end to this nonsense."

"Do you mind if I look about?" she asked. "I've always loved horses."

"Of course," Manson replied. "Shall I show you around?"

"That's nice of you to offer, but I don't want to intrude," she said. "I'll just look them over and then come and find you. I'd be interested in your thoughts."

"Very well," the squire replied. "You'll find me in that office down yonder. Now, I must be off to chase down that young stable boy and give him a good thrashing for not doing his job."

He left her, rushing off on his search. Albreda turned her attention to the horses.

Aldwin sat, nursing his ale. Nearby, a group of four knights were drinking deeply of their tankards. Their swords looked expensive, and the young smith wondered who had forged such weapons.

"Like what you see?" called out one of them, a large fellow with a bushy black beard.

Startled out of his reverie, Aldwin managed to stutter, "What?"

The knight drew his sword, laying it on the table before him. "It's the finest Wincaster steel," he declared. "Come and have a look."

Aldwin looked across the room, taken aback by the sudden interest. He stood up, walked over to the group and stopped at their table. "It's a fine blade," he said, "though I wonder why the crossguard is so plain."

"Hah!" exclaimed a fellow knight, this one with closely cropped red hair. "I told you so, Sir Galway. You should pay more attention to such things."

"Shut up, Balfour," the bearded man replied, then turned his attention back to Aldwin. "How do you know such things?" he asked.

"I've always admired weapon work," he replied.

"You've the look of a fighter to you," said Balfour. "Ever been a soldier?"

"No," admitted the smith, struggling to decide how to talk his way out of things.

"He looks strong enough," offered a blond man, "perhaps we should recruit him. Ever handled a horse?"

"I can ride if that's what you mean," offered Aldwin, "but I'm a commoner."

"We're not suggesting you be a knight," said Sir Galway, "only a noble can be that."

"I thought ordinary folk could be knighted," said Aldwin.

"He's got you there, Galway," offered Sir Balfour.

"Don't be absurd," said his companion. "Yes, in a few rare cases someone can be knighted on the battlefield, but they seldom make good knights."

"What makes a good knight," interrupted Aldwin, "if I may be so bold as to ask?"

"A good knight is noble born," began Galway, warming to the task, "an expert horseman and lethal with a sword."

"What about an axe?" interjected Aldwin.

"An axe?" asked the knight.

"Shouldn't a knight be able to use a variety of weapons?"

"Why? Do you think a sword wouldn't be enough?"

"I'd just heard that knights could use all sorts of weapons."

"He's got you again," uttered Sir Balfour.

"Not at all," replied his companion, now growing irate. "While it's true that some knights use axes, far more use the sword; it's the very symbol of our order."

"What about women?" pressed Aldwin, unable to hold his tongue. Perhaps he had sipped too much of his ale, but he found himself unable to stop.

"What about them?" uttered Galway. "Are you trying to suggest that a woman could be a knight? Preposterous."

"And yet there have been female knights," Aldwin persisted.

"None of them amounted to anything," interjected Sir Balfour. "A waste of armour, if you ask me."

"I heard," pushed Aldwin, "that Dame Beverly Fitzwilliam bested all who opposed her."

"Where did you hear that?" asked Sir Galway, his face growing red.

"It's utter nonsense," added Sir Balfour. "A woman could never defeat a man, and as for Dame Beverly, she was nothing but a whore."

Aldwin hadn't meant for things to become so heated, but the next thing he knew, his fist slammed into the knight's face. Years of toiling at the forge had given him a superior strength, and the force of the blow was such that it knocked Balfour back on his chair, causing it to tip over, landing the knight on his back upon the floor.

The next thing the smith knew, he was surrounded by noise while fists flew everywhere. Someone grabbed his arm, trying to take him off balance, but Aldwin easily pulled his assailant from his feet. Next, he kicked out, landing a foot in Balfour's groin, causing the knight to collapse and let out a whimper as he fell to the floor.

Balfour might have been stunned, but Galway wasn't. He rose to his feet, sending a fist Aldwin's way, but the smith ducked the blow, throwing his attacker off balance. He then dropped to a crouch, grabbing one of the table legs and heaved, upending the entire thing and shoving it into his attackers.

Standing back up, Aldwin paused as he felt hands clutch his arms. He strained to pull free, but now it seemed the entire tavern had jumped into action, and several soldiers grabbed him in an attempt to restrain him.

Yelling broke out all around him, and then the hands pinning him in place suddenly released, leaving him to fall to the floor, unsure of what had transpired. He cast his eyes about only to see hordes of mice skittering along the floor and climbing up men's legs. It was almost comical, seeing the mighty Galway screaming in fear at such small animals. A hand tapped him on the shoulder, and he looked up to see Albreda.

"I see you've been busy," she said. "I think it's time we left."

He rose to his feet, watching in disbelief as knights ran about, trying to divest themselves of vermin.

Albreda dragged him out into the sunshine. "I rather suspect they'll be busy for some time," she said, "but we shouldn't linger. I thought I told you to just listen."

"I was," he defended, "but they were saying some unkind words."

Albreda paused, stopping him in his tracks, "What sort of unkind words?"

The smith blushed, "The kind of words I shouldn't like to repeat."

"About Beverly?" she asked.

"Yes," he admitted.

She continued walking, and he hurried to catch up. "Aren't you going to call off the mice?"

"I was going to," she admitted, "but based on what you just told me, I think they deserve a little more punishment, don't you? I'll let it continue for a bit longer."

They wandered down the street while townsfolk drifted toward the tavern, eager to see what the commotion was all about.

Albreda led him down an alleyway, stopping to get her bearings.

"What now?" asked Aldwin.

"We make our way out of the city. We've got what we came for."

"We did?"

"Well, I did, anyway. I found the stables that house the knight's horses."

"And?"

"And nothing, I simply talked to them. They can be quite reasonable on occasion."

"The knights?"

"No," said Albreda, "the horses. It seems the Knights of the Sword are generally not liked by their mounts."

"That's surprising," said Aldwin. "I thought they looked after them."

"Some do," offered the mage, "but the vast majority of them have servants for such things."

"Doubtless Beverly wouldn't think much of them," he offered.

"I don't either," admitted Albreda. "And might I remind you it's Dame Beverly or Lady Beverly. Have you become so accustomed to her that you forget her title?"

Aldwin blushed, "No, sorry, I forget my place."

Albreda touched his arm lightly, "Don't be ridiculous, Aldwin, I meant it in jest. You will marry her, after all. It's only right that you should call her by name. Now, come along, we must take our information to the baron."

. . .

"Shouldn't they be here by now?" asked Sir Rodney.

"Give them time," replied the baron. "It may be a while before they return."

"Are you sure it was a good idea, Lord," asked Sir Gareth, "sending a woman and the young lad into Tewsbury alone?"

"Good Gods, man," replied Fitz, "Aldwin is a grown man now, he hasn't been a young boy for years. And Albreda is...well, Albreda is Albreda, need I say more?"

Sir Rodney laughed, sounding much like a horse.

"What's so funny?" demanded Sir James.

"I haven't seen the baron so worked up about a woman since Lady Evelyn," he replied.

"She's not just a woman," replied Sir James, "she's a witch as well, remember?"

"Her power doesn't make her less of a woman," defended Sir Rodney. "I'm sure if you took the time to know her you'd appreciate her finer talents."

"Like what," asked Sir James, "needlecraft?"

"That's enough, gentlemen," said Fitz. "I would remind you that Albreda is a powerful mage and our ally. I will not have you speak ill of her."

"Is that all?" asked Sir James.

"What do you mean?" said Fitz.

"I mean, Lord, that you spend quite a lot of time in the company of Lady Albreda of late."

"What of it?"

"We mean no disrespect, Lord, but it's obvious you hold her in some affection," continued Sir James.

"And," added Sir Rodney, "it is clear she feels the same about you."

"Get to the point, man," said the baron.

Sir Rodney turned to the baron's second in command. "Sir Gareth?" he said.

Sir Gareth turned red, "I think Sir James should make the suggestion."

"That isn't what we agreed to," stuttered Sir James. "It was Rodney's idea."

"To do what?" asked the baron.

"Well," said Rodney, "we've been discussing your situation for some time."

"That's becoming quite clear," stated the baron.

"Well," he continued, "we think you should woo Lady Albreda."

"Woo her?" asked Fitz in disbelief.

"Yes," agreed Sir Gareth, "court her. It's been many years since Lady Evelyn passed away. Perhaps it's time you remarried."

"This is none of your concern," said Fitz, turning crimson.

They were interrupted by the timely arrival of Sir Heward, leading Albreda and Aldwin down the path toward them.

"My lord," called out Sir Heward, "we have returned."

"It's good to see you safe," offered the baron, "and a timely arrival it is." He glanced around at his knights before continuing, "The conversation around here was growing quite uncomfortable. What have you learned?"

"The enemy numbers are large," said Albreda. "They have at least a hundred knights, and I would estimate at least fifteen hundred foot."

"You learned all that from entering Tewsbury?" asked Sir Rodney.

"I also had some aerial scouts," she replied. "Aldwin, here, was more interested in mingling with the locals."

The baron's gaze swept over the smith, "Is that a bruise I see on your face, Aldwin?"

"It is," interjected the druid, "though I daresay the knights that he fought are in far worse shape."

"You fought a knight?" asked Sir James in disbelief.

"I did," admitted the smith.

"Why would you do that?" asked Sir Rodney.

"I was defending a woman's honour."

A smile crept over Sir Rodney's face, "You mean Lady Beverly's honour."

"I do," he admitted.

Sir Rodney trotted his horse over to the smith, extending his hand. "No one can fault you for that, young Aldwin, let me shake your hand."

The smith shook the knight's hand in surprise.

"For Saxnor's sake, Rodney, he's not young. He's the same age as Beverly, and she's twenty-seven."

"I know," defended Sir Rodney, "but I'm over sixty, so everyone's young to me."

"He has a point," added Sir James.

"I often wonder if having these knights arrive at Bodden is a blessing or a curse," muttered the baron. "Can we get back to the matter at hand?"

"Of course, my lord," said Sir Gareth. "How would you like us to proceed?"

"I should like to make a demonstration outside of the city. Is Valmar in command?"

"Yes," said Albreda, "his standard was flying."

"And," added Aldwin, "his name was mentioned quite a bit in the taverns. It seems his men don't think very highly of him."

"What do we know of him?" asked Sir James.

"He's vain," began Fitz.

"Can we use that against him?" asked Sir Rodney.

"I think so," the baron replied. "I intend to draw him out."

"What do you have in mind?" asked Albreda.

"That depends on how you made out," said Fitz. "Were you successful in your quest?"

"What quest?" asked Sir Rodney.

It was Albreda who answered the question, "The baron and I discussed a number of possibilities and yes, to answer your question, I did manage to find what I was looking for."

"Excellent," said the baron, rubbing his hands together. "Sir James, proceed back up the road and call the rest of the cavalry forward. We'll parade in front of the city walls, out of bow range, of course."

"And then?" asked Sir Rodney.

"And then I shall call on Valmar to parley."

"Will he do such a thing?"

"Why not?" defended the baron. "He has nothing to lose and everything to gain."

"What do you hope to achieve by this?" asked Sir James.

"I shall attempt to convince him to come out and do battle."

"Surely not," said Aldwin, "he outnumbers us to a considerable degree."

"Precisely why I think he will take the bait. He can't ignore the chance to crush me once and for all."

"And how do we prevent that from happening, Lord?" asked Sir Gareth.

"We have a little surprise in mind for the duke," replied the baron. "When we counter-attack, we only need to wound a few people. They have no healers so any injured will strain their resources."

"Counter-attack?" exclaimed Sir James. "Have you gone mad?"

"Trust me," said Fitz, "their attack will be scattered and lack cohesion. Isn't that right, Albreda?"

"It is, Richard. It is."

"Very well," said Sir James, "then we shall take up our positions."

Marshal-General Roland Valmar, Duke of Eastwood, sat in a chair, his feet propped up while his hands clutched a goblet of fine wine. He was just starting to doze off when he was rudely interrupted.

"Your Grace," the servant was saying, "you are needed at the wall."

"What nonsense is this?" he demanded.

"The enemy has sent someone to parley," the servant answered.

"Oh, he has, has he? And which enemy might that be?"

"Baron Fitzwilliam, Your Grace."

The duke sat up immediately. "Now that IS interesting," he declared. "I shall be there directly."

Shortly thereafter, he appeared at the walls of Tewsbury, resplendent in his gilded armour. He leaned forward, looking down on the two riders who sat waiting below.

"Who dare come before me?" he called out.

Much to his surprise, it was a woman's voice that answered. "I am Albreda, Mistress of the Whitewood. I come on behalf of Lord Richard Fitzwilliam, Baron of Bodden."

"Has he come to surrender?" asked the duke.

"He has come seeking battle," offered the woman. "He invites you to sally forth and settle the matter once and for all."

"Then he wastes his time," called out the duke, "for I am safely behind these walls while he skulks about the countryside. The baron must be mad, and the fact that he has sent a woman to speak with me is insulting. Tell him to send a real lord to negotiate, and I shall have words."

A new voice called forth from below, "Then perhaps, Lord, you will treat with me?"

Valmar gazed down on the knight that accompanied the woman, but his eyesight was not what it used to be. "Who is that?" he yelled at someone on the wall.

"It is Sir Heward," the man replied, "also known as 'The Axe'. His fame has travelled far."

"It has, has it? Well, it shall travel no farther this day." He raised his voice to yell down at them. "You are a dishonourable knight, Sir Heward, and have brought nothing but shame to the order."

"It is not I that has brought shame," defended the knight, "but the likes of you who serve a dishonourable king."

"That is treasonous," spat out Valmar, his voice rising.

"And rebelling against the crown isn't?" called back Heward.

"Enough of this," yelled the duke. "If the baron seeks battle then I shall be pleased to give it to him." He turned to his aides. "Mount up the knights," he commanded.

"How many, Lord?"

"All of them! I would see the rebel army destroyed this day and then victory shall be ours."

"It will take time, Lord, the men are not prepared."

Valmar turned in fury on his unfortunate aide, "Carry out my command or by Saxnor's beard I'll have your balls hanging from my belt."

The aide scurried off as Valmar fumed.

The Knights of the Sword poured forth from the gates of Tewsbury. The sun was shining, the wind mild, as more than a hundred men rode out to bring death and destruction to the enemy. The duke's orders had been simple, ride forth and destroy. This was to be no grandiose battle, no careful manoeuvring of troops, just a glorious, epic cavalry charge to crush the enemy once and for all.

Sir Charles of Haverston rode at their head. As an experienced warrior, the sight of the paltry few horsemen that the traitor baron had arrayed against them gave him a sense of relief. Barely thirty horse were lined up, and only a handful of them knights. He spurred on his horse, his men following closely behind. The thunder of the hooves pounded in his chest, and he felt the elation of the charge, his blood singing.

They drew closer, the horses now at full gallop, the enemy unprepared for the coming storm. This would be a day that would live in his memory forever! The details grew clearer the closer they drew, and Sir Charles grinned in triumph, raising his sword over his head, then something strange happened.

The knight commander's horse began veering off to the left. He struggled to control the beast, but the mighty Mercerian Charger ignored him. Digging his spurs in deep, he pulled back on the reins to correct the course, but the horse wouldn't have it.

Sir Charles spotted a woman in the enemy ranks; she sat astride a horse, waving her hands in a strange pattern. When his mount suddenly reared up, he had to ignore the woman and concentrate on maintaining his position in the saddle. He cast his eyes about to witness his men, his knights, all having the same problem. The whole charge ground to a halt as all the knights fought with their horses.

His mind couldn't register what was happening, tried to reason things out, but all he could do was stare, open-mouthed, as the well-trained Mercerian Chargers went galloping in all directions.

The thunder of hooves was replaced by a distant sound, that of the enemy advancing. Sir Charles panicked, tried to wheel his charger about to retreat, but the beast just would not cooperate. He never saw the weapon coming. One moment he was pulling back on the reins, the next his head was cleaved cleanly from his body by an axe, falling to the ground to be kicked by hooves in the onslaught that ensued.

. . .

Fitz watched the melee unfold before his eyes. "That's enough," he yelled. "Sound the recall."

Sir Gareth put the horn to his lips, the notes calling out clearly across the field.

"They're returning, Lord," said Sir Gareth. "It worked."

"Yes," admitted the baron, "we have bloodied their nose, but nothing more." He turned to Albreda, "You have done your part, Albreda, now we must do ours. It is time to retreat, pulling them out of their hiding place and luring them back to Bodden."

"Are you certain they will follow, Lord?" asked Sir Gareth.

"We shall make sure of it," he replied. "We have struck them, and they have not been able to strike back. Knights are proud people, they won't let this insult go unanswered. Ride eastward, Sir James, just as we discussed. We will leave a thin screen behind us to guard our rear. I don't imagine Valmar's men will get very far today. We have the advantage of speed, but we must remain within sight, or they will lose interest."

"You're tempting fate, my lord," warned Sir Gareth. "Should they defeat our rear guard, we would be overwhelmed."

"Then it is imperative that we remain disciplined. Give the order."

"Aye, Lord," replied Sir James.

"Richard?" called out Albreda.

"What is it?" asked the baron.

Her eyes were closed as she sat on her horse, gripping the saddle with both hands as she did so. "I can see the city. There's a massive army south of Tewsbury waiting to march. I fear it's even bigger than I predicted."

"How much bigger?" he asked.

"I would say nigh on two thousand."

"Then let us pray that our allies are successful in Redridge, for if not, we are doomed."

NINETEEN

The Battle of Redridge

SPRING 962 MC

"The scouts report that Redridge is in sight, General."

"Thank you, Captain Worthington. Have your men pull back until the rest of the army catches up." Gerald watched as the man rode off to relay his orders.

"How do you plan to proceed?" asked the princess.

"Revi's report was rather detailed," he replied. "It seems we will have little choice but to attack their centre."

"Won't they be expecting that?" she asked.

"Yes, but the ends of the lines are both fortified, and we can't afford the casualties a full-scale siege would bring."

"What about the tower?"

"I've been thinking about that," Gerald responded, "but we have no siege engines. It's a circular keep, quite well fortified from Revi's description. I daresay the Trolls could toss rocks at it all day to little effect. At least at Colbridge, the walls were in a state of disrepair. Here, the keep looks much more formidable."

"So then, what's the alternative," Anna asked, "an assault?"

"I'd like to think they'd surrender once the army is defeated, but I'm afraid it's going to have to be a frontal attack. Luckily, there's little in terms of outer defences, just a thick door to a very well built tower. We'll send the Trolls in with a battering ram."

"And to protect them?"

"We'll use the Dwarven arbalesters, they're heavily armoured and can pack a punch. Hopefully, they can provide enough covering fire. The main assault will be carried out by the heavy cavalry. We'll dismount them, and their job will be to take the keep once the main door falls."

"You mean IF the door falls," the princess countered. "This could result in heavy casualties."

"I know," the general replied, "but time is of the essence here. By now, Fitz should be at Tewsbury. We need to be marching north by the time he starts his withdrawal, or we won't be at the crossroads in time."

"Couldn't we just bypass Redridge altogether?"

"And leave an enemy army to our rear? No, we have to protect our supply lines. We must take Redridge."

As they were talking, Arnim Caster rode up.

"Ah, Arnim," greeted Gerald, "just in time, we were just discussing the attack."

"I take it you have orders for me, General?"

"Yes, I want you to tie down the troops guarding the north end of the enemy line; they're dug in and well protected. Your job will be to keep them busy so they can't support the defence of their centre."

"What troops will I have?"

"I'll give you the Elven bow and the Weldwyn foot. If you see a chance to assault, take it, but we need to keep casualties to a minimum. We still have a long march and another battle to carry out. I'll leave the deployment of your men up to you, Commander."

"Aye, General," confirmed the knight, then turned his horse about and rode off.

"Who will command the centre?" asked Anna.

"I'll take care of that myself," Gerald responded.

"Is that wise? You're the general, we can't afford to lose you."

"I have trusted commanders on both flanks, Anna. I need to be close to the lines to spot any opportunities to take advantage of."

"You're thinking of Hayley's little escapade, aren't you?" she asked.

"Yes, with a bit of luck it'll weaken their line."

"And who will you be leading on this assault of yours?"

"Orcs and Mercerians, mostly, though our Kurathians will be waiting to exploit an opportunity if we can punch through their lines. Their bowmen will also be supporting us during the initial advance. I want you back with the rest of the troops, in reserve. You'll have to decide whether or not to commit them. If the attack goes badly, you're to withdraw the army to Kingsford."

"Understood," Anna replied. "How long till the battle commences?"

"We've only just started moving into position. The battle likely won't begin until noon."

"Plenty of time for Hayley," the princess mused.

"We'll see," said Gerald. "It's a long shot. I'm not counting on it."

"Our ranger is a resourceful woman, she'll come through."

"I hope you're right, Anna. We need to minimize our casualties as much as possible."

Hayley Chambers peered over the edge of the cliff. Below, she could see the open pit that was the iron mine.

Kraloch crawled up beside her to add his eyes to the observation. "It doesn't look too bad," he speculated.

"The trick will be to take out the guards quickly. If we can keep the element of surprise, we'll have them on the run."

"Aren't you afraid that your escaped prisoners will get hurt? Surely you don't expect them to fight?"

"No, I just want to create chaos behind enemy lines. I'm hoping that in the heat of battle, all they'll realize is that someone is behind them."

"A wise plan. How do you want to start?"

She used her hand to shield her eyes from the sun. "There's a man over there," she pointed. "We'll need him removed, but it'll be difficult to get to him."

"I can take care of that," said the shaman. "I have a spell that will be particularly useful, I think."

"I doubt a sleep spell will work from this range."

"Not the spell I was thinking of," he defended.

"I thought you were a Life Mage."

"I am, what of it?"

"What kind of healing would let you take out a guard?"

"Life Mages are about more than just healing, Hayley Chambers. I shall call upon the spirits of our ancestors."

"You can do that?"

"Yes, that and so much more, but we have little time to discuss such matters. Revi's message indicated the battle would be starting soon. We must act before it's too late."

"Very well," she said. "I'll take three of your hunters and move that way, off to the left. There's a track leading down into the pit. You take the remainder, eliminate that guard and then take that track to the right. With any luck, we'll meet in the middle."

"Good hunting, Ranger," said Kraloch.

"And to you," Hayley replied.

She made her way to the left, soon finding the meandering path that led down toward the pit. The Orcs followed, their steps soundless despite the rocky terrain. She silently thanked Saxnor that she had learned a few Orc phrases as she moved downhill. They descended half the distance and then paused, for the guard they had seen earlier would have a clear view of the remaining path. Hayley peered around a rock to spot the sentry in the far distance.

A tap on her shoulder drew her attention to look for Kraloch. She spotted him standing on the cliff, his hands raised in the air as an aura of magic enveloped him, and then a streak of light burst into the sky. A moment later, the same beam came down, landing beside the startled sentry.

Hayley blinked in astonishment, for where the beam struck now stood an Orc, the likes of which she had never seen. He was tall, his broad shoulders armoured with chainmail, his head encased in an iron helm. He wielded two axes, which twirled in the air in perfect harmony as he stepped forward. There was no fight, not even an attempt at a defence as the sentry went down beneath the fury of the Orc champion.

Hayley barked out a command, and her small party rushed down the path. If anyone in the pit had witnessed the attack, they gave no indication, for the mine workers had not paused, merely continued to shuffle back and forth pushing carts and barrels.

They left the pathway to enter the pit itself. The mine had been worked for hundreds of years, and rows of steps had been carved into the side of the pit over all that time. She stopped at the first ledge and looked down, picking out the guards. Her Orc companions knelt, letting loose a volley as she swung her arm down. Two guards fell as the hunters quickly reloaded.

An undulating cry rang out from the edge of the pit and Hayley risked a glance. Upon the outcropping, the strange armoured Orc yelled out a defiant call. She watched Kraloch, who once again was in the throes of casting, a shimmer in the air surrounding him, then strange, ghostly creatures began to manifest in the pit. She watched in amazement as they formed into Orc warriors. There were dozens of them, and they swarmed into the pit, their weapons seeking enemies.

"Come on," she yelled, then repeated the command in Orcish. *"Remember the plan!"*

Down she rushed, the Orcs in hot pursuit. The first group of startled prisoners lay just below her. She jumped off the ledge, dropping the six feet to the next level, landing next to a guard and quickly swung her bow, clipping him in the face, knocking him back. The startled man struck out with his whip, but Hayley was faster. She rolled out of the way, and then stood, dropping the bow and drawing her sword.

She was about to strike out when an arrow took the man in the chest, and he fell over backwards, toppling down to the next level. Yelling erupted in the background, lower down in the pit, and she peered over to see the ghostly Orcs slashing their way through the enemy. She tore her gaze away, looking to the prisoners that stood before her in bewilderment.

"Who are you?" asked an old man.

"I'm Hayley Chambers," she said, "and I work for the princess. We're here to rescue you."

"Wait," came a voice, "I know you. You sent me to this place."

A grumbling of resentment began to build amongst the prisoners as they were pushed aside by a large man with a patchy beard.

"Fenton Landry?" she said in surprise. "What in the Afterlife are you doing here? Your sentence should have ended years ago."

"No one ever leaves this pit alive," the man growled. "It's all your fault I was sent here, you and the rest of the rangers."

The crowd grew ugly, murmurings of their discontent increasing. The Orcs dropped down behind her, their bows covering the prisoners.

"Give me one good reason why I shouldn't kill you where you stand?" demanded Landry.

Hayley lowered her sword. "You have been wronged," she said, "and have paid more than the price you should have. Help us, and we will grant amnesty."

"Amnesty? From the crown? You must be daft if you think we'd believe that."

Hayley looked on in confusion and then realized the problem. "You haven't heard? The kingdom is in the throes of a civil war. We're fighting to take back the crown. Join us, and you'll be rewarded."

More muttering came from the crowd as the words sank in. "Why should we believe you?" he demanded.

"I have no reason to lie," she responded. "I treated you fairly, despite your crimes. I could have hanged you by the roadside like other rangers do."

"That's true," said Landry, "but we have no weapons, how can we help? It would be suicide to attack formed troops."

"You don't need to," she replied. "Take what weapons you can from the guards. All you need to do is harass the rear of their lines; avoid combat, ransack their supplies, create havoc, we'll be right there with you. Our army is attacking Redridge even as we speak."

Landry looked around at the crowd who watched him expectantly, "Well lads, it looks like our time is at hand. Who's with me?"

They all yelled their assent and Hayley, finding she had been holding her breath, exhaled. "Grab that," she said, indicating the whip.

The tall man stooped, taking up the weapon while others searched the body, producing a knife.

"Come on," she said, "we've work to do. There are still more prisoners to free."

The sun was high in the sky as Arnim, along with Nikki, rode behind their lines giving his final orders. His archers, the men of Weldwyn, were primed for the assault.

"You should get to safety, Nik," he said. "This will be dangerous work."

"I'm used to danger," she said, "and I can look after myself."

"This is not an alleyway. Besides, arrows and bolts will be flying everywhere, and you don't have armour. I need you to be safe."

She looked around at the troops. "Very well," she acquiesced, "I shall return to the princess, but you must promise me you'll come back."

"I'm not ready for the Afterlife just yet," he grinned. "I shall do my best to return to you."

"You'd better," she replied. "I think while you're enjoying yourself here, I'll go and see Herdwin."

"The Dwarf? Why?"

"To see about getting some armour, of course. I don't want us separated again, Arnim. The next time we face battle, it'll be side by side."

"Agreed," he said, "now get going, I have work to do."

She rode off, pausing only long enough to look back and wave. He returned his attention to the troops. "Telethial," he called out.

The Elven maid jogged over to him. "Yes, Commander?"

"Are you ready to commence the attack?"

"We are, Sir. Shall I give the order?"

"Yes, begin your volleys now. We need to soften them up before we advance."

Gerald sat, watching, as the northern flank moved forward.

"They've started the assault," he said, rather unnecessarily.

"Yes," agreed Anna, "how long will we wait before hitting the centre?"

"We'll wait till Arnim has fully occupied their attention."

Beverly rode up, surprising Gerald.

"What are you doing here?" he asked. "You should be preparing to assault the tower."

"The princess sent for me," she said in explanation.

Gerald looked at Anna, "What's this about?"

"I know you won't like this, Gerald, but you can't lead the assault. Beverly will command the centre."

"I command the army here," he said, stubbornly.

"And I command you," she reminded him. "I can't afford to risk my general unnecessarily. Beverly is more than capable of leading the attack. You're needed here, to oversee the battle. You're the key to winning this war, Gerald, and I won't lose you."

His face turned red, and, about to lash out, he paused as he realized the logic in her decision. "Very well," he said. "Beverly, you know the plan?"

"Yes, General. We'll drive into the centre, keeping clear of the tower, if we can."

"And the tower?" asked Gerald.

"Once we've taken the centre and rolled up their northern flank, we'll see if they'll surrender. If not, we can still assault the tower using the original plan."

"Very well," he said, "though it goes against my blood to be here while my men are fighting."

Anna put her hand on his arm. "You are a general now," she soothed, "and must begin acting like one. You were successful in Weldwyn because you could see the developing battle, could react to it as needed."

He nodded his head. "You're correct, of course. Where's Revi? We shall need his help."

"I'm right here, General," came the mage's voice. "I have Shellbreaker circling overhead, ready to report."

"Then I see no reason to delay any further. Beverly, get into position. When Revi can see the north flank is occupied, you'll launch your attack. Look for the signal."

"Aye, General," she said as she turned and rode off.

"Any sign of Hayley's group?" he asked.

"Not yet," said Revi, "but I'm keeping Shellbreaker's eyes peeled. If she was successful, they should be flooding out of the hills shortly."

"Then we must hope they arrive in time."

The earthworks that anchored the north end of the line were extensive and backed up by catapults. As the Elves moved forward, their arrows flew, driving the defenders behind the security of their earthen walls. The catapults, safe behind the defences, started their own barrage, the stones arcing over the defenders to land in the area before them.

Arnim drew his sword, its blade catching the noonday sun. He had dismounted to join the footmen in their assault. "Forward," he yelled, pointing his weapon in the direction of the enemy.

The line began to move, more than two hundred men of Weldwyn, their swords and spears thirsty for blood. From Arnim's point of view, the enemy defences were little more than a ridge with the occasional head peeking over the rise. Forward he pushed them, and then the stones began to strike. It started with a whooshing sound as they flew overhead. One landed in front of them, ploughing up the land as the rock struck, and then it bounced, slewing through the lines, leaving a red stain where warriors had once been.

"Keep moving!" Commander Caster yelled, his sword held aloft. He knew that once they were close enough, the catapults would be useless, unable to perform at the steep arc needed to hit them. He broke into a jog, his armour jangling in protest.

The Weldwyn footmen surged forward like a tide, as fast as their feet could carry them. Arnim felt an arrow career off of his shield, saw a soldier beside him go down, a bolt taking him in his leg. The ridge before him seemed to grow as he drew closer. He pumped his legs, trying to climb the steep incline.

About him men were crawling on all fours, grasping the dirt in an effort to make progress. He heard a bark of command and the enemy suddenly rose from behind cover, their spear tips glinting in the sun.

"For Weldwyn!" he called, pushing himself forward. Onto the ridge he climbed, standing as he reached the top. Spears came at him, and he quickly parried with his sword. There was a whistling sound as Elven arrows flew into the enemy lines.

Down into the trench he dropped, his sword striking out in a fury of blows. Soon, others were there with him, their distinctive blue surcoats easy to spot. Arnim's blade rose and fell, blood covering him as he hewed his way down the lines, the men following him like a pack of dogs.

Beverly sat astride Lightning, the great beast shifting about, eager to start. She was watching the battle unfold when an aide spoke.

"The signal, Commander."

Turning her head, she looked back toward the general where Revi's ball of light could clearly be seen rising high into the air. She returned her attention to the men around her.

"This is it," she said. "Sound the advance."

The cavalry began trotting. To their flanks, the Kurathian archers moved forward and began loosing their arrows. This was not accurate fire, but a maelstrom of shot meant to confuse and intimidate the enemy.

She held Lightning back, his powerful legs easily able to outdistance the rest, if necessary. All around her, the heavy cavalry moved, flanked by the horsemen of Weldwyn and the remainder of the Mercerian riders. The advance started out slowly, the disciplined riders keeping a solid formation. Ahead she saw the enemy; there were no prepared defences here, just a line of footmen, their spears set to receive the charge.

Time seemed to slow, and Beverly felt as though it took forever to reach the enemy, while their spear tips stood ready, mocking the advance. She lifted her sword high, and held it, waiting.

The Kurathian archers suddenly switched targets. Now, instead of a shower of shots, they honed in on one part of the line. It was a short barrage, for soon the cavalry would block their view, but it was effective. The spearmen, needing two hands to wield their weapons, were unable to shield themselves from the arrows that flew forth. The line wasn't decimated, but enough went down that a small gap formed; a gap that the cavalry was counting on.

Beverly swept her sword down, and the disciplined line of horsemen changed course, urging their horses into a full charge. The enemy drew closer. This was it, the moment of impact.

Lightning surged ahead, and she struck out at a spearman that tried to impale her. The sword bit deep into the wooden shaft, sending her attacker staggering back. Other horsemen rode into the gap, widening it as their blades rose and fell, dealing out death and destruction.

From her vantage point atop her mount, she caught sight of the enemy's reserves. The defenders sent a new crop of soldiers forward to reinforce the line, and suddenly her riders were facing twice the numbers.

Lightning struck out with a hoof, pushing a man to the ground as her sword struck another. She felt herself jostled as horses careened into her, the close proximity of the fighting crushing them together in a massive melee that stretched left and right.

Troops were starting to flank the attack now, and she recognized the danger they were in. They had pushed partway through the line, but the enemy had pulled back, drawing them in. Now their flanks were exposed, and reinforcements were beginning to encircle them.

She gathered her wits, looking down at the hammer that hung from her saddle. She jammed her sword back into the scabbard, the blood clogging it as she did so. Unhooking the hammer, she swung it a few times to get a feel for it, then launched Lightning forward.

She struck out with Nature's Fury, the head easily crushing a spearman's helmet. Back and forth the weapon flew as she swung it, crashing through a spear, smashing it to splinters and driving into someone's chest. Then, she backhanded it, again crushing her opponent, this time driving into a shoulder.

The noise was tremendous as the sound of fighting intensified. The clang of sword against sword, of weapons striking armour, of men and horses horribly mutilated, rang in her ears. A distant shout grabbed her attention, and then the enemy began to give way. She rose in her stirrups, glancing east to see a flood of people pouring into the rear of the enemy lines. She looked behind her and saw the Kurathian horse, breaking the encirclement. It had worked!

All around her the enemy fled, some dropping their weapons while others simply sank to their knees, their hands held up high. Beverly pushed through the confusion to spot a new group of men behind the enemy lines and immediately recognized Hayley. The ranger was with the Orcs who were firing off arrows into the melee.

Spotting a Weldwyn flag flying from the northern rampart, she realized the victory was complete. Turning to congratulate her troops, a wailing shriek cut across the battlefield to send shivers to her very core.

TWENTY

The Tower

SPRING 962 MC

G erald heard the sound, for it was impossible to miss. It cut through the din of battle, reverberating throughout the Margel Hills. It grated the nerves, sent shivers up everyone's spine and as one, the soldiers turned their gaze south, to the stone keep.

High atop it, a screech issued forth again and then a nightmarish creature emerged, peering above the battlements. At first, it appeared to be a giant man, its head, torso and arms very humanlike, but as Gerald's eyes watched, it dragged itself over top of the crenellations and started crawling down the side of the tower, head first. It was then that its lower torso came into view to the disgust of those watching. It looked as though the giant creature had been ripped apart at the waist, trailing a sickly green ichor that clung to the stones of the keep as it descended.

When it reached the ground, almost the entire head opened to reveal razor sharp teeth, the mouth some obscene mix of shark and man.

More keening issued out from on top the keep, and then three more creatures appeared, each pausing to let out their terrible shrieks.

"What in Saxnor's name are those?" called out Gerald.

Everyone watched in horrified silence as the next three creatures crawled down the stonework. The first waited for its companions and then raised itself on its arms, scurrying toward the gathered armies, the others following along behind. Despite its ungainly appearance, it moved rapidly, making a straight line for the Mercerian horsemen.

"Gods help us," uttered Anna.

. . .

Beverly looked on in disbelief. The vile creature charged, plowing into the cavalry. She saw horses flying through the air, and then the strange creature struck out with one hand, its rake like claws ripping flesh from bone.

She tried to wheel Lightning around, but the press of horseflesh here was too tight, leaving no room to manoeuvre. A scream burst out, and then a heavy cavalryman flew through the air, hitting the ground beside her. Horses panicked, rushing past with wild abandon. She saw someone take a swipe at the creature, but the sword bounced harmlessly off its back. The thing twisted its neck at an impossible angle and plucked the soldier from the ground, leaving behind only the man's legs as it tore him asunder.

"Back, back!" she screamed.

The nightmarish monster lunged forward again, now joined by its companions. She watched in horror as they moved through the warriors like a scythe through wheat, cutting them down where they stood.

Off to the right, a small group of riders had abandoned their horses and were trying to form a small knot of resistance, but the first creature simply ran into them, snapping up one in its great teeth while it pummelled the others with its strange arms.

A stench overwhelmed the red-headed knight as the fumes from the green slime reached her. She raised her visor and turned to the side to retch. Death and destruction surrounded her; their victory had just turned into a rout.

Other horses fled, but Lightning held his ground. She urged him on, her hammer grasped firmly in her hand. The lead creature drew closer and let out a shriek, its open mouth spewing forth spittle that covered her helmet, splashing her face. On she rode, Nature's Fury at the ready. She swung with all her might, the hammer taking the creature in the shoulder. It let out an ear-piercing screech, snapping at her as she rode by.

She cleared the first creature, having inflicted a wound, but suddenly Beverly was pitched from the saddle. She hit the ground hard, her left shoulder taking the brunt of the force. Her head spun as she lay there a moment, but then a sickening wail brought her upright. The monster had attacked as she rode by and now the creature's mighty jaws snapped shut, tearing the leg from her steed. Lightning collapsed to the ground, blood gushing forth, even as his body skidded forward.

Beverly forced herself to rise, stumbling slightly when her vision swam. As she focused, all around her was chaos; men and horses ran, desperate to get to safety, but the creatures were faster, picking them off in groups.

She staggered forward, reached Lightning, but the poor mount's eyes were wild with pain. The lead creature moved closer, took a look at her and opened its maw, revealing the rows of teeth waiting to take her life.

Beverly reacted without thinking, swinging the hammer with all her might. The head of Nature's Fury hit the creature squarely in the mouth, breaking off a portion of its jaw. It pulled back its head, swiping at the knight with its arm, and Beverly swung again. This time the hammer struck its claw, the sound of bone breaking echoing across the field. Again and again, she attacked, her weapon seeming to take on a life of its own.

She stepped forward, heedless of the danger and swung out once more. It clipped the thing's arm, tearing off a chunk of flesh. The hammer was glowing now, its head almost afire with light. Faster and faster she lashed out, driving the weapon onto the mocking face. Finally, the creature collapsed, letting forth a terrible wail that echoed in Beverly's head.

She stood panting, her breath ragged, muscles aching with the effort. A sound behind reminded her she was not yet done, and so she turned to see the three that remained. They were in a rough line abreast, running toward her with inhuman speed. Beverly swung the hammer over her head, striking the area before her. She wasn't sure why she did so, but the ground reverberated, and then vines shot out of the place she hit, crawling across the intervening distance to wrap themselves around one of the creatures, holding it in place.

The last two didn't so much as blink. They kept coming, and the knight dove aside as they sailed past. She swung as she rolled, feeling the hammer strike flesh, but as she came to her feet, Beverly could detect no wound on either of her enemies. The creatures, moving so swiftly, overshot her and now, as they turned, she rushed forward. Her left arm was useless, her shoulder torn, but she gripped the hammer in her right, ready to attack.

It wasn't until they had completed their about-face that she saw where the damage had been done. A section of abdomen was missing from the left one, the flesh hanging loosely as a thick fluid oozed out. The stench of the slime burned her lungs, but she continued onward. They were heading straight for her, and at the last moment, she dropped down, landing on her back and swinging the hammer over her head in desperation. It sank into flesh even as jaws of death reached out for her.

The hammer caught on bone, and she was jolted as the creature's momentum dragged her forward. It tried to turn on her, but its own body protected her. The monstrosity pivoted in place now, desperate to remove the unwanted knight. She managed to rise to her feet, tore the hammer from its anchor and swung again. She struck the open wound, the hammer sinking farther into the putrefying flesh. The creature lurched to the side and then collapsed, almost crushing her.

There were two left now as she staggered away from the body. The fourth lurched toward her, barely slowed by the hole in its side. She stood her ground, waiting. Its teeth, dripping with blood and gore came at her, ready to tear her limb from limb. Beverly went to one knee, bracing herself for impact as she lunged forward, driving her hammer into the side of the creature's head. Nature's Fury struck deep, penetrating through bone and muscle.

The creature reared up, dragging her off her feet. She flailed about wildly, trying to keep her legs free of the grasping mouth. She was tossed into the air as it reared its head, with only the hammer keeping her anchored. Down she came with a tremendous crash, her legs wrapping around the creature's head. She hauled back on the hammer, pulling it free, almost tumbling from her perch, but before the creature could react, she struck again, sending Nature's Fury through its brain.

It fell heavily, throwing her to the ground. She felt her leg snap with the impact, knew her shoulder was dislocated, but something drove her on. She rolled as best she could, the body almost crushing her beneath its weight.

Her vision blurred, her body in anguish, she pulled the helmet from her head, tossing it to the side in an attempt to breathe. The last creature loomed above her, having broken free of its restraining vines. Its teeth hovered over her, ready to end her life. Her head spun, and she glanced over, but Nature's Fury had fallen from her grasp to lie just out of reach. All she could do was raise her arm in a pitiful gesture to shield herself.

The maw came towards her but missed. Beverly scooted backwards with her uninjured arm and leg, disbelieving her eyes. It snapped at her, just out of reach and she looked to see Lightning. The creature had run past her horse, but now, despite losing its leg, her mighty Mercerian Charger bit what passed for the creature's lower torso, using his teeth to hold it in place.

The hammer came into sharp focus, and she knew what she had to do. Her leg broken, she did the only thing she could and rolled directly beneath the vile monstrosity. Her hand instinctively grabbed the hammer, and a sense of calm came over her.

When the creature turned on Lightning, Beverly struck. The hammer swung as she yelled, "Leave..." she struck again, her breath ragged, "my horse..." a third time she struck, "alone!"

There was a flash from the head of the hammer as the light caught it and then the creature fell on top of her, dead. An eerie silence descended, punctuated only by her ragged breathing and the laboured cries of her horse. Then she heard her name being called. Her lungs were burning, eyes tearing up as the fumes from the hideous beasts took their toll.

Time seemed to stand still. There were shouts of alarm and then people came closer. She saw Revi Bloom standing over her, saying something, his voice harsh and cracking.

"Lightning..." she stammered.

Revi knelt, his hands glowing as he laid them on her leg. She felt the warmth spreading through her, but her lungs were still on fire.

"Let's get you out of here," he croaked, "it's hard to breathe."

Helping hands lifted the creature off of her, then bore her away from the scene. "Where is my horse?" she asked.

"I have him," came a familiar voice.

A group of men carried her now, kerchiefs over their faces to shield them from the burning fumes. A figure hunched over Lightning, the mighty charger in his last throes of death. Tears came to her eyes, not from the fumes this time, but from immense sadness.

"No!" she tried to yell, "not Lightning! Put me down, I must see him."

Revi nodded, and they carried her back to him, where he lay on his side, the ground soaked with blood. Beverly pulled forth her dagger. "I'll do it," she said, "it should be me that releases him."

"Not so fast, Cousin," Aubrey stood there, looking over the noble beast. "I can save him."

"What good is a horse without a leg?" asked a warrior.

"I'll grow him a new one," she replied.

Revi looked up in surprise, "You can regenerate flesh?"

Aubrey looked at him, "I learned quite a few new spells, Master Bloom. I am, after all, a healer, like my great-grandmother." She began casting a spell.

"What's she doing?" asked Beverly.

"That's not regeneration, it's a simple healing spell. Aubrey needs to stabilize Lightning so we can get him away from these..." Revi waved his hands around, "fumes. Regeneration takes time we haven't got at this moment. Now, let's get you to safety. Don't worry, Aubrey will do her best to save Lightning."

Beverly looked up from the bed. She lay in Princess Anna's tent, off to the side while others discussed matters of great importance.

"Bev, you're awake," said Hayley, looming over her. "We thought we'd lost you."

"You did it," said Anna, "you saved the army."

"You seem to be making a habit of that," added Gerald. "Perhaps next time you can do it without almost killing yourself."

"Those creatures, what were they?" she asked.

"Nightmares," called out the voice of Arnim Caster, "at least that's what I'd call them."

"Not this time, Arnim," countered the princess. "Those creatures have names already; they're called Blights."

"I've heard of those," said Revi. "Aren't they supposed to guard the Underworld?"

"Yes," Anna agreed, "according to legends, anyway."

"Why Blights?" asked Beverly.

"They blight the land," explained Anna. "That ichor they produce will prevent anything growing for years. You're lucky you weren't exposed to it for too long."

"Wasn't I covered in the stuff?" asked Beverly.

"Yes, but I was there," added Revi. "The damage was undone thanks to my ability to remove toxins. I'm afraid you're going to need to rest a few days, the battle still took its toll on you."

"What about Lightning?" she asked. "Is he still alive?"

"Yes, Aubrey assures me he'll recover. She's in the process of regenerating his leg. It takes some time, several days at least, perhaps as long as a week. You can't regenerate a leg in a day."

"What about the tower?" she asked. "There could be more creatures inside."

"Yes," agreed Gerald, "precisely what we've been discussing. For now, we've been victorious, although we almost lost everything. Those creatures-"

"Blights," corrected Anna.

"Yes, those Blights tore into us, inflicting tremendous casualties. I'm afraid they did more damage than the rest of the army. We don't have much left to march to Bodden's aid."

"But we still need to take the tower," protested Beverly.

"That we do," replied Gerald, "but we must be careful."

"I have a plan," said Beverly.

"You need to rest, you've taken a beating," interjected Hayley.

"Gerald, listen to me," the knight pleaded. "I have to lead the assault. I'm the only one that can use that hammer."

"But who would accompany you?" asked the general.

"The Dwarves," said Anna.

"The Dwarves?" asked Gerald.

"She's right," added Beverly. "Remember the creature back in Loranguard?"

"The Soul Eater?" said Hayley.

"Yes," continued the red-headed knight. "The princess's Dwarven sword cut its flesh. The Dwarves have lots of weapons like that. It's the only way we can take the keep."

"But you're too weak, Bev," pleaded Hayley.

"Get Kiren-Jool," she replied. "He can give me the energy to carry on. I'll rest once the keep is clear."

"I hate to say it," said Gerald, "but she has a point."

"I don't like it," said Anna, "but I don't see any other way."

"Let me take the hammer," said Arnim.

"I admire your courage," said Gerald, "but a hammer is not an easy weapon to wield. I'm afraid Beverly is correct. Send for the Kurathian Enchanter."

They stared across the field at the tower that stood in defiance of their presence. The bodies of the Blights were still visible, giving off a stench that drifted toward them; even the crows wouldn't approach.

Kiren-Jool completed his enchantment, lowering his hands as the glow faded. "It is done," he said, "but I warn you, Dame Beverly, when this is over, you will have to rest for a long time."

"How much time?" she asked.

"Many hours, perhaps days. The effects of the spell should last long enough for you to take the tower, Saints willing."

Beverly turned to Gerald, "Are the troops ready, General?"

"They are," he confirmed. "We've cut down a tree to make a battering ram, and the Dwarves gave it a crude metal head for extra measure. The Trolls are ready to march forward on your command."

"Then we'd best get going," she said, "before this spell wears off."

"I'll be moving the arbalesters into position as you advance," offered Hayley, "and the Dwarven axes will be just behind the Trolls."

"You remember the plan?" asked Gerald.

"Yes, the Trolls take out the door, the Dwarves enter with me," confirmed Beverly

"You're to hang back and only engage if there are more of those creatures. The Dwarves are used to close-in fighting, let them do the clearing, understood?"

"Understood."

"Good luck, Beverly, and may Saxnor's strength be with you."

She made her way down toward the waiting Trolls. Gerald watched the knight, her hammer hanging loosely in her hand, her shield in the other.

"Will it work?" asked Anna

"It has to," he replied, "the rendezvous with Fitz is drawing near. We don't have time for anything else. And even then, it may be too late."

"We took a lot of losses," she said.

"Yes, perhaps too many, but we promised him we'd be there and we will. I only hope we have enough troops left to make a difference."

Beverly made her way to the Trolls. Their leader, Tog, stood amongst them, a head taller than his eight-foot high brethren.

As she approached he moved toward her, "We are ready to march, Commander."

"Very well," she replied, "let's get this underway."

The company began moving forward, directly for the tower. Despite the massive tree log, the Trolls moved swiftly, and Beverly found herself jogging to keep up. On their flanks, the Dwarven arbalesters had moved up and were now beginning a rain of bolts in an attempt to keep the defending crossbowmen at bay.

They drew closer to the tower, and she found it difficult to breathe. The miasma here penetrated her nostrils with its stench, burning her. She shook it off while beside her she noticed the Trolls making similar movements. Looking back, she saw the Dwarven axes following at a slower pace. Although outdistanced, they knew the door would take time to collapse and had chosen to conserve their strength for the final push into the tower.

Tog gave a yell in his native tongue, and the Trolls surged forward. Beverly moved to the side, out of their way as they swung the massive log. It struck the door dead centre with a loud bang, and she saw the stone structure shake slightly, showering her with particles of dust. She was up against the tower now, her back to it, while she watched her troops advance. Another strike of the ram brought more dust raining down on her helmet.

Crossbow quarrels flew from the battlements, landing short of the arbalesters. The defenders were outranged by their opposites but soon the Dwarven axes came into sight, and they switched targets. The Dwarf foot was heavily armoured in the finest chainmail, but some bolts still penetrated. She saw three go down in the first volley, one with a shot to the leg. There was a brief pause as they reloaded and then another shower of bolts flew forth.

Again and again, the mighty timber struck, the ringing echoing in Beverly's ears. The door was reinforced with metal, but when she risked a glance, she noticed it was beginning to buckle. She looked up, to the top of the tower where someone was tipping something over the parapet. She yelled out a warning.

The Trolls backed up as boiling water cascaded down from the tower, drenching the opening.

"Ready the Dwarves," yelled Tog. "The door should break in three more strikes."

Beverly ran toward the Dwarves to pass on the message.

"One," yelled Tog, the strike echoing across the field.

"Two," he yelled again, this time to the sound of wood splintering.

"Three." The log surged forward with a tremendous crashing noise

"Back," came the cry and the heavy ram was dragged out of the doorway and tossed to the side.

"Forward," yelled Beverly, rushing through the opening to see a line of footmen, their shields forming a short wall of defiance. Beverly didn't pause but struck out with the hammer. Someone lunged out with a spear, but she easily brushed it aside and rammed her shield into the unsuspecting target's face. Behind her the Dwarves followed, their axes chopping down any resistance.

Beverly finished off her opponent and looked around. She stood in a circular chamber, with a staircase that wound its way up to the second floor. Dwarves immediately flooded up the stairs, driving all before them. She waited, letting the warriors carry the day, remembering her orders. More than thirty Dwarves had climbed the stairs by the time she followed. The second floor was divided into rooms off of a central corridor, and she observed the Dwarves searching room by room, hunting down their prey.

She walked by dead bodies, noticing they were all Humans. Off in the distance echoed the sounds of fighting and then a Dwarf came toward her, his helmet revealing a blood-soaked face. "Commander," he said in common, "we've reached the top floor. They've barricaded themselves in."

"I'm coming," she said, rushing forward.

Up the stairs she flew until the sounds of chopping wood drew closer. The tower here was divided in half, the stairs on one side, an ornate looking door leading to the other.

The Dwarf captain, Gelion, acknowledged her presence as his troops hacked away at the door. "We'll have it down soon enough," he said. "We've already cleared the roof."

"Be careful," she warned, "we have no idea what else they might have in store for us."

"Foul necromancy," spat the Dwarf. "If we find the mage?"

"Take him down as quickly as possible, we can't afford for him to get a spell off."

"My thoughts exactly," he said, then smiled grimly. "This is close-in work, just the sort we Dwarves like."

"We're glad to have you here, Captain."

Splinters began to fly off the door, and soon a small hole appeared. Light glowed from within; the flickering of a flame. The Dwarves paused a moment, while one of them peered through.

"What d'ya see?" asked Gelion.

"They're just standing there," the Dwarf replied. "There's four of them, with one standing behind the other three."

"Bring down that door and be cautious," said the Dwarf captain, "they have something planned."

A flurry of axes leaped into action. The door splintered even more, and then a large chunk fell to the ground to be pulled away by someone in the back row. Two larger Dwarves pulled the remainder from its hinges and tossed them aside. They flooded into the room, Beverly in close pursuit.

As they entered, they clustered around the door, surprised by the sight before them. Beverly, taller than the rest, looked over their heads to see the last defenders of the tower. In the rear stood a richly dressed man, and though she had never met him, she had no doubt it was the Baron of Redridge. Before him, however, was a sight that chilled her to the bone.

Three armoured knights stood in front of the baron, weapons drawn, visors down. It wasn't the presence of knights that froze her, however, but the crest each bore on its shield; they were all Knights of the Hound!

Beverly's mind tried to take in the meaning of this; she remembered the dead bodies, in the dungeons of Wincaster. She had seen them tortured to death, and yet here they were, standing before her in opposition.

The baron simply pointed at the intruders. "Kill them all!" he yelled.

The knights stepped forward, and the Dwarves responded in turn. The tallest knight swung its sword, cleaving through chainmail and severing an arm. Another Dwarf drove his axe into the knight's breastplate, splitting it. It should have killed the knight, but it kept on swinging. Beverly wanted to fight, was ready to, but in the close confines of the room, there was no space.

The Dwarves were whipped up into a frenzy, axes swinging left and right, hacking away to little effect. She witnessed wound after wound as axes chopped into the knights, but still, they kept fighting. Someone struck the tallest one in the head, knocking the visor clean off. The eyeless sockets of Dame Levina stared back at her.

The Dwarf in front of her fell, and finally, she stepped forward, striking overhead with her hammer. In the low ceilinged room, it hit a rafter,

ruining her blow. Nature's Fury came down with little force, bouncing off
of Levina's shoulder pauldron.

The undead knight struck back, bashing Beverly's shield. The force was
otherworldly, sending her reeling. She backed up to get her bearings but
another knight, this one shorter, stepped forward bringing down a mace
onto her shield, creating a huge dent.

"Abby," she called out as the mace struck again. She tried to strike back,
but the two knights, heedless of the Dwarves, had focused on her as their
target. Beverly attempted to parry the blows, but the close confines
restricted the hammer, and she could do little to use it effectively.

Gelion leaped onto Dame Abigail's back, his legs locked around her
waist, and brought his axe crashing down onto her head. The knight
collapsed, a strange black liquid streaming out of her helmet.

As the Dwarf fell atop his victim, Levina struck out, but Beverly, trained
for years as a warrior, was faster. She lashed out with an overhead swing,
this time from her knees, confident the rafters wouldn't interfere. The
hammer missed the knight's head but crashed into the shoulder with the
full force of the blow. Nature's Fury smashed through the pauldron, driving
deep. There was little resistance after the metal defence, and the weapon
tore the limb from the vile undead minion.

Levina staggered back, her balance momentarily disrupted and then
surged forward again while her arm, which lay on the floor, still grasping
her sword, kept moving, trying to wield the weapon. Employing her shield
as a weapon, she used its edge to smash into Beverly. The red-headed
knight countered the blow, using her own shield to deflect while driving
the hammer forward, this time at the legs. She felt her weapon crush the
armour, saw a leg buckle as the full force of the blow hit, and then watched
as Levina fell to the floor.

About to finish off the former Knight of the Hound, Beverly felt an
intense pain. Tendrils of green light wrapped around her, crushing her and
pinning her arms in place. She yelled out in alarm, fighting to free herself
from its grasp.

The Dwarves were finishing off Levina, but then the green tendrils
began to reach out farther, grasping Dwarves left and right, pinning them
in place as well. She could only stare at the baron as he backed up, his hands
glowing, the green light reaching out like tentacles.

She managed to free her right arm, but the tentacles were crushing her.
The last undead knight struck out, cleaving a Dwarf in two with a single
strike. Another Dwarf dropped to his knees and struck, taking out the
kneecap of their opponent. The undead knight fell to the floor while three
more Dwarves hacked at the body.

The tendrils were growing thicker now, entangling more and more of the Dwarves. Beneath Beverly, the floor glowed, and she suddenly understood. She had never seen a magic circle before, but the glowing light could be nothing else. The mage was out of her reach, but the circle wasn't. She called on the power of nature and struck the floor, hoping to disrupt his spell.

She only expected to interrupt his attack, but the hammer acted like it had a mind of its own. As the floor split beneath her feet, the beams that supported it cracked under the onslaught of the blow. With a sudden crashing sound, Beverly felt herself falling to the floor below, no longer bound.

Hearing cries of alarm, she wiped the dust from her eyes as she crawled out of the wreckage, surveying her surroundings. The fighting had ceased, but she knew the battle was not over.

"Where's the Necromancer?" she called out.

"Over here," came the reply. Beverly made her way through the dust and debris to where the Baron of Redridge lay, impaled on a piece of timber. Even as she watched, his eyes clouded over and then a strange transformation took place. Before all of them, the body returned to its natural form; that of an Elf.

TWENTY-ONE

The Circle of Death

SPRING 962 MC

~

R evi Bloom surveyed the devastation. "Did you have to bring the entire floor down?" he asked.

"We were fighting for our lives," Beverly defended. "What did you want me to do, ask him politely to surrender?"

He bent down to examine a floorboard that held strange markings.

"What is it?" she asked.

"Remnants of a pentagram," he said, "or rather a circle of death. They are much like our own magic circles, though tuned to the art of necromancy. It's a good thing you destroyed it when you did, though I'm surprised it worked."

"What do you mean?" she asked.

"It takes great power to construct such a thing, and they are almost impossible to destroy without great magic."

"I had the power of Nature's Fury," Beverly responded.

"You did," Revi agreed. "A far more powerful weapon, it seems, then I realized."

"What of the rest of the keep?"

"We're searching it now," replied the mage, "but our first priority is seeing to the wounded." He wandered over to the corpse of a knight, its sandy hair spilling out from beneath its helmet. "Dame Juliet," he remarked.

"She was the daughter of the Earl of Tewsbury," said Beverly. "He disowned her for her choice of profession."

Revi shivered, "It seems Lady Penelope likes to keep her enemies nearby. I've never seen the like of this before. You say they fought well?"

"They were difficult to defeat," she admitted.

"Did they act with intelligence, or just mindlessly hack away?"

"They seemed to be able to react, if that's what you mean," she responded. "Why?"

"These were no ordinary animated corpses. It appears our necromantic enemy has discovered a way to give them some modicum of intelligence."

"You think the baron, whoever he is, imprisoned their souls?" Beverly involuntarily shivered.

"I'm of two minds," he replied. "Either, he imprisoned their souls and made them do his bidding, or he placed some sort of creature into their bodies."

"Creature?"

"Possibly. A kind of possession, if you will. I know so little about Death Magic."

"What happens now?" she asked, starting to feel the effects from her wounds.

"The army marches north. We'll keep a small group here to look through the wreckage and take care of prisoners, but we need to make our rendezvous. There is still another battle to fight, even though our numbers are depleted."

"And likely many more before the war's over," added Beverly.

"True enough. I'll be remaining here for a few days, as will you."

"I can ride," she protested.

"So you can, but your horse is out of commission for the foreseeable future, and you must rest. The enchantment placed on you will soon expire, and you'll have no energy left. Aubrey will see to Lightning, have no fear."

"What of the princess? She'll need a healer."

"Not for several days. You're needed with the army, but Lightning's leg will take a week or so to regenerate."

"Though it pains me to leave him behind," said Beverly, "I can take a spare mount and catch up with them once I've rested. How soon do they march?"

"They've already started. The Kurathian horse left this very evening." Revi looked around at the carnage, "I'm afraid the Dwarves have been decimated. I'd hate to run into more of these...," he kicked the undead corpse, "things." He stared down at the ruined shield. "How many of the Knights of the Hound are unaccounted for?" he asked.

"They tortured and killed six in the dungeons," Beverly replied. "Why, you think we'll have to face them again?"

"Possibly," he replied, "though I rather suspect it takes great power to animate them."

Beverly nodded her head in the direction of the baron's body. "He was quite powerful, but I suspect Penelope is even more so."

"I daresay you're right," said Revi. "Now get some rest. I have some exploring to do."

It took most of the night to recover all the bodies, for when the floor had fallen, part of it had crashed through the level beneath. By morning, the injured had been seen to, and the two healers sat for a moment in the dawning sunrise.

"That was very tiring," said Aubrey.

"It was," admitted Revi. "I must say your skills have increased tremendously. Tell me, what other spells have you learned?"

"Variations of healing, mainly," she confessed. "I can mend wounds, regenerate limbs, even remove poisons and toxins."

"Oh, I had hoped to teach you that one, I learned it myself. We shall have to compare notes and see if there are any differences. Anything else?"

"Yes, I managed to enter the spirit realm."

"You did?" he responded in surprise. "Then you're far ahead of me."

"In some ways, yes," she said, "but I heard you've become an Enchanter on top of being a Life Mage, I think that outshines me."

"It's not a contest, Aubrey. We have both been very busy with our studies. Now, are you ready to continue?"

"Continue with what? We've healed everyone we can."

"Ah, but we have to investigate the tower. The Dwarf captain, Gelion, tells me they've found a study of sorts."

She quickly rose to her feet, "Why didn't you say so sooner. Shall we?"

"Very well," he replied, likewise rising from his seat. He arched his back, making a cracking sound. "I fear I am getting too old for this sort of thing?"

"You're not that old, Master Bloom."

"True enough, though I sometimes feel ancient. It must be all we've been through, it wears on a person. Where's Hayley?"

"She's dealing with the escaped prisoners. Some of them want to join our army."

"At least we have that," he said, "though I doubt many of them are trained."

"They'll be good enough to garrison Redridge," she replied.

"True enough," he admitted, "and that will free up men for us to march north, a win all around if I do say so myself. Now, let's see what they've found inside, shall we?"

They approached the keep, nodding at the Dwarves guarding the entrance, while two more were taking measurements at the door as they walked through.

"What are they doing?" asked Aubrey.

"They're making a new door," he replied. "Now that we have Redridge, we have to protect it. I believe Gerald is going to leave the Dwarves in control here, at least for the time being."

They climbed the steps, avoiding the damaged section where the roof had collapsed.

"It's a good thing she doesn't use that hammer too often," mused Revi, "or we'd have no fortifications left." He barked out a laugh at his own jest.

Aubrey was about to defend her cousin when they stopped suddenly.

"Here we are," said Revi. "The Necromancer's secret laboratory."

"Secret?"

"Yes, it was hidden beneath a spell of concealment."

He opened the door, revealing a small room, much like any other. Indeed, at first glance, it was not dissimilar to Revi's own study back in Wincaster.

A desk, littered with notes, along with a leather bound book with a clasp, sat against the far wall. Hanging above it was a rather ornate mirror.

"Runes," Aubrey pointed out, "here, around the mirror."

"Yes," he agreed, "I rather suspect it's a scrying device of sorts."

"Or a method of communication," offered Aubrey.

"I hadn't thought of that," he admitted, "but now that you mention it, it makes perfectly good sense, the Dark Queen was masquerading as the baron's sister."

"So what happened to the real Penelope Cromwell?" she asked.

"A good question. I rather suspect they were both killed and then replaced by these Elves. We'll likely never find their bodies." He looked through the papers and then turned his attention to the book. "Tell me, do you remember the spell of tongues?"

"You never taught me that one," she replied, "and besides, that's an Enchantment, not Life Magic."

"So it is," he replied. "Let me cast it on both of us and then we'll take a look at this book."

He put it down and stood back to give his hands space to trace the patterns in the air.

Aubrey watched as the area around him lit up and then she felt a tingle as the spell took effect.

"Now," said Revi, "let's see what we have here, shall we?" He unsnapped the clasp holding the book shut, then slowly opened it, revealing the first page.

"I can't make it all out," said Aubrey, "but it looks like some type of journal."

"Yes, unfortunately, the spell only grants us a rudimentary understanding."

"You should learn Elvish," she replied, "then the spell would boost your knowledge even more."

"I have been rather busy of late," he said in irritation. "You make it sound like I have lots of free time for these sorts of things."

"Sorry," she replied, "but the princess has learned multiple languages."

"Well, I'm not the princess, and I have other things to attend to. It's all well and good for her, she simply sits back and lets the others do all the hard work."

"That's hardly the case," defended Aubrey. "She has to plan and run an entire kingdom. You should be more appreciative, without her there'd be no rebellion."

"Sorry," he said, "I know you're right, of course, but I'm just so drained. Healing takes a lot out of me."

"As it does any mage," she reminded him. "Now, shall we get back to the book or do you need a nap?"

Gerald watched as the heavy cavalry rode past. "I wish we had more of them. They took quite a beating at the hands of those Blights."

"As did the foot," added Anna. "I'm afraid our numbers are depleted."

"Yes," he agreed, "and we will lose more so that we can keep a garrison here."

"How many men can we march?" she asked.

"We should be able to field a thousand, but the real question is if we can reach the crossroads in time."

"And what do we think the enemy has?"

"That's the big unknown. We know the baron has about five hundred men, all told. What we don't know is how many Valmar has."

"What would be your estimate?" the princess asked.

"I would hazard a guess at about fifteen hundred. That would give him a three to one advantage over Bodden. I can't see him marching with less."

"So our numbers should be even," she mused.

"If we're lucky, yes, but there's always the chance he'll have reinforcements from the capital. We'll know more as we get closer. Albreda will be keeping tabs on them and will keep us informed."

Another group of riders filed past, followed by Revi Bloom, who pulled over to meet them. "Your Highness, General," he said in greeting.

"Master Bloom," said Anna, "have your investigations borne fruit?"

"They have, Highness, though I wish it were better news. The Necromancer's notes have revealed a much larger organization at work, something called the Shadow Council."

"What do we know of it?" asked Gerald.

"Not much, I'm afraid. The notes are short on details. I rather gather the organization has been around for a very long time, possibly longer than Merceria itself."

"What is it they're after?" asked Anna.

"Power, I think, and I don't mean political power."

"But they wish to control the throne, don't they?"

"They do, but that is a means to an end, they're after something else. I think controlling the crown is just the beginning."

"Any ideas of what their long term plans may be?" she asked.

"As a matter of fact, I've been thinking on that very topic."

"And?" prompted Gerald.

"And I believe they covet the power of magic. Blood Magic, to be exact."

"I've never heard of that," said Gerald.

"I'm not surprised," Revi countered. "I'd never given it much thought until Penelope held me prisoner."

"So what is Blood Magic, precisely?" asked the princess.

"Mages harness their innate magical energy," he began.

"We understand that, Master Bloom," she said, "but how is Blood Magic different?"

"Simple," he responded, "Blood Magic harnesses the power of those around the mage."

"Meaning?"

"Meaning there is no longer a limit on how much power they have access to. They can, if they have enough victims, create much more powerful spells."

"More powerful how, exactly?" asked Gerald.

"Those creatures, for one," said the mage.

"The Blights?"

"Precisely. It would take a lot of power to summon such creatures, likely much more than a single person would have, and let me remind you, he summoned not only one but four of them."

"This does not bode well," offered the general.

"No," admitted Revi, "it doesn't."

"Well," added Anna, "we shall have to hope there are not too many members of this 'Shadow Council' you spoke of."

"There is the off chance that the baron and his sister, Lady Penelope are the most powerful of them. Perhaps the rest are lesser mages?"

"I hope you're right," said Gerald, "or we'll discover more of those things when we assault Wincaster."

"We have to deal with Valmar's army first," said Revi, "but I doubt he'll have a Necromancer with him."

"Let's hope you're right," said Anna.

TWENTY-TWO

The Retreat

SPRING 962 MC

Sir Heward watched the enemy soldiers march by. He and Sir Rodney were at the tree line, while their men waited deeper in the woods.

"Valmar's not much of a general," observed Rodney. "He hasn't even deployed scouts."

"He's not just a general, he's the marshal-general, remember?" offered Heward.

"He still doesn't know his business."

"Agreed, but at least it works to our advantage."

"I'm rather curious," mused Sir Rodney, "why he would send his footmen out in front. Surely that's a job for his cavalry?"

"It is," Heward replied, "but his only horsemen are knights. Any decent general would have lighter cavalry to guard the march, but Valmar is little more than a jumped up sergeant."

"Everyone has to start somewhere," mused Rodney, "even Gerald started as a sergeant. Now, he's the princess's general. In theory, he outranks the both of us."

"I suppose he does," offered Heward in response. "Though I've never met the man. Is he the one that was the baron's Sergeant-At-Arms?"

"That's him."

"And where did he learn his trade?"

"He was trained by Fitz," said Rodney, "need I say more?"

"You've convinced me," said Heward. "I assume he has some experience?"

"Scads of it," offered Rodney. "The man has spent years fighting Norlanders."

"So what do you suggest we do about them?" Heward nodded to the soldiers marching by.

"We let them proceed unmolested. We'll wait till the second group arrives and then strike."

"Valmar will likely have his knights nearby to reinforce."

"Precisely what I was thinking," said Rodney. "I rather suspect he's dangled these men out front to lure us into an attack. My guess is that we'll see his knights soon enough, or a few of them, at least."

"We can but hope," replied Heward.

They sat in silence as the enemy moved westward toward Bodden. In theory, the road ran east to west, but the terrain here was rough and wooded, the road often meandering to make the path easier. They didn't see the next group of soldiers so much as hear them, the distinctive clopping of horses' hooves pounding against the ground.

"Hear that?" asked Sir Rodney.

"It seems you were correct," replied Heward. He looked over his shoulder at the men behind. "Prepare yourselves," he said, "they'll soon be in sight. Remember, we strike quickly and then withdraw. No heroics."

The men all nodded their understanding. They were nervous, Heward could tell, but he couldn't fault them. Other than Heward and Rodney, they were regular horsemen about to go up against heavily armoured knights.

Rodney inched his horse forward to get a better view. The Knights of the Sword appeared around the corner, strung out in a ramshackle line, riding only two abreast. Many were not wearing their helmets, and at least one drank from a bottle as he rode.

The riders drew even with the ambush point and continued westward, unaware of the lurking warriors. Rodney waited until two-thirds of the column passed before he raised his arm, holding it still. The raiders watched him in anticipation, waiting until his arm sliced down.

Twenty riders burst from the woods, heading directly for the trotting knights. The enemy reacted slowly with a few at the rear shouting a warning, but by the time their companions turned to look, the riders were in amongst them.

Heward struck out with his axe, cleaving the arm from his first foe and sending his shield whirling through the air. The knight continued on, intent on the next target. Sir Rodney, resplendent in his armour, rode up to a Knight of the Sword offering his left hand in greeting. The confused enemy held out his hand as Rodney struck with his sword, driving it into the man's armpit.

Heward saw at least four knights fall on the first pass before the riders were across the roadway, driving their horses into the trees. The enemy captain, keeping his wits, ordered his men to follow and the Royal Knights crashed into the woods behind the raiders, screaming threats of retribution.

Heward halted, letting the other men ride by. When he was sure they were safe, he followed, nodding to the woman who stood nearby. The Knights of the Sword were close behind, the sound of their mighty steeds echoing through the glen.

Albreda raised her hands, uttering an incantation. A moment later, tree branches extended with thorns growing from the limbs. The armour of the knights was impervious to such a small thing, but their mounts were not. In battle, the Mercerian Chargers would wear barding, metal armour to protect their flanks and face, but on the march, such protection tired them. Now, this worked to their disadvantage as thorns dug into the relatively soft flesh of the beasts.

Albreda listened to the sounds of surprise and the whinnying of the horses. She hated to inflict pain on such noble creatures, but this was war, and thankfully the injuries would soon mend.

She lifted her staff into the air, calling forth a word of power, then struck down. The ground undulated for a moment as if the Gods themselves came up from the Afterlife. The shockwave carried through the trees, felling branches and shaking leaves loose. The horses, incapable of understanding such things, panicked.

Back the knights went in fear. This was no easy slaughter of the enemy, but a nightmarish contest of wills with a magic far older than man.

Albreda watched as the last of the enemy returned to the road. She glanced to her left, where the great wolf sat. "Well, what do you think, Snarl? Enough damage for today?"

In answer, the wolf let out a howl. It echoed through the woods, to be repeated by others. Soon, the entire forest reverberated with the sound.

Valmar shuddered. He sat safely in his carriage, but the sound of howling echoed from all around him. "What was that?" he asked.

"Wolves, Your Grace," replied Captain Davis, who sat opposite him.

"I can tell that," he snapped. "I meant why now, of all times. Shouldn't they be skulking away from an army this size? Why are they even here?"

"I don't know, sir. I've never heard of wolves being so bold before. It's this cursed forest, the whole north is thick with it."

Valmar peered out the window. "This is nothing," he warned, "wait until we get closer to Bodden and you see the Whitewood."

"You've been there before, sir?"

"I have, though not for some years. The Whitewood is both a marvel to behold and a terrible sight."

"I've heard it's haunted," offered the captain.

"I don't know about haunted, but I know that horrible things live there. It's said that the very denizens of the wood hunt any Humans that dare enter."

"And yet Bodden somehow thrives, Your Grace."

"Yes," said Valmar, "though I rather suspect Fitzwilliam has made some ungodly deal to do so."

"You think he's in league with Death Mages?"

"Or worse," he replied. "We've heard the enemy has Orcs among them."

"I've heard that, too," added the captain. "I understand there were many of them at Colbridge."

"It's true," confirmed the marshal-general. "I read the reports myself. We were lucky. In the aftermath of the siege, some of our men managed to escape and bring word to the capital. It seems we've been underestimating our enemy."

"How so?"

"We assumed they were a small, ill-disciplined lot, but that has been proven incorrect, so now we march with the largest army ever assembled. We shall crush this uprising, once and for all."

A rider appeared at the side of the carriage, leaning down to tap at the window.

"What is it?" demanded Valmar.

"The enemy has ambushed us, sir."

"Casualties?" asked the captain.

"Six knights dead, another four wounded."

"And how many of the enemy were slain?" asked Valmar, leaning forward.

"None, as far as we can tell, Your Grace."

Valmar sat back in disgust.

"Orders, Your Grace?" asked the captain.

"Send word to the head of the column to slow until the rest catch up. It seems our little ruse has been spoiled."

"Shall we pursue, Lord?" asked the rider.

"No, let them have their tiny victory," said Valmar. "We'll be in Bodden soon enough, and then they'll pay the price for their insolence."

. . .

Sergeant Dryden had been a soldier for as long as he could remember, having served with distinction in the northern wars. Now, as he wandered through the camp, he took pride in his accomplishments. The army commanded by the marshal-general consisted of the finest soldiers in the kingdom, many of them battle-hardened.

He paused to warm his hands by a fire as his warriors looked at him. "We'll have them soon enough," he told them, "and then there'll be plenty of plunder to go around."

His remarks brought smiles to their faces, for the common soldier made little enough coin.

"Is it true we're going to reduce Bodden?" asked a youthful-looking archer.

"It's true, lad, we're going to turn it into rubble. There won't be a living soul left there once we've done."

"And women?" asked another.

"Plenty to go around," he replied, "and they'll all be widows, pining for their loss and looking to the safety of a warm bed." He chuckled at his own remarks. It was an old habit, promising everything a soldier could desire, but he didn't mind. Many of these men would die in the coming days, but those that survived would wear their experience like a badge of honour.

"What happened today, Sergeant?" asked the youth.

"Nothing to worry about, lad, just a couple of raiders that surprised us. We dealt with them already. If you look carefully tomorrow, you may see their heads on spikes." The lie came easily to his tongue for he knew by tomorrow it would be forgotten. "Now get some rest, men, we still have a long way to march before we get that plunder."

The men grinned, slapping each other on the back in anticipation. Sergeant Dryden withdrew from the fire, wandering farther through the camp.

He heard a strange noise to the north as if a heavy weight had been dropped, and then halted, peering through the darkness. The sound of talking around the fire drifted toward him from behind, but nothing to the north, not even the buzz of insects. His heart began to pound, for in his experience, it could mean only one thing; raiders!

He drew his sword, but at that precise moment, a spear flew towards him, striking him in the chest. Sergeant Dryden silently collapsed to the ground, dead.

Lorgar ran forward, pausing only long enough to withdraw his spear from his target. The other Orcs dashed past him, their eyes seeking out prey. He took one last look at the man lying on the ground, then ran on, his face a mask of calm.

He heard yelling coming from the campfires and turned as an arrow flew in his direction. The bolt went wild, likely shot in panic and Lorgar grinned, his white teeth in stark contrast to his dark green skin. His comrades were striking out now, the sound of melee growing, increasing around him. Running to the nearest campfire, he plunged his spear into a footman. His target fell heavily into the fire, sending a shower of sparks into the air.

He looked at the blaze, noticed one of the logs was only burning at one end, and he picked it up. Nearby stood a group of wagons stacked with supplies, so he ran toward them, tossing the burning branch into the back of one.

The fire didn't take right away, but he didn't care. Lorgar ran on, jabbing out again with his spear, forcing a soldier to back up. He swung the spear like a staff, taking out the man's knees, collapsing the soldier to the ground, then ran on, screams echoing behind him.

The camp was in chaos. Humans were yelling everywhere, and Lorgar knew there wasn't much time left before the heavy horses of the knights responded.

He caught sight of Gorlag and waved his hand in the air, signalling the withdrawal. Gorlag pulled the horn from its sling and blew the notes. The sound echoed through the darkness and the Orcs withdrew, their work done this night.

Valmar surveyed the damage in the early morning light, his captain following him obediently.

"They caught us by surprise," muttered Captain Davis.

"I can see that," Valmar fumed. "Weren't the sentries posted?"

"They were, Your Grace, but the greenskins killed them all."

"And not one of them was able to sound the alarm?"

"I'm afraid not, sir."

"Who commands here?" he asked.

"Captain Conners, Lord."

"Bring him here, to me, right now!" he demanded.

Captain Davis ran off to find him.

Valmar looked at the dead bodies. They were scattered all over the place, many of them at the edge of the tree line. "They ran," he said, more to himself than anyone in particular. He walked toward the trees to examine the dead men in more detail. There were three here, all of them with wounds in the back. He shook his head in disgust, then spit on the corpses.

"I found him, Your Grace," came Davis's voice.

Valmar turned to see a young soldier, "Are you Captain Conners?"

"I am, my lord," the man replied.

"And you command here?"

"I have that honour, Your Grace."

"Give me your sword," he ordered.

"Lord?"

"You heard me, man. Give me your sword!" Valmar demanded, his voice rising in anger.

Captain Conners drew the blade, hesitantly handing it to the marshal-general hilt first.

Valmar took the handle, holding it up before his eyes to examine the metalwork. "A fine blade," he mused.

"It was a gift from my father, Lord."

"Tell me, Captain," said Valmar, "what do you make of these men?" He used the tip of the blade to point to the bodies.

"They were killed by the Orcs, Your Grace."

"Is that all?" he asked.

"I'm not sure what you mean, Lord," said the captain.

"These men," said Valmar, "were running from the fight. Do you know why a man runs from battle, Captain?"

"They are cowards?" he offered.

"They are led by cowards," Valmar clarified, plunging the tip of the sword into the hapless Captain Conners, whose eyes grew wide in surprise. Valmar felt the man's breath on his face and pushed harder, the blade now protruding from the man's back. "I will have no cowards in my army, Captain!"

The duke stepped back, pulling forth the sword, and then the helpless Captain Conners fell to the ground, clutching his wound. As an ever-increasing pool of blood formed around him, he looked up at the marshal-general with pleading eyes.

Valmar smiled, then knelt by the dying captain.

"Why..." the man uttered.

"I have nothing against you, personally," whispered Valmar, "but I must make an example. Your punishment will inspire the men to fight to the death, if necessary."

He watched the captain's eyes glaze over and then the breathing stopped. Rising to his feet, he pushed the corpse with the toe of his boot to ensure no life remained. The marshal-general stared at the body for a moment longer, then turned to his aide. "Captain Davis, send word of what happened here. Tell all the officers that any man that fails in his duty will be executed for treason."

His aide swallowed and then nodded his head, too afraid to speak.

"Come," said the marshal-general, "it's time we were on our way."

Valmar turned to look back at the camp. Soldiers milled about while others helped with wounded, but without a Life Mage, they were a liability.

"Any man who cannot walk is to be left behind," he snarled.

Captain Davis nodded his head, "Aye, Your Grace."

Valmar smiled, a look that sent shivers down the captain's back, then turned toward his carriage in the distance. He began moving toward it, the men giving him a wide berth.

TWENTY-THREE

The Battle at the Crossroads

SPRING 962 MC

Baron Fitzwilliam brought his mount to a halt. Before him lay the crossroads where Sir James waited with the footmen and archers from Bodden Keep while the horsemen rode past, Sir Rodney at their head.

"Take them to the northern flank," Fitz commanded, answered by Rodney's nod. The baron looked eastward, but the enemy troops were still out of sight.

"Any sign of our allies?" he asked, looking to Albreda.

"Not yet, Richard, though I have agents out looking."

"Agents?"

"Birds mostly," she replied. "Don't worry, at the first sign of them I'll let you know."

The baron turned and rode on until he was before his footmen, then halted again, this time dismounting and passing off the reins.

Sir James quickly approached, "I have deployed the men as directed, Lord. Archers to the north, a few to the south in that group of trees and the footmen in the middle."

"Any defences?" he asked.

"I'm afraid not," replied Sir James, "but they all have shields, and even horses can't break our shield wall."

"They can if there's enough of them," countered Fitz. "Let's hope Valmar is as incompetent as I remember."

"We are vastly outnumbered, Lord. Would we not be better to withdraw back to Bodden? Surely we would be safer within its walls.

"It's too late for that," said the baron. "They're too close now, I'm afraid the choice has been made for us."

"Any word on our allies, Lord?" asked Sir James.

"I have spotted some in the distance," offered Albreda, "but they are still a long way off, and I fear their numbers are lower than expected."

"They must have suffered stiff resistance at Redridge," said Fitz.

"What do we do now?" asked Sir James.

"We do what we always intended to do, we fight."

"We are still outnumbered, my lord."

"Is there anything you can do, Albreda?" asked Lord Richard.

"Not much, I'm afraid. My spells are useful against small groups, but against these types of numbers, they're not very effective.

"What about a stampede?" Fitz asked. "It worked once before."

"There's no time to prepare that," she said. "I can't produce an entire herd from thin air, and the last time I did that it cost us dearly; a lot of animals died that day."

"Then we shall have to do what we can," he replied. "I suspect Valmar will aim directly for the centre of our line. He'll attack in three waves with his knights."

"How can you be so sure?" asked Sir James.

"He has no respect for his footmen so he'll be counting on his knights to do all the heavy work. The first two waves will try to disrupt the line, then he'll charge home with the third. It's a simple strategy, but sound considering his numbers."

"How shall we counter?" pressed the knight.

"The men of Bodden are highly disciplined. They'll hold the line, you can be sure of it."

"I might be able to help after all," offered Albreda.

"How?" Fitz asked.

"I can make the ground here uneven to break up their charge. It won't stop them, but it will take some of the bite out of their strike."

"Do what you can."

"And the cavalry?" asked Sir James.

"Break them into two groups. Heward will command one group, Rodney the other. They'll be to the north of our line. Tell them to use their best judgement when to attack. I'm afraid we'll be too busy to send messages back and forth, and we have no other effective method of signalling."

"Yes, my lord. Anything else?"

"As a matter of fact, yes," Fitz replied. "Send three men with Albreda to keep her safe. When the enemy appears, make sure she gets to safety."

"I can take care of myself, Richard," she declared.

"I know you can," said the baron, "but it would give me peace of mind."

"Then you take care as well, Richard, I shouldn't like to see you fall this day."

"Nor I, you," he replied. "You are ever in my heart of late." He took Albreda's hand and kissed it.

Roland Valmar gazed across the field to take in the rebel army. "Is that all they have?" he asked out loud. "I'm surprised he would make a stand when he's so obviously outnumbered. It's not like him."

"A trap perhaps, Lord?" offered Captain Davis.

"Doubtless," he agreed, "but who does he expect to arrive? And better yet, how many?"

"There could be reinforcements coming up the Redridge road," suggested the captain.

"A valid point. Let's deploy some footmen to the south to block the way while our knights finish off this feeble excuse for an army."

"And the archers, Your Grace?"

"We'll send half of them south, to reinforce the foot. I want the rest of them behind us, watching our rear."

"Our rear?"

"Yes. The last thing we need is Orcs attacking us from behind," said Valmar, "Send two companies of foot to reinforce them. We'll make a line there, back by that hill. We've already deployed the rest of the army to this side. Perhaps our overwhelming numbers will convince them to surrender."

"I doubt it, sir. They're already facing the death sentence as traitors, what would they have to gain?"

"A good point," mused Valmar. "Perhaps we'll try a different option."

"Sir?"

"We'll send a messenger out under a flag of truce and give them the option of surrendering."

"You think the baron would consider it?"

"The baron is a sentimental old fool. He'd surrender himself to spare his men, I'm sure of it. We'll promise to spare the men if he surrenders himself."

"And will we, Lord? Spare the men, that is."

"No, of course not, but if we can convince them to lay down their arms, so much the better. Then we'll be able to destroy them at our leisure."

. . .

Sir James reached out to adjust a footman's grip on a spear. The soldier, looking over his shoulder at something in the distance, caught the knight's attention. He twisted his head to see three men riding toward the lines with a white flag. He immediately turned his attention to the baron. "My lord," he called out, "someone approaches under a flag of truce."

Baron Fitzwilliam swept his gaze eastward where the riders were approaching. "Now that IS unexpected. Shall we see what he wants?"

Sir James returned to his horse, hauled himself into the saddle then spurred his mount forward to match gaits with the baron. They began riding towards the approaching enemy, that had halted halfway between the two armies. Fitz heard some hoof beats, and suddenly Albreda was beside him.

"You're coming with us?" he asked.

"I can't allow you two to have all the fun, now can I?"

"I suppose not," he said, "and truth be told I'm happy to have you with us."

"What do you think they want?" she asked.

"I rather suspect they want us to surrender," replied Fitz. "Wouldn't you agree, Sir James?"

"More than likely," said the knight.

They halted a horse's length away from the other riders and sat, patiently waiting.

"I am Sir Alard," called out the messenger, ignoring his companions, "here representing His Grace, the Duke of Eastwood, Lord Roland Valmar, Marshal-General of the Royal Army of King Henry of Merceria."

"And I am Lord Richard Fitzwilliam, Baron of Bodden and these are Sir James and Lady Albreda."

Sir Alard bowed his head in greeting, then waited, as if unsure of how to proceed.

"What is it Valmar wants?" asked the baron.

"The same thing as you, Lord," replied the knight, "to avoid unnecessary bloodshed."

"Then march your army away," said Albreda, "and none shall be shed this day."

The enemy knight showed a look of distaste. "You should keep your woman under control. A parley is no place for a female."

"She is not my woman," the baron replied, "but a powerful ally. Have you never heard of the Witch of the Whitewood?"

The baron was pleased to watch Sir Alard visibly pale.

"The etiquette of battle leaves no place for magic," said Sir Alard.

"Spoken by someone who has none," said Albreda.

"You seem to be under the illusion that this is a meeting of gentlemen," remarked Fitz.

"Can we not be civil?" replied Alard.

"Civil?" said Fitz. "This is war, not a game. It is a struggle for survival."

Sir Alard looked past their group to the thin line of troops that waited to the west. "You are vastly outnumbered, Lord. Would it not be better to avoid the slaughter? Have your men lay down their arms and they shall be spared."

"And the baron?" asked Albreda.

"The baron must surrender himself to face the king's justice."

Baron Fitzwilliam looked back to his own line, his hand instinctively going to his chin to rub his beard. He returned his gaze to the envoy, "I must admit your proposal has merit. Allow me to consider the offer. I shall give you an answer by mid-afternoon."

Sir Alard, pleased with his success, bowed deeply, a smile creasing his face, "By all means, Lord."

They each turned, heading back toward their respective lines.

"Richard, you're not seriously considering surrendering yourself? I didn't rescue you only to have you taken away in chains."

"No, of course not," he replied, "but we need to buy some time. I don't think Valmar will attack while he believes I'm seriously considering his offer."

"He's cunning, our baron," added Sir James. "We like to call him 'The Fox'."

Fitz looked at him in surprise, "When have you ever called me 'The Fox', Sir James?"

"Lots of times," the knight retorted, "just not to your face."

Baron Fitzwilliam broke into a grin.

"Now you've done it," said Albreda, "he likes it."

They returned to their lines to wait. The afternoon wore on with little taking place; then, about the time they expected the parley to reconvene, the enemy began to move. They deployed their troops in a line opposite those of the baron's, the same width as the defenders, but deeper ranks thanks to their numerical superiority.

"I don't see their archers," commented Fitz.

Albreda opened her eyes, focusing them on the baron. "My agents tell me they've placed crossbowmen to the north with the bulk of the archers to the rear, though he's sent some to the south, along with some footmen. I think they may be trying to outflank you."

"Any sign of our allies?" he asked.

"Reports indicate horsemen to the south, though they're still some distance off. There's perhaps one hundred to one hundred fifty, moving quickly. I suspect they're the Kurathians."

"Sir James," called out Fitz, "send riders to them, warn them of the enemy's location."

"Aye, sir," replied the knight, who then began barking out orders.

"Will Valmar wait much longer, do you think?" asked Albreda.

"No, he's an impatient man. He's already started shifting men south. It's his opening move."

"What will he do next?" she asked.

"He'll try to hit us as hard as he can."

"How?"

"With a mass of knights, I suspect. He's not the type to take his time. He'll try to crush us as fast as possible."

Even as they talked, there was activity amongst the enemy. Their foot soldiers had lined up in groups, with gaps between them. Now knights were riding through these gaps, their armour glinting in the afternoon sun. As they made their way forward, they turned, forming a line in front of the infantry. More knights poured forth, forming a second, and then a third line of heavily armoured warriors.

"What's he doing?" she asked.

"Preparing for the assault," Fitz answered. "He's going to launch them at us one group at a time to try to wear us down, bit by bit. All he has to do is break our line, and he will have the run of the battlefield. How many knights did you say he had?"

"One hundred," Albreda replied, "or so I thought. He must have received reinforcements from somewhere; there has to be almost three times as many now. Why doesn't he get the attack over with?"

"He's making a show of force," said Fitz, "but it won't work."

"It won't? Why is that?"

"The men of Bodden have been under threat of attack for years. They're defending their homes, they won't give ground easily."

"They've started moving," called out Sir James.

"So they have," replied Fitz.

~

Captain Lanaka, commander of the Kurathian horse, looked back at the long line of troops following him. There were two hundred of them, the finest light horse in the land, and yet he worried for their future. They rode to battle as they had done many times before, but this time he knew they were outnumbered. It was not that he feared death; he had lived his life as a mercenary with death a constant threat, but his honour demanded he do his duty. The army of the princess had been badly mauled at Redridge, and now only a small portion of it was able to reach the crossroads.

He heard a yell, and one of his men pointed ahead where the road meandered through fields of wild grass and thickets. A bird circling above a group of trees caught his attention as it let out a loud caw that carried across the distance. Lanaka knew it was meant for him.

"Enemies in the woods," he said in Kurathian. *"Bear left and let the Orcs take care of them, we must get to the defenders as quickly as possible."* It went against his nature to leave an enemy to the rear, but he knew today's success lay in the men of Bodden surviving this battle.

He turned his men to the left, riding northwest. The troops were not in sight yet, for the trees interfered with his view, but he knew, deep down inside, that they were getting close. The riders tore across the open ground, great clumps of earth flying forth from the hooves of their horses.

~

Dame Hayley saw the signal from Shellbreaker. The Kurathians ahead of her started turning off the road. A copse of trees lay ahead, and she directed her Orc archers into the safety of the underbrush. Once the Orc spears caught up, they would move forward, seeking out their enemy, but if she advanced too soon, she would find herself overwhelmed.

She used a hand signal to indicate her intent, and the Orcs began weaving through the trees. The hunters moved swiftly and quietly as if they were ghosts, lending an air of otherworldliness to the situation.

She crouched at the edge of the woods, peering northward toward the expected enemy. The afternoon sun cast shadows, and Hayley wondered if perhaps Shellbreaker had been wrong, but then something moved. It was a momentary movement, likely to be missed by anyone else, but to her trained eye, it told her all she needed to know.

"Bowmen," she muttered to herself then turned to the Orcs nearby, reverting to their language, *"There are archers up ahead."*

"We see them," replied the hunter beside her. *"What would you have us do?"*

"Wait till the spears arrive. Once they're even with us, we'll commence loosing arrows on the enemy."

"A good idea," the Orc said. *"We will have their flank, but what of the other side?"*

"Telethial should be advancing with the Elves. They'll take care of the right flank."

The Orc nodded in agreement. Hayley was impressed, for it wasn't so long ago that the Orcs and Elves had stood on opposite sides of a fire yelling at each other. Marching and fighting together had fostered a mutual respect.

She moved eastward, down the line, to get a better view of the road. To the south, she spotted the Orc spears, Kraloch at their head.

~

Unlike most other commanders, Telethial was on foot, like her archers. The Elves were in small groups, some pausing with their bows ready, while others moved forward like a giant game of leapfrog.

She looked westward to see the Orcs marching up the road, their shaman leading. Down the road, farther south, she knew the princess's cavalry rode hard, but she wondered, not for the first time, if they would arrive in time.

~

Baron Fitzwilliam shifted uncomfortably in his saddle. "Why don't they hurry up and attack?" he asked.

"I thought you wanted them to wait," said Albreda.

"I do, but I don't. I understand it's to our advantage for them to wait, but they're making me nervous. I want Valmar to commit to battle, then we'll be sure of his attack plan."

"His knights have already formed up," she retorted, "what more can you expect?"

"He's waiting for something," he replied. "But I don't know if it's reinforcements or if he's just finishing his lunch."

"Shall I find out?" she offered.

"If you would be so kind."

She closed her eyes and began uttering strange words that lingered in the air. Fitz watched as her fingertips glowed slightly when she traced the arcane patterns needed for her spell.

"I can see them," she said. "I'm just flying over their lines now."

"Tell me, can you see any activity?"

"The knights are just sitting there. I can see some of them drinking from wineskins. Most of them don't have their helmets on, and there are other men on foot, running amongst them."

"Squires, most likely," offered Fitz.

"Yes, I believe you're right. They're tightening harnesses and making adjustments to belts and such."

"That means they'll be moving forward shortly," said Fitz. "It appears they're about to make their opening moves."

"What's this?" said Albreda.

"What's what?" asked Fitz in alarm.

"I see activity to the south. It seems the Life Mage, Revi Bloom, has sent his familiar circling around a group of trees."

"A signal to our allies?"

"Likely, there's movement below him. I rather suspect Valmar has put some troops in there to guard his southern flank."

"Can you make out how many?"

"No, but I can see our allies in the distance. They've sent horsemen and some Orcs."

"Can you tell how many?" asked Fitz. "We are vastly outnumbered here."

"A few hundred, no more," said Albreda. "Their horsemen are heading northwest, toward our lines. They should reach our southern flank before too long."

"Thank Saxnor for that," said Fitz.

"I'll circle back around the enemy lines," offered Albreda.

The baron waited patiently, watching the mage with intense interest. She opened her eyes, and for the briefest moment he saw them glowing, then the light faded. "The knights are moving," she announced.

Fitz snapped his attention to the east. The Knights of the Sword were advancing in three waves, each separated from the others by several dozen horse lengths. "Valmar's showing some cunning, for a change," he explained. "Three waves, just as I thought."

"Will the line hold?" she asked.

"It will have to, though it doesn't look good. I've never heard of footmen holding off three waves of knights."

"Have faith, Richard," she said, placing her hand on his forearm.

Lanaka's horsemen cleared the trees, and he turned right. Off to the north, he could make out the end of the baron's line of battle, the princess's standard displayed proudly. The baron had insisted they use the distinctive flag, rather than his personal one and the captain had to admit, it was easy to identify from this range.

The Kurathians were trotting, conserving their horse's energy, for they knew they would soon be engaging the enemy. The general had told him to 'improvise', a term he was finding more and more common within this army and now he understood its necessity. Before him, the enemy advanced toward the Bodden line, the heavily armoured knights kicking up dust and dirt as they rode.

Lanaka realized there were three sections of cavalry, separated by a short distance and immediately understood the tactic. Though Kurathians didn't employ knights, they had fought them on the battlefield before, and he knew their strengths and weaknesses. Few troops could withstand their fury, and he silently prayed to the Saints to protect the men of Bodden that stood waiting for the storm to descend upon them.

~

Hayley gave the command and arrows poured forth. They flew through the air and she watched in fascination as the quiet of the afternoon was broken by the screams of people being hit.

Arrows struck branches, the vast majority doing little damage, but at least one man staggered forth from the trees, falling to the ground with an arrow through his chest.

She watched Kraloch and his spears approaching the edge of the wood. The shaman raised his staff on high, and then his brethren rushed forward, letting out a roar of challenge. This was no orderly advance of spears, but a mad charge of hunters seeking their prey.

The ranger kept up the volleys until the Orcs disappeared into the tree line then halted. There would be little more they could do in their present position; the risk of hitting their own was too high. She gave the command, and the archers began their advance.

~

Sir Alard held his sword up high, bellowing out a challenge as the Knights of the Sword advanced. The enemy line drew closer, its chainmail clad footmen gripping their spears and shields tightly, hoping these would protect them. He dug in his spurs, and the mighty warhorse picked up speed. Looking left and right he saw the other knights following his lead. His cavalry, the finest in the land, would rip into the traitorous baron's line and carve them to pieces.

His mount stumbled, and he looked down to notice the ground strewn with rocks. Cursing, he slowed, his men dropping their speed to keep the line intact. It wouldn't matter, he thought to himself, we will still crush them. The knights were drawing closer to the enemy now, and the anticipation of battle rushed through his veins.

He gave a yell of triumph as he smashed into the enemy line. A spear struck his horse's chain barding, but the armour held, deflecting the blow. He pushed forward, his sword seeking out the astonished warrior. Down crashed his weapon, cutting deeply into the man's neck. Not waiting to see the result of his blow, he pushed his horse forward and struck again. Risking a glance, he saw the other knights repeating his movement. The line was already being forced back, the enemy unable to withstand the awesome fury of the king's finest warriors.

Baron Fitzwilliam saw the impact, saw his men fall. He yelled out a command, and those to the rear moved up, spears at the ready.

The cavalry had spent its charge, the impetus pushing his troops back more than twenty paces, but now it was his turn. Spears reached forward, stabbing at the heavily armoured enemy.

It was a desperate fight, but the future of the kingdom was at stake. To a man, they all knew what would happen if they lost this day; their entire lives, their families and homes, would be destroyed. The men of Bodden fought back with the fury of desperation.

Lanaka gave the command, and the Kurathian horse broke into a gallop. The second wave of knights prepared to charge into the Bodden lines, but he ignored them. He knew that if he attacked the second line, the third would crash into him, decimating his troops and so he headed directly for the third wave.

The knights were trotting slowly, waiting for their brothers to launch the second assault. As the Kurathians came into view, a few knights noticed them, pointing, and some began to move, but the light horses of Lanaka's men were swift and closed the distance rapidly.

The knights managed to turn their mounts to face this new threat, but they were unprepared for what came next. The Kurathians rode in amongst them, slashing left and right. The heavy armour of the enemy protected them, but their line became disordered as the foreign mercenaries mingled in. Soon, it broke down into a mass of individual combats as the bewildered knights, their vision restricted by heavy helmets, struggled to defend themselves.

Lanaka struck out with his weapon, his sword deflecting off of a chain covered leg. He attacked again, this time with the tip, and felt it penetrate flesh. His men were screaming defiance as they clashed, but the knights began to fight back. He noticed a knight slice into a horse, toppling its rider, then swing at another target, all while his horse stomped the unlucky Kurathian rider to a pulp.

All about him, his men were dying, but Lanaka knew he must buy the princess's army the time it needed to arrive.

~

Leaving the woods with the Orc archers in tow, Hayley spotted a swarm of cavalry off in the distance, near the crossroads. As Kurathian fought knight, she broke the archers into a run, rushing northward, desperate to arrive in time to help.

To her right, she heard the fighting die down as enemy archers broke through the trees streaming north with Kraloch and his troops followed in pursuit. Knowing that reinforcements were desperately needed, she moved to the side to let her Orcs run past while searching for the Mercerian cavalry to the south, but her view was blocked by the very same trees that had given her cover.

~

The first wave of knights withdrew, trotting back to the northeast to make way for the next. Baron Fitzwilliam moved fast, ordering the wounded moved, replacing them with fresh men. They had taken a beating, far worse than he had imagined possible. "We can't take another charge like that," he declared.

"We must," asserted Albreda, "our very survival depends on it. If they break through our lines, Bodden will be wide open."

"I know," he retorted, "but it seems I've underestimated Valmar, and now my men will pay the price."

"Is there no hope?" she asked. "Surely our allies are here?"

"Too little to be of aid," he said, "and, I fear, too late."

Albreda saw the look of defeat on the baron's face. "Have faith, Richard, the day is not over yet."

~

Another of his companions fell as Lanaka struck out yet again. His men were being worn down, but for now, the enemy was being held at bay.

"Captain," yelled an aide, "we cannot continue. We are being slaughtered."

"Back!" he yelled. "Withdraw!" The Kurathian horse, their numbers decimated, began withdrawing to the southwest, the knights in pursuit.

TWENTY-FOUR

The Desperate Fight

SPRING 962 MC

~

R evi Bloom opened his eyes, "The Kurathians are retreating."

"And the knights?" asked Gerald.

"Are pursuing, but they're much slower. It looks like they've inflicted heavy casualties on our mercenaries," offered the mage.

The command group were riding at the head of a long column of men that stretched to the south.

"Redridge cost us too much time," growled Gerald.

"You couldn't help it," offered Anna. "We had no idea they would unleash the Blights."

"I should have sent men north sooner. They could have been riding while we attacked Redridge."

"Don't start second-guessing yourself, General," offered Revi. "We cannot change the past."

"Yes, but now our allies are depending on us, and all we can do is trickle troops in piecemeal."

"There is still time," said Anna. "You can take the Weldwyn horse ahead. Arnim and I will bring up the footmen as quickly as we can."

"It's worth a try," said Revi. "Valmar's knights are pounding the baron's men; we must do something."

Gerald looked at the troops behind him. "You're right," he said at last. "Arnim, you take command of the foot. Bring them north as fast as you can. I'm riding ahead with the cavalry."

"What of the heavy cavalry?" Arnim asked.

"Tell Beverly to use her best judgement. We can't wait for them, they'll only slow us down."

"I'm coming with you," interrupted Revi.

"You're needed here," said Gerald, "to protect the princess."

"Aubrey will look after her, you may need me with you."

"Very well, but we ride hard." He forced his mount to a faster pace, the men behind following suit. "For Weldwyn!" he called and soon the cry was taken up, echoing down the line.

~

Hayley rushed into cover as what remained of the Kurathian horse rode by. She observed the Knights of the Sword pursuing, their larger horses falling behind the swift-moving mercenaries.

"Form a line," she called out, pointing to a space just in front of the tree line. In her rush to get out her command, she forgot to use the Orcish tongue, but the hand gestures sufficed, and they fell into position quickly.

The knights, triumphant over the trouncing of the light horsemen, trotted along slowly, intent on their distant prey but conserving their strength for an opportunity to charge. As Hayley drew her bow, she heard the soft intake of breath as the Orcs all along the line did likewise.

She waited for the enemy horses to draw closer. The knights rode past them, ignoring the archers until a single rider turned his attention toward them. With his yell of alarm, Hayley let fly her arrow. It sailed through the air, suddenly joined by an entire volley. The rider saw the shot, tried again to alert his colleagues, but the jangle of harness and the footfall of the horses drowned out his words.

Hayley's arrow struck true, driving through the breastplate. The rider gazed down at the injury, then slowly started tilting to the right and fell off his horse. A moment later, the rest of the volley hit home with a clatter of arrow tips striking armour

Almost a hundred archers had let loose at short range, and the arrows tore into the packed ranks of the knights. She watched riders fall to the ground, riddled with arrows. She loosed shot after shot, taking little time to aim. Orc bows twanged in the afternoon sun as arrow after arrow flew forth to create a hail of death.

Horses staggered about, arrows protruding from their flesh, for even their chain barding was not proof against such close range fire.

Hayley's arms ached with the effort. She reached for another arrow only to find her quiver empty. Dropping her bow, she drew her sword and waited as the rest of the archers used up their projectiles.

On the field, the knights were quickly reduced to little more than wandering individuals. Past them, she saw the second wave of knights amongst the Bodden line, in a furious melee. She wanted desperately to help them but knew her part was done. Their arrows expended, all they could do was watch the battle unfold before them.

Hayley heard the sound of horses to her side and looked in time to recognize the Weldwyn horse. They were riding north, directly through the fleeing knights, General Matheson at their head.

~

Sir Heward looked across at Sir Rodney. They could clearly see the first wave of enemy knights trotting back to their own lines as if returning from a Sunday picnic. A nod of acknowledgement was all it took and then the two warriors surged forward, their men taking up a yell of battle.

Save for their leaders, the Bodden horse were not knights, but they might as well have been. Years of fighting on the frontier had honed their skills, and now, after being forced to stand back and watch their comrades face the fury of these knights, they unleashed all their pent up energy.

Crashing into the rear of the retreating knights, their swords dealt out death and destruction. The enemy, already tired from their exertions, turned to fight, but their horses were blown, their movements sluggish. The riders of Bodden ripped through the enemy ranks.

~

Gerald Matheson may have spent the last year being a general of an army, but long before he led many patrols in the wilderness surrounding Bodden. Now, as his cavalry headed northward over the field of battle, he caught sight of a small group of riders, decimated by Hayley's volley.

What was left of the Knights of the Sword meandered about the field, trying to regain some sort of order. He urged his mount on, directing his men toward a knot of survivors. The knights turned at their approach, determined to fight to the end.

The Weldwyn horse took up the cry once again. "For Weldwyn!" they yelled, their voices carrying across the field.

Someone was trying to organize the knights and Gerald headed straight for him. His enemy struck out, his sword reaching far, but Gerald, by instinct, leaned to the side, and the blade passed harmlessly by him. He struck back with a short, efficient thrust, driving into the closest target of opportunity, in this case, the man's thigh. As he withdrew the blade, blood gushed down the knight's leg. The general struck again, this time into his foe's stomach and the rider fell, his horse galloping off in fear and confusion.

Gerald turned in his saddle, seeking another target, but the small band of resistance was defeated. Now, his men were in the middle of the battle-field, and he quickly surveyed their position. To the east stood an unbroken line of royal foot troops, while to the west the men of Bodden were in a violent melee with the second wave of knights. Gerald heard fighting to the north and looked to see a fierce cavalry melee where the remainder of the enemy's first wave had been engaged by the Bodden horse. He immediately saw the danger they were in and ordered the Weldwyn troops forward, hitting the first wave from the rear.

Beverly advanced the heavy cavalry to the north at a steady trot, prepared to deploy where needed. It was strange, she thought, to be riding a horse other than Lightning, but her valiant steed had yet to complete his healing. In the distance, she spotted the Orc spears which had pushed Valmar's archers back and were now assaulting the southern tip of the enemy footmen.

Just to the right of them, the Elves, under Telethial, were pouring fire into the enemy line. The defending troops were caught between a rock and a hard place. Moments before they had been facing westward, their line securely anchored by a group of trees, but now the Orcs were threatening their rear, moving up from the south.

Beverly brought the horsemen to a full gallop and aimed straight for the enemy line. The Elves, seeing the charge, began concentrating their fire, pouring volley after volley into the intended target, halting only moments before the horsemen arrived, crashing through the line of defenders. The heavily armoured horsemen continued their charge, pushing through the startled footmen and forcing their way north, into the thickest part of the enemy's defences.

Beverly struck blow upon blow with her hammer, the tip of her weapon becoming a blur. Time felt as if it stood still while she attacked; Nature's Fury smashing down, splintering a shield and driving the footman back. Her horse struck out with a hoof, knocking a man to the ground. Around her the men, her men, fought with efficiency and professionalism, breaking the enemy's morale and driving them away in fear.

As the enemy line began to give way, the mass of defenders become thinner and thinner while they tried to avoid the vengeful blades of the heavy cavalry. These men were armed and armoured as knights, but they fought with ruthless efficiency, having been trained for weeks under Beverly's watchful gaze, and now they did her proud. These were not individual knights, each with their own concerns over honour and chivalry, but a professional unit of horsemen, highly disciplined and adept at keeping each other safe. They had practiced in pairs, and now she watched in admiration as she saw them doing their work, each aware of their partner, warning them of any danger and protecting each other.

∾

Telethial stopped her volley just before Beverly's cavalry struck the line. As soon as the horsemen obscured their view, she began searching for other opportunities. Moving the Elves forward, their leader honed in on a small group of men to the north. She paused, letting her eyes take in all she could see.

A group of mostly mounted men surrounded their standard, and she spotted one in particular with an elegant cape. There could be no doubt in her mind as to the identity of him. The distance was great, even for the mighty Elven bows, but she couldn't surrender the chance, no matter how small, of potentially robbing the enemy of their general.

She gave the command, and arrows began to fly.

∾

Valmar watched the battle with intense interest.

"The knights are in danger, Your Grace," said Captain Davis, rather unnecessarily.

"We still have the foot," snarled Valmar, "and the bulk of our archers remain unengaged. This day may yet be ours. What's happening to the west? Have they broken the Bodden line?"

"I cannot see, Lord, too many block our view. However, they are pushing us back in the north, and the southern end of the line is under attack by horsemen."

"More of those accursed mercenaries?"

"No, my lord, they look like knights."

"Knights," spat out Valmar. "Impossible, the enemy doesn't have any knights."

"Perhaps from Westland, Your Grace?" suggested the captain.

"Nonsense, Merceria is the only realm with such troops. It must be some sort of trick."

He was staring south now, trying to make out the distant fight, when an arrow struck the ground nearby.

"What was that?" he called out in alarm.

"Archers to the southeast, my lord."

"I don't see them," Valmar cursed. "Where in the Afterlife are they?"

Captain Davis pointed, "There, my lord, far in the distance, do you see?"

"That's an impossible range," Valmar sputtered, then it dawned on him. "They must be Elves. They've hired the God-spawned Elves. How many do they have? Can you make it out?"

"A small group," replied Captain Davis, "and yet they have our range."

As if in answer, another arrow struck the ground, soon followed by two more.

"We must get you out of here, Lord."

"Nonsense, Captain," replied Valmar. "The range is great, and we have our armour to protect us."

Captain Davis didn't reply, so Valmar turned in annoyance only to see an arrow protruding from his arm.

"Good Gods, man," said the marshal-general.

Captain Davis gave a yell of pain and then slumped forward in the saddle.

"Davis," yelled Valmar in concern, "are you all right?"

The captain sat back up, grimacing in pain. "We must get you out of here, Your Grace, it is far too dangerous."

"I'm inclined to agree," said Valmar. "Come, let us be gone from here."

"But the men..." began Davis, his words trailing off.

"The men be damned," said Valmar. "This battle is lost. It is our duty to inform the king of our victory."

"Our victory?" said the captain in disbelief.

"We have worn down their army," said Valmar, "and blunted their attack. Though it's true they hold the field, they have little to continue the war with. We shall regroup in Tewsbury and prepare for a siege. One way or another, we will bleed this traitorous army dry."

The footmen of the princess's army arrived too late for the battle. They reached the crossroads just as the Bodden foot began their advance into the enemy line, which immediately disintegrated, flooding the field with men tossing their weapons to the ground or fleeing eastward.

Anna spotted a small group of horsemen approaching and smiled in relief as she recognized Gerald at their head. She rode out to meet him, Arnim and Nikki following.

"Gerald," she exclaimed, "I'm so glad to see you well. Are you hurt?"

The general looked over his armour. "The blood's not mine," he said. "I am pleased to report the enemy is defeated, Your Highness."

"You could have saved some for us," grumbled Arnim.

Gerald laughed aloud, releasing the pent up stress. "Never fear, Sir Arnim, there'll still be plenty of fighting."

"Where's Revi?" asked Arnim.

"He's back with Sir Heward, dealing with the injured and trying to corral the prisoners. The enemy is in retreat, a small number, at least."

"Should we pursue?" asked Anna.

"No, though shattered, they could still rally and put up a fight, and we need to take care of this mess." He swept his arms to indicate the field.

Anna looked northward, at the bodies that lay strewn about the battle-ground. The sound of men and horses in pain echoed across the blood-soaked field. "It's a terrible sight," she said.

Gerald nodded his head in agreement. "It is indeed," he said, "but I fear we have worse to come. Wincaster is a large fortified city. It won't fall easily, and we have yet to take Tewsbury."

"Still," said Anna, "we have won a victory this day. Let us be thankful for that."

"Agreed," said Gerald. "Now, we must find the baron and see how he fared."

"Could Revi not spot him with Jamie?" she asked.

"The mage is too busy," replied Gerald, "but Bodden's lines are nearby. Even now, his men are advancing to round up the prisoners."

"Have we any word of Valmar?" she asked.

"Not as yet," he said, "but the field is still chaotic. We'll know more soon enough."

"Then let us seek out the baron and ensure he is well."

"Where do you want the footmen?" asked Arnim.

"Bring them north," answered the general, "and have them assist with the prisoners. We'll need someone to watch over them and then we'll have to decide what to do with them."

"We could take them to Redridge," suggested Arnim.

"A good idea," said Anna, "but we'll have to detach troops to march them there. We'll need a temporary place to guard them."

"I'll see to it, Highness," replied the knight.

"Thank you, Arnim. Now come along, Gerald, we have a baron to find."

Baron Fitzwilliam sat on his horse while Albreda bandaged his arm.

"You need this looked at, Richard," she chided, "and your armour will have to be repaired.

"It is a minor wound," he replied.

"That could easily fester. Did you have to charge into battle yourself? Surely your men were more than capable of holding the line."

Fitz looked at her in shock, "I would never expect my men to do something that I was unwilling to do. I lead by example."

"Well," she responded, "you should try to do it without getting wounded. It was very nearly the death of me."

The baron noticed the look of concern on her face and the tears that were forming in the corner of her eyes. "I'm sorry, my dear."

Albreda wiped away the tears, "And well you should be. Now, let's get you over to the princess and see where their healers are."

"Healers?" he said in surprise. "They have more than one?"

"Yes," she responded, "didn't I mention it? That niece of yours, Aubrey Brandon, has taken up magic."

"Aubrey is with the princess? I thought she was in Hawksburg."

"I'm sorry, Richard, I couldn't tell you earlier, but Hawksburg has been sacked."

"Robert?"

"I'm afraid Valmar killed them all, save for Aubrey."

"Why didn't you tell me?" he asked.

"I thought it best to wait," she replied. "All of this developed so fast." She used her hands to indicate the field. "I didn't want to distract you. I'm sorry, I know you were very close."

Fitz looked to the ground, unable to meet her gaze. "I understand," he said at last, "and it wouldn't have brought them back."

"Look at me, Richard," she said, using her hand to tilt his head back up to meet her gaze. "You are very important to me and will always be so. Lean on me if you wish, I am here to share your sorrow."

"Thank you," he replied. "Their loss weighs heavily on me, but I have not the time to grieve just yet. You did the right thing. I would have been too overcome by their deaths to carry out this battle. You have saved me. More than that, you have saved our army, for I daresay I would have been useless as a commander."

"I think you underestimate yourself," said Albreda, "for you are the strongest man I know. Now come, let us compose ourselves, for I see the princess is approaching."

She passed a handkerchief to the baron, who wiped his eyes, then tucked it into his sleeve.

"Baron," called out Anna.

"Your Highness," he replied. "It is good to see you safe. And Gerald, pardon me, General," he corrected himself, "you look reasonably fit for an old man."

Gerald grinned at the compliment, "Need I remind you, my lord, that you are older than I?"

"I am indeed," Fitz replied, "and happy to be so. I must say you arrived just in time. Another line of those knights would have finished us off."

"You can thank Captain Lanaka for that," Gerald replied. "I understand he kept them busy so that our archers could finish them off. Though I fear they took heavy casualties doing so."

"Remarkable," said Fitz, "that such lightly armoured troops would contemplate such a move. I can well imagine the bravery it must have taken."

"Are you wounded, Baron?" asked Anna.

"A minor wound," he replied.

"Well, have it seen to. Lady Aubrey is close at hand, helping with the wounded. Seek her out and get it looked at."

"When I find the time, Your Highness,"

Anna looked at him with a stern expression, "That is not a suggestion, Baron, that is a command."

"Yes, Highness," the baron said, rebuked.

"I like her," said Albreda.

Gerald moved his horse forward to look at the baron's arm. He held it, looking at the rent in the mail when he noticed something. "What's this?" he asked, pulling forth the kerchief.

"Well, er..."

"For goodness sake," said Albreda, "have you never heard of a lady's favour?"

Gerald looked to the baron, who was blushing furiously. "A favour? Well, it seems more has been happening at Bodden than I thought, my lord."

"You must stop calling me 'my lord'," said Fitz, trying to change the subject, "you're a general now."

"And you're still a baron, my lord," he said, winking at Anna.

"Lady Albreda," said Anna with a smirk, "would you be so kind as to escort Baron Fitzwilliam to a Life Mage?"

"I should be delighted," replied the witch.

TWENTY-FIVE

The Ride East

SPRING 962 MC

They all met that evening to discuss their future strategy. The weather was warming, and they stood around a fire while others continued to clear the battlefield.

"Where do we stand?" asked Anna.

"I'm afraid our army is greatly reduced," said Gerald. "We'll have to rebuild our strength."

"Yes," agreed Beverly, "though we now have my father's troops."

"Perhaps enough to take Tewsbury," offered the baron, "if we act quickly."

"Agreed," said Gerald. "Word won't have reached them just yet, and with any luck, we can convince the garrison to surrender the town."

"It's worth a try," said Anna. "Gaining Tewsbury would let us control the north."

"Yes," agreed Beverly, "and it would give us a base of operations where we could rest and recover our strength."

"The garrison there might still resist us," advised Arnim.

"What if we send an advance party?" offered Albreda. "A show of force to prove we defeated Valmar."

"What are you suggesting?" asked Anna.

"We send a group of horsemen, perhaps only a hundred or at least what we can spare. If we have the baron at their head, there can be no doubt of Valmar's defeat."

"What do you think, Baron?" asked Anna.

"A good strategy," he replied. "When would we set out?"

"As soon as possible," suggested Albreda. "First thing in the morning, if we can."

"That sounds good," added Gerald. "Who would you take?"

"I was thinking Sir Heward and Sir Rodney," said Fitz, "along with what's left of the Bodden horse."

"I think we should add more," offered Beverly. "Let me take the heavy cavalry."

"Won't they slow you down?" asked Nikki, who until this time had remained silent.

"No," said Beverly, "we're not rushing eastward at great speed, but a sensible marching pace to conserve energy."

"My daughter is correct," said Fitz, "and I think the presence of the princess's horse will lend weight."

"Your thoughts, Gerald?" asked Anna.

"It makes sense," he agreed. "We'll still have the Weldwyn horse here along with the Kurathians and these prisoners will keep us busy for some time. We'll march the rest of the army in a few days and meet you there. If you run into trouble, you can come back up the road and join us."

"Who else should go," asked Anna, "other than Beverly and the baron?"

"Well, I'm going," announced Albreda, "and I think Lady Aubrey should as well."

"Aubrey?" asked Gerald. "She's still busy healing people."

"Revi can take over her duties," said Albreda. "I think it's important for them to see a Brandon in our midst. It shows a unified north."

"Very well," said Anna, "have the men get some rest. You'll ride out at first light."

The group began to disperse, leaving Gerald and Anna by the fire. Soft snoring drew their attention.

"It seems Tempus is comfortable," said Gerald.

"So it does," she agreed, stooping to pet her faithful hound. "He's getting grey around the muzzle."

"He's getting old, like all of us," Gerald suggested.

Tempus opened one eye, then closed it again as she petted him. "How much longer will he live, do you think?" she asked.

"I think he has a few years, yet," said Gerald. "Revi's magic keeps him healthy enough."

"Good," she said, "I'd like to see him live a life of comfort once this is over, he certainly deserves it."

"As do we all," agreed Gerald.

The road to Tewsbury was twisted and little more than a cart track. They hadn't been riding long when they came across some men sitting by the side of the road. It was Beverly that saw them first, calling a halt to the small column.

"What is it, my dear?" asked the baron.

"Soldiers by the look of it," she replied. "They must be stragglers from the royal army."

"Are they a danger?" asked Aubrey.

"No," said Beverly, "there aren't enough of them."

"Then I suggest we move closer," said Baron Fitzwilliam, "and see what they are up to."

Beverly and her father rode forward with a couple of cavalrymen. Albreda, not to be left out, trotted after them, leading Aubrey to do the same.

"Who are you?" called out the baron.

"We're soldiers," replied one of the men. "My name is Sergeant Kendall, of the Third Wincaster Archers."

"And what are you doing here?" asked Beverly.

"We guard the sick and wounded, my lord," said the man.

"Where is the rest of your army?" asked Fitz.

"They have abandoned us, Lord. The marshal-general has fled with those that can keep up. The rest of us have been left to fend for ourselves." The look of dejection on the sergeant's face told the whole story.

Fitz looked at the man incredulously, "Are you saying Valmar abandoned his wounded?"

"He did, Lord," said the sergeant.

"You say you have wounded?" interrupted Aubrey. "Show me, I am a healer." She dismounted, passing the reins to Beverly.

"They're over this way," said Kendall, "I'll take you to them."

"We cannot afford this delay," offered Albreda.

Fitz looked at her in surprise. "They are wounded men," he said.

"They are enemy soldiers," she corrected, "who, not one day ago, were fighting against you."

"They had little choice," said Beverly, "the king commanded it."

"Need I remind you, the king also commanded the death of your father."

"They still need our help," Beverly persisted. "What say you, Father?"

"I'm inclined to agree," said Fitz, "but Albreda has a valid point. If we are late to Tewsbury, we may find it locked up tight, and that would mean a siege."

"I think Aubrey has shown us another way," said Beverly. "Perhaps, if we look after their wounded, they might, in return, help us."

"It's worth a try," offered her father.

They dismounted, passing their horses off to the cavalrymen. Making their way through the makeshift camp, Fitz found himself overcome with grief as he saw the state of the wounded. "War is horrible," he said at last.

"War is necessary," offered Albreda. "It is the very epitome of nature."

"There is nothing natural about war," countered Fitz.

"On the contrary," the druid replied, "it is all about survival of the fittest."

"You are a model of contradictions," said Fitz. "On the one hand you abhor the loss of life, but on the other, you say that war is necessary."

"Necessary does not mean desirable," she corrected him. "If we are to prevent the darkness from ruining the kingdom then yes, the war is necessary. I should much prefer the corrupt king to simply remove himself from the throne but I don't think that's likely to happen any time soon, do you?"

"No, of course not," said Fitz, "but you show a callous disregard for Human life."

"You should know me better than that, Richard. I detest death of any type, but death is part of life. Without it, life would be meaningless. It is the very spectre of death that drives us forward."

"You are quite the philosopher, Albreda," said Fitz.

"I've told you before, I read Califax."

"He was a poet, not a philosopher," argued the baron.

"Can he not be both?"

"I concede the point."

"If you two are done discussing the classics," said Beverly, "perhaps we can return to the subject at hand?"

"By all means," said Fitz. "Albreda?"

"Yes, of course," she agreed.

Beverly cast her eyes around the camp, noticing her cousin casting a spell of healing, her hands glowing with the effort.

"Sergeant Kendall," she called out.

"Yes, Dame Beverly?" the man replied.

"You know me?" she asked in surprise.

"Of course," replied the sergeant, "your fame has travelled far and wide, and I know of no other red-headed lady knight."

"Hah!" cried out the baron. "He's got you there."

"Tell me, Sergeant," asked Beverly, ignoring her father, "is the way to Tewsbury open?"

"I would think so," responded the man, "though I'd be happy to show you."

"You would take us to Tewsbury?"

"I have no love for the king, not after the way we were treated. To be abandoned like this is unforgivable."

"We shall look after you," offered Beverly. "We'll send word back to our army, and they'll come and collect you."

"Why would you do such a thing?" asked the sergeant.

"We are all Mercerians," said Beverly, "and though we don't always see eye to eye, we all want the same thing deep down; a fair and just ruler. I invite you and your men to pledge service to the princess. We shall restore the throne and bring back the rule of law to the land."

"Take me to Tewsbury with you," offered Sergeant Kendall, "and I will do my best to see the gates opened wide for you."

"Agreed," said Beverly. "Have you a horse?"

"No," answered the sergeant, "though I can ride when needs be."

"Then we shall find you one," she replied.

"I'll leave some of the Bodden horse here to help with the wounded," said Fitz. "He can take one of their mounts."

"Very well," said the sergeant, "when shall we leave?"

The baron looked up at the waning sun, "It's too late to make much more progress today. We'll head out first thing in the morning. That gives Aubrey time to heal the more seriously wounded."

"I cannot thank you enough, Lord," said Sergeant Kendall.

"You can thank me once we're inside Tewsbury," said the baron in reply.

They set out early the next morning, three royal soldiers in their company. Aubrey had done her best, healing the more severely wounded, and was now back aboard her sturdy horse, though looking the worse for wear.

"How are you holding up?" asked Beverly.

"I'm exhausted, Cousin," Aubrey admitted. "The spells take a toll on me, and I didn't have much time to rest."

"You did the right thing."

"I wish I could have done more."

"We have limited time, they will understand," soothed Beverly.

"I wish this war were over," said Aubrey. "It wears on me to see so much pain and suffering."

"You and me both," added Beverly.

They rode on in companionable silence, Beverly keeping a close watch on her cousin, lest she fall from the saddle. Their progress was unopposed, and three and a half days later they stood before the gates of Tewsbury.

True to his word, Sergeant Kendall came forward, convincing the garrison of the city to surrender to Baron Fitzwilliam. Soon, they were within its walls and discovered that Valmar had fled south, back to Wincaster, along with everything he could carry.

TWENTY-SIX

Tewsbury

SUMMER 962 MC

A ldus Hearn entered the Earl of Tewsbury's estate, a bundle of papers tucked beneath his arm. The two guards standing station here, used to his presence, ignored him, allowing him to enter the earl's residence unchallenged.

He made his way down the hall, turning at the end to enter the dining room. Here, scattered across the table were numerous reports and maps, carefully being scrutinized by various individuals.

Princess Anna looked up from her notes at his entrance, "Master Hearn, so good to see you again."

"Your Highness," he replied in greeting.

"What have you there?" asked Gerald.

"Some information I have become aware of," he replied. "You remember that captain that was in Mattingly?" He looked to Revi Bloom, who was deep in a book.

"What was that?" asked Revi.

"Captain Griffon?" put in Hayley.

"Yes," agreed Hearn, "that's the one. It seems he had kept a journal. We didn't see it at first, he'd hidden it away for safe keeping. We only found it by accident."

"I take it," said Anna, "that it's something of interest?"

"Indeed it is," said Hearn. "In fact, you might describe it as troublesome."

"Wickfield and Mattingly are both under our control now," said Gerald. "We even reinforced their garrisons. What could be so concerning?"

"It seems that early last winter, an expedition was mounted from Wincaster. Its sole purpose was to investigate some ruins that were found southeast of Mattingly."

"Southeast, you say?" asked Revi. "What kind of expedition?"

"A large one, by the sounds of it. It seems it was led by a scholar, with orders from Lady Penelope."

"Not from the king?" asked Anna.

"No," he replied. "I think it was a private excursion."

"The person in charge," asked the princess, "what was his name?"

In answer, the elderly mage dropped the papers to the table and began rifling through them. "It's here somewhere, let me see... Ah, here it is." He held it up, squinting to read the fine hand, "A man named Summers."

"I know that name," said Anna. "He's a scholar from Shrewesdale. An expert in history, if I'm not mistaken."

"The very same," said Hearn, "it's mentioned in these notes. He came to Mattingly seeking assistance, mostly tools and such."

"What type of tools," asked Revi, "does it say?"

"Shovels, pickaxes, that sort of thing. He also had the authority to take some of the captain's men."

"How many?" asked Gerald.

"It doesn't say, I'm afraid. Why? Does it matter?"

"It does," said Gerald, "if there's a group of enemy soldiers somewhere in the north, they could cause all kinds of trouble."

"I think they're likely to be busy elsewhere," offered Revi. He had grabbed one of the papers and was examining it when the princess looked up at him.

"What is it, Master Bloom?" asked Anna.

"A rather crudely drawn map," the mage responded. "But unless I miss my guess, they've found a confluence."

"A confluence?" asked Gerald.

"Yes, a meeting of the ley lines."

"Like the magic flames?"

"Yes, we identified coordinates near that area, but were unable to contact them," offered Revi.

"Meaning?" asked Gerald.

"Meaning the Dark Queen may know of a gate location. It's imperative that we stop her. If she discovers how to utilize them, it will give her tremendous power."

"Is that likely?" asked Anna. "It took you months to discover how they work, and that was with the aid of intact temples."

"True," admitted Revi, "but we don't know who else might be working with her or what knowledge she already possesses. Need I remind you that the disc we used to discover the location of Erssa Saka'am was in her possession?"

"That's true," she said. "So the big question is, what do we do about it?"

"We must send an expedition of our own," suggested Revi.

"Can we afford to do that?" asked Hayley. "After all, we're preparing to march on Wincaster."

"We've replenished our strength," said Gerald, "but the newer recruits still need training, and the smiths are struggling to get them equipped. I think it will be another month, maybe two, before we're ready to march."

"That settles it then," said Anna. "We'll send an expedition."

"Very well," said Gerald, "but who shall we send?"

"I must go," declared Revi, "for I'm the one with the greatest knowledge of such things."

"You'll need help," said Gerald. "I think Hayley and Beverly should accompany you, along with some troops. Hayley will provide you with the woodland knowledge you'll likely need and Beverly will be there with some horsemen in case you run into a fight."

"I'd like to go as well," said Hearn, "if I'm not needed here."

"Your company would be most appreciated," said Revi.

"Very well," said Anna, "but no more, I can't allow all our leaders to go gallivanting off across the north."

"Who's to be in charge?" asked Hayley.

"Do I really need to designate someone?" asked Anna, somewhat annoyed. She looked to Gerald, who shrugged his shoulders. "You're not being much help," she said.

"Very well," he said, "Beverly is in charge. You'll defer to her in all matters."

"What about the dig," said Revi, "surely I should be the one in charge?"

"Do you have a problem not being in charge when I'm around?" asked the princess.

"No, why?"

"Then you shouldn't have a problem when Beverly is in charge. She will obviously defer to you in matters pertaining to magic, but your safety is of the utmost importance."

"When would you like us to leave?" asked Aldus Hearn.

"First thing tomorrow should do," said Anna.

"I'll go and find Beverly," offered Gerald, "and fill her in on what's happening. How many men do you think you'll want, Hayley?"

"A dozen archers should do," she replied. "I have a number of Orcs I've worked with before."

"Pick out a dozen," said Gerald, "and let us know who you're taking. Will they ride?"

"Orcs don't ride," said the ranger.

"Do you think you should take horsemen instead?"

"No," said Hayley, "the Orcs are almost as fast on foot as a horseman. I think they'll be able to keep up."

"Good. I'll leave it to Beverly to see how many men she wants to take, though I suspect it will be a similar number. Draw your supplies for the journey and coordinate with Beverly."

"Aye, General," said the ranger. She rose to leave but noticed the Life Mage still staring at the map. "Something wrong, Revi? Surely you're not upset with Beverly being in charge?"

"What, no, it's not that. I'm worried about this enemy expedition. If they've managed to unlock the secrets of the gates, it will not go well for us. They could get in behind our lines and create havoc."

"What can we do to alleviate the problem?" asked Anna.

"I think it's time we started posting guards on all the known gates," said Revi.

"And in the main temple in Erssa Saka'am," added Gerald, "but we'd need the permission of the Saurians for that."

"Yes," agreed Revi, "but we can't do that at the moment, we're nowhere near a gate."

"It's true," offered Hayley, "in fact, we're almost equidistant from three gates; Uxley, Wickfield and the Margel Hills."

"We'll send dispatch riders to those we can reach," said Gerald. "Captain Lanaka has been using his men as scouts, and his reports indicate Uxley has no troops."

"So the way to Wincaster is clear," said Anna.

"Yes, but we're not ready to march yet," warned Gerald. "We'll need supply wagons and lots of food. A siege can last months, and we have to be properly prepared."

"We'll send a small force to Uxley," said Anna. "They may be able to garner some more information, and it would give us access to the gate there."

"What of the king?" asked Aldus Hearn.

"It appears he's pulled all his forces back to the capital. I doubt he'd trouble Uxley, it's of no consequence to him, after all, and he doesn't know of the gate there."

Revi looked torn, "Though I'm needed on this expedition, I'm worried you may need my expertise here."

"You taught Aubrey how to work the gate, did you not?" asked Anna.

"I did," he said. "As a matter of fact, she mastered it quite quickly."

"Then we're all set," said Anna. "Now, you'd best get going. You'll need to draw whatever supplies you deem necessary. I'd hate for you to get there and find you're missing something."

Revi rose, following Hayley from the room.

"I will leave you to your work, Highness," said Hearn, bowing deeply. He turned, leaving Gerald and Anna alone.

"What was that all about?" asked Gerald.

"What? Revi?"

"Yes, I've never seen him like that before."

"You forget," said Anna, "he's faced the Dark Queen in person. She undoubtedly left him with a grave impression. He's worried, aren't you?"

"I have a war to run," said Gerald. "I can't let matters of magic concern me, that's for others to deal with."

"And if magic is being used to defend Wincaster?" she asked.

"Then we shall have to prepare as best we can."

Beverly was easy to find. She was exercising Lightning. The great warhorse ran around her as she watched, kicking up dirt as he did so.

"He looks like he's back to normal," observed Gerald.

"Yes, his leg was still a bit tender when they brought him to me, but he seems to be back to his old self now."

"Good, you may have need of him."

Beverly stopped watching her horse and shifted her gaze to Gerald, "We're marching on Wincaster?"

"Not yet," he said, "but we have a little expedition for you to lead."

"Say the word, and I'm ready," she said.

"You're going north. There's an area that likely contains the ruins of a Saurian temple."

"Fair enough," she replied. "Is that all?"

"No," he said in response, "the Dark Queen sent an expedition of her own, so we don't know what to expect. If one of those Blights show up, or an undead knight, they'll need your help."

"Who's going?"

"Revi, Hayley, a dozen Orcs and Aldus Hearn. You'll take some horsemen with you, as many as you like."

"I'll take a dozen of the Bodden horse, if it's all right with you."

"You'll have to ask your father for those, they're his troops, though I doubt he'll object. Are you sure they'll be enough?"

"If we do face Blights, more men won't help, they'll only get in the way."

"I suppose you're right," said Gerald. "There's one other thing."

"What is it?"

"Revi seems shaken, I think there's a chance that the Dark Queen herself may make an appearance."

"Penelope? You think that likely?"

"Quite frankly I just don't know, but you must take precautions."

"You have something particular in mind, I can tell," she said.

"I do. I won't mention this to anyone else, but you must ensure Revi is kept safe. If he were to fall into enemy hands, they might find out about the gates."

"You think he'd talk?"

"No, but she practices dark magic. For all we know, she might be able to force the information out of him with a spell."

"Can I tell Hayley?" she asked.

"If you see fit, but don't tell too many people, and whatever you do, don't tell Revi. The last thing we need is for him to be looking over his shoulder."

"Don't worry, we'll keep him safe."

"Make sure you do, he's more valuable than a gate location. If things go sour, get him out of there at all costs."

"I'll do as you say, General."

"This is not a command, Beverly, it's a request from one friend to another."

"Understood, Gerald. Don't worry, we'll look after him."

"Get the men sorted out quickly. You'll set out at sunrise."

"I'll find my father and make arrangements," promised the red-headed knight.

As it turned out, the baron was most accommodating, though he insisted he send his own man to help. So it was that early the next morning a dozen of the Bodden horse stood ready to ride, Beverly and Heward at their head.

"This mage of yours," said Heward, "he must be valuable."

"He is," she assured him. "He's the reason we can use the gates."

"A fascinating thing, those gates. I shall have to see one someday. What's it like when you travel through them?"

"Actually, it's a rather strange sensation. Perhaps, when we get back, I'll get Aubrey to take us through. You can see the Saurian home temple."

"I'd like that," said Heward. "Tell me, how is that smith of yours?"

She smiled, "He's well. My father brought him with us to Tewsbury. His smithing duties have kept him busy, but we've managed to spend some time together."

"I'm surprised you didn't want to bring him on this expedition," he said.

"No, I'd rather he were safe here with the army. I'd hate to put him in danger."

"But it's all right to put me in danger?" he added with a grin.

"That's different, and you know it. You're a knight. Aldwin knows how to take care of himself, but he'd be a distraction for me in battle, I'd be constantly worrying about him."

"I can understand that," said Heward. "Don't worry, he'll be safe enough." He looked around conspiratorially, "After all, there aren't THAT many good looking women here."

"Very funny," she said. "When this war's over you should become a bard."

"You think so?"

"No," she said. "Now, where are the others?"

Heward looked westward, where the road curved around the old church. "Here they come now, if I'm not mistaken."

Beverly turned her gaze to see the rest of their party. Hayley and Revi were trotting in the lead, a dozen Orcs following along at a jog.

"Don't they get tired?" asked Heward.

"No," said Beverly, "at least I've never seen them so. They can run at that speed for hours."

"I wish we had more of them in the army," observed the Axe.

"So do I, Heward, so do I."

"Bev," called out Hayley, "I see you're all ready to go."

"Yes," she replied, "though I don't know if you've met Sir Heward."

"The Axe, isn't it?" asked the ranger.

"Yes," replied the knight, "and you must be the archer that Beverly told me about. A fellow Dame of the Hound, if I'm not mistaken."

"Indeed I am, and this is Master Revi Bloom."

"Your reputation precedes you, Master Bloom," said Heward. "We are most fortunate to have you on this expedition."

"You serve the baron, don't you?" asked Revi. "I seem to remember you did your part at the Battle of the Crossroads."

"Is that what we're calling it?" asked Heward. "Yes, I suppose I did, but then again, we all did. If I remember correctly, it was your skills that helped many of our men survive their wounds. We are grateful to have you."

"If we're done extolling each other's virtues," said Hayley, "can we be on our way?"

"Certainly," said Beverly. "Why don't you ride up front with me, Hayley, then the men can spend all their time complimenting each other."

Hayley grinned at Revi, "I believe that's an excellent idea." She urged her horse toward the head of the column, the nimble Archon Light almost prancing as she did so. "Where's Aldus?" she asked.

"He's ahead of us. He left early to commune with nature," Beverly replied.

They set off at a slow pace, waiting to clear the city gates before picking up speed. The women rode in silence for some time while the two men chatted away, then Hayley turned to her companion, "Tell me, Bev, now that you've had time to spend with Aldwin, how was it?"

Beverly merely smiled and rode on.

TWENTY-SEVEN

The Ruins

SUMMER 962 MC

～

The group headed north, through the remains of Hawksburg, and then took the road to Mattingly. A week after leaving Tewsbury they reached the coordinates that Revi had calculated as a gate location. It wasn't hard to tell where the dig was; the noise of the workers alone was enough to give it away. The first sound that caught their ears was that of a whip.

As they drew closer, large mounds of freshly dug dirt blocked their path, requiring them to dismount. Beverly, Hayley, Revi and Aldus Hearn moved forward on foot, leaving Heward in command of the troops.

A group of tents were set up to the east of their present position, but the freshly dug earth ahead promised a greater prize. They crawled forward, using the mounds as cover as they peered over. At first glance, they spotted a shallow pit, only about a Troll's height in depth, but looking further, they discovered it stretched across an area the size of a jousting field.

"They've been busy," said Hayley.

"Indeed they have," agreed Revi. "It appears they have unearthed a Saurian Temple."

"It looks strange," commented Hearn.

"That's because they're normally under a hill," said Revi, "like at Queenston."

"Fascinating," mused the Earth Mage. "I can clearly see corridors and chambers. It looks like a series of tunnels."

"I rather suspect the Saurians created the structure and then moved the earth around it for extra security."

"It makes sense," said Hearn. "I, myself, can move earth. I take it these Saurians you speak of are powerful mages."

"They are, or at least, they were," said Revi. "It appears that is no longer the case. We found no evidence of any remaining spellcasters in their capital, though the high priest was able to work the flame once we showed him how."

"Fascinating," mused Hearn again.

As they watched, a group of six workers exited the structure carrying heavy wicker baskets with a soldier escorting them, or more precisely, watching them. They approached a small mound that was just before the temple entrance, then halted and began to empty the contents of their burdens.

"They're stripping the temple of its artifacts," said Revi.

"Yes," agreed Beverly. "I remember we found similar items at Uxley."

"Look, someone is approaching them," whispered Hayley.

Sure enough, a man drew closer to the pile created by the workers. He wore a rather plain looking tunic but carried himself like a noble.

"That must be Summers," said Hearn. "I think I've seen him before."

"You know him?" asked Revi. "Why didn't you say so sooner?"

"I didn't remember the name, but I met that man in Shrewesdale years ago."

"What were you doing in Shrewesdale?" asked Beverly.

"I studied under the great Sage Mezin. That man down there approached the sage with his theories, which, if I recall, were rather strange."

"What theories?" asked Revi.

"Something about the destiny of men to rule over all the other races. Mezin didn't take him seriously."

"How long ago was this?" asked Beverly. "I spent some time in Shrewesdale myself."

"Oh, quite some time ago, more than twenty years in fact, though I don't recall the exact date. Does it have relevance here?"

"Not really," she said. "Of more import to us is how we are to proceed."

"Let's get back to Heward and make our plans," suggested Hayley.

They were soon safely returned to their horses where Heward had posted lookouts. Sitting beneath a small cluster of trees, safe from prying eyes, they began to plan their next move.

"We need to get into those ruins," said Revi.

"Why don't we just attack the place," offered Heward, "we've enough soldiers."

"No," said Revi, "if we do that they might destroy something important. We need to see what they've been up to and what they've learned."

"We also need to find their notes," said Beverly. "I don't think they're going to keep those down at the dig."

"They'd be in the camp somewhere," suggested Hayley.

"Precisely," Beverly replied.

"Then we have to get into those tents," announced Aldus Hearn.

"During the day they're more likely to be down in the pit," said Beverly, "but at night they'll be in camp."

"I would suggest an infiltration of the camp first," said Hayley. "It would have to be during the daylight, and we'll need to watch for guards."

"I'm far more interested in that Saurian Temple," confessed Revi, "but I see your logic. The temple will have to wait for nightfall."

"We have to scout out their camp before we go in," said Beverly. "We don't know the layout, or how many guards they have."

"That guard down in the pit," asked Aldus, "what kind of armour was he wearing?"

"I'm not sure," said Beverly, "I've never seen its like before."

"Can you describe it?" asked Heward.

"Yes," said Aldus. "It looked like fish scales, small overlapping plates of metal."

"It sounds like scale mail," said the Axe.

"You're familiar with it?" asked Hearn.

"I've heard of it, though I've never seen it. I'm led to believe it's a foreign invention. I rather suspect these guards are foreign mercenaries."

"Like the Kurathians?" asked Revi.

"Yes, but from a different area. I'm not familiar with the world outside of Merceria, but I've heard tales of great kingdoms and empires."

"If the king has contacts outside of Merceria, it bodes ill for us," said Beverly.

"Indeed," added Revi, "it means our enemy's influence is quite considerable, but I doubt it's the king that has arranged things. I rather suspect it's the work of the Dark Queen."

"I assume you mean Lady Penelope?" asked Heward.

"I do. You might not know this, Sir Heward, but Lady Penelope is an Elf."

"She looked Human to me," defended Sir Heward. "She was at court as we passed through Wincaster on the way to Bodden."

"Yes," said Revi, "but she uses some type of magic to conceal her true appearance. I believe she's also a Necromancer."

"In the court of Merceria? No wonder we're fighting the crown. Do you suspect the king is one as well?"

"No," said Beverly, "but we think he's being controlled. I'm sure the princess would like to capture him and release him from whatever hold has taken him over, but it's doubtful that will happen. I rather suspect he'll fight to the bitter end."

"And so this foul Necromancer controls the kingdom?"

"She does," said Beverly, "though not for much longer. We'll take back Wincaster, and when we do her dark reign will come to an end."

"Do you think she's here?" asked Heward.

"I hope not," said Revi, shuddering. "The mage that was purported to be her brother conjured some very dangerous creatures at Redridge. If Penelope is here, we're all doomed."

"That doesn't sound like you, Revi," remarked Hayley, "you're usually much more positive."

"Don't worry, she's not here," assured Beverly.

"How can you be so sure?" asked Hayley.

"There would be more guards. Penelope doesn't travel anywhere without lots of protection."

"Good," said Revi, "that makes our job much easier."

"So where do we start?" asked Heward. "We want to sneak into camp, but we also need to get into the ruins. Have I missed anything?"

"No, that about sums up everything," said Hayley. "Let's start by observing the camp as Beverly suggested."

"Shellbreaker can help with that," added Revi.

"Here's what I propose," said Beverly, "We'll begin with the Bodden horse in reserve..."

The discussion went on for some time as they made their plans.

Hayley looked out from the trees. The Orcs were spread out in a thin line to either side of her, each one intent on the camp. She waved her hand, and then Beverly advanced, coming up to crouch beside her. "It's all clear," the ranger announced.

Beverly crept forward. "Wish me luck," she said, moving past Hayley. Revi and Aldus followed a few yards behind, each quickly crossing the distance to the first tent. They paused behind the shelter before looking back to where Hayley, her hand in the air, watched as the guard finished his circuit and then began moving north again. She silently chopped her hand down, and then Beverly advanced past the edge of the tent.

In the centre of the camp lay a much larger shelter, a pavilion of sorts, and it was to this that they made their way. Standing just outside the doorway, Beverly moved her head close to the canvas to listen. "I don't hear anyone," she whispered. "I'll go in first."

Drawing her hammer, she stepped inside. A moment later she reappeared. "It's safe," she said.

Following her in, they at first noticed a pile of furs, but what held everyone's attention was the table set up in the middle. Papers littered the surface, most held down with a stone to stop them from blowing away should a breeze enter.

"What do we have here?" muttered Aldus Hearn, picking up a note to examine it.

Beverly began rifling through the furs, looking for anything that might be of interest while the two mages looked over the table.

"This is interesting," said Revi, lifting a stone.

"What is it?" asked Aldus.

"It appears to be a rune stone."

Aldus Hearn looked at the object in Revi's hand. "I've never seen a rune like that."

"It's a new one," he explained, "or rather, new to us here in Merceria. I discovered a number of them when we studied the gate at Uxley."

"Fascinating," said Hearn. "These new runes, I take it they're what enable the gate to function?"

"Partially," said Revi in reply. "It's actually much more complicated. Each gate has a unique address that identifies it. After a starting sequence, you have to touch the appropriate rune stones in the correct order to activate the gate, then you can step through the flame."

"I'm confused," admitted the Earth Mage. "Is it a portal or a flame?"

"Both," said Revi. "We call them gates because they open and allow us to walk through them, like a gate, but in appearance, they're a green flame that you step through."

"Fascinating," said Aldus, and then returned his attention to the papers before him. "There are plenty of notes here, but none seem to indicate any knowledge of gates or flames."

"I agree," said Revi. "They talk mainly of artifacts, though there is some mention of solving a puzzle of some sort, whatever that may be."

"Perhaps the temple itself will provide the answers we seek."

Beverly, who had been looking through a bag of clothes, stood. "We haven't much time. The guards will be wandering back through camp soon. Have you two got what you came for?"

"It would take hours to sort through this lot," admitted Hearn.

"We'll take this stone," said Revi. "At least that way they'll be missing a rune. I doubt they've had time to identify it and even if they did, without it in their possession they won't be able to activate the gate."

"Fair enough," said Beverly, "but we need to move, now."

She opened the tent flap, peering outside. Off in the distance, she spotted Hayley, hiding amongst the trees. The ranger noticed her and gave a hand signal. Beverly backed into the tent, standing to one side of the flap and putting her finger to her lips.

The others froze. Outside, they heard a guard walking past. He paused a moment just beyond the doorway and then continued on his way.

Beverly counted to ten, before carefully peering outside again. The guard's back was toward her as he wandered away to the south. She waited for him to turn at another tent then waved the two mages forward.

They made their way past the other tents to find safety once again in the trees. Hayley let them pass, then brought up the rear after making sure they weren't being followed.

Later that afternoon, Revi sat in a small clearing examining the rune stone. "I'm not sure what type of stone this is," he said, "but I don't think it's from around here."

"I would agree," said the Earth Mage. "Do all the temples use the same?"

"Yes, at least all those we've seen."

"Interesting, it must have magical properties we're not aware of," said Aldus.

"I've seen runes etched on stone before," said Revi, "but not like this. It reminds me of the stonework we saw in Tivilton."

"Tivilton? Where's that?"

"Back in Weldwyn," said Revi, "what you would call Westland. We found an ancient ruin there."

"This is a most interesting mystery you've discovered," said Hearn. "I should love to help you unravel it."

"I look forward to it," said Revi, "but we must get this accursed war over with first."

"Agreed," said Hearn, "war spoils everything. Why can't we just all get along, it would make things so much easier?"

Just then a rustle among the trees interrupted them as Hayley stepped into the clearing.

"They're returning to camp," she announced.

"And?" asked Revi.

"And nothing. No one seems to have raised the alarm. They must not know you took that stone."

"Or something else is occupying their mind," suggested Aldus.

"Like what?" asked Hayley.

"I don't know," admitted Aldus, "but I'm thinking the temple will tell us what we need."

"Did you see the scholar?" asked Revi.

"Yes, he was talking to one of the guards. Their leader, I should think."

"Could you tell his mood? Was he angry?"

"No," replied the ranger, "quite the contrary, actually, he seemed quite pleased with something."

Revi looked to Aldus Hearn who nodded gravely.

"We need to get into that temple as soon as possible," said Revi. "I know it sounds trite, but they could be on the verge of a monumental discovery."

By the time the sun set, they were in position. The rune stone was in Heward's possession, the better to safeguard it should they be discovered. He waited some distance away, ready to charge in if he should be called. The other four were back to their original position, behind the pile of dirt, with Hayley peeking around it, watching the dig as the sun disappeared over the horizon.

"The workers are leaving now," whispered the ranger, "though for some reason they've left all the torches lit."

"Convenient for us," said Revi.

"A little too convenient if you ask me," said Beverly. "It could be a trap."

"I don't think so," said Aldus Hearn.

"Why do you say that?" asked Beverly.

"You remember I mentioned Mezin earlier?"

"The sage?" said Revi.

"Yes, I was apprenticed to him for some time, long before I discovered the magic within me. He was obsessed with the great Archmage Meghara. Have you heard of her?"

"You mean THE Meghara," corrected Revi. "Yes, we've heard of her, or rather all of them."

"All of them? What do you mean?" said Aldus in surprise.

"We learned from the Orcs that Meghara is a title, not an individual," said Beverly.

"Fascinating," mused Aldus, "you must tell me more of this."

"You're getting off target," said Hayley. "You were telling us about the sage, Mezin?"

"Yes, that's right," the elderly mage continued. "Anyway, Mezin was obsessed with finding her tower."

"Her tower?" said Hayley, turning to Revi. "It appears that you're not the only one missing a tower."

"How does one misplace a tower?" asked Aldus.

"It's not missing," replied Revi, "but my master, Andronicus didn't have a chance to tell me where it was before he died."

"How unfortunate," said Aldus.

"Please," said Beverly, "can you keep on topic?" She turned to Hayley for help, "Are all mages this easily distracted?"

"I'm afraid so," the ranger replied, "it must be in their blood."

"Master Hearn," said Beverly, "concentrate. You were talking about Meghara's Tower."

"Yes," the old man continued. "Scholars have been searching for it for years. Mezin thought he'd discovered the location through an old tome he found in the great library at Shrewesdale, and so we set off on an expedition. His set up was very similar to what we see here, though perhaps fewer people."

"I see," said Beverly, "but how is this relevant?"

"Well," continued Aldus, "he kept the dig lit at all times. He would often wander down there at night, while the workers were sleeping. He said it was easier to concentrate without all the distractions."

"So you're saying there's a chance that our scholarly friend might wander down there tonight?" asked Beverly. "Why didn't you just say that?"

"I just did," defended Hearn.

Beverly shook her head, "All right, so we'll have to be on the lookout for this man, Summers. Anything else we should know?"

"Not that I can think of," said Hearn.

"Nor I," added Revi.

"Hayley?" asked Beverly.

"All set, Bev. Give the order, and I'll lead the way."

"Consider it given," said the knight.

Hayley rose, making her way around the mound of dirt. The ground dropped where the earth had been removed to reveal the temple, but the descent was gradual, more of a slope than a drop. Hayley led, with the others following, keeping to the shadows where possible.

It didn't take long to reach the entrance. The expedition had not only removed all the dirt from around the temple, but they had also removed the doors. Hayley could see the strange indents where the door used to pivot on its centre.

A stack of unlit torches and a lantern sat beside the entrance. The ranger took one, entering the dark corridor before her. She waited till she was down the hall and around the corner before stopping to light it. Beverly saw the sparks as steel met flint and then a small flame leaped to life as the fire took hold.

"You know I could have used my orb of light," Revi reminded her.

"It might draw attention," said Hayley. "It's too bright."

"That's the trouble with being a powerful caster," said Hearn, "it's so hard to reduce magical effects."

"It is, isn't it," agreed Revi.

"Here we go again," said Hayley, shaking her head.

"Yes," agreed Beverly, "this mutual admiration is getting a little thick, don't you think?"

The ranger led the way, the two mages following while Beverly brought up the rear, keeping an ear open for any activity.

"There should be a four-way intersection just up here," said Hayley, holding the lantern before her. "We'll cross through and head into the waiting room. Just beyond that should be the room with the magical flame."

"How do you know it's a waiting room?" asked Hearn.

"We don't," said Revi, "but we had to call it something. It seemed logical that people would wait somewhere before stepping through the portal, so the name made sense."

"I'm surprised there's no glow here," said Beverly.

"I'm not," said Revi. "All indications are that the flame here was extinguished. I believe that's why we couldn't open a gate to this location."

"Here we are," announced the ranger. "Watch your step, there are stones all over the floor."

"Time for my spell, I think," said Revi. "We're far enough into the temple now, no one will notice." He uttered an incantation, and a ball of light appeared, hovering over his hand.

In Uxley, there had been a pedestal of stone with a green flame floating above it, but here it was disassembled. Instead, the stones were spread about the floor, their runes facing upward. Some had parchment beneath them with hastily scribbled notes.

"What's this?" asked Hearn.

"I think they're trying to decipher the meaning of the runes," said Revi.

"By the looks of it they've had some success," added Hearn. "More than three-quarters of them are labelled."

"Indeed," agreed Revi.

Aldus Hearn turned his attention to the rest of the room. "What's down this corridor?" he asked.

"That leads to another chamber," replied Beverly. "In Uxley we found slates there."

"Slates?"

"Yes, it's how the Saurians kept records. Thin slabs of stone with writing on them. Sometimes the writing is scratched, other times painted, but always in their tongue."

"Fascinating," said Hearn, "I should like to take a look if I might."

"I'll take you," said Beverly. "Hayley, give me the lantern while you stay here and look after your mage."

"I like that," said Hayley, handing over the light. "Revi, did you know you're my mage?"

"What?" asked Revi, still staring at the rune stones.

"Never mind," said Hayley, "I can see that you're busy."

Hearn stepped through the archway that led to the other chamber, which was the same size as the flame room. At some point in time, there must have been a structure here for evidence of a shelf remained, its wood mostly rotted away.

"There's a casting hall down there," said Beverly, "and then it dead ends. We think it was used to train mages in ranged magic." She pointed at the corridor that ran to the east.

"There seems to be something glowing," observed Hearn. "Let me shield this." He stood before the lantern, blocking its light. Sure enough, a blue glow emanated from the casting hall.

Beverly drew closer, and Hearn, who had now placed the lantern on the floor, followed. At the end of the short corridor was a glass cylinder with metal caps at each end and a glowing blue liquid held within.

"What is it?" she asked.

"Essence of magic," said Hearn in awe, "or mana, if you prefer that term." He turned to call out, "Revi, you must come and see this."

It didn't take long for the Life Mage to appear, Hayley quick on his heels. Revi brought his orb of light, revealing the cylinder in more detail.

"Good Gods," said Revi in astonishment.

"I don't understand," said Hayley. "What, exactly, is it?"

"It's pure magical energy," said Revi, "the same thing that gives a mage their power. It's the essence that's within us."

"Where would they get that from?" asked the ranger.

"They presumably took it from a mage. I can think of no other place it exists."

"More than one mage, I suspect," added Hearn. "It would take many to fill a container of that size."

"Agreed," said Revi.

"How would they do that? Remove it from a mage, I mean?" asked Hayley.

"A good question," said Hearn. "Through a spell, I would suspect. We know that Necromancers can leech power from other mages, perhaps it's a variation on that."

"Why is it here?" asked Beverly. "You don't think they found it here, do you?"

"No," said Revi, "this cylinder looks more recent."

"Yes," agreed Hearn, "though I cannot fathom where it came from, its purpose seems clear. They must have thought to use it to power the flame."

"Would that even work?" asked the ranger.

"They likely thought it would," said Revi.

"How rare is that stuff?" asked Beverly.

"Very rare," said Hearn, "perhaps the rarest of all liquids. It must have taken a lot of work to gather so much."

"Then we take it," said Beverly.

"To do what?" asked Hearn.

"To deny it to our enemies, they must value it highly. If we take it, it will cripple their plans, don't you think?"

"I do," agreed Revi, "though we must take care when transporting it. There's no telling what might happen if the container were to break."

"What do you mean?" asked Hayley.

"That is raw magical energy," said Revi. "It could open a rift or bring forth foul creatures beyond our understanding."

"Or it could just make a mess," added Hearn. "They are all possible outcomes."

"You're not exactly filling me with confidence," said Beverly, "but we need to get moving. We can't linger here all night."

"I'll take it," the ranger said, pulling off her cloak.

"Wrap it carefully, Hayley," said Revi.

"Yes," said Hearn, "we don't want it to break."

"You've made that abundantly clear," she replied.

"Let's go," said Beverly, "we need to get back to camp and make some plans."

Heward held the cylinder, examining its contents. "This is quite the discovery you've made. Do we return to Tewsbury now?"

"No," said Revi, "we need Summers."

"You have these, isn't that enough?" asked Heward, hefting the cylinder and looking to the rune stone before them.

"Yes," agreed Revi, "but we don't know how much has been passed on to Penelope."

"And," added Hearn, "we need Summers' notes."

"Then let's attack their camp in the morning and take them," said Heward.

"He might have time to destroy his notes," pleaded Hearn.

"I have a better idea," said Beverly.

"We're listening, Bev. Tell us what you're thinking."

"Revi, imagine you're this scholar, Summers. Your camp is attacked. What is the first thing you do?"

"I grab my research and run," said the mage.

"Wouldn't you be more interested in getting away?" asked the ranger.

"Without my research?" Revi replied. "I think not!"

"Precisely," said Beverly. "What I propose is that we have Heward and the horsemen attack the camp from the west. We'll deploy Hayley and the Orcs to the east. They'll keep an eye out for Summers fleeing the scene."

"Wouldn't he just go after a horse?" asked Hayley.

"I can take care of that," offered Hearn. "Rest assured, he won't be riding anywhere."

"That's it then," said Beverly. "First thing tomorrow morning we'll carry out the operation."

"The princess always likes to name her operations," said Hayley. "How about operation 'Rock and a Hard Place.'"

Beverly grinned, "I like it. Now, let's get some sleep, people, it's going to be a busy day tomorrow."

TWENTY-EIGHT

The Raid

SUMMER 962 MC

~

H eward and Beverly sat on their horses, waiting for the early morning mist to dissipate.

"How much longer?" asked the Axe.

"Till we see Shellbreaker," Beverly replied. "When he circles the camp, we'll know the others are in position."

"What about Hearn?" he asked.

"What about him?"

"How do we know he's in position?"

"Revi will know, he can see through the bird's eyes."

"I still can't get used to these mages," said Heward.

"They're not so bad once you get to know them," she replied.

The mist grew thinner, and soon they could make out the shapes of tents in the distance.

"Any time now," said Heward. "I can see a group of people over by the fire. One of them looks like that scholar of yours."

"Keep an eye on him," she said, "while I watch for the bird, we don't want to miss the signal." A moment later Beverly spotted Shellbreaker, his black wings letting him coast on a current of air. "I see him. It's time to move forward."

They rode forth, the other Bodden horse to left and right forming a ragged line.

"Loosen up the formation," she called out, "we're supposed to be raiders, not professional soldiers."

The horses drew closer to the camp, the distinctive jingle of their harnesses breaking the stillness of the early morning air.

Someone, perhaps a guard, shouted out a warning and soon the call was taken up throughout the camp. Men were running back and forth, seeking weapons. Beverly's eyes locked on the scholar who rushed towards a tent. She adjusted her angle of approach to give him some time, and her men followed suit.

Heward had already drawn his axe, and now he spurred forward. A sentry tried to spear him, but the knight's weapon cut through the flimsy wooden shaft and buried itself into the man's chest. The knight gave a mighty heave, freeing it, and continued his advance.

Beverly stabbed out absently, cutting into a soldier's arm. The man fell back, clutching the wound while she scanned the area once more for the scholar.

She spotted him emerging from a nearby tent, a book tucked securely under his arm. He looked around wildly in a state of panic. Beverly cut to the south then roared a challenge. Summers heard the sound and fled northward, toward the horses.

~

Aldus Hearn looked across the field to where the horses grazed. He heard cries of alarm in the distance, so he raised his hands and began casting. The familiar buzz drew closer and then he released the spell. He felt the wave leave him, could almost see it as it travelled across the field to the waiting horses.

One moment they were grazing happily, the next they were looking up in his direction. He continued the incantation, and the beasts started trotting toward him, beckoned by his magic. The horses were quite cooperative, but the guards were less so. A cry of alarm rang out as soon as the mounts started moving. Moments later, two soldiers came running toward the Earth Mage.

Hearn watched them come closer, his spell of animal summoning now complete. Holding his hands up in the air again, he used the words of power. Small lights gathered around his fingertips, and then he lowered his hands, pointing them at the ground before him. The lights sank into the earth, to be replaced by four figures of light that gradually took form.

The guards slowed as they witnessed the power of his magic, then stopped as the lights coalesced into the forms of wolves. It didn't take long for the guards to react; they quickly turned and ran in fear. Hearn thought to send the wolves in pursuit but decided against it. After all, they might be needed elsewhere.

Revi's eyes were shut while Hayley waited beside him, watching the camp from the east. "Can you see him?" she asked.

"Yes," he said, his head bobbing up and down. "He's heading north toward the horses, then again, maybe not."

"Why, what's happening?"

"Someone's running south, toward him in a panic. They're waving him off."

"Aldus must be doing his part," she mused.

"He's turning toward us," said Revi. "You'll see him any time now. In fact," he opened his eyes and pointed, "right about there."

On cue, Summers appeared, running for all he was worth, but instead of heading for the woods, he picked a large fallen tree to dive behind. He turned his back to the woods and watched the camp.

"What's he doing?" complained Revi. "He's supposed to run into the woods."

"He's scared," said Hayley, "he's looking for help."

"Well, I'm not waiting any longer," said the mage, and began casting his spell. The air buzzed with energy as he called forth the magic within him.

Hayley had seen it all before, of course, but never tired of watching him exercise his arcane power. A moment later the scholar fell to the forest floor in a deep slumber.

"*Go,*" yelled Hayley, pointing. Four Orcs leaped to their feet. Two ran with their bows notched, ready to take down any opposition, while the other's headed straight for Summers. Soon, they were standing over him, binding his arms and legs. They hefted the unfortunate scholar into the air, carrying him back to the wood line as the others covered their retreat.

"We have him," said Hayley.

"Good," said Revi. "Get him back out of the way, and I'll give the signal." His hands began to move again, and the familiar orb of light rose into the air.

Beverly noticed the brilliant light hanging over the woods. "Time to finish it up," she yelled.

The attack now began in earnest as the horsemen of Bodden hunted

down their enemies. Most of the soldiers surrendered while the mercenaries fought to the last man. They made a final stand near the centre tent,
but it was more of a slaughter than a battle. Hayley brought the Orcs closer
and finished them off by bow shots after they refused to surrender.

Beverly looked down at the bodies in disgust. "What a waste of life," she
stated.

A new group of people started making their way into the camp, Aldus
Hearn at their head. "I took the liberty of releasing the slaves," he called out,
"though I daresay they could use a heal or two from Master Bloom."

Beverly turned to Heward, "How many prisoners?"

"About a dozen, all of them soldiers of the king, no doubt from Mattingly's garrison. The man in charge of them is only a sergeant. I doubt he
knows much about the expedition itself."

"We'll take them all with us to Mattingly first and get these commoners
returned to their homes," she said. "Then take the prisoners with us back to
Tewsbury, along with the scholar, but first we'll have to have a word or two
with him."

"What about the dig?" he asked.

"Hearn said he could move earth. Let's see if he can re-bury the temple.
It's best it remain undiscovered for now."

"But won't the Dark Queen already know it exists?"

"Yes," said Beverly, "but we're about to march on Wincaster. Things will
be far too hectic for her to organize another expedition."

Two days later they had returned to Mattingly. At Beverly's suggestion, they
had not yet interrogated the scholar, letting him fret over his fate as they
rode. The villagers of Mattingly were overjoyed to see the return of their
loved ones, and the new garrison of footmen, sent by Gerald, were more
than happy to put the prisoners to work.

They kept Summers in a locked room while they made their arrangements. By late evening, they were finally ready to question him. Beverly
brought him to the tavern, which had been cleared of villagers for the occasion. Revi, Hayley, Aldus Hearn and Captain Foster, the local garrison
commander, were all in attendance.

Beverly sat the man down at the table, his interrogators arrayed in front
of him like a jury. By agreement, they had decided that Revi should lead the
proceedings since he was the one most familiar with the Dark Queen and
her methods.

"You are Mathias Summers," said Revi, "is that correct?"

"It is," the man replied, "but surely there's been some kind of misunderstanding."

"You were hired, were you not, to undertake the excavation at the behest of Lady Penelope Cromwell?"

"I was, but there is nothing unusual in that. She is a patron of the arts, after all."

Revi looked to Hearn in surprise, but the old mage merely shrugged.

"What is the purpose of your expedition?" asked Hearn.

"As you may or may not know," began the scholar, "for many years I have been researching the ancestry of Humans in this land. Not our mercenary forefathers, mind you, but the original Human inhabitants."

"And what have you discovered?" asked Revi.

The man leaned forward, his excitement evident to all. "It was a most fortuitous circumstance that led me here. I was at the Great Library in Shrewesdale when I received word that my expertise was sought in Wincaster. Someone was interested in my research and, quite frankly, the request came with a generous donation of coins."

"And so you travelled to Wincaster," said Hayley, "where you were surprised to meet Lady Penelope?"

"Yes," he admitted. "She told me she had read my work on our Human ancestors and she agreed with my findings."

"Wait," said Beverly, "what findings do you speak of?"

"Well," he continued, "it is my theory that all of the mages that live within the realms today are descended from these ancient Humans."

"So your entire hypothesis," said Revi, "is that the mercenaries that came here had no mages?"

"Precisely," the man replied, sitting back and smiling.

"And what led you to this conclusion?" asked Aldus.

"I have searched through ancient records," he said. "I can tell you it wasn't easy, but I found muster lists from our original mercenary ancestors, but there was no mention of mages."

"That's it?" asked Revi.

"What do you mean, that's it? Of course, that's it. What other conclusion could I make?"

"Did it ever occur to you," asked Revi, "that a simple muster list wouldn't have that information?"

"A list like that," added Beverly, "wouldn't even specify if someone was a horseman or a footman."

"Now, had you managed to find pay records," said Hayley, "they would have been much more informative."

"But you don't understand," said Summers, "the ruins, they prove my hypothesis."

"How so?" asked Revi.

"The ruins are clearly the work of early Humans."

Revi sat back in astonishment. "Why would you say that? Couldn't another race have made them?"

"When the architecture so closely resembles our own? I think that unlikely."

"How do you explain the strange writing on the slates?" asked Aldus.

"Obviously an ancient tongue," the scholar replied. "When our mercenary forefathers came, their own language naturally took precedence."

Beverly leaned forward, "Then how do you explain the fact that Weldwyn speaks the same language as us? They were never conquered."

The scholar looked stunned, "I have no explanation for that, but it doesn't invalidate my research."

"You're research is flawed at the most basic level," offered Hearn, "though I must admit it's of some interest to us. You say that Lady Penelope agreed with your conclusions?"

"She did," he said with pride. "She related to me how she had received word of an ancient ruin that might serve as proof and offered to fund an expedition there."

"Did she say who informed her of the site?" asked Revi.

"Unfortunately, no," he replied, "and the location wasn't precise, but luckily we were able to find it using my calculations."

"What calculations are those?" asked Revi. "You have me intrigued."

"Are you familiar with the concept of ley lines?" asked Summers.

Revi looked nervously at Aldus Hearn and saw the look of shock on his face. He returned his attention to Summers and tried to appear calm. "Vaguely, why?"

"Ley lines," began the scholar, "are lines of power that run north and south. They are said to carry great energies that mages can tap into."

"And these 'Ley Lines'," said Revi with emphasis, "what have they got to do with the ruin?"

"The ruins lie directly over one of them," Summers said with satisfaction. "That is what led me to the area."

"I thought you said Penelope gave you the location?" asked Beverly.

"She did, in a very general sense. It was my calculations that pinned down the precise location. Once we arrived, it was a simple matter of looking for a mound."

"A mound?" asked Hayley.

"Yes, a mound of earth. Our Human ancestors built temples underground."

"We looked through the ruins," said Revi. "How do you explain the pictures of lizard men on the walls?"

"Simple," said Summers, obviously pleased with himself, "our ancestors worshipped gods that took that form. It's only natural for a primitive people to do so."

"An interesting theory," said Aldus. "You've given us much to consider. Tell me, we found bricks with runes on them, what do you propose their purpose was?"

"They confused me at first. They were stacked in a sort of miniature pyramid, you see, the runes facing outward. I rather suspect the room might have been a classroom of some type. We may have found evidence of Humans developing the written word!"

"Astounding," said Revi. "And what of the container of blue liquid we found?"

"The liquid?" asked Summers. "Oh, yes, I'd forgotten about that."

"What is it for?" asked Aldus Hearn.

"It was supplied by Lady Penelope," explained Summers. "She indicated it was a Dwarven invention; a mechanical device that produces light. She was going to come and demonstrate its use once the ruins were fully excavated, but we never got to that point."

"I think we're done here," said Revi.

"No, wait," said Aldus Hearn, "just one more question?"

Revi nodded, and the old mage continued, "How much of this did you report to Lady Penelope?"

"I wrote a number of times," Summers responded, "telling of our initial discovery and its location. I filed my last report about a month ago, just before we breached the ruin."

"You didn't enter the ruins right away?" asked Hearn.

"No, I wanted to clear the dirt away first, so that we could determine its layout."

"So you never told your benefactor about the rune stones?" asked Revi.

"Rune stones? Why would you call them that? It is an ancient alphabet, nothing more," defended Summers.

"NOW I think we're done," said Aldus.

"Agreed," said Revi. "Take him back to his room."

Beverly marched him off while the others waited for her return.

Once she sat down, the conversation continued.

"The man has absolutely no idea it's a gate location," said Hearn.

"Agreed," said Revi, "nor does he know the magical alphabet when he sees it. A surprising lapse for a scholar."

"He must be self-taught," said Hearn. "I knew the arcane symbols long before I discovered my inner magic."

"He has strange ideas," said Beverly. "Where does he get them from?"

"Not so strange when you consider things," said Revi. "After all, he does not know of the Saurians."

"I have looked through his notes," said Aldus, "and I think I can safely say the man is... How shall I put it?"

"Convinced that Humans are the superior race?" suggested Beverly.

"Yes, precisely. His prejudice has blinded him. Every piece of evidence, every discovery has been twisted to support his claim. I've read about others who thought this way. Back when Merceria was expanding, they'd come up against the Elves of the Darkwood and had taken heavy casualties. There was some talk of a peace agreement, but the king wouldn't have it. He decreed that Humans were a superior race and then ordered his scholars to find proof. Of course, most of that research is discredited today."

"So where does that leave us?" asked Beverly. "Do you think Penelope knows about the gates or not?"

"I think we can assume that she knows about the existence of them, though perhaps not their precise locations. We saw evidence in Westland that the Elves had destroyed the Saurians, wiping them out."

"Or so they thought," added Hayley.

"Yes," Revi agreed, "they didn't know there were survivors."

"If they knew of the gates," asked Hearn, "why didn't Penelope go searching for the others, like Uxley?"

"I'm guessing her information was incomplete. The war that eliminated the Saurians was fought a very long time ago, perhaps even generations before Penelope's birth. She might have assumed they were all destroyed."

"Then why the sudden interest now?" asked Hearn.

"A good question," said Revi, "one to which we might never know the answer. It's clear that Summers knows nothing of value to us."

"Other than confirming Penelope has failed," corrected Hayley.

"Thank Saxnor for that," said Hearn. "I shouldn't like to contemplate the alternative."

"Perhaps we'll learn more when we reach Wincaster," suggested Beverly.

"Yes," agreed Revi, "a search of her tower might prove most illuminating."

"Tell me," said Aldus, "you mentioned the tower of Andronicus. Should we be able to find it, do you think it might reveal anything of this mystery?"

"I doubt it," said Revi. "Andronicus didn't impress me as the type to take an interest in such things. He was more interested in perfecting his spells."

"What type of spells?" asked Hearn.

"Many," replied Revi, "but the one that drove him mad was teleportation."

"Which is?" asked Hayley.

"It would be like using the gates but could be cast anywhere. He started showing signs of insanity shortly after he began his research."

"Albreda can do that now," Beverly noted. "She called it a spell of recall. I saw her use it in Queenston."

"Astounding," said Hearn. "I've heard of Albreda before, of course, but until I came to Tewsbury, I'd never met her. Who was her mentor?"

"She had none," answered Beverly. "She's a wild mage."

Aldus Hearn sat back in response, a look of shock on his face. "A dangerous breed."

"Why," asked Beverly, "because she wasn't trained?"

"There are safeguards that all mages are taught, all trained mages, that is. Without these safeguards, control could be lost."

"What kind of safeguards?" asked the knight.

"Mental exercises, mostly," he replied.

"I think you're missing the point," said Beverly, defensively. "Without these limitations she's been able to create powerful spells. Perhaps these mental exercises you speak of are limiting your own power."

"That's an interesting premise," reflected Revi. "I must give it some thought."

"Surely you're not suggesting we abandon our teachings?" asked Hearn.

"Abandon? No, of course not, but perhaps it's time we re-evaluate them."

"I don't understand," said Hayley. "Don't you just let the magic flow through you?"

"No," replied Revi. "If we let all that raw power spill forth, we'd likely die, or at least that's been the reasoning for generations. The flow of magic must be tightly controlled, just as Beverly will tell you that sometimes a blow with a weapon must be controlled. Without these exercises, the energy would pour out in an uncontrolled manner."

"I'm still not sure I understand," she said.

"Imagine a river of water," said Revi. "To harness the power of the river, we build a water wheel. Surely you've seen those?"

"Yes, of course," Hayley replied.

"Well, the water wheel only harnesses a portion of the river. If we diverted the whole river toward the water wheel, the force of it would likely break it."

"I suppose that makes sense," said Hayley.

"I'd have to disagree," said Beverly. "I'm no mage, but I've seen Albreda's magic. I think she could take a whole river and more."

"Your loyalty to her is commendable," said Aldus Hearn, "but we can only speculate at the moment. No one knows for sure, but it is definitely a subject worth exploring at a later date."

"I agree," said Revi, "and I think Albreda would be more than willing to assist, but for now we must temporarily put it to rest. There are far more important things to see to."

"On that, we are in agreement," said Hearn. "We must examine the vial of mana in more detail once the capital has been retaken, and there's the matter of possibly restoring the Mattingly Mound."

"The Mattingly Mound?" queried Hayley.

"It's as good a name as any," added Revi, "what else would we call it? You know, I have some thoughts on how it might be repaired."

"Fascinating," said Aldus, "I may have been thinking along parallel lines."

"I think it's about time we were on our way," interrupted Hayley. "Bev, how soon can we ride?"

"First thing in the morning," the knight replied, "but what do you want to do with Summers?"

"He's not much use to us," said Revi. "We'll leave him here. I take it that's all right with you, Captain?"

Captain Foster, who had dozed off during the interrogation awoke with a start. "Pardon me?" he said.

"We wondered," said Beverly, "if we might leave our prisoner in your care while we return to Tewsbury."

"Is he dangerous?" asked the captain.

"Only in his opinions," said Revi.

"Then I see no problem. I'll keep him locked up with the others."

"I doubt he'll be much use as a worker," said Beverly.

"Then he won't do labour like the rest of the prisoners."

"It's important that he is unable to send word to anyone," added Beverly.

"Understood," replied the captain. "Anything else?"

"No, that's all," said the knight. "We ride in the morning."

"Then I wish you safe travels," said Captain Foster.

TWENTY-NINE

The Army Marches

SUMMER 962 MC

⁓

G erald stabbed down with his fork, puncturing the skin of the sausage. "This looks delicious," he said as the juices dribbled out.

"Careful, they're hot," said Anna, who delicately sliced her own. "How are yours, Aubrey?"

"I'm waiting for mine to cool down a bit," the young mage replied, "but the rest is very nice. Do you do this every day?"

"What, have breakfast?" asked Gerald.

"We try to have breakfast together whenever possible," said Anna. "It lets us catch up on things. Gerald keeps very busy these days, what with the army and everything."

"And what do you do to keep busy, Highness?"

"There's a lot for me to do," Anna replied. "I have to plan out all the changes I need to make once this war is over. I thought I might enlist you to give me a hand, actually."

"I should be delighted," responded the mage. "What kind of things are you looking at?"

"I've given it quite a bit of thought," began Anna, "and so there are both short term and long term goals. Where would you like to start?"

"How about the short term?"

"Of course the results of the siege will have a big effect since we don't know what we'll find inside the capital, but one of the first things will have to be an amnesty for all nobles, at least those that surrender."

"Just like that? You're going to pardon them?"

"As I said," said Anna, "only for those that surrender. I won't negotiate with anyone that holds out. After that, the next step will be to repopulate the ranks of the nobility. We've lost nobles on both sides. The titles will have to be given to someone. We'll need that complete to form a proper noble's council, then we can start changing laws."

"I rather gather you've some particular laws in mind," said Aubrey.

"I do," said Anna. "The first thing I'm going to do is change the law of succession and rulership."

"How so?"

"My firstborn child will rule after my death, regardless of whether it's a boy or girl."

"I expect you'll see some opposition to that," commented Aubrey. "I can't see it going easily."

"Oh, I don't know, I think we have broad support. I've already brought it up with a number of important people, and Baron Fitzwilliam agrees with me."

"On that, I have no doubt," said Aubrey. "He's made no secret of the fact that he wants Beverly to inherit. I can't see him happy with her husband taking all the power."

"I doubt Aldwin would be like that," said Anna.

Gerald, who was halfway through a sausage, looked up in alarm, "Who told you about Aldwin?"

"I saw him with Beverly in town, right here in Tewsbury. It was pretty obvious the affection they have for each other. Does that shock you?"

"No, I've known about it for years. I'm just surprised you knew about it."

"I'm a very observant person," said Anna. "Did you know about it, Aubrey?"

"I did, Highness," replied the mage. "I learned some years ago when my cousin came to visit. I was very young at the time, but I could tell she was in love."

"Then I see no problem here," said Anna. "I think Beverly should be able to marry whomever she pleases, don't you?"

"I do," agreed Gerald, "but she IS a noble. By convention, it requires the king's permission, or queen's, in this case."

"I would hardly object to the marriage," said Anna, "but I shouldn't have to approve it. Marriage should not be at the whim of the monarch. That's another change I intend to make."

"Tell her about the crown," suggested Gerald.

"The crown?" said Aubrey. "What about the crown?"

"In the past," said Anna, "when a queen is crowned, it is usually her husband that rules. I intend to change that."

"Intriguing," said Aubrey. "How, precisely, would you change it?"

"When I am crowned queen, it will be for life. My husband..."

"Alric," interrupted Gerald.

"Yes, Alric. He will not rule as king."

"What will he be then?" asked Aubrey. "He should have some sort of title, don't you think?"

"Yes," agreed Gerald, "and I'm curious if you've discussed this with King Leofric. I'd be interested in his opinion. He is, after all, Alric's father."

"I have discussed it with Alric," Anna confessed, "though I have not breached the subject with his father."

"And," asked Gerald, "how did Alric take it?"

"Remarkably well," she replied. "He has never seen himself as a king. After all, he's third in line to the crown of Weldwyn. He's quite happy to be a prince."

"Prince Consort then," suggested Aubrey. "That has a nice ring to it."

"It does, doesn't it," said Anna. "I think I'll suggest that."

"You'll need to give him something to do," said Aubrey. "If he's not going to rule, you need to keep him busy."

"I can use him in the army," said Gerald. "I think he'd like that."

"You'd have to be clear on the chain of command," said Aubrey.

"Don't worry," said Anna, "Alric respects Gerald. I don't think that will be a problem. You're full of good ideas Aubrey. I think I'll keep you close."

"Fine by me, Highness," said Aubrey. "I can eat food like this every day without any worries at all."

Anna laughed, and Gerald smiled. It was good to see her in a relaxed atmosphere around friends, without the stress and pressures of ruling.

"You know," said Gerald, "you should enjoy this peace and quiet while you can. Once you're queen, your days will be filled with problems."

"They will, won't they," mused Anna.

"Don't worry, Highness," said Aubrey, "we'll keep you entertained." She stuffed the end of a sausage into her mouth and made a face.

Gerald laughed so hard he almost choked on his food.

"Are you all right, Gerald?" asked Anna.

He held up his hand as he coughed. "I'm fine," he finally said, "I just wasn't expecting that."

"Now that our general has finished almost killing himself," said Aubrey, "what are some of your long term plans?"

"I want to alter the legal system. Our laws only favour those in power. I want justice for all."

"Fair laws for the common man. Very interesting," said Aubrey.

"Yes, I've been thinking on that one for some time. Currently, the magistrates are all appointed by nobles. That gives the earls and dukes considerable power. I've never heard of a trial that wasn't in a noble's favour, have you?"

"No," replied the mage, "but my father seldom used the courts. He believed in fair and just rulership."

"As does Baron Fitzwilliam," added Anna, "but they are few and far between. Beverly experienced that herself, back in Shrewesdale."

"I don't think I've heard that story," said Aubrey.

"She was sent to chase down some bandits," Anna began, "but instead she found a bunch of starving farmers. The Earl of Shrewesdale had driven them from their homes."

"That's terrible. What happened?"

"They were led by a mercenary," she said.

"Yes," added Gerald, "the dreaded Bandit King."

"That's right," said Anna. "She killed him and put an end to his reign of terror."

"What happened to the farmers?" asked Aubrey.

"Beverly sent them to Bodden, where they still live. One of them even joined the baron's archers."

"A very interesting tale," said the mage, "though I rather suspect there's more to the story."

"Oh, there is," said Gerald. "You'll have to get Beverly to tell it to you sometime."

"I shall," she confirmed, "providing I can pry her away from Aldwin."

"That reminds me," added Anna, "I received some good news today from Kingsford."

"Oh," said Gerald, "what news is that?"

"More reinforcements are on the way. King Leofric has been kind enough to offer them to us. They're waiting for permission to cross the border."

"That IS good news," said Gerald. "Any idea as to numbers?"

"Yes, a thousand men, mostly footmen and archers."

"I see," said Gerald, winking at Aubrey, "and do we have any idea who might be commanding them?"

Anna blushed, and Gerald broke into a smile. "I take it that means Prince Alric, himself?"

"It does," confirmed the princess.

"Excellent news," said Gerald. "It means we can accelerate our plans."

"I agree," said Anna. "I'd like to start by liberating Uxley. I wish to pay a visit."

"I can understand our interest in freeing the place," said Gerald, "but why now. Can't it wait until after the war is over?"

"No," said Anna, "there's something I need to take care of."

"What is that?" he asked.

"I've been talking to Aubrey here, and I think she might be able to heal Hanson."

"Alistair? Is that true, Aubrey?"

"From what Her Highness has told me of his affliction, I think I can. I believe a regeneration would do the trick. My great-grandmother had notes on such things."

"The same spell you used on Lightning's leg?" he asked.

"Yes, that's the one."

"But it took a week to cure Lightning, didn't it?"

"True, but I had to regenerate an entire limb. I rather suspect that in Hanson's case it might only take one or two castings."

"Couldn't you just cast it multiple times in one day?" suggested Anna.

"The magic doesn't work that way, Highness. The spell takes time to take effect. Though I can cast the spell multiple times, it will only affect a patient once a day. It would be like bandaging a wound that was already bandaged. Does that make sense?"

"I think I see now," said Anna.

"I don't," grumbled Gerald.

"When she casts the spell, the body begins its own regeneration. Until that is complete, another casting will have limited or no effect. Did I get that correct?"

"You did, Highness."

"Now THAT I understand," said Gerald. "It's like my teeth."

"Your teeth?" asked Aubrey.

"Yes, I had them regenerated by the Orcs after the guards at Wincaster removed them."

"How awful," said Aubrey.

"That wasn't the half of it," said Anna, "they almost killed him. It was actually Kraloch, the Orc shaman that cast the spell."

"I should very much like to swap notes with him," said Aubrey.

"That's a marvellous idea," added Anna. "You mages should do that more often."

"Up until now there haven't been many mages to share information with," said Aubrey.

"I shall have to change that under my rule," said Anna.

"You're not queen yet," warned Gerald. "May I remind you we still have a challenging task ahead, the taking of Wincaster."

"True," said Anna, "but I know we'll be successful."

"And how do you know, Highness?"

"Because Gerald is here with me." Anna ended the conversation by stuffing a piece of toast into her mouth. She chewed it slowly, and Aubrey could almost see the princess's mind working as she looked around absently at the room.

"She's thinking," explained Gerald.

"I noticed," added Aubrey.

"Is it that obvious?" asked Anna.

"Tell me, Anna, what is it that occupies your mind this time?"

"I was thinking about the heavy cavalry."

"What about them?" asked Gerald.

"The name doesn't do them justice. They're more than just heavily armoured horsemen; we need a new name."

"Such as?" asked Gerald.

"Such as the Royal Guard?" suggested Anna.

"You already have a Royal Guard. Foot soldiers, remember? Granted they're not the original guard. We lost those poor souls when we were taken prisoner."

"How about 'Guard Cavalry'?" suggested Aubrey.

"I like that," said Anna, "and I believe Beverly would like it as well. What do you think, Gerald?"

"It's a good name," he answered, "and it'll give them a sense of pride. You're good at this Aubrey, have you been taking tips from Arnim?"

"Sir Arnim Caster?" said Aubrey. "No, why?"

"He likes to name things," explained Anna.

Gerald, finally finished with his meal, placed his knife and fork on the table. A servant scurried forward to carry it away.

"Well," he said, "if we're to move forward, I must be off. I have orders to issue and a supply chain to organize."

"That sounds like a lot of work," said Aubrey.

"I have Baron Fitzwilliam to help, he's very good at that sort of thing."

"Don't work too hard," said Anna, "and remember to take a break from time to time. I'll send Sophie around later to check up on you. I can't have you passing out again."

"Does he need a heal?" asked Aubrey.

"No, but sometimes he gets so busy he forgets to eat," chided Anna.

Aubrey looked down at her plate, still half full from her breakfast. "A meal like this will last me all day."

"Yes," said Anna, "but you're not a soldier."

Gerald rose from his seat and was about to leave when Anna interrupted him.

"There's still some scones left. Why don't you take them for later."

He scooped two of them up in his hands and grinned.

"I'll expect you here for dinner," she said.

"Of course," he said, then left the room.

The room fell quiet, but for the sound of snoring.

"What's that?" asked Aubrey.

Anna looked down beside her chair, "That's Tempus. He never leaves my side."

"Does he sleep all the time?" asked Aubrey.

"No," she responded, "but the older he gets, the more he does. He sometimes finds it hard to move about, particularly if he's been sleeping on a cold floor."

"May I try a regeneration on him?" asked the mage. "I'm sure it would help."

"What a marvellous idea," said Anna. "You mean right now?"

"I can think of no better time, can you?"

"Very well," said Anna. "I've only seen regeneration cast once, back with the Orcs, though I heard all about Lightning, of course."

"There's not much to see," said Aubrey. "You've watched a heal before?"

"Of course."

"It's very similar, but my hands will turn orange while I cast."

"Whenever you're ready, then," said Anna.

Aubrey rose from her seat, coming round the table to where Tempus lay asleep at Anna's side. She began casting the spell, uttering the words to bring forth the power from within her. The air buzzed and then her fingers began to glow bright orange as if they were on fire. Her casting complete, she placed her hands onto the faithful dog and the colour soaked into the mighty mastiff's skin, dissipating quickly.

Tempus opened his eyes, barked and wagged his tail.

"He likes that," said Anna.

"We'll give him another treatment tomorrow," said Aubrey, "if you think he's up to it."

As if in answer, Tempus sat up, barking again.

"Well I must say," said Anna, "I haven't seen him this energetic in quite some time."

"How old did you say he was?" asked Aubrey.

"I'm not sure," said Anna. "I first met him when I was a little girl, and he was old even then."

"Then I would recommend regular treatments, perhaps once a month or so. There's no reason he shouldn't live for years yet, barring misfortune."

"Thank you, Aubrey, you've made me very happy. You know, I think I'm going to like having you around here again. You're probably the closest person to my age that I know."

Gerald sat on his horse while the troops marched by. It promised to be a sunny day, and the roads were dry; things were looking up. Hearing the sound of a galloping horse, he turned to see Beverly approaching.

"I heard you were back," he said. "How did your little expedition go?"

"It went well," she replied. "I just finished filling in the princess. She tells me we're finally moving south."

"Yes, we are," he responded, "and we have new troops joining us, thanks to Weldwyn."

"That's excellent news," she said.

"It is, isn't it. Did you hear about the Guard Cavalry?"

"I did. I like the name."

"I knew you would. We've sent the light horse south, to scout the outskirts of Wincaster."

"So," Beverly mused, "the final phase of the war is starting."

"Yes," said Gerald. "Nervous?"

"Of course," she replied. "Wincaster is a large city; a siege there will be difficult."

"And time-consuming," he added. "Of that, I have no doubt."

"Do you have a plan for the siege?"

"I do, but I'll have to modify it once we see the city. It's hard to plan things when your knowledge is based on memories rather than maps."

"We'll need siege engines," she suggested.

"All in good time. We have to seal up the city first, and that's where you come in."

"Go on," she urged.

"I'm giving you overall command of all the horse. Your job will be to force them to close the gates to the city. Do you think you can do that?"

"How many horsemen do I have? It's a big city."

"In addition to the Kurathians, you'll have the Weldwyn horse, the Mercerians and, of course, the Guard Cavalry. Oh, and don't forget the Bodden horse."

"Any particular instructions?" she asked.

"Yes, I want you to try to keep the farmers from entering the city, if possible. Assure them we mean no harm, but I don't want the king getting any more food inside their walls."

"They've likely been stockpiling for some time," said Beverly.

"Yes, but Wincaster is the largest city in the realm, that's a lot of mouths to feed. The more we limit their stocks, the better, and the farmers will be out of harm's way if they stay clear."

"Agreed," said Beverly, "but I'll need a second in command in case I go down."

"You have someone in mind?"

"Yes, I'd like Sir Heward. He's professional, and I know I can count on him."

"I'll clear it with your father," said Gerald. "Anything else?"

"How long till the footmen follow? I can't block the gates with just cavalry."

"They're already moving. I suspect you'll have a day's head start on them. We'll be arriving from the west. The real problem will be the east gate. If the king's going to try a breakout, that's where he'll go."

"Don't worry," said Beverly, "we'll seal it up tighter than a bottle of wine. What about a healer? We may have to fight. Can I take Aubrey?"

"The princess needs her here for the short term, but Revi can go with you."

"Good, I'll take Hayley as well," Beverly added. "You know those two are inseparable."

"Cleverly played, my friend, I should have thought of it. She can scout out positions for the archers while you're there. The footmen will be marching quickly under your father and Arnim. Alric will be arriving with the reinforcements from Kingsford, but they still have some distance to travel."

"Prince Alric?"

"Yes, but don't worry, you'll still take your orders from me."

"Understood," said Beverly. "When do we start?"

"You already have," said Gerald. "Your men are moving south, you'll have to hurry to catch them. I'll find Heward and send him along to join you."

"Aye, General," she said, then urged Lightning forward.

"Remember," called out Gerald, "seal the gates!"

He watched her as she easily outpaced the troops that were marching by, the great warhorse tearing across the field.

THIRTY

Uxley

SUMMER 962 MC

"There's the main gate," said Gerald. "It hasn't changed a bit."

"A few more weeds than I remember," said Anna.

They passed beneath the immense archway that housed the gate. Lady Aubrey looked around at the grounds as Tempus ran down the pathway.

"He seems in fine form," said Gerald.

"He does, doesn't he," the princess confirmed. "Aubrey's magic has done wonders for him. Look at him, running through the long grass. What do you think, Aubrey?"

"It's nice," replied the mage. "Is this where you were born?"

"No," Anna replied, "I was actually born near Hawksburg, or so I'm led to believe, but I did grow up here. This is where I first met Gerald. He came to look after the grounds."

Aubrey returned her gaze to the choking weeds, "It appears they miss you, General. The grounds hereabouts are quite overgrown."

"So they are," he agreed. "We'll have to see who's in charge these days."

"My couriers tell me Margaret and her guards are no longer here," said Anna.

"Just the staff, then," he replied. "I rather suspect that the estate has fallen into disuse, what with the war and such."

"Yes," said Anna, "I don't imagine they've had funds for some time. I would think a lot of the staff have left."

"True," said Gerald, "though I still think we should have brought Sophie."

"She enjoys helping out with the army. We'll get her here eventually.

Once I'm queen, I intend to make this my official residence. I'll use it anytime I want to get away from the capital for a few days."

"It looks nice," said Aubrey, "though I daresay it needs some repairs."

"Nothing a few coins can't cure," said Gerald.

"Are we sure this place isn't deserted?" asked Aubrey.

"Our scouts reported seeing lights in some of the windows the last few nights," said Gerald. "Perhaps we should have sent some troops inside?"

"No," said Anna, "the king's people have long since fled, and I'd like to be the first to set foot back in Uxley Hall."

They were nearing the house now. The roadway turned into a loop that ran to the front door. Tempus tore across the ground, running in circles and barking loudly. Gerald brought his horse to a stop, the others following his lead. Tempus barked one more time then ran back to them.

"It doesn't look like anyone's home," said Anna.

Just then a figure emerged from the stables, and the familiar looking man made his way toward them.

"As I live and breathe," the man called out, "if it isn't Gerald Matheson."

"Jim Turner, you old rogue," called back Gerald, "it's good to see you."

"Do you not remember me?" asked Anna.

Turner turned to examine her face then suddenly bowed. "My apologies, Highness, you've grown so much I didn't recognize you."

"I'm not a little girl anymore," she mused, a smile coming to her face.

"Indeed not, Your Highness," the man fumbled.

"This is Lady Aubrey Brandon," she continued, "Baroness of Hawksburg."

"Baroness?" said Aubrey in surprise.

"Yes, with the unfortunate demise of your family, the title falls to you. Did you not realize?"

"I suppose I didn't think of it," said Aubrey.

"I know it's a shock," said Anna, "but it's important to recognize your title. Hopefully, we will soon be rebuilding a kingdom, and we'll have to deal with the trials and tribulations of court. Your title will come in handy."

"May I take your horses?" asked Turner.

"Have you no stable boys to help?" asked Gerald.

"I'm afraid not," the stable master apologized. "The funds have ceased, you see."

"How do you get by?" asked Gerald.

"Cook grows some vegetables, and we sell them in the village."

"Come," said Gerald, "I'll help with the horses while the ladies go inside."

They started heading toward the stables while Anna and Aubrey entered the house.

"I take it there are no guests at present?" asked Gerald.

"No," said Turner, "there hasn't been a guest here since Princess Margaret left last fall."

"How many staff are left?"

"Me, Hanson, Cook and two maids, it's all we can afford."

"I'm glad to hear Alistair's still here. How is the old man?"

"He gets about the house with help, but the side of his face still doesn't work, and at times he can be difficult to understand."

They walked through the large stable entrance. "Tell me, Gerald, what brings you back to Uxley?" asked the stable master.

"The princess remembers the great loyalty and affection of the staff here. She brought Lady Aubrey to heal Hanson."

"The young lady is a healer?" asked Turner.

"More than that," Gerald replied, "she's a powerful Life Mage. We're hoping she can restore him to his former self."

"That IS good news," said Jim, "though I fear there has been little of it of late."

"Why, what's happened?"

"Most of the men of the village have been pressed into service. Only the very old and the very young remain."

"When did this happen?" asked Gerald.

Turner led a horse into a stall, "Just this last spring. Right after some high ranking officer rode through with his staff."

"This officer, did he have a name?" asked Gerald.

"He did, though I don't rightly remember what it was."

"It wasn't Valmar, by chance? Marshal-General Valmar?"

"That was it. I remember, now that you reminded me. You've heard of him?"

"Oh yes, he's been a thorn in our side for some time. He visited Uxley once, along with the king, do you remember?"

"I must confess I remember the king's visit," said Turner, "but there were so many nobles, I couldn't possibly remember them all."

"He wasn't a noble at the time," said Gerald, "he was in charge of the king's bodyguard."

"I think I remember him now, wasn't he a bit of a horse's arse?"

"That's the man."

"Tell me," said Jim, "how goes the war? We've heard so little. I can only assume that, since you're here, it goes well?"

"It does," Gerald confirmed. "In fact, our armies have pushed the king's forces back to Wincaster. The north has been secured, and even as we speak, we're marching to the capital with new troops."

"That's good news."

"Yes, hopefully by the end of the summer this war will be over. I know you're short of funds, but you must hold on a little longer. Once Anna takes the throne I'm sure she'll want to look after Uxley Hall, she sees it as her home. When we return to the army, I'll see if we can spare a little coin. It won't be much, mind you, but it should see you through to the end of the summer."

"That would be appreciated," said Turner. He had now placed the last of the horses in their stalls and began removing their saddles.

"I should get back to the Hall," said Gerald. "I'll leave you to finish up here."

"Of course," said Turner, "it's good to have you back, even if it is a short visit."

Aubrey followed Anna into the estate. The entrance looked large, far larger than Aubrey's own home, and she marvelled at the massive staircase that led up to the balcony above the great hall.

Tempus trotted in behind them, his nails tapping away on the wooden floor.

"Hello?" called out the princess. "Is anyone home?"

"It looks empty," added Aubrey.

The patter of distant feet drifted towards their ears. "Someone's coming," said Anna. "I wonder who it could be?"

A moment later a portly woman appeared from the hall to their left. She stared at the visitors in disbelief.

"Is that you, Highness?" she called out. "I can't believe it!"

"It is indeed, Mrs. Brown," said Anna, delight evident on her face. "Sophie would have come too, but she's busy with the army. I'll bring her on my next visit, I promise."

The old woman came closer, "My goodness, look at you." Her eyes wandered to Aubrey, "And who's this you've brought with you?"

Aubrey bowed slightly as she introduced herself. "Lady Aubrey Brandon," she said.

"Lady Aubrey is being modest," said Anna, "she's the Baroness of Hawksburg."

"Well, I never," said Mrs. Brown. "Shall I make some food? We weren't expecting visitors, but I can pull something together if you like?"

"No, it's all right, we can't stay for long. We've come to visit Hanson. I assume he's still here?"

"He is, Highness, though he spends most of his time in his bed these days. He'll be tickled pink to see you. Shall I take you to him?"

"No," said Anna, "I think I'd like to surprise him. Don't worry, I remember the way."

"Very well," the old woman replied. "My goodness, you've grown so much. Look at you, the very model of womanhood. I expect you'll be getting married soon."

Aubrey chuckled.

"Not for some time yet, Mrs. Brown," said Anna, blushing profusely. "Perhaps you might bring some drinks. Do you have any of that sweet cider you used to make?"

"I'll go and fetch some," said the cook, toddling off down the hall.

"That was quite interesting," remarked Aubrey. "She's obviously very devoted to you."

"Cook was always one of my favourites," she confessed. "She used to make the most magnificent scones."

"Stop it," said Aubrey, "you're making me hungry. We're here to see Hanson, remember?"

"So we are," Anna replied. "Follow me."

They began making their way through the manor.

"Remind me what his symptoms were," said Aubrey.

"The right side of his face fell, I don't know how else to describe it. Oh, and his right arm wouldn't work properly."

"I've read of this sort of thing before. I assume his speech was slurred."

"Yes, it was quite disturbing when it happened."

"You were there?"

"Yes, he and Gerald had come to talk to my tutor. I was in the middle of a lesson, you see. Gerald started to say something and then Alistair, that's Hanson's first name, he grabbed onto Gerald's arm and fell to the floor."

"That must have been terrifying," said Aubrey.

"It was. I was only ten at the time. Of course, I insisted he remain here at Uxley so we could care for him."

"Didn't you have someone looking after you? Your mother, or an uncle or something?"

"No, just Gerald and the rest of the staff."

"And Tempus, I assume," added Aubrey. "Speaking of which, where is he?"

"He's likely made his way to the kitchen, don't worry he'll show up later."

They arrived at a simple wooden door. "This is it," said Anna. "Hanson lies just beyond." She knocked timidly, "Alistair? Are you in there?"

Aubrey heard a faint reply, and then Anna opened the door to a room that was on the small side, big enough only for a bed and a small nightstand on which sat an unlit candle. There was a window here, its glass thick and dirty, but light still managed to struggle in, bathing the room in the orange glow of the afternoon sun.

"Your Highness," came a reedy voice.

Anna stepped inside, Aubrey close behind. The young mage saw an old man lying in bed. He looked ancient, with a bald head and strands of wispy white hair to the sides. The man had slurred his words, and Aubrey could see why for the right side of his face was slack.

"It's good to see you, Hanson," said Anna.

"And you, Highness," squeaked out the old man.

"I've brought a friend to see you, Alistair. This is Lady Aubrey Brandon."

"To see me? Why?"

Aubrey saw tears coming to the princess's face and stepped forward. "I'm a healer. I'm going to use magic to make you feel better. Do you understand?"

"I'm afraid I'm naught but an old man," said Hanson. "I doubt there's anything you can do for me."

"We shall see," said Aubrey moving to the side of the bed. "Now, I'm going to cast a spell, then I'll touch your face and right arm. Will that be all right?"

The man nodded weakly.

"Very well, let's begin, shall we?"

She knelt by the side of the bed and held her hands before her as if she was staring at the back of them. The familiar buzz in the air could be felt as she started her incantation. Stray strands of hair poked loose from her head and began to stand on end as the spell continued. Soon, her fingers glowed with a deep orange hue, and then she went quiet, placing her hands upon her patient. The light flowed from her hands into Hanson, the orange glow transferring into his face and arm and then the colour travelled to the top of his head, lingering for a moment before dissipating.

"It's done," said Aubrey, letting out a long breath. "How does it feel?"

"I don't feel..." the old man's words trailed off. "Good Gods, I can talk properly again! By Saxnor's beard, you've healed me!" He held up his right arm, clenching and unclenching his fist before his tear-stained eyes. "I can use my arm! How can I ever thank you?"

Aubrey looked at Anna to see tears of joy running down her face. "It is I that should thank you," said the young mage, "you've brought such happiness to Princess Anna."

"You'll have to rest a few days," warned Anna.

"Yes," agreed Aubrey, "your body has been afflicted for some time, it will be a bit of an adjustment returning to its natural state. You might find your-self a little clumsy for a few days. I would suggest you start with short walks and simple tasks."

"Will he need another treatment?" asked Anna.

"I don't think so," Aubrey replied. "I felt him being cleansed of his affliction."

"But how is that possible?" asked Anna. "Surely the entire lame arm would have had to be regenerated?"

"I think not. Did you notice how the colour stayed in his head for a moment longer?"

"I did, why?"

"I think his brain was damaged, not his arm. There are some that say the brain controls everything. I don't know if that's true, but he seems to be back to his old self."

"I won't forget this, Aubrey; it means the world to me. Now, how can I repay you?"

"How about you show me around the estate, Highness?"

"Now that, I can do," Anna replied.

Anna and Aubrey found Gerald outside, on the grounds, tossing a stick for Tempus.

"Some things never change," said Anna. "Tempus still likes to chase sticks."

"I imagine you have fond memories of this place," said Aubrey.

"I do," Anna admitted, "though it feels like a lifetime ago. You know I never told anyone this, but Gerald and I planned to run away together and live out our lives as a family. He really is a father to me."

"What changed your mind?" Aubrey asked.

"The war," she replied. "Just as we were planning to leave, your cousin showed up and told us the kingdom had been invaded."

"That sounds like Beverly," said Aubrey. "Do you ever regret your decision?"

"Once or twice," she replied, "but things happen for a reason. Call it fate if you will, but I've learned that when Gerald and I are together, we can overcome anything, and now you're part of my family, too."

"Me?" said Aubrey in surprise.

"Yes, you, Beverly, Revi, and all of my advisors, to tell the truth. I know you lost your family, Aubrey. And I know how painful that can be, but we're here for you now, I want you to remember that. If you have a problem, no matter how large or small, you must feel free to come and talk it over with us."

"I'll remember that, Highness, I promise."

Arlo Harris leaned on the parapet, looking down on the farms that lay to the west. The cool afternoon breeze was a welcome respite from the morning's heat, and he took off his helmet to let the sweat evaporate.

"Cold?" came a familiar voice.

He turned to see Sam Collins approaching.

"No," he replied, "just nervous. We're a long way from Uxley."

"That we are," Sam agreed. "What I wouldn't give to be back home safe and sound."

"Yes," agreed Arlo, "given a choice, I'd much rather be behind the bar at the Old Oak, but fate has dictated otherwise, and instead, here we are in this godforsaken place."

"Not fate," said Sam, bitterly, "but the marshal-general."

"Regardless," said the old man, "this will end badly, mark my words."

"Agreed," added Sam. "There'll be a terrible siege, and then we'll all die."

"You should have more faith," said Arlo.

"In who?" asked his companion. "We've been drafted into this army with little training," he looked down at his threadbare tunic, "and this useless garb. They might have at least given us some armour."

"At least you have an axe, all I got was a spear."

"Perhaps they won't attack this part of the wall," said Sam.

"If we're lucky," Arlo said, then fell into silence.

"I miss Jax," said Sam.

"He was following us when we marched," said Arlo. "What happened to him?"

"The sergeant doesn't like dogs and chased him off."

"Riger?"

"Yes," said Sam, "miserable excuse for a man."

"I'd have to agree," said Arlo. "He deals out fists as often as orders. Who does he think we are, prisoners?"

"We are, if you think about it."

"What do you mean?"

"We were forced here, we didn't volunteer."

"It's our duty," said Arlo, "or have you forgotten the law. Each able-bodied man is to provide arms and armour according to their station, and up to thirty days service."

"You really think they'll let us go after thirty days?"

"No," said Arlo, "not when they're expecting a siege."

"I miss Gerald," said Sam. "He would know how to deal with this."

"Gerald Matheson? Now, there's a name I haven't heard in a while." He went silent for a moment and then started to laugh.

"What's so funny?" asked Sam.

"It just occurred to me," said Arlo, "that he'll be here after all."

"Gerald's here?"

"He will be. Or rather, he'll be out there," he pointed westward.

"What's that supposed to mean?"

"Don't you keep up on gossip, man? He serves the princess. Rumour is he heads up the rebel army."

"Gerald does? But he's just a sergeant."

"I heard they call him general now. He fought in the west and word is he was at the marshal-general's defeat in the north."

"I thought that was Baron Fitzwilliam," said Sam.

"They were both there," Arlo swore.

"Well, that's just great. Not only are we here to defend the city, but we'll likely be killed by our friend. Anything else you'd like to tell me?"

"You need to relax," said Arlo.

"Relax? How can I relax when they're coming to kill us?"

"It'll likely be weeks before they arrive," said Arlo. "Talk is they won't attack till the end of summer, so you've still got some time left."

"You two," yelled a voice, "shut yer gobs and keep an eye out. Yer not being paid to gossip.

"Yes, Sergeant," they both replied in unison.

THIRTY-ONE

The Siege Begins

SUMMER 962 MC

~

Beverly sat astride Lightning as she waited for her captains. Lanaka, as usual, was late but still arrived before the morning mist had a chance to evaporate. He joined the others, who, to Beverly's mind, were still half asleep.

"Orders?" asked Sir Heward.

"We're very close to Wincaster now," she replied. "We'll be there before noon, but I want to make sure everyone is clear on their responsibilities."

"I'm to take the Guard Cavalry," said Heward, "and keep the west gate busy."

"And I the east," said Lanaka, "though it will likely be quiet.

"I take the Bodden horse to secure the south," said Sergeant Blackwood.

"And I'll take the Weldwyn horse to threaten the north," added Beverly.

"Shouldn't you take more with you?" asked Heward. "After all, it's the north gate that leads to Eastwood. Surely reinforcements would come from that direction, if at all."

"I doubt there'll be much help coming from Eastwood," said the red-headed knight. "Valmar is their duke, and he likely has any available troops with him in Wincaster."

"What about us?" interrupted Revi. "Which group should we go with?"

"I think," said Beverly, "that it's best we keep you with Heward's group. The army will be arriving from the west, and that's our anchor point."

"I'll mark out the area for the footmen," offered Hayley, "so that when the troops arrive, they'll know where to set up."

"An excellent idea," commented Beverly. "Coordinate things with the general once he gets here."

"Since I'm going to be superfluous to this expedition, perhaps I could carry out a reconnaissance?"

"What did he say?" asked Blackwood.

"He means," said Hayley, "that since we don't need him, he'll use his familiar to scout out the city."

"Why didn't he just say that?" asked the sergeant.

"I did!" argued Revi.

"Be careful," Beverly warned, "we don't want your bird getting too close to danger. Only long-range observation for now, Master Bloom."

"Very well," the mage agreed.

"Now," continued the red-headed knight, "does everyone know their orders?" There were nods of agreement as she looked around. "Remember" she continued, "all we have to do is stop people from entering or leaving the city, so no heroics. I don't want anyone trying to assault a gate."

"But what if one is open?" asked Blackwood. "Surely we should make an attempt?"

"No," she responded, "we don't have the troops to follow up; the footmen won't be here for some time."

"How long?" asked Heward.

"I'm hoping they'll arrive by nightfall, but they won't all be into position until tomorrow. Is everyone clear on their orders?" She glanced around the group looking at each leader in turn. Satisfied they were ready, she continued, "Lanaka, you have the furthest to travel. You have to get to the other side of the city, so you better ride out first. My group will go next, followed by the Bodden horse and then Heward's group. Good luck gentlemen, and may Saxnor bless us. Except for your group, Lanaka, the Saints will look after you."

Lanaka smiled at the compliment. "May you all fare well this day," he replied, "and may the Saints watch over all you heathens." He turned his horse, heading off into the mist.

"Isn't he the heathen?" asked Blackwood.

"Everyone's a heathen to someone," said Beverly. "Now, get back to your units and prepare to march."

"In this fog?" griped the burly sergeant.

"You've seen enough patrols in Bodden," said Beverly, "I know the fog doesn't frighten you."

"I'm a sergeant," said Blackwood, cracking a grin, "it's my job to complain." He rode off, leaving Beverly and Heward.

"Well," said Heward, "it looks like we're going to have a busy day. Good luck to you Dame Beverly, I pray things go smoothly."

"I would hope luck has nothing to do with it," said Beverly, "but I know the enemy we face can be treacherous and dangerous so I will accept your prayers. Now, I must be off. It wouldn't go well for me to be late when I'm the one that gave the orders."

Heward smiled, watching as she rode off. He made his way to the back of the column. The Guard Cavalry was the most heavily armoured horsemen but, as a result, they were also the slowest. There would be no rushing them today.

Captain Lanaka led the way. His men rode south and then cut eastward, across the farmland that lay beneath the city. He crossed the Burrstoke road then began riding northeast, his men spread out and moving quickly.

They weren't expecting to see much, for the eastern road led to the Darkwood, the mysterious home of the Elves and they were no friends of the king. As a result, the road should have been empty, but much to the captain's surprise, he saw troops to the east.

He brought the column to a halt, straining to make out the distant soldiers. "*Maravan,*" he called out in Kurathian, "*take two companies and block off the gate. I'm going to investigate our visitors here with the rest of the men.*" His aide confirmed the order and rode on while Lanaka turned eastward.

The strangers were on the march, a line of foot soldiers marching in ranks. As he drew closer, he heard the synchronized footfalls of disciplined troops. Their armour was peculiar, to the Kurathian's eyes, but there was no doubt it was made of metal, for the early morning sun reflected off of it.

He halted on the road and waited as his men formed a line to the left and right of him, their swords at the ready. The strange troops drew closer and then those in the lead stopped, the rest fanning out to either side to form a line. The bark of a command was heard, and then spear tips whipped forward, presenting a wall of steel.

Lanaka held his hand up in the air to signify he was no threat and advanced, his men remaining stationary.

"Who are you?" he called out in the common tongue of Merceria.

"A question I might well ask you," came the reply. "Who are you that you would block our way?"

"I am Captain Lanaka of Kurathia," he responded. "Who are you?"

"I am Lord Arandil Greycloak, Lord of the Darkwood."

"And I am Falcon," came another voice, "a former King's Ranger. Whom do you serve?"

"I serve the true ruler of Merceria," said Lanaka, "Princess Anna."

"Then we are on the same side," called back the ranger. "I would speak with her."

"I'm afraid that would be difficult," replied the Kurathian, "for she has not yet arrived. We are the advance scouts, the army is half a day's march behind us, but if you would wait, I'm sure she would be pleased to receive you."

In answer, the Elf lord bellowed an order and spears returned to shoulders. The ranks parted, and two riders came forward. The Human was heavily wrapped in a great cloak, his face mostly hidden by his hood.

The Elf lord, however, sat resplendent in ornate chainmail that seemed to reflect even the tiniest morsel of light. He removed his helmet, revealing his Elven features. "We are pleased to meet you, Captain Lanaka," he said, extending his hand in greeting.

Lanaka urged his horse forward and shook the hand of the Elven lord. "You look familiar," he said.

"No doubt you have met my daughter, Telethial," the lord replied.

"I have had that pleasure," the Kurathian responded, "and she has brought nothing but honour to your people."

Lord Greycloak nodded his head in acknowledgement. "How may I assist you?" he asked. "I have four companies of spears and two of bows."

"My men are tasked with watching the eastern gates to the city. We are to let no man enter or leave without challenge.

The lord looked to the capital, which still lay some distance off. "I shall move my men directly opposite the gate then, and assist where opportunities may present themselves."

"I need to ride to the princess," said Falcon. "I have news that may be of benefit to her."

"You shall have a hard ride," offered Lanaka, "for she is still some way off. You'll have to cross to the other side of the city."

"I have information on the king's forces," insisted the ranger.

"Then I will send two men to escort you," said Lanaka, turning and barking out orders in Kurathian. Two men rode forward, waiting just behind their leader.

"Thank you," said Falcon.

"I only hope the information you bring proves fruitful," said Lanaka.

"I'm sure it will," he replied. "Tell me, who guards the north gate?"

"Why?"

"I have reason to believe a large force of cavalry will try to disrupt your plans, and they'll ride from the northern gate."

"What makes you think that?" asked the captain.

"I've spent the best part of the last two months in the capital," said Falcon. "The king recalled all the rangers, and I answered the call." He saw Lanaka move to draw his sword and held up his hand, "Only to learn their intentions, I assure you."

Lanaka's hand relaxed.

"Their cavalry commander wants to hit back. He's a most insistent man."

"Who is this commander?"

"Lord George Montrose, the Earl of Shrewesdale."

Lanaka swore a Kurathian oath, "Any idea of numbers?"

"I can't be sure," replied the ranger, "but I would suspect two hundred or so. The king is eager to make a statement, and horsemen aren't much good in a siege."

The look of indecision on Lanaka's face must have been obvious for it was Lord Greycloak that provided the solution. "Take your men north," he said, "we will cover the east gate."

"You don't have horsemen," said the captain.

"True, but we have Elven bows, and their range is great."

"Very well," said Lanaka, "I shall ride there immediately."

Beverly brought the Weldwyn horse eastward. They were north of the city where the ugly grey walls were easily visible to the south as the cavalry made their way across the fields. The terrain was quite flat here, ideal horse territory, making their progress swift.

They were trotting at a sedate speed to conserve their mounts' energy, but as she looked south, she spotted some sort of activity by the north gate of Wincaster, and so she urged them on faster, the better to deal with whatever was developing.

Slowly the gates opened, revealing a mass of horsemen that began filing out in fours. She kept her eyes on them, though they were still some distance off. Glancing around at her men, she could tell that they had seen the threat as well. Many of them were drawing their swords in preparation. She slowed the pace while everyone unslung their shields, then confirmed all were ready before launching the attack.

The enemy horsemen had filed out in good order, surprising Beverly. She stared at them, trying to determine who they were. Their armour was not the heavy armour of the knights, and yet they were not as lightly armoured as the Kurathians, meaning they were the Wincaster horse, for they could be no other. These horsemen, like their Bodden counterparts, were professional soldiers, disciplined and efficient. They wore a mix of armour, many with chainmail shirts or vests, yet they rode horses smaller than those of the knights.

She gave the command, and her own men slowed as those behind rode faster to form up. They would attack in two lines, to prevent the enemy from getting into their rear. Pulling forth Nature's Fury, she gave the command, and the line surged forward.

In response, the Wincaster horse mirrored them, and Beverly realized their lines were wider, outnumbering her by some degree. She spotted a flag in amongst the enemy force and was shocked to recognize the banner of the Earl of Shrewesdale. Undaunted, she kept formation, resisting the lure of taking on her nemesis face to face.

The enemy spurred their horses forward, kicking up dust that lingered in the air, drifting westward in a dense cloud.

The lines met with a titanic crash. One moment the thunder of hooves drowned out all other sounds, next it was the clatter of steel on steel as men hacked and slashed at their enemies.

Beverly swung her hammer, knocking a man from his mount. His horse kept running, the herd instinct forcing it closer to its companions. Lightning shoved forward, pushing another beast out of the way. The startled rider grabbed his reins in an effort to control it while Beverly struck out, driving the hammer down onto his shield arm, using her legs to urge her Mercerian Charger forward.

Again and again, she attacked, the dust thick and blinding. All about her, she heard riders, but the distinctive blue tabards of the Weldwyn horse were hidden from sight.

A horseman struck her shield, the blade sliding across it. She pushed out with her left arm and felt resistance as the edge of the shield struck home. Lightning reared up, kicking out with his hooves. She heard the impact as a metal helmet rang out like a bell, and then she saw the rider topple from the saddle.

She cursed the lack of wind that caused the dust to linger. Somewhere in this morass of fighting were her troops, but she had pushed too far forward, and now found herself surrounded. The hammer rang off of an arm, deflecting her blow. She withdrew the weapon, going for an overhead strike, but as she raised it, a sword struck her, jabbing in from her right, hitting her just below the armpit. A fraction higher and it would have sunk into flesh, but the side of her metal breastplate tempered the blow. Nature's Fury came down on the man's head, knocking him from his horse.

Beverly glanced about, trying to get a feel for her situation, but all she saw were enemy soldiers and dust flying everywhere. She kept striking out, horse and rider functioning as one. Parry here, swing there, back and forth, her muscles doing everything by instinct. She felt the magic gripping her now, driving her ever faster and faster, the weapon becoming a blur in her hand.

In front of her, a group of riders came at her with lances couched. She braced for the impact, knowing there was nothing she could do about it, but just before they struck a sound emerged; a high pitched yelling. Suddenly, the enemy turned, trying to meet the new threat to their rear.

She forced her way through and struck while they were distracted, knocking one man from the saddle and hitting another in his side. Lightning pushed forward, and as she was about to swing, she saw the cause; Kurathian horsemen. They surged past her, intent on their prey. Beverly brought her horse to a halt and then waited, hoping for the dust to settle.

The clear sound of a horn blew from the city walls, and then the enemy horse began to break away from the fight. Beverly wanted to attack them while they retreated, but without knowing the state of her men, it would be too big a risk. She watched the king's men ride off to the safety of Wincaster and trotted back into the massive dust cloud that was finally starting to dissipate.

A cheer went up from the troops at the sight of their retreating foes. Beverly spotted Lanaka while his men gathered up stray horses. She rode over to him, his face covered in dust and blood.

"Are you injured?" she asked.

"I am fine," he said, pointing, "but you need to see the healer."

She looked down at her side, the blood flowing onto her saddle.

"It seems I was hit," she said. "Strange, I didn't feel it." She looked back to the Kurathian. "Why aren't you at the east gate?"

"It seems a friend of yours is looking after it," he replied, "an Elf named Lord Greycloak."

"The Elves?" she queried. "I thought Elf didn't fight Elf?"

"I don't know anything about that," offered the Kurathian, "but he has a Human with him, a man named Falcon. I sent a couple of riders to escort him to the princess. He's not dangerous, is he?"

"No," replied Beverly, "at least not to us."

"Good, he's the one that warned us about the enemy cavalry. You should take your men back westward. My men will keep an eye on things here."

She was about to object, but her gaze wandered to the Weldwyn horse. They had taken a beating and close to half of them were either dead or wounded. "Very well," she said, "I'll return with them once the Life Mages have done their part."

She turned Lightning, and her men fell into line behind her as she made her way westward.

. . .

The rest of the army arrived that evening. The Life Mage, Revi Bloom, had ridden with Heward's group and Beverly had been healed by the time she arrived at their camp. She dismounted, handing Lightning's reins to a nearby aide and entered the farmhouse that functioned as their headquarters.

Inside, Princess Anna sat at a table with the rest of her entourage standing around it. The room was crowded, and Beverly was very conscious of the amount of space her heavy armour occupied.

"Ah, Beverly," said Gerald in greeting, "I'm glad you're all right. We heard you had a little bit of a dust-up today?"

"I did," she replied, nodding to Revi Bloom, "though thanks to Master Revi, I'm back in fighting shape. What have I missed?"

"We've been going over the troop dispositions," said Anna. "Nothing as exciting as your cavalry escapades, I'm afraid."

"Everything's important," Beverly replied.

"We were just discussing how we are to proceed," said Gerald. "I'd be curious what ideas you might have?"

Beverly squeezed in to look down at the crude map of Wincaster someone had drawn on the table.

"I'd say a lengthy siege," she offered, "and try to starve them out."

"Why would you say that?" asked Arnim.

"Wincaster is large," she explained, "and there are a lot of mouths to feed. They'd likely be starving by late summer with no hope of getting in the fall harvest."

"Exactly what Gerald thought," said Anna. "Did he tell you?"

"No, Your Highness, I've only just arrived."

"It's her training," offered Baron Fitzwilliam. "She can't help it. She was reading maps before she could speak."

"Not quite true," offered Gerald, "though she did like playing with the little wooden horsemen."

"It's true," said Beverly, "what can I say? Even at an early age, I liked horses."

"How ARE we to proceed, Your Highness?" interrupted Arnim.

In answer, Anna looked to Gerald.

"We'll start," he said, "by setting up some trenches to stop them from popping out again. Thanks to Falcon here," he pointed at the retired ranger, "the Elves have come in force to help us."

"What changed their mind?" asked Arnim.

"I think I did," offered Telethial.

"You were in communication with your father?" responded Arnim.

"No, but my actions in support of this rebellion may well have swayed him."

"How many Elves did he bring, Falcon?" asked Anna.

"About three hundred," the man responded, "a third of them Elven bowmen."

"Excellent," said Gerald. "That means, between the Elves and the Dwarves, we can deliver long-range archers to each of the gates. That should prevent any further sallies on their part."

"When do we assault?" pressed Arnim.

"Not for some time yet," said Gerald. "We've already started building siege engines, but it's a time-consuming task, and it will be the end of the week before we can commence bombardment. The Trolls are gathering stones for ammunition and to keep our options open, I've ordered the construction of rams and ladders."

"The walls are too high for ladders," declared Arnim.

"True," said Gerald, "but if we can reduce the top half of a wall, we can climb up to it. It's a long shot, but we should prepare for every eventuality."

"Any news on when Prince Alric and his men will arrive?" asked Hayley.

"Any time now," said Gerald. "I suspect the faster units will start arriving late tomorrow. The main army camp will be behind our lines to the west of the city. It's nice and flat with plenty of trees to the north for raw materials."

"What are your orders for the meantime?" asked Fitz.

"Baron, I'd like you to take command of the forces to the south. You'll have your own troops with you, but I'll add some reinforcements once Prince Alric arrives."

"And am I to attack?" asked Fitz.

"Not for a while yet. I rather suspect we'll have weeks of bombardments before we're ready to assault."

"The walls of Wincaster are thick," warned the baron.

"They are," Gerald agreed, "which is why I'm open to other ideas if anyone has them."

"What about mining?" asked Herdwin. "We could tunnel under the wall and collapse it."

"That would take quite some time," said Anna.

"Yes," agreed Gerald, "but it's a definite possibility, and one, I admit, I hadn't thought of."

Arnim glanced at Nikki and, when she nodded, turned his attention to Gerald. "How about subterfuge?"

"I'm open to the idea," said the general, "but I'd need more detail."

"I'd rather talk about it in private," replied Arnim. "It does no good to talk of these things openly."

"Very well," said Gerald, "once we're done with this meeting we'll talk over the idea."

"I may be of some help in the siege," offered Aldus Hearn, "and I think that Albreda could be as well."

"How?" asked Anna.

"In many ways," added Albreda. "We can animate trees, for one thing."

"How would that help us?" asked Arnim. "Can they tear down the walls?"

"No," replied the witch, "the walls of Wincaster are far too thick for that. But we can move trees to provide cover."

"Or," added Hearn, "we could move them forward like siege towers."

"That would have to be some very large trees to top the walls," said Gerald.

"I agree," said Hearn. "But it's not outside the realm of possibility, though I daresay I could only control one such tree at a time."

"I concur," added Albreda.

"Can we use some sort of spell to get inside of the city?" asked Gerald. He looked at the mages, but none was quick to answer.

"I can look inside the city," offered Aubrey, much to everyone's surprise.

"I can use Shellbreaker for that," said Revi, "no need to put yourself in danger."

"No," persisted Aubrey, "with all due respect, I don't think you understand what I mean. I can use a spell called spirit walk to enter the city in a ghostly form and look about. It might be useful to determine where the best troops are."

"I like it," said Gerald. "That could give us a much better idea of where to attack."

"I can help," said Kraloch, "I too, can use such a spell, and I can conjure forth aide from the beyond."

"It's true," said Hayley, "he conjured an Orc hero back at the Redridge Mine."

"It's called hero of the past," offered the shaman, "but it only lasts for a short period of time."

"We could also cast a vines spell," added Albreda, "strong enough for soldiers to scale the walls."

"I'll consider it," said Gerald, "but I think we'll start on a more traditional plan of reducing the walls for now. Once the catapults are in action, we'll take a second look at all these other options. Does anyone have anything else they'd like to add?"

He looked around the room before continuing, "Then we'll call an end to this meeting. If anyone should come up with anything else, I'm always available. For now, you should get some sleep; the morning will be quite busy."

They began filing out in small groups.

Arnim and Nikki waited till the room was empty, save for Anna and Gerald, before continuing the description of their plan.

"Go ahead," prompted Gerald, "tell me what you're thinking of."

"Nikki and I have plenty of contacts in Wincaster," he began.

"I fail to see how that helps us," said Gerald in response.

"If we can get a message to them, we might be able to take a gate from the inside."

"It would be dangerous," warned Gerald. "How well armed are these friends of yours?"

"Not very well," offered Nikki, "but they wouldn't have to be. You can have an assault column waiting to march in as soon as the door is in their hands."

"How would you get a message in?" asked Anna.

"We have a couple of options," said Arnim, "but the real question is timing. It would have to be coordinated with an outside assault."

"We could use Aubrey's spell," suggested Anna. "She could be inside the gate, in spirit form, during the attack, and then relay their success to the assault group."

"I'll consider it," said Gerald.

"It's a chance to wrap things up quickly," pressed Arnim. "Surely you can see that?"

"I understand it's an option," said Gerald, "but it also carries, potentially, a high price. If the attackers are too soon, they risk being killed, and if they're too late, the relief column will be cut to pieces waiting for the city gate to open."

"So you won't approve it?" asked Arnim.

"I'll consider it," said Gerald. "You have my promise, but you are to take no action until we have made our final plans. Ideally, I'd like to try a number of things, but they have to be carefully coordinated, or else we won't succeed."

"Very well," said Arnim, "then by your leave, Your Highness, we shall retire."

"By all means," said Anna.

The couple left the room, leaving Anna and Gerald alone.

"What are you thinking?" she asked.

"I'm thinking we have a multitude of options available to us, but if we try something that fails, our support may dwindle."

"You don't like Arnim's plan?"

"Not without further details," he warned, "and it would be nice to have it coincide with a wall assault."

"And for that," added Anna, "we have to have catapults ready."

"Precisely."

THIRTY-TWO

Preparations

SUMMER 962 MC

⁓

The line of Weldwyn troops marched past, led by a contingent of horse.

"A fine body of troops," offered Jack Marlowe.

"Indeed," agreed Prince Alric, "but I wish we had more cavalry."

"Foot soldiers are more useful in a siege, Highness," the cavalier reminded him.

"True, but nothing is quite as splendid as armoured horsemen; they're the finest troops in our army."

"I'm surprised your father let you have them," mused Jack. "After all, he wasn't too keen on the idea of sending Weldwyn troops into Merceria in the first place, as I recall."

"Nonsense," said Alric. "He already sent the volunteers to help, why not send more?"

Jack looked at the young prince carefully, "Surely it was a little more difficult than simply asking?"

Alric grinned, "You know my father well. Yes, it took quite a bit of convincing to send these men."

"And how much more to convince him to allow you to accompany them, Highness?"

Alric blushed, "Well, let's just say that I had help."

"The queen?"

"Naturally, she's the only one that can make the king see the sense of it."

Alric's horse shuffled its hooves as the young prince adjusted his position slightly.

"How much longer, Jack?"

"We should be there by noon, Highness."

"It's almost noon now," Alric noted. "We should get to the head of the column to greet our hosts."

"By all means," agreed Jack, urging his horse forward into a trot.

Alric rode up beside him, matching his pace. "Have we word on their deployments?"

"Yes, they've surrounded Wincaster," said Jack, "and sent word that a delegation will be waiting to welcome us."

"Then it seems there is little for us to do."

"You mean, other than greet the princess?" suggested the cavalier.

Alric broke into a smile, "Yes, precisely."

Jack continued, ignoring the prince's obvious enthusiasm, "I know how much of a burden that is for you, Highness, I'll look after the troops. I imagine it will take hours, maybe even a day or two to ensure a proper welcome. I shouldn't like to distract you from your duties."

Alric cast a glance at the cavalier, trying to maintain a serious expression. "It is, of course, my duty to keep a friendly relationship with our Mercerian allies."

"And," offered Jack, "dare I say, a pleasure?"

"Of course," grinned the young prince.

Jack nodded his head in understanding, "We shall have to pick up the pace if we are to get in front of these troops, Highness."

"Very well, Jack," said Alric, spurring his horse into a gallop, "let us not be tardy."

Gerald sat on his horse. The beast shifted slightly, perhaps sensing the anticipation in the air.

Beside him, Anna sat, staring off into the distance. She stood up in the stirrups for a better view. "Can you see them yet?" she asked.

"Not yet," he replied, "but then again, at this range all we can see is a column of people. They're not close enough to make out faces yet, but they soon will be."

"I should ride out," she said. "It's been so long since I saw him."

"You should wait," called out Arnim from behind, "it's only proper etiquette. After all, you're the receiving royal."

The princess looked around, seeing the people lined up to greet the foreign prince. They were all fidgeting, eager to meet their allies. Anna returned to her gaze to the approaching Weldwyn troops. "Etiquette be damned," she said, then turned to the general. "Race you there, Gerald!" she called out suddenly as she pushed her horse forward.

Gerald, who had been expecting just such a move, followed her almost instantly but the retinue behind was caught entirely by surprise. There was a moment of shock and panic before they all started advancing.

Anna urged her mount on, quickly gaining the lead. She looked over her shoulder to see Gerald just behind her and smiled in glee. The only other horse even close was Beverly, who had also been taken by surprise, but her mighty Mercerian Charger quickly made up ground. The red-headed knight was soon riding beside Gerald, just behind the princess, slowing her gait to match his.

As they drew closer to the Weldwyn column, Gerald noticed a couple of riders breaking off from the rest, and it soon became apparent it was the prince himself, along with his bodyguard, Jack Marlowe.

"Alric," called out Anna, her face beaming.

The young prince slowed his pace, his face equally animated. "Your Highness," he said, rather formally, "it's so good to see you again."

"And you," she replied.

They sat on their horses, gazing at each other as the rest of Anna's followers caught up.

"Perhaps," offered Gerald, "Prince Alric would like some refreshment to wash away the dirt of the march? We have a tent set up nearby for just that purpose."

Alric tore his gaze from Anna a moment to acknowledge Gerald, "A marvellous idea. Lead on, Gerald."

The general turned his horse, guiding them back toward the Mercerian camp. Anna's retainers, finally having caught up, found themselves immediately turning around as the young princess led Alric away.

Gerald trotted across the field watching Anna, who was deep in conversation with the prince. He looked to Beverly, but the red-headed knight was scanning their surroundings, always on the lookout for danger.

They finally reached the tent, dismounting while servants ran forward to take their horses. The two royals entered together, while Gerald remained outside, as did Jack.

"So, the war goes well then?" asked the cavalier.

"It does," admitted Gerald, "though we've suffered some losses. Your reinforcements arrived just in time."

They stood by, watching as the rest of the riders arrived and began noisily dismounting.

"Do you think that's enough time?" asked Jack.

"I think they've had enough privacy for now," replied Gerald. "Let's head inside."

Gerald watched as another stone arced overhead, flying through the air to strike the walls of Wincaster with a solid cracking noise.

"Saxnor's balls, it did nothing," he grumbled. "The damn walls are too thick, we can't seem to affect them at all."

"I understand the frustration," offered Baron Fitzwilliam, "but after all, the walls of Wincaster have never been breached."

"That's because no one has ever attacked them," said Gerald in defence.

"True," admitted Fitz. "Still, they are a formidable obstacle."

They had been at it for almost a month now, lobbing stone after stone to little avail. Even Prince Alric, who was eager to learn the ways of siegecraft, had fallen by the wayside, bored with the unending rain of the catapults.

"Perhaps the trebuchet will do better," offered Fitz.

Gerald looked up at the giant construction. "Perhaps," he mused, "it certainly took a lot to build."

"Thank Saxnor for those Dwarves," said Fitz.

"I'd be happier if Saxnor would let us knock a wall down. These siege engines are far too inaccurate for my tastes. It would be nice if two stones could at least hit the same section of the wall."

"It can't be helped, General," said Fitz. "The men do what they can. How's morale holding up?"

"The men are happy," said Gerald, "and why not? No one is in any imminent danger except for the poor souls within the city."

"They'll surrender eventually," said Fitz, "after all, they have to. They have no hope of reinforcements and their food can't last forever."

"In the meantime," said Gerald, "we'll keep hammering away at them, though it feels like throwing stones into a lake."

"I must say," said Prince Alric, "it's a much more pleasant experience being on the outside of a siege for a change."

"You wouldn't say that," said Anna, "if you were charging into a breach."

"Doubtless I wouldn't," he agreed, "though it's going to take months for that wall to come down at this rate."

"We have the advantage of time," said Anna. "While they're putting up with this, they'll be going through their food stocks with no hope of replenishment."

"And you have plenty of your own?" asked the prince.

"We do," she confirmed, "thanks to your father, we can last for months. The food shipments have proven most useful."

"My father understands the requirements of warfare," he said.

"Speaking of your father," Anna said, "have you talked to him any more of our wedding?"

"He's all in favour of it, you know that."

"Yes, but does he know you won't rule as king?"

"Not exactly, no."

"What do you mean, 'not exactly'? What exactly did you tell him?"

"Things have been busy back home," he deflected, "and with all the Clansmen to deal with he's had a lot on his plate."

"Alric, you have to tell him."

"I will, in time," he promised, "meanwhile, I've enlisted the help of someone. Someone who has his ear."

"Not Jack?" she said in mock horror.

"Did someone say my name?" came a call from behind them.

Anna looked back to where Alric's champion rode. "No, Jack, we weren't talking to you."

"But you were talking about me," he proclaimed.

"Yes," confirmed Alric, "as a matter of fact we were, only we weren't."

"What's that supposed to mean, Highness?" quipped Jack.

"It means," said Anna, "that your name came up but not as the principal subject."

"But it still came up," said Jack, wearing an impossible smile.

"Sometimes I wish his hearing wasn't so keen," said Alric.

"Agreed," said Anna. "Now, tell me who you've enlisted to the cause."

"My mother," confided the prince, "she's always been on my side. She'll work on Father while I'm here in Merceria. Don't worry, it'll all be sorted out by the time we're married, whenever that may be."

"I told you, Alric, I have to change the laws first. If I marry you before that, I lose my position as queen."

"Surely as the wife of a king you'd still be queen?"

"Of course," she said, "but what I meant was I'd lose my power as queen. I'd essentially become just a decoration."

"I understand," replied Alric, "though I wonder which will take longer; convincing my father, or convincing your earls?"

They watched as another rock sailed overhead toward the distant city. It cracked into the top of the wall, breaking off a section of crenellations.

"Good shot," said Alric.

"Indeed, Your Highness," agreed Jack, "though I rather suspect it was more luck than skill."

"We'll take it," said Anna. "Luck or skill makes no difference providing the wall breaks."

"Something's happening at the west gate," announced Jack.

They all swivelled their gaze to the west gate of Wincaster. As the great doors swung open, a nearby group of cavalry mounted up to repel the expected sortie.

"So," mused Alric, "they've decided to attempt another counter-attack."

"It'll be just like the last," said Anna, "and they tried two times the week before. Do they not realize we stand ready to fight? What do they hope to achieve?"

"I rather suspect they're striving to build up morale," suggested Jack.

"I'd agree," offered Alric.

They watched as the gate opened, but instead of horsemen riding out, a gaggle of people on foot exited.

"Hello, what's this?" asked Alric. "They don't look like soldiers."

Sure enough, with the doors wide open, a group of grubby looking commoners left the city. It started as a trickle but soon grew until the archway that made up the gate tower was jam-packed with them.

"By Malin's hand," said Alric in astonishment, "there must be hundreds of them."

"But why are they leaving?" asked Anna.

The answer soon became obvious, for among the poor folk rode horsemen, driving the crowd forward with the flats of their blades.

"What are they doing?" asked Jack.

A grim look settled over Anna, "They're pushing them out of the city, so they don't have to feed them. They're of no military significance. I'd wager they've been plucked from the slums."

"Why aren't our archers firing?" asked Jack. "The enemy horsemen are drawing nearer."

"They can't fire without hitting innocents," explained Anna, "and the crowd is getting in the way of our horsemen."

"They've planned this carefully," offered Alric. "They must have been watching our troops during their last sorties. See how the refugees are heading for our lines?"

∼

The mass of refugees advanced, panicking as horsemen from the city drove them on. "Run!" commanded a voice and the throng surged forward. Sam tried to keep his bearings, but the press of humanity carried him like a current. He had thrown off his threadbare soldier's tunic, hoping to blend in with the crowd, but now all semblance of order was thrown to the wind as people stampeded in their haste to escape.

He spotted rebel horsemen ahead. The crowd parted, fearful of being cut down, yet still seeking safety. Someone fell in front of him, to be trampled mercilessly by those coming after. Sam stopped, helping the battered woman to her feet as the city folk pushed their way past.

A horseman rode by, striking out with the flat of his blade, raising a welt across Sam's back as the Uxley native was knocked to the ground. The woman ran off, leaving him rolling on the ground, desperate to avoid the fate he had just saved her from.

The saddle maker managed to get to his feet and run. There was no east or west, no friend or foe as fear drove him onward. A ditch appeared in front of him, and he jumped over, only to find soldiers there, swamped by the sudden press of people.

Sam stumbled forward, his feet finding purchase on the far side and he rushed onward, his lungs burning, his throat parched and dry. Finally, he halted, bending over to try to catch his breath while riders streamed past him. He looked up, not sure whose side they were on, but no longer caring if they ran him down.

A nearby horseman halted, reaching into a satchel strung over his neck. Sam watched as the man pulled forth a clay pot, no bigger than a tankard of ale. Mesmerized, the saddle maker stared as the rider threw this strange object through the air. He jumped back in surprise as it struck a siege engine and burst into flames.

Sam tried to get his bearings, but before he had even a moment to determine what was happening, he heard screaming to his left and turned to see a mass of refugees tearing into wagons and sacks. Joining the starving crowd ransacking stocks of food, he dropped to his knees and grabbed a loaf of bread, biting into it; his first food in days.

All around him soldiers yelled, trying to chase back the looters, but these people were desperate and starving. The soldiers backed up, forming into a line with their weapons drawn. Sam staggered towards them, his hands in the air. He tried to call out, but his parched throat let no sound pass.

The footmen began moving forward at a steady pace, their weapons extended. Slowly, the underfed crowd began to take notice, pausing their feeding frenzy. Sam dropped to the ground, feigning dead. Lying motionless, he listened to the soldier's footsteps as they advanced, even felt a foot briefly step on him as they moved past, ignoring him. Waiting for but a moment more, he stood up, his hands above his head in surrender.

He was grabbed roughly by the arms and turned around to come face to face with a grim looking soldier.

"Take me to Gerald," he managed to croak out. "Gerald Matheson, I have important news."

~

Heward struggled to move his riders forward, even the bulk of the horses was not enough to force their way through the press of people. He spotted the enemy horsemen clustering near the edge of the crowd, but he could do nothing when they spurred forward.

The great knight cursed as the enemy rode past, his men still hopelessly engulfed by the throng of commoners. When he drew his weapon, the action brought terrified looks from those nearby. Expecting a slaughter, they began to flee, creating an opening. Spurring his horse, he moved forward, finally clearing the refugees with a small trickle of his original force.

The enemy horsemen were in full gallop now, and Heward swore again. They were in among the catapults, and he watched, helplessly, as flames leaped onto the wooden frames. Finally, the enemy turned, intent on making their way back to Wincaster and Heward knew he had them.

A few more of his men had cleared the crowd, and now they formed a small, but disciplined line of heavily armoured horsemen. He gave the order, and they began moving forward at the trot. The enemy, tired from their exertions, wished only to return to the safety of the city gate. Breaking into small groups they each tried to make their own way back; this proved to be their undoing.

The Guard Cavalry rode forth, smashing into them like a tidal wave. Heward swung his axe, meeting little resistance as he sliced into a man's chest. The weapon sunk in, wrenching it from the knight's hand, and he cursed as his victim fell, taking the axe to the ground with him.

Heward had no time to find another weapon as an enemy horseman swung a mace at him. He deflected the blow with his shield and then lunged out with his hand. The knight was a giant of a man, more than six feet tall, with a reach that exceeded that of most others. He gripped the man's weapon arm and pulled him from the saddle. The unfortunate victim fell, his arms flailing about until he landed and then was promptly trampled by a multitude of hooves.

The line of Guard Cavalry passed through the enemy, thinning their ranks considerably. Now, only a scattered few remained, speeding desperately for the safety of the walls of the capital.

. . .

Alric watched as the princess's Guard Cavalry decimated the enemy horsemen; fewer than a quarter of the king's riders returned to the gate.

"A valiant effort by the enemy," offered Jack, "but a wasted one. They have taken heavy losses and only lightly diminished us."

"Warfare isn't valiant, Jack," admonished Anna, "it's a game of life or death."

"And yet it requires courage and honour, does it not?" Jack persisted.

"Bravery, certainly," agreed Anna, "but honour? It certainly wasn't honour that put me into the dungeons of Wincaster, nor was it honour that resulted in the invasion of your kingdom."

"I concede the point, Your Highness," said Jack.

A commotion behind the lines grabbed Anna's attention, and she cast her eyes westward toward their supply wagons. "They've broken into the food stocks!"

"That can't be good," said Alric, spurring his horse forward.

They galloped toward the disturbance to see soldiers advancing with weapons drawn.

"Stop!" yelled Anna.

"They're destroying the food," yelled a captain. "We have to stop them."

"They're starving," she replied.

"Then what do we do, Highness?" asked the man. "Let them have free rein?"

"Secure the wagons," said Alric, "and then hand out the food. Make them form lines. It will lessen their panic." He turned to Jack, but words were unnecessary.

"I know what is required, Highness," said the cavalier, and then looked to Anna for permission.

"Take command," she said, turning her attention to the footmen. "You take your orders from Lord Marlowe now, he knows what to do."

It was a grim night as they met around the table. Everyone had heard of the terrible tragedy that had befallen them, and now they all knew what the inevitable outcome would be.

"We are low on food, Highness," said Revi. "I've conducted an inventory on our remaining stocks, and it doesn't look good. We've lost more than half our food, and we now have many more mouths to feed."

"Drive them off," suggested Lanaka, "and keep the food for ourselves."

"We are not at war with the commoners," asserted Anna. "This war is fought on their behalf. I will not leave them to starve."

"What say you, General?" asked the Kurathian.

"I agree with the princess," he replied. "The whole reason we initially got involved with the rebellion, all those years ago, was to save the commoners. It is our duty to protect them, our obligation if you will."

"Where have I heard that before?" asked Baron Fitzwilliam.

"Your own words, Father," said Beverly. "You taught us well."

"So we must assault after all," said Fitz. "I knew it would end that way, it was inevitable."

"But not an ordinary siege," declared Gerald. "We still have a few surprises in store. I think it's time we accelerate our plans."

He was just about to explain himself when a guard entered the room. "General," the man said, "we captured an enemy deserter. He claims to know you."

"He knows me?" said Gerald. "I suppose it's possible, I did spend some time in Wincaster as a sergeant. Bring him in."

The guard disappeared, leaving the others looking around in confusion.

"A deserter?" said Arnim. "That sounds suspicious. I suspect a trap."

"You may be right," said Gerald, "but let's hear the man out. He might slip up and give us some valuable information."

"I would never take the word of someone who deserts," announced Jack. "They'll say anything to save their skin."

"How do we know he's not here to kill you?" asked Arnim.

"He'd have a tough time," said Beverly, "in a room full of armed soldiers, not to mention they would have searched him first."

"It could be dark magic," warned Arnim.

"He has a valid point," said Revi. "We know so little about the ways of Necromancers. Perhaps we should have weapons ready?"

"Agreed," said Anna.

Beverly pulled Nature's Fury from the loop on her belt and moved to stand at the princess's side.

"Is all this quite necessary?" asked Anna.

"Just a precaution, Highness," promised Beverly. "I'd hate to see all this work fail because we got complacent."

The guard reappeared, "We have him here, General."

"Bring him in," he commanded.

The guard stood aside while two men hauled in the prisoner, each grasping an arm to prevent any action.

"Sam?" said Gerald in disbelief.

"Sam Collins?" added Anna. "Let him go, for Saxnor's sake."

"Gods man, what happened to you? You look awful," said Gerald.

"The marshal-general ordered the militia raised and marched us to Wincaster. We've been on the walls for more than two months."

"I heard about that in Uxley," said Anna. "Tell me, Sam, what's it like in the city?"

"It's dreadful," he replied. "There's little enough food, and the militia gets the scraps while the poor townsfolk are starving. This morning we were ordered to empty the slums. That's who rushed out the gate."

"That's terrible," said Albreda.

"Arlo suggested I try to get word to you," Sam continued. "The men of Uxley have been kept on the same section of wall for the whole time, save for the excursion to the slums."

"Which section?" asked Gerald. "Can you show me?"

Sam looked down at the crudely drawn map. "Roughly here, if I read this right."

"Hmm," said Gerald, "north of the west gate, in a reasonably straight section of wall. Are you thinking what I am, Arnim?"

"A chance to get in?" suggested the knight.

"Precisely," confirmed the general.

"You obviously have a plan," said Anna. "Care to share it?"

"Remember Arnim's suggestion?" he replied. "Now we have a chance to use it, if you're still willing?" This last part he directed towards Arnim.

"Of course," said Arnim, "I'll do whatever I can."

"Me too," added Nikki.

"Good," continued Gerald, "because once you're inside the walls, it'll be all up to you."

"What can I do to help?" asked Prince Alric. "The men of Weldwyn stand ready to help their allies."

"I'd prefer the assault not be conducted by your men," explained Gerald. "If the defenders see us as foreigners, they'll fight that much harder."

"Surely there must be something for us to do?"

"Indeed there is," continued the general, "I'd like you to take your men to the eastern side of the city and start making preparations. You'll construct siege towers and ladders, all in full view of the city walls."

"I thought you said you didn't want us to assault?" Alric said in surprise.

"I don't, but the mere threat of your existence will be enough for them to send extra troops to the east wall, giving a western assault a higher chance of success."

Alric smiled, "It will be our pleasure."

"I can help too," added Sam.

"I hoped you'd say that," added Gerald, "because we'll need you too. Here's what we're going to do..."

It took all afternoon to work out the details.

. . .

"Are you ready?" asked Gerald.

"We are," said Arnim, looking around. It was the middle of the night, and only the glow of the moon revealed their faces. Arnim, Nikki and Sam wore dark coloured clothing while Albreda and Baron Fitzwilliam stood by.

"Good luck to you," the general said as they disappeared into the dark of the night.

Arnim moved quickly, while the others struggled to keep up. As Wincaster drew closer, he saw the torchlight on the walls throwing up shadows. Crouching, he waited for the others to catch up.

"Up here, Sam," he said.

The saddle maker hunkered down beside him, his breath laboured in the chill evening air.

"Can you see where Arlo should be?" asked the knight.

Sam started counting the crenellations atop the wall. "Seventeen north of the tower," he said. "He has a rather distinctive helmet, an old one with a flat top."

"I see him," whispered Nikki, pointing, "halfway along that section of wall."

"Then that's our target," said Arnim. "Did you get that, Albreda?"

"Of course," replied the mage. "Should be simple enough."

"Won't your magic alert them to our presence?" asked Fitz. "The air does glow when you cast, does it not?"

"It does," she said, "but I'm counting on you lot to tell me when no one is watching."

"What of your incantation?" asked Arnim.

"I can keep that quiet," she assured him. "Surely you're not worried about it now, of all times. These are things you should have mentioned earlier. Do you really think I'd agree to do this if I thought I'd be detected?"

"My dear," soothed Fitz quietly, "they're worried, that's all. You don't need to take it out on them."

"Of course," she retorted, "my apologies. Now lead on, Sir Arnim, we have work to do."

Arnim glanced at the top of the wall and waited. The guard walked back and forth, pausing as he reached the end of his circuit. The knight moved forward in a crouch, advancing toward the base of the wall with the others following, one by one.

Soon, they stood with their backs against the walls of the city, all save for Albreda; she looked upward, at the steep incline before her. Taking a deep breath, she began moving her hands about in an intricate pattern.

Small fireflies of light appeared before her. Fortunately, they were too close to the wall for the sentries to spot them before they sank into the ground. Suddenly, the earth shook slightly as small tendrils began to issue forth, winding their way up the wall like ivy.

"Wait till it's anchored at the top," she whispered, "or it won't take your weight."

Fitz watched in fascination as the stalks grew thicker at the base, while more vines crept their way upward until Albreda paused them near the top, waiting.

Arnim moved out from the wall, and whispered, "Now," as he spotted the guard walk past.

The vines gripped the battlement as she completed her spell.

Arnim tapped Sam on the shoulder. "Go," he whispered.

Sam began the climb, thankful for the dark that hid his exposed position. If the guards on the neighbouring tower had been alert, he would have been dead, but they were more concerned with their comfort than actually standing watch.

Halfway up, he paused for breath, looking below to spot Arnim and Nikki following, ascending rapidly. Picking up his pace, he stopped again when the crenellations were just above him. He poked his head up above the wall.

"Psst," he hissed.

The guard looked in his direction.

"Arlo," Sam called out, "is that you?"

"Sam?" came back a whisper. "What are you doing here?"

"Give me a hand," he called back, "my arms are tired."

The tavern keeper ran forward, pulling him over the wall. "What in Saxnor's name are you doing?" he asked.

"I brought friends," Sam announced.

Arnim crawled over the wall, followed closely by Nikki.

"What are you doing?" repeated Arlo. "I can't help you, Sergeant Riger is nearby."

"Don't worry," said Arnim, "we're only passing through. Just act like nothing is happening. Go back to your regular patrol, we don't want to raise suspicion."

"Easy for you to say," grumbled Arlo, "you're not the one who would be in trouble."

Sam brought his mouth close to Arnim's ear. "There are steps down there," he pointed, "that lead into the city streets. Watch out for soldiers though, there's a couple of them that play cards, but they're usually drunk this time of night."

Arnim nodded his head and looked back to Nikki who was framed by the moonlight, her pale face smeared with mud to blend into the darkness. She nodded her understanding, then moved ahead of him to lead the way.

Sam waited for them to disappear into the night and then began climbing over the parapet once more.

"What are you doing?" asked Arlo.

"I'm leaving," explained Sam. "My work here is done. The assault will commence two days hence, at daybreak. Make sure you stay at your post."

"What about the catapults? I don't want to be smashed to bits."

"Don't worry," said Sam, "we're going to create a bit of a diversion."

"Good luck," said Arlo.

"And to you, old friend." He passed the tavern keeper a note and added, "Make sure you read that in private," then dropped below the parapet, using the vines to descend.

When the saddle maker reached the ground, Albreda dismissed the spell and the vines withered, shrinking into nothingness.

"Come along, you two," she whispered, "it's time we return to the camp."

THIRTY-THREE

Into the City

SUMMER 962 MC

~

The siege engines renewed their bombardment at first light. It began with a single stone hurled across the field, leaving a slight trail behind it as it sailed through the air, impacting the wall just south of the western gate.

Kiren-Jool looked on in satisfaction.

"Well done," said Revi. "Right on target."

"I should have thought of this myself," the Kurathian mage confessed. "After all, if I can make archery fire more accurately, why not a catapult?"

"Are you sure you'll have enough energy to keep this up?" asked Revi.

"No doubt I'll be tired by the end of the day, but the rate of fire of these things is not great, even with Trolls reloading them. I'll have plenty of time to recover." He glanced back at the massive creatures who lifted another rock while others pulled the lever back to the firing position.

"Handy, aren't they?" said Revi.

"Yes," he replied, "though I think we should have built bigger catapults for them."

"We'll try to remember that for next time."

"Hopefully there won't be a next time," said Kiren-Jool. "This is not something I ever want to experience again."

"I thought you were a battle mage?"

"I am, but sieges are terrible. Think of all the people suffering in that city of yours."

"I can well understand your reticence," said Revi. "How long will your enchantment last?"

"Some time yet," he replied. "I think I'll have to recast mid-morning and again at noon. Of course, each casting only affects one catapult, so I have my work cut out for me."

"Send someone to find me if you find yourself getting tired," offered Revi. "Remember, this is a diversion, but we need to make it look like we mean business."

"I don't see why you had to endanger yourself by going to the wall, Father."

"I told you, my dear," explained Fitz, "Albreda needed someone to keep an eye on her."

"Richard," corrected Albreda, "you know that's not true."

"I'm a warrior," retorted Fitz, "and I need to set an example for my men."

"I don't think the men had anything to do with it," chided Beverly.

"Well, it's all done now," replied the baron. "Now, correct me if I'm wrong, but aren't I the parent here?"

"Yes," said Beverly, "though if you persist in taking these unnecessary risks, you might not be for much longer. You had me worried."

"You needn't be," offered Albreda, "I had things under control. You know your father meant well, he is a baron, after all. You and he have a lot in common."

They looked at her in confusion.

"You're both headstrong on occasion," she added.

"I'm not headstrong," said Fitz.

"Nor I," said Beverly.

"If you say so," offered Albreda. "Now, don't you two have places to be?"

"Not until this evening," said Fitz. "The attack won't commence until first light tomorrow."

"True," said Albreda, "but you still have to ride all the way over to your men. You don't want to be doing that in the dark, and you want to set a good example, don't you?"

"Yes, of course," he muttered.

"Well then, off you go."

Beverly wore a smug look as she watched her father ride off.

"What are you looking at?" asked Albreda. "I believe you're the one that's supposed to be seen preparing the assault troops for the breach."

"Yes, of course," Beverly replied, blushing.

"Take care, Beverly, and give my regards to that smith of yours," called out the mage.

"Aldwin?" she questioned. "How did you know I was going to see him first?"

"I know that look," said Albreda.

"What look?" the knight replied innocently.

"That look you get whenever you think of him. Do you think I see nothing? Now, be off with you, and good fortune."

"And you, Albreda," the knight replied.

It had been almost one year ago that 'Handsome' Harry Hathaway had come to the Gryphon to meet the knight, Hayley Chambers. Now, he sat in the very same seat, nursing an ale, this time in the company of Nikki the Knife. He let his eyes wander the room, noting the presence of his people.

"Are you sure about this, Nik?" he asked, for the third time.

"I told you, Harry, it's safe," assured Nikki. "You need to relax a little, you're even making me jumpy."

The door opened, and Arnim Caster entered, followed by a dozen men.

"What's this?" demanded Harry, rising to his feet.

"Don't worry," soothed Nikki, "it's not what you think."

"He brought the watch with him," cursed Harry. "I knew he couldn't be trusted."

"Sit down, Harry, you're creating a stir."

Harry sat, looking alarmed. Arnim walked over to their table, his men taking up seats nearby.

"What's the meaning of this?" demanded Harry.

"These men are trustworthy," insisted Arnim. "Do you vouch for yours?"

"Of course," Harry replied, "I only picked men I trust completely. What's this all about?"

"You know the city is under siege," started Arnim.

"Tell me something I don't know," said Harry.

"The assault is coming soon."

"And?"

"And the attackers will come against the west wall," said Arnim.

"What's that got to do with us?" asked Harry.

"We're going to take the south gate," he replied, to be met with silence.

"Are you insane?" Harry finally said. "It would take trained soldiers to assault a gatehouse!"

Arnim leaned in close, lowering his voice, "The enemy will be concentrating their defences on the west wall. They'll be distracted and vulnerable. They'll never be expecting an attack from within the city."

Harry looked at the knight in disbelief and then finally shook his head, "You're serious."

"Very," said Arnim.

"And just how long would we have to hold it?"

"Not long," said Arnim. "Cavalry will be closing in from the south. Once they arrive, our job will be done."

"And you want us to work with the Town Watch?"

"I know what I'm asking, Harry. You'll need to put aside your differences for the time being. Until this siege is over, we're all on the same side. Unless, of course, you like being on the receiving end of those siege engines?"

"All right," Harry said at last, "I'm in."

"Good," said Arnim. "How many men did you bring?"

"Twelve."

"Excellent, that matches the dozen I've recruited. I'd hoped for more, but it'll have to do. We'll rendezvous on Pennington Ave, it's only two blocks from the gate."

"I know the street," said Harry. "There's an old candlemaker's shop there, do you know the place?"

"Yes," replied Arnim, extending his hand. "I've been there many a time. We'll meet there, just before dawn."

"Agreed," said Harry, shaking the knight's hand. "We'll see you there."

At the midnight changing of the guard, a shadowy figure sidled up to the Palace gates, where he was quickly admitted. Making his way into the Palace by means of the back door, he passed through the courtyard to enter the building, knowingly navigating the route to the office of Marshal-General Roland Valmar. He knocked on the door.

"Enter," came a voice.

He opened the door to see the marshal-general himself, sitting at his customary desk.

"Saunders," said Valmar, "this is rather unexpected. You have news?"

"I do, Your Grace," the man replied.

"Well, get on with it, man," said Valmar, rather irritated.

"Beggin' your pardon, sir, but it's just as you thought, Caster has called on his old friends in the watch. He's in the city, even as we speak."

Valmar sat back, a smile creasing his features, "That's good news, Saunders. Or should I say, Sergeant Saunders?"

"Thank you, my lord," said Saunders. "What shall we do? Do you want us to arrest him?"

"No, not at this time," said Valmar. "I think we'll let him carry out his plan. Do you know what that is?"

"I do, Lord, I was there as one of his men."

"Excellent! We shall let them believe their ruse has been successful and draw them in. Once their comrades have entered the city, we'll unleash our ambush."

"They'll be trapped like rats in a barrel," offered Saunders.

"Precisely," said the marshal-general.

A stone struck the rampart, sending shards of brick flying into the city. Arnim instinctively ducked, as did most of the people on the street, even though the attack was blocks away. Across the way, Nikki, waiting in the alleyway, had her people lined up behind her. Ever since the bombardments started, the soldiers had sought out refuge in the towers, leaving the streets clear of troops. Now, a very select group of individuals made their way toward the southern gate.

Arnim waved Nikki and her people forward. They left the safety of the alley, moving down the street, parallel to his own advance. A shopkeeper opened the door, saw the advancing group, and hurriedly rushed back inside, closing it quickly. As they drew closer to the gate, Arnim gave the signal to halt and wait.

The sun had just begun its daily ascent, stretching shadows as it climbed in the east. The guard tower was still closed up from the night before, the portcullis down. Even the great double doors of the city were closed, the massive drop bar holding them in place.

Arnim drew his blade and waited as two of the watchmen moved forward, meandering slowly, so as not to raise suspicions. They stopped, knocking on the door to the tower and waited. A moment later it opened to reveal a bored looking soldier. The knife was quick, slicing through the man's throat and the watchmen pushed their way past the body

Arnim broke into a run, the rest of his men following. Across the street, he saw Nikki's people, waiting to rush for the same structure. Pushing through the doorway, he heard the sound of fighting in the floor above. Looking up, he spotted a dead watchman lying on the stairs, blood pooling beneath the body. He rushed past and cursed as his foot slipped, sending him crashing to his knee.

A few of his men ran past him as he staggered back to his feet. "Guard the door!" he yelled at the ones below, then continued his climb. The top floor held the winch for the portcullis. He arrived in time to see two of his men working the mechanism, raising the large iron gate that prevented access.

There was an opening here, a window that looked down into the tunnel beneath them. He hurried towards it to see Nikki and her people moving forward to remove the wooden beam which held the great doors closed.

~

"I wish I knew what was happening," said Fitz.

"We must be patient, Lord," said Sir Rodney. "They are doing all they can. Even now, your niece is watching them."

The baron looked to where Aubrey lay on the ground as if she were sleeping, while guards kept her safe.

"The sun is rising in the east," he said. "It's almost time to move. If we wait too long, it'll be too late."

A gasp from behind alerted him that Aubrey had returned from her spirit walk. "They're in the gatehouse," she announced

"Now," yelled Fitz, spurring his horse forward. The Bodden horse advanced with the footmen following. Fitz knew this was the moment of greatest danger, for if the attack failed, they would be cut to ribbons by archers on the wall, unable to strike back. It all hinged on getting to the gate in time.

They began closing the distance, but it felt agonizingly slow. The plan was to dismount once they reached the gate, for the fighting there would be no place for horses.

He spared a thought for Albreda. He knew she was busy to the north, and he prayed for Saxnor to protect her.

~

Albreda stood beside Aldus Hearn at the edge of the wood, watching the action in the distance.

"I see Beverly is moving the men forward," she said. "It's almost time."

"Get ready," yelled Hearn. The Elves emerged from the woods, their bows nocked and ready to let fly.

"Now," yelled Albreda.

As she began calling forth the power of nature, Aldus Hearn's deep voice rang out with his words of magic, almost harmonizing with her own. The trees shook as a terrific noise burst forth from the woods, startled birds fleeing from branches. The air surrounding Albreda buzzed with energy, and lights swirled around her while her hair, which had come loose from its braid, stuck out in all directions.

Before her appeared a pillar of light, and she willed it to move, slowly advancing it toward the tree line where a tall redwood stood waiting. The beam flared briefly as it enveloped the trunk, and then the ground rumbled as the roots tore loose, sending dirt flying.

The Elves all moved to stand clear as the great tree began to shamble forward, towering more than one hundred feet into the air. As its roots hit the field, it began to pick up speed, and the Elven archers had to break into a run to keep up.

Albreda looked to her right to witness another tree, this one a tall ash, emerge from the forest as Aldus Hearn beckoned it forward.

Beverly was halfway to the walls of Wincaster before she halted the men. She looked to the top section of the wall where the catapults had done their damage. Troops crammed the battlements, standing ready to repel the attack. Even as she watched, the early morning sun began to rise, dispelling the darkness.

She turned to her men who stood ready with ladders. "That's it," she called out, "they've taken the bait. We'll hold still here for a moment, then begin our retreat."

The two great trees lumbered forward, accompanied by the Elves who were loosing off the occasional arrow as they rushed to keep up. Albreda ran beside the great redwood now, preparing for the next phase. She kept her eyes on the walls, looking for the telltale sign. There was activity up there, as the defenders struggled to grasp what was happening.

Then she saw it; white linen draped across a section of the battlement. Suddenly, fighting broke out on the wall itself. She gave the command, and the mighty tree bent its trunk until the very top lay across that exact spot on the wall, creating a ramp. She waved her hands, and the branches moved, forming steps.

Up went the nimble Elves, their swords at the ready. On her right, she watched Hearn's tree performing a similar action. The druid waved his hands, casting another spell, and then a flock of ravens appeared above his head.

"Show off," she said, more to herself than to anyone in particular. She moved to the base of the redwood, letting the Elves precede her. She waited a moment, giving them time to finish their climb, then started her own spell. The air buzzed with energy and then six small lights descended into the earth. A moment later, half a dozen large wolves appeared. She pointed at the tree, and they began running up it, with Albreda following closely behind.

A clash of steel greeted her ears as she finally reached the battlements. The soldiers defending here were all Human, but a small group had tied a white cloth around their arms, identifying them as allies, and she ignored them, targeting their opponents instead. Small stones flew through the air, propelled by her magic, striking a defender, sending him tumbling from the wall.

~

Baron Fitzwilliam drew ever closer to the walls of the city. He was nervous, for the king's soldiers atop the gate had spotted their advance and were now readying to repulse them. The only thing that saved them from the first barrage of crossbows bolts headed their way was that the early morning shadows had interfered with their aim.

They would not be so lucky with the next wave. At the very last moment, the gates swung open and Lady Nicole waved him forward. He rode into the archway and dismounted, his men following suit. They charged into the tower with their swords out, seeking to disrupt the enemy's next barrage. Looking behind him, the baron made out his footmen coming safely through the gate. Sir James had them in hand, so Fitz turned his attention to the city itself.

The gate opened into one of the poorer sections of town, the main road heading north, with many side alleys visible. He directed his men up the road while he remained to help secure the gatehouse.

Arnim approached from the tower to greet him. "It worked," announced the knight. "Now, we must push north as quickly as we can."

Above them, someone yelled a warning, and then the portcullis started coming down.

"What's happening?" called Fitz. "I thought you had the gate secured?"

"I did," yelled Arnim as a clash of steel echoed down the stairwell. They both ran for the stairs, Arnim in the lead. He caught sight of an enemy knight above him and stabbed out with his sword. The fine blade easily penetrated the man's armour, and his foe staggered back. Arnim pushed forward, pressing the attack, but the knight parried his blows.

Fitz tried to get around him, but the confined space was his enemy.

"They must be coming from the battlements," he said, suddenly realizing the danger. "We have to stop them."

Arnim lunged again, driving his foe back into the wall. With no place to go, the blade easily found him, and the king's knight fell to the floor, clutching his wound.

"You raise the portcullis, I'll take the wall," yelled the baron.

Arnim stepped into the room, only to find three enemy knights standing there while his people lay dead on the floor. The largest one paused before the chains that ran through the floor to the portcullis below. Before Arnim could move, the man's axe came down, severing the chain and releasing its burden with a great crash.

With no time for thought, Arnim struck out at the two closest knights. The tip of his sword plunged forward, scraping across a breastplate to dig into a soft armpit. The enemy cried out in pain as he slid down the wall to lie on the floor, a pool of blood growing beneath him.

With one down, Arnim shifted his focus to the second knight. This one, who had a large two-handed sword, stepped forward, his blade slicing menacingly left to right. Arnim dove to the side while the weapon passed harmlessly over him. He rolled over and swung at the man's legs, feeling the tip slice through boot leather.

Looking up, Arnim determined that the knight's wild swing had left him vulnerable, and he struck again, this time a jab into the man's belly. The tip of the blade drove deep, and as he pulled back, his enemy fell, clutching his wound, trying to stem the flow of blood.

The axeman, surprised by this chain of events, moved towards where another door lay, but sounds of footsteps beyond changed his mind. He turned to face Arnim, his axe and shield ready to do battle.

The shouting beyond the other door told Arnim that the baron had been successful in his endeavours. Risking a glance at the two combatants on the floor to see neither presented a threat, he stepped forward with another jab, this time at his target's face. The remaining knight lifted his shield to fend off the blow even as he was driven back. Arnim used the enemy's momentary distraction to redirect his attack and stab down at the man's foot, driving the blade deep into the floor beneath.

The axe-wielder gave a bellow of rage as he brought the battle axe thundering down towards Arnim, hitting his right arm with a glancing blow, scraping the armour and continuing its momentum until the axe bit into a wall brace. Arnim moved forward using his elbow to smash into the man's face, causing the knight to crumple to the floor.

He rushed to the winch assembly, but it was plain to see there was nothing that could be done to repair it. The chain hung, limp and broken.

The heavy iron portcullis below blocked anyone from entering or leaving the city.

They were trapped!

Baron Fitzwilliam swung out, driving his enemy back. His foe, now precariously perched on the edge of the battlements, had nowhere to go. Fitz pushed forward with his shield, causing the unfortunate knight to tumble over the edge. The man fell with a scream, the echo of his voice only stilled when he struck the ground, silencing him forever.

His own men flooded out of the guardhouse behind him, along with Sir Rodney, who ran up beside him.

"We have them on the run," said Fitz.

"There's trouble below, Lord," reported Rodney. "The men that went north are returning; the enemy has set up barricades. They were waiting for us."

"Take command here," ordered the baron. "I'll see what can be done." He made his way back down through the gate tower. Arnim was just coming out of the winch room when their eyes met.

"The portcullis?" asked Fitz.

Arnim shook his head, "There's nothing to be done, they've cut the chain. We're trapped."

"Worse than that," added the baron, "it seems the attack was easy for a reason. They've set an ambush and are coming for us in strength."

"What do you suggest we do?" asked the knight.

"We do what we must," declared Fitz. "If that means dying to the last man, then so be it."

The fighting on the wall grew more intense. All around Albreda was the din of battle as wolves and soldiers fought within the close confines of the battlements.

A streak of flame shot out, and she instinctively ducked while it struck the ash to send splinters of wood flying while enveloping the top branches in flames. Thick black smoke began billowing out, filling the sky.

Albreda looked back to where the enemy caster was preparing another spell, but she was quicker. With a deft flick of her wrist, along with a word of power she pointed her finger at him. Small specks flew forth, each growing into a stone the size of a walnut, striking the mage full in the chest, propelling him backwards. He lost his balance, flailing his arms about as he tumbled down the stairs. Albreda ran forward to spot him lying at the bottom of the steps, a large pool of blood forming beneath his head.

A shout pulled her attention back from the stairs, and off to her right, two men approached, swords in hand. She called on nature once more, this time kneeling to strike the walkway beneath her feet. A ripple appeared in the stone, travelling away from her, creating a shockwave which sent the enemy soldiers tumbling.

A yell behind caused her to turn again. This time, she saw the group of Elves defending that section fall to the blades of the enemy. Fresh royal soldiers flooded onto the battlements.

The Earth Mage raised her hands, but a fiery pain lanced through her shoulder before she could call upon her magic once more. She scanned the area, trying to locate her attacker, finally spotting a dark-haired woman at the base of the stairs.

Albreda acted quickly, conjuring more stones and sending them flying towards her target, but watched in horror as they bounced off the woman, falling harmlessly to the ground.

A smile creased the woman's face as she uttered the words of power. Dark specks flew across the intervening space, expanding into a black cloud. The air around the Earth Mage grew dark and noxious. Albreda fell to the floor, gasping for breath as the woman ascended the stairs.

"Foolish mortal," the woman said, staring down at her, "no person in this world can kill me."

At that moment, Albreda knew who she faced. "Penelope," she managed to spit out through gritted teeth.

"Yes, I am Penelope," said the Necromancer, "or the Dark Queen, if you prefer. I've tolerated your interference for the last time, Witch. Prepare to die!"

Penelope raised her hands to cast a spell, but Albreda desperately lunged toward the battlements, diving over the wall and plunging silently into the darkness.

A soldier ran up to the Dark Queen, his sword covered in blood. "The wall is secure," he reported.

"Good," she replied. "Now, it is time to finish off those at the south gate. Release the rest of the knights."

THIRTY-FOUR

The Fall of Wincaster

SUMMER 962 MC

~

Tog watched as the Bodden foot swarmed about in front of the south gate. "Something is wrong."

"The gate must be down," said Aubrey. "There's an iron gate, called a portcullis, that keeps people out."

"How does it work?" asked the Troll.

"There'll be a room above, in the gatehouse, with a winch; a sort of drum that has a chain curled around it."

"Can it be raised?" he asked.

"It's likely very heavy," she answered, "and only the winch would work."

"Not too heavy for Trolls," he said, then turned to his people, issuing commands in their own tongue.

Aubrey watched as they began moving north. "Wait, I'm coming with you!" she hollered. "You may need me." She ran to catch up.

Across the field they went, their long legs carrying them swiftly. Crossbow bolts started flying at them from the walls, but the range was great and most bounced off harmlessly. Aubrey knew their luck wouldn't hold, and as the range dropped, the bolts began to take their toll. She saw Tog in front, two quarrels sticking out of his shoulder. He jogged now, his laboured breath steaming in the chill morning air.

They finally reached the gate, and the Bodden footmen quickly moved aside. Tog placed his hands between the iron bars of the portcullis, gripping as hard as he could and tried to bend them to no avail.

"Lift," yelled Aubrey.

Tog reached down to grasp the iron crossbar firmly in his hands and then straightened his legs. The gate groaned with the effort, moving only a handbreadth above the ground. Other Trolls, seeing the effect, leaped to his assistance, and soon there were six of the massive race, lifting the gate. Slowly it rose, and the men of Bodden began crawling beneath it.

Aubrey moved closer. The bottom of the gate had spikes of iron that recessed into the ground. She pointed at one on the left side and told a watching Troll to bend it, using a stick as an example. The Troll mimicked her action, then grabbed the leftmost spike and pushed until the metal began to twist slightly. A few others lent their strength, and soon it jutted sideways at an angle. They repeated the action on the right, and then Tog and the others slowly released the gate. It scraped down the stone a ways, digging into the archway until it seized up, caught on either side.

The Trolls rushed in, leaving Aubrey to follow. Walking through the gate, she saw the way lined with wounded and immediately began casting her spells, healing the most critical first.

Arnim swore as he crouched behind a makeshift barricade that they had hastily assembled. Enemy knights stood waiting at the far end of the street simply watching. While his men pulled together what defences they could, he wondered why the knights hadn't charged right away. When arrows started raining down on the men of Bodden, he understood. The king's archers had been making their way across the rooftops, and now they were letting loose with everything they had.

The man beside him gave a yell, then fell back, an arrow through his shoulder. Arnim was getting desperate as he saw soldier after soldier go down.

"The pig," said Nikki.

He looked at her in confusion.

She pointed "The tavern, the pig; we can reach the rooftops from there."

He cast his eyes in the direction she indicated. The Boar, as it was called, was a large tavern, popular among the lower classes. He saw the wooden sign, swinging in the breeze, its boar head mocking him with a slight grin. "Follow me," he yelled, then rushed for the doorway.

Arrows fell all about him, but he ignored them, crashing through the door into the common room. The place was deserted, emptied, no doubt, by the same people that had created this death trap of an ambush.

Nikki was right behind him. "To your right!" she called out.

He ran up the stairs, two by two, Nikki close behind, along with a few others following their lead. He reached the top of the stairs to see another set, heading upward.

"Keep going," said Nikki. "At the end of the hallway is a door that leads to the roof of the building."

"How do you know all this?" he yelled.

"This is my part of the city, remember? I know all the alleys and shortcuts."

He reached the top, the doorway clearly visible before him. Throwing his weight into it, he forced the timber from its hinges. As luck would have it, he fell, the door beneath him; it was an act that saved his life for an arrow sailed over his head and into the hallway.

Arnim rose, running for all he was worth. The startled archer grabbed another arrow and was nocking it when Arnim struck. Rather than hitting with his sword, he clotheslined the man, causing his unfortunate victim to lose his balance. The archer slipped, grasping in vain at the clay tiles, but they ripped from the roof as he fell, dropping to the ground and shattering, along with his body.

The lone knight tore across the rooftops towards the next archer. Nikki paused long enough to take in the scene below. The baron's soldiers were still pinned down, but the archery fire would soon lessen as they struggled to deal with the new rooftop threat.

Arnim reached the end of the building and jumped. Nikki held her breath until she heard his feet hit the next rooftop, a jump of some distance. He was yelling now, his sword flashing as he ran. Another archer went down while a third, holding his fire to avoid hitting his companion, suddenly turned and ran.

Nikki followed suit and leaped, clearing the gap to land safely. She plucked a bow from a dead man and began firing across the road at archers on the other rooftops.

The men following her took their cue from Nikki and began hurling tiles across the street. It wasn't accurate fire, but it was enough to convince them to take cover. In the street below, Nikki spotted Baron Fitzwilliam rallying the troops, and now they rushed forward, abandoning their barricades.

The king's knights, on their horses to the north, were shifting nervously and looked like they were about to charge, but something changed their minds, and they withdrew, turning the corner and disappearing from sight.

~

Beverly, seeing the tree erupt in flames, knew the assault was in jeopardy. The fighting on the battlements looked to be thinning out, the defenders gaining the advantage. Suddenly, she spotted Albreda, unmistakable given her lack of armour. Beverly watched in horror as the mage tumbled from the wall, disappearing into the shadows below.

"No!" she cried out, charging toward the debacle, her men following.

The Elves were withdrawing, bringing their wounded and burned comrades back down the mighty redwood. Beverly galloped up, leaping from the saddle and pushing past them, her hammer firmly in hand. She started up the tree at the run, her feet firmly planted as she made her way along the incline.

"For Bodden," she called out, her voice husky with emotion. Full of anger now, her hammer glowed with energy as she reached the top. There, she beheld a mage on the wall, his shoulder covered in blood and glowing light at his fingertips. He was about to let loose with a spell when an arrow took him in the eye.

"Gotcha," yelled a familiar voice and she turned to see Hayley on the burning ash tree. She had paused to let loose her arrow, and now continued on her way, the Orc archers close behind.

Beverly reached the end of the tree and dropped to the battlements. The air here was harsh, but the cool morning breeze wafted the fumes away. Someone loomed up before her, and she instinctively swung the hammer, driving into their shoulder and knocking them from the wall. She deftly blocked a sword that stabbed out at her, then used her shield to push back. Her foe fell to the side, to be finished off by another.

The path ahead was blocked by the enemy. She smashed the hammer down, striking the stone, sending vines creeping along in front of her. Four men were quickly entangled in the spiny growth, but she ran past them, letting her soldiers dispatch them.

She reached the stairs to find them deserted. Halting to catch her breath, she saw some of her men nearby. "Head south, along the wall," she said. "Secure the western gatehouse and open the gates."

Her soldiers ran by, their swords dripping with blood.

"They're on the run," called out Hayley.

"Yes," Beverly replied, "but we must make haste, or Penelope will get away."

"Where's Albreda?" asked the ranger.

"I'm afraid we've lost her, I saw her fall from the wall. There's no way she could have survived that."

∾

Albreda felt herself falling. Her arm was on fire, the acid burning through skin, and it was all she could do to not scream from the agonizing pain. She lay back, looking upward, awaiting the sweet release of death, but instead of hitting the ground, she found herself landing in a thick bush, crashing through the branches. Finally coming to a halt, she lay still, her shoulder throbbing, her body feeling as if it had a thousand cuts.

"Albreda, are you all right?" came a familiar voice.

She turned her head as best she could to see a fuzzy shape approaching. "Aldus, is that you?"

"It is," he said, coming closer. "I conjured a bush to break your fall, it's all I could think of in the moment."

"It seems to have done the trick," she said, through gritted teeth.

"Let's get you out of here," he said.

"No!" she replied. "I can't move. I think I've broken something. More likely lots of things."

"I'll get the healer."

"Make it quick," she added, "I don't think I can last much longer."

With the ambush broken and the gate now open, Baron Fitzwilliam led his men north. Still wary of the enemy, he advanced cautiously, his men spread out in a rough line.

Arnim joined him, his task on the rooftops complete.

"You need to get to the Palace," said Fitz. "Grab some horses and ride off. We'll clean up here."

"We don't have any horses," protested Arnim.

"Nonsense," said the baron, "we left them at the gates, remember? Head back and round up some men."

"It will take too long. We can't afford the delay."

Baron Fitzwilliam looked up the road. The knights had returned, this time intent on a charge. "It seems the Gods have provided."

The king's knights broke into a trot, but the confines of the street and the short distance prevented them from reaching a full gallop.

The first strike was at Arnim. He ducked to the side reaching up with his blade. The sword of King Dathen slashed through his opponent's arm, the blade glowing slightly. "It's magic," said Arnim, in disbelief.

"So it would seem," yelled back Fitz as he pulled a man from the saddle. He stabbed down with a dagger, silencing his foe. Around them the men of Bodden struck out, taking out their vengeance on this haphazard group of knights.

It was all over in a moment, leaving Arnim and the baron looking at the carnage before them.

"That wasn't too difficult," said Arnim.

"I suspect they were newer knights," replied the baron. "Rather poor fighters they were, if you ask me. I'll never understand why someone is knighted without being trained properly."

"Not all of us have the luxury of your instructions, Baron."

"If you're referring to my daughter," said Fitz, "I might remind you it was Gerald that trained her, not I."

"True," agreed Arnim, "though I'm told it was your decision."

"I must admit that's true," he said, turning his attention to the horses. "Now, seeing how Saxnor himself delivered these fine mounts to us, take them and ride to the Palace, there's still an enemy to defeat."

Arnim mounted a horse while Fitz detailed men to accompany him. The knight turned his horse, ready to gallop off when someone jumped on behind him.

"I'm going with you," said Nikki, wrapping her arms around his waist. "Now hurry, we've no time to lose."

~

"They've broken through at the wall," said Anna.

"Are you sure?" asked Gerald. "I can't make out much at this range."

"The princess is correct," said Revi, "I can see through Shellbreaker's eyes. Our men are making their way north and south, clearing the battlements."

"Good," said Gerald, "with any luck, they'll soon have the west gate in their possession."

"I should be there," said Revi. "People need healing."

"Not yet," said Anna. "It's still too dangerous, and we can't afford to lose you. Once the wall is secure, it will be safe."

"Someone's approaching," announced Gerald.

An exhausted looking Elf ran up to them. "We need the Life Mage," he said through gasps for air. "The druid, Albreda, is gravely injured."

Gerald turned to Revi. "Go," he said, "meet us inside when you're done."

"How will I know where to find you?" asked the mage.

"We'll be at the Palace," called out Anna, as Revi vanished into the distance.

"Where is Sir Heward?" called Gerald

"Here, General," came the reply.

"Take the horse," Gerald commanded, "all of it you can gather, and head to the west gate. I rather suspect it will be opening soon. Stay out of bow range until you see the doors begin to open, then make your way into the city as quickly as you can. We'll rendezvous at the Palace."

"Yes sir," responded the giant knight, turning to yell out commands.

They watched the horsemen trot by.

Gerald looked to the gate which even now began to open. "Time to get closer, I think."

"Is that wise?" asked Anna.

"I can't direct the attack from here anymore, I need to see what's happening. We'll follow the cavalry."

"Very well," said Anna, "but I'm coming too."

A tremendous bark erupted from beside her.

"It appears Tempus is joining us," said Gerald.

"She's in a tremendous amount of pain," beseeched Aldus Hearn.

"I can well imagine," replied Revi, dismounting. He moved closer, looking carefully over the prostrate witch. "The wounds look quite severe. Can you hear me, Albreda?"

She nodded her head weakly.

"I'm going to heal you," he continued. "I can't repair the more seriously broken bones, but it will keep you alive until we can get Aubrey here. Do you understand?"

Again the head nod, this time with a grimace.

He began casting his spell, the air buzzing with the familiar feeling. His hands glowed with a pale yellow light, and then he placed them on Albreda, watching as her body absorbed it. "How do you feel?" he asked.

"It still hurts," she replied huskily.

"We need to get her out of this bush," said Revi. "She's entangled, possibly even impaled."

"I can take care of that," said Aldus. "Hold on a moment."

Now it was the elderly mage's turn to use his magic. He uttered the words of power, and the bush came to life, lowering Albreda carefully to the ground. A moment later the bushes receded into the dirt, all traces of them quickly gone.

"That's much better," said Albreda, "though I can't feel my legs."

"I suspect you've broken your back," said Revi. "From what they've told me you've suffered quite the tumble."

"Better to die in a fall than suffer at the hands of that vile Necromancer," she said.

"Penelope was on the wall?" Revi said in astonishment.

"Yes," said Albreda, "and I tried to wound her."

"It's too bad you didn't kill her," said Hearn.

"I can't," said Albreda, "no one can."

"What do you mean?" asked Revi.

"She said there is no person in this world that can kill her."

"And you believed her?"

"I do," said Albreda. "You didn't see my spell. Even at low power, it should have at least hurt her, but she just shrugged it off. It would have felled a lesser mortal."

"I believe you," said Revi, "though I shudder to think of the ramifications."

"You need to go," said Albreda. "You too, Aldus. You're both needed within the city. You must chase down the Dark Queen before she can make an escape. I'll be fine here until Aubrey can be brought, I promise."

"I'll wait here," said Hearn, "my magic is not likely to be very useful in a city. I'll watch over you."

"Very well," said Revi, "I'll send help as soon as I can."

～

Arnim and his horsemen rode through the city at full gallop. Stray soldiers were running in fear, but none opposed them. They turned north onto the Royal Promenade, the main street that headed directly to the Palace.

The stores were locked up tight, many with shutters nailed shut. As they drew closer to the Palace, its massive iron gates and high walls were clearly visible.

"The gates are open," said Nikki.

"The Gods favour us again," said Arnim as he noticed the line of horsemen just inside. "The knights forming up in the courtyard must have just arrived."

"I'll leave that to you," she said.

She held on to his shoulders as she stood behind him, then jumped, rolling as she hit the ground. Arnim looked back over his shoulder to spot her coming to her feet with a wave indicating she was all right. He drew his sword but didn't slacken his pace, crashing into the waiting knights, along with his men.

～

To the east of the city, Prince Alric stared at the eastern gate, waiting impatiently.

"I can't tell what's happening, Jack. How go the attacks?"

"I'm afraid we have no news, Your Highness. Perhaps we should send a rider south to Baron Fitzwilliam, I believe he commands there?"

"I doubt you'll find him. If everything is going according to plan, he should have assaulted the southern gate and be well inside the city by now."

"Or still struggling to take the gate," suggested Jack. "We have no way of knowing which."

Alric sat for a while, staring at the wall before them. "Is it just my imagination," he asked, "or have the defenders thinned out before us."

Jack stood in his stirrups, struggling to focus on the distant defences. "I think you may be right, Highness. I would say there's only half the number we saw at dawn."

The prince turned to his bodyguard. "It can only mean one thing," he said, "they've thinned the men down by sending some to repel the attacks. We must send troops to help."

"How many?" Jack asked. "We don't want the enemy escaping through the east gate."

"We have plenty enough to bottle them up," Alric replied. "Let's send half our men to the south gate to reinforce Baron Fitzwilliam."

"Which troops, Highness?

"Keep the horse and bowmen here, along with a hundred foot. That should be more than enough to deal with anything that tries to escape. Send the rest to the south gate. Wincaster is a large city, if the baron has broken through, he'll need all the men he can get."

"And shall you command them?" asked Jack.

"Much as I'd like to, I need to remain here," said Alric. "I must do my duty to prevent the enemy from escaping. I'm afraid I'll have to delegate that responsibility. Do you think you're up to it?"

Jack looked at him in surprise, a smile creasing his lips, "Are you serious, my liege? You're honestly asking if I'd like a chance at fame and glory?"

"Does that mean you don't want to, Jack?" said Alric with a smile.

"I accept the honour with all my heart, my prince."

～

Beverly and Hayley pushed through the city, the Orcs spread out in front of them. There was no opposition here, and the fighting in the distance was sporadic.

"We're almost there," said Beverly.

"You know this area well?" asked Hayley.

"I spent quite a bit of time here with the other knights."

"How much farther, Bev?"

"It should be just up ahead."

"Yes," replied Hayley, "I can see the spires in the distance."

They arrived just in time to witness Arnim and the others dealing with the prisoners.

"Those are my father's men," said Beverly.

The sound of galloping to the south grabbed their attention, and they looked to see Heward at the head of the Guard Cavalry.

"It seems we're all getting here just in time," she observed.

"Dame Beverly," called out Heward, "it's good to see you safe. And you too, Dame Hayley."

The horsemen entered the courtyard while they chatted. At the tail end of the line rode another pair of friends.

"Your Highness," said Beverly.

"Dame Beverly," replied Anna, "it's good to see you fit and hale."

"Your plan worked brilliantly, General," said Hayley.

"It worked yes," agreed Gerald, "but it very nearly turned into a disaster."

"Over here," came a voice. They all turned to see Nikki waving frantically, "We have to find the Dark Queen. We must search the Palace."

"Where's Revi?" asked Anna. "He should know where to look."

"I am here," he called, astride his horse which was lathered in sweat.

"You move quickly," said Anna.

"A fast horse that doesn't have to worry about carrying a lot of armour," explained the mage. "Albreda is seriously injured. Where's Aubrey?"

"To the south," called back Nikki. "She's helping with the wounded while the baron clears the streets."

"I'll send someone to fetch her," offered Heward.

"Come on," called Arnim, "we have no time to lose."

They dismounted, rushing for the doors to the Palace. Anna insisted on leading the way. "The great hall," she said, "that's likely where they'll make a stand."

They entered, turning down the passageway towards the audience chamber known as the great hall. Gerald nodded, and two soldiers pushed open the doors revealing a unique sight. The room was empty save for a single chair in the centre of the room, its occupant still and brooding, the warrior's crown of Merceria upon his head.

"Sire," called out Arnim, "your reign is at an end. I call on you to surrender."

There was no response. The figure remained seated, unmoving.

"Henry, it's Anna," called out the princess, stepping into the room.

"Something's wrong," warned Beverly. "He's not moving."

"I think he's dead," said Gerald.

"I smell something," said Hayley, "a burning smell of some type."

"Acid," said Revi, moving closer. "If you look at his chest you can see the small puncture wound where the acid stream hit. It seems Penelope likes her deaths to be painful."

They all gathered around the body of the fallen king, his crown balanced upon his head at an angle while his sword sat at his side, still sheathed.

"He's been posed like this," said Gerald.

"It's a message," said Anna, "from the Dark Queen."

"So it's over," said Nikki.

"No," said Anna, "we still have to find Penelope."

"Her tower," shouted Revi. "Follow me, I know the way."

They rushed through the Palace, soldiers following in their wake. Revi knew where Penelope's tower was located, having escaped from it some time ago. He led them to the room that served as its ground floor, but when he opened the door, there was a surprise waiting for them; three knights wearing the livery of the Order of the Hound.

"Not again," cursed Beverly stepping forward. She swung the hammer at Dame Aelwyth, but the undead knight blocked with her shield.

An arrow punctured the knight's breastplate but didn't appear to have any effect. Arnim stepped forward, swinging at the creature that used to be Sir Barnsley. The blade bit deep, slicing off a chunk of flesh, but the former Knight of the Hound returned the blow, sending its attacker sprawling.

The last of the princess's departed knights, Sir Howard, launched itself at Gerald, who parried the blow. It sent a shock up his arm, and he staggered back.

"Keep them busy," yelled Revi, "we must get past them." He stepped forward, trying to edge along the wall, but a sword hit just in front of him, sending fragments of brick flying.

Gerald stepped forward, braced for an attack. His sword stabbed out, sinking into the chest of Sir Howard, but the undead knight didn't even flinch. "Go for the legs," he yelled.

Beverly dropped to her knees, swinging the hammer in a wide arc. It struck the kneecap of Dame Aelwyth, making a sickening sound and causing her to topple to the floor. Hayley stepped forward, plunging her sword into the eye socket of the possessed knight's helmet.

Anna, appalled at the sight of her departed knights being used this way, turned her head to see Gerald in danger and stepped forward, stabbing out with her Dwarven sword. It sliced into Sir Howard's arm, cutting it loose, the limb still moving as it hit the floor.

Gerald struggled to keep Sir Howard busy, taking a terrific pounding to his shield. He felt a heavy blow that sank him to his knees, buckling his shield. He held up his sword to stop the next blow as a large bulk sailed over him.

Tempus tore into Sir Howard as he landed, ripping the other limb from the vile creature which fell back, thrashing about on the floor.

Beverly, now free of her opponent, swung the hammer in an overhead strike, pummelling its helmet until the creature lay still.

Now only one knight remained, Sir Barnsley. It had forced Arnim back with a heavy blow, but suddenly it changed its tactics, backing up to block the door behind it.

Revi let out a curse and then began casting. A moment later, the creature that had been Sir Barnsley dropped to its knees, letting out an otherworldly shriek. Arnim stepped forward to finish it off.

"What was that?" asked a surprised Gerald.

"A heal," said Revi. "I wasn't sure if it would work."

"A heal did that?" said Anna.

"It's undead," defended Revi, "the very antithesis of life. It only makes sense that curing the flesh would hurt it."

"The door," called out Anna, "we must hurry."

Gerald grabbed the door, but it wouldn't budge. "It's locked," he cursed.

"I have it," said Nikki, pulling forth her lock picks. She knelt by the door, her fingers working feverishly.

Revi had his ear to the door, "Hurry up, I can hear her casting something."

"No more of those foul creatures, I hope," said Anna.

There was a satisfying click, and then Nikki backed up. "Got it," she said.

Revi pushed open the door, but the only thing visible was the faintly glowing runes of a magic circle. "Saxnor help us" he called out, "we're too late. She escaped."

"She has," said Anna, "but the kingdom is now finally free of her shadow."

THIRTY-FIVE

A New Beginning

SUMMER 962 MC

Mid-afternoon saw soldiers still searching the city, but things were beginning to calm down. With a sense of relief, Gerald made his way through the Palace to the great hall. King Henry's body had been borne away, and in its stead, the room was now a refuge for the wounded. Revi and Aubrey healed the most critical, while Sophie made her way through the soldiers, helping where she could.

The general heard a bark and looked to see Tempus sitting beside his old friend Jax. It took a moment for Gerald to register the presence of Arlo Harris. The Uxley tavern keeper lay propped up against the wall, his arm in a sling. Sam Collins sat chatting with him while the two dogs wagged their tails.

"I see you made it through the siege," said Gerald.

"I did indeed," replied Arlo, "though I had my doubts there for a moment that we would survive."

"You did us a great service, Arlo. If it hadn't been for you, we could never have secured the west wall. You and the rest of the villagers of Uxley held the line long enough for us to get there."

"Don't thank me," he replied. "If it hadn't been for Sam's note, I would have never thought to mark the wall with a sheet, not to mention wearing the armbands to identify us."

"I didn't want you getting cut down by friends," offered Sam.

"Is it true?" asked Arlo. "Are you really a general now, Gerald?"

"I am," he said, "though I fear we have little enough of an army left, but the city's ours and hopefully, the rest of the kingdom will soon submit."

"I'll drink to that," said the tavern keeper.

Jax barked, and Gerald looked down at the old dog, "How did you find him?"

"He was wandering the battlefield," said Sam. "I caught him trying to steal food."

Gerald reached down, scratching the dog's head. Tempus watched, then forced his head forward, seeking similar attention. "If Tempus is here, the princess can't be far away," he mused.

"She's over there," said a familiar voice, and Gerald turned.

"Sophie," he said, "I haven't seen you for ages."

"I've been busy helping Lady Aubrey," she replied. "There are far too many wounded for her and Master Revi to look after by themselves."

Gerald's eyes scanned the room, "You seem to have enlisted a lot of help. Is that Jack Marlowe I see over there?"

"It is," she said. "He and Prince Alric have been visiting the injured, keeping them in high spirits."

"Lord Jack doesn't look too happy."

Sophie chuckled, "No, he's not."

"Why? What happened?"

"He brought reinforcements through the south gate, but the battle was over before he got a chance to fight. He's trying to make the best of it."

"If only more of us had that problem. How are things going here?"

"We do what we can to make the injured comfortable until the healers can use their magic," she explained.

"You are a remarkable woman," he said. "The princess is lucky to have you."

"I'll be happy when this is over, and we can get back to some semblance of normal."

"So shall we all," Gerald agreed. "Where did you say the princess was?"

She pointed to the north end of the hall. "Over there," she repeated.

"Thank you," he said, making his way toward Anna, who sat at a table littered with papers and books.

"What's that you have there?" he asked.

Anna looked up from where she was examining a book. "It's Henry's journal. It seems he kept detailed accounts. I would never have expected it."

"I see you've marked some pages," he said, noting pieces of paper poking out.

"Yes, there's all sorts of things in here."

"Such as?" asked Gerald.

"Listen to this," said Anna, searching through her bookmarks. "It was written some years ago."

"I must admit that I knew Father had something special in mind for me when I hit my 16th birthday, but the revelation that he was behind the Black Hand was quite astounding. By creating the terror of the Black Hand, he said, he could justify his increase in power and gain more control over his nobles. Now, I find that I have been placed in command of these rogues, the better to advance our agenda, whatever that might be."

"So your father engineered the whole idea of the Black Hand?" asked Gerald.

"I'll remind you he's not my father," said Anna.

"You know what I mean."

"Wait, there's more. I think Henry started to have doubts. Listen to this."

"Father is using the Black Hand rather effectively, but I fear that his attacks on my sister are misplaced. While she is expendable, should one of the attacks succeed in killing her it would do irreparable harm to the notion that we are untouchable. Father will not listen so I shall have to find someone to protect her, a knight of renown who will safeguard her with his life."

"And so, in his own way, he did just that," said Gerald. "After all, he sent Beverly to protect you."

Anna shuddered involuntarily. "Think how things would have turned out if you hadn't shown up at Uxley all those years ago. I would be dead and the kingdom in the grip of a Death Mage."

"Your brother wasn't all bad," he reminded her. "He still had enough humanity in him to try and protect you."

"Agreed," she replied, "and I can't help but feel for him, despite the actions he took."

"What do you mean?" he asked.

"Listen to this," she said, "it's his last entry."

"I fear I no longer have any influence over Penelope. She has revealed her true nature, and I have damned the throne. Even my dear sister Margaret has succumbed to her influence. I now await the death I deserve at the hands of the Dark Queen."

"Your sister?" he asked.

"We haven't found her," said Anna, "and now I fear she is in the grip of Penelope."

"A terrible fate, to be sure."

"How's Albreda?" asked the princess, changing the subject.

"She's doing well," said Gerald. "Aubrey tells me she'll make a full recovery. The baron is looking after her. We've put her in one of the guest rooms here in the Palace."

"And the others?" she asked.

"We lost Sir Rodney in the fighting, and our troops took a beating, but the capital is secure. I doubt the cities to the south will hold out for long."

"No indeed," she responded. "We've already received word that Shrewesdale has recognized my claim to the throne."

"What of Valmar?" he asked. "Any word of him?"

"No," said Anna, "but things got chaotic once we entered the city. I suspect he's given us the slip."

The door behind Anna opened, revealing Dame Beverly and a man wearing expensive looking robes accompanying her. "Your Highness," she said in greeting, "this is Holy Father Angelis, the Bishop-Supreme of Saxnor."

"Your Holiness," said Anna, dipping her head slightly. "What brings you here?"

"I bring you the greetings of the church, Your Highness. The Gods have seen fit to bless you with a victory this day."

"It was not the Gods," said Anna, "but the men and women who gave their lives this day that determined the fate of the crown."

Epilogue

AUTUMN 962 MC

~

Margaret walked through the darkened corridor, shivering as shadows cast by the torches danced around her.

"It has been a long road, child, but we are almost there," said Penelope, halting at a great wooden door. She knocked, paused a moment, and then knocked again, letting the sound reverberate down the hall.

"Enter," came a voice from within.

The Dark Queen opened the door, revealing the room beyond; a circular chamber, with steps leading upward in all directions, reminding Margaret of the stadium seating in Shrewesdale. There were seven seats arranged about the centre, only one of them empty.

Penelope advanced to the middle of the circle and stopped, looking around at those assembled. Margaret watched from the doorway as the six that sat there looked with interest at the woman who now stood in judgement.

"You have failed us, Kythelia," said one of them, a bearded man. "You promised us Merceria and have delivered us nothing but failure."

"Failure?" said Penelope in response. "I have brought you no such thing. Have I not neutralized the military might of two kingdoms? Merceria and Weldwyn now lie in a weakened state, ripe for the plucking."

"You wished a seat on this council," said a dark-haired woman, "and yet you try to claim victory when it is clearly a defeat."

"I promised you I would lay the groundwork for the coming storm,"

Penelope retorted. "I have done just that. When our forces launch their attack, it will be against a weakened enemy."

"Is this true?" asked the woman, glancing at another council member.

"It is true that both kingdoms are diminished," a fair-haired Elven maid responded. "It will take them many years to rebuild their strength."

"And what of Norland?" asked another.

"Malkar assures us things are proceeding as planned," said the bearded man.

"You see?" said Penelope. "The plans are progressing well."

The first man leaned forward to emphasize his words, "You had the crown of Merceria in your grasp, and you lost it."

"I lost nothing," retorted the Dark Queen. "Henry wasn't as malleable as his father and had to be removed. In his place, I have obtained a far more valuable resource."

"The secret of the gates?" asked the dark-haired woman.

"The lost ravings of a long-dead race," Penelope replied. "No, something of much more value to us."

"Which is?" the woman pressed.

"With your permission," said Penelope, "I will show you." There were nods of agreement throughout the room, and Penelope turned to face the doorway, "Come, girl, none here will harm you."

Margaret stepped forward, her legs shaking, her breathing ragged.

"This woman holds a power that will determine the fate of the four kingdoms. With my help, she will unleash that power and a true Death Mage shall rule the lands. May I present Princess Margaret, a Necromancer in training and the true heir to the crown of Merceria."

"Very impressive," said the bearded man.

"Yes," agreed the dark-haired woman, "it has been decades since we have seen a new member of our order."

"I can feel her inner power," commented the Elven maid.

The woman looked around at her fellow council members, each nodding their assent. "Well done," she said at last, "you have truly brought us a most precious gift." She pointed at the empty seat, "Now, take your rightful seat on the Shadow Council and tell us your plans."

<<<>>>

REVIEW FATE OF THE CROWN

~

ONTO BOOK SIX: BURDEN OF THE CROWN

If you liked *Fate of the Crown*, then *Temple Knight*, the first book in the *Power Ascending* series awaits.

START TEMPLE KNIGHT

A few words from Paul

Fate of the Crown brings an end to the first part of the Heir to the Crown series. The Kingdom of Merceria is safe for now, and the darkness has been vanquished or at least kicked out of the realm.

Anna, Gerald and the others will face new challenges, ones that might not necessarily be solved by armies and warfare. Revi still needs to find the tower of Andronicus, and there are many more secrets waiting to be revealed.

The next book in the series, Burden of the Crown, continues the tale. Merceria is at peace, at least in theory, but old loyalties remain, and though the presence of the shadow has been removed, new players will arise seeking power and influence and someone will face the fight of their life, but not on the battlefield. All the while, events to the north will bring the kingdom inexorably closer to war.

I should like to thank my wife, Carol, for her excellent work as editor, as well as her suggestions and ideas. I could not have written any of these books without you.

In addition, I would once again like to thank Christie Kramburger, for her work on the cover, Amanda Bennett and Stephanie Sandrock for their support and enthusiasm, along with Brad Aitken, Jeff Parker and Stephen Brown for bringing some of these characters to life.

Thank you, also, to my Beta readers who provided excellent feedback and allowed me to enrich the storyline. Rachel Deibler, Tim James, Stuart Rae, Don Hinkey, Mark Dawson, Phyllis Simpson, Mark Tracy, and Paul Castellano, you all rock!

Lastly, I must thank you, the reader, for the wonderful reviews and encouragement I have received for this series.

I look forward to entertaining you with further tales of Merceria and the people that inhabit the land.

About the Author

Paul J Bennett (b. 1961) emigrated from England to Canada in 1967. His father served in the British Royal Navy, and his mother worked for the BBC in London. As a young man, Paul followed in his father's footsteps, joining the Canadian Armed Forces in 1983. He is married to Carol Bennett and has three daughters who are all creative in their own right.

Paul's interest in writing started in his teen years when he discovered the roleplaying game, Dungeons & Dragons (D & D). What attracted him to this new hobby was the creativity it required; the need to create realms, worlds and adventures that pulled the gamers into his stories.

In his 30's, Paul started to dabble in designing his own roleplaying system, using the Peninsular War in Portugal as his backdrop. His regular gaming group were willing victims, er, participants in helping to playtest this new system. A few years later, he added additional settings to his game, including Science Fiction, Post-Apocalyptic, World War II, and the all-important Fantasy Realm where his stories take place.

The beginnings of his first book 'Servant to the Crown' originated over five years ago when he began running a new fantasy campaign. For the world that the Kingdom of Merceria is in, he ran his adventures like a TV show, with seasons that each had twelve episodes, and an overarching plot. When the campaign ended, he knew all the characters, what they had to accomplish, what needed to happen to move the plot along, and it was this that inspired to sit down to write his first novel.

Paul now has four series based in his fantasy world of Eiddenwerthe, and is looking forward to sharing many more books with his readers over the coming years.